THE Corpse WITH THE Turquoise Toes

CATHY ACE

FOUR TAILS PUBLISHING LTD.

PRAISE FOR THE CAIT MORGAN MYSTERIES

"In the finest tradition of Agatha Christie…Ace brings us the closed-room drama, with a dollop of romantic suspense and historical intrigue." – *Library Journal*

"…touches of Christie or Marsh but with a bouquet of Kinsey Millhone." – *The Globe and Mail*

"…a sparkling, well-plotted and quite devious mystery in the cozy tradition…" – *Hamilton Spectator*

"…If all of this suggests the school of Agatha Christie, it's no doubt what Cathy Ace intended. She is, as it fortunately happens, more than adept at the Christie thing." – *Toronto Star*

"Cait unravels the…mystery using her eidetic memory and her powers of deduction, which are worthy of Hercule Poirot." – *The Jury Box, Ellery Queen Mystery Magazine*

"This author always takes us on an adventure. She always makes us think. She always brings the setting to life. For those reasons this is one of my favorite series." – *Escape With Dollycas Into A Good Book*

"…a testament to an author who knows how to tell a story and deliver it with great aplomb." – *Dru's Musings*

"…perfect for those that love travel, food, and/or murder (reading it, not committing it)." – *BOLO Books*

"…Ace is, well, an ace when it comes to plot and description." – *The Globe and Mail*

Other works by the same author
(Information for all works here: **www.cathyace.com**)

The Cait Morgan Mysteries
The Corpse with the Silver Tongue
The Corpse with the Golden Nose
The Corpse with the Emerald Thumb
The Corpse with the Platinum Hair
The Corpse with the Sapphire Eyes
The Corpse with the Diamond Hand
The Corpse with the Garnet Face
The Corpse with the Ruby Lips
The Corpse with the Crystal Skull
The Corpse with the Iron Will
The Corpse with the Granite Heart

The WISE Enquiries Agency Mysteries
The Case of the Dotty Dowager
The Case of the Missing Morris Dancer
The Case of the Curious Cook
The Case of the Unsuitable Suitor

Standalone novels
The Wrong Boy

Short Stories/Novellas
Murder Keeps No Calendar: a collection of 12 short stories/novellas
Murder Knows No Season: a collection of four novellas
Steve's Story in "The Whole She-Bang 3"
The Trouble with the Turkey in "Cooked to Death Vol. 3: Hell for the Holidays"

This book is dedicated to all those who have volunteered their time and energy to our community of crime writers and readers

Serene Turbulence

If we survive this trip, I might never leave home again, was what I thought; "I hate turbulence," was what I said. I've never been good at not being in control, and when you're a passenger in a small aircraft that's being buffeted by what feels like a cyclone, you're about as helpless as a person can be.

My husband was already holding my hand across the narrow aisle, but gave it an extra squeeze. "I'm sure this sort of thing happens all the time. Look at Mike, our attendant – he seems pretty cool. Used to it, I guess. We'll be through it soon, Cait, like the pilot said."

I'd thought the freckled redhead had dumped the champagne and strapped himself in pretty sharpish when the juddering had started, and reckoned his smile was more curated than spontaneous, but allowed myself to be soothed by my husband's words, even if the tiny muscles in his jaw flexed tellingly as he uttered them.

"It's been ten minutes already, Bud. The pilot said no more than five." I had to deflect my own guilt; I was the one who'd talked him into this journey, after all. He hadn't been keen from the beginning, so this was all my fault, in a way.

"Close your eyes, that might help," suggested Bud.

I replied with a "Hmm", grabbed the plush cream leather upholstery of the armrests, and squeezed my eyelids shut, blotting out my view of the walnut veneer trim of the private aircraft that had been chartered to deliver just the two of us to our destination. This was supposed to be the fabulous start of an indulgent week or so in Arizona, where Bud and I were to be guests of honor at the opening of a restaurant set up by the insanely wealthy Soul family, but – at that precise moment – I wasn't feeling the glamor of the experience one little bit.

I told myself that everything would be fine – probably – and focused on the reason for our trip: Sammy Soul, the big-hearted ageing rock legend, and his once-groupie wife Suzie, had financed the eatery where we were to be feted for their daughter, Serendipity. It was her attempted murder we'd managed to foil, and whose attacker we'd brought to justice, when we'd been in Kelowna investigating a so-called suicide almost exactly three years earlier, and this was the Soul family's chance to thank us for the role we'd played in that dreadful drama. To be fair, Bud hadn't been averse to the honored guest part of the proposition; indeed, he'd been delighted that we'd get to see Serendipity again because we'd both taken a shine to the hard-working and talented chef when we'd first got to know her.

No, what had led my husband to baulk at the prospect of the trip was the fact we'd be staying at what our hostess had described as "the recently-opened luxury resort" being run by the folks who espoused the practices of the Faceting for Life movement. He'd said the whole thing sounded like a recipe for disaster – that they were bound to try to recruit us, and he didn't like that idea one little bit. I'd assured him they wouldn't dare – though I'd admitted to myself at the time that the idea of debating the whole Faceting thing with the odd zealot or two held more than a little allure for me, given my background in psychology, and my love of a good discussion.

We'd first come to know about the Facetors when we'd originally met Serendipity; she and a couple of her friends in Kelowna had introduced us to what I understood to be a fairly simple, if slightly whacky, set of behavioral patterns designed to give structure and meaning to the lives of folks who felt their existence needed some direction. I'd said as much to Bud, and had reminded him of how the Facetors merely believed the need to consciously focus on attending to a number of aspects of their life every day, without any prescriptive mystical or spiritual content to their ethos.

I'd gone on to enthuse about the chance to visit Taliesin West, Frank Lloyd Wright's jewel in the Arizona desert, as well as maybe traveling to the Petrified Forest and Monument Valley National Parks, which were both just further along the route we'd be taking if we went to stay with Serendipity. It was only then that Bud had relented.

We'd set up all the arrangements for the trip so that we'd arrive at a hotel in Phoenix in time for a lovely dinner, a good night's sleep, then a trip to Taliesin West on the way out to the Desert Gem, which was what the boutique resort where we'd be staying for a week was called – to differentiate it from the Gem, which had been the original Faceting headquarters in Sedona. Then we'd head off to the National Parks on our own for a few days.

As I tried to keep down my lunch – caviar, grilled salmon, and lemon mousse, all accompanied by Dom Perignon champagne (who knew one attendant in a small private jet could rustle up such a feast?) – I reminded myself that air travel is one of the safest forms of transport. Then the plane lurched downward, and my eyes flew open in terror; I caught a glimpse of the smile sliding from our attendant's face.

"Sorry about that last bit of bucking around there, we're just getting through it now; shouldn't be too much longer before Mike can pop another cork for you both." The pilot's voice sounded cheery enough; was she an accomplished actor, or did she posses that Zen-like quality so many of her type always radiate?

"See?" Bud was looking a little pale. "Not long now."

I looked at my watch. Fourteen minutes had passed since the beaming Mike had high-tailed it back to his seat – and I was beginning to think they were the longest fourteen minutes of my life. I was also beginning to understand why the Pope kisses the tarmac after his plane lands; I was considering doing the same thing, assuming we managed to reach *terra firma* without further incident.

To be fair to the pilot, it really was only a couple of minutes later that Mike seemed to receive a secret signal, unbuckled, stood, smoothed down his skinny navy pants over his jolly striped socks, and headed for the galley. He returned with a second bottle of champagne and two crystal flutes; Bud and I took the glasses with slightly trembling hands.

"We should be wheels-down in about an hour," he said as he headed out of sight. Before he disappeared, he turned, beamed, and added, "If you need anything else, just ask."

Bud checked his watch. "We'll only be about half an hour late," he said. "Plenty of time for a lovely evening to ourselves. When are we being collected in the morning?"

"Ten. Serendipity is sending a friend of hers to pick us up. Her text spelled the name KSUE – not a name I've ever seen before, so it might be a typo. If not, I'm not sure how to pronounce it."

Bud sipped his champagne. "Kay-Sue? Or possibly she's just Sue, and the K was a thumb-bumble."

"A thumb-bumble?"

Bud smiled. "That's what I call it when my thumbs are too big for the tiny letters on my phone." He raised his glass. "To landing safely, and an enjoyable break in the sun, knowing that Marty's romping around happily with Jack and Sheila's dogs – and their new puppy – on their acreage. Doggie heaven on earth." We both swigged. "You did remember to pack the sunblock, didn't you?"

"Factor 50. Yes. But we'll still need to be careful – our poor little bodies haven't glimpsed real sunshine for months, and I don't want to burn."

"There'll be no burning for us, Wife. We're sensible, right? Besides, it's only the end of March, it won't be that hot."

"Could be. Certainly a good deal warmer than at home, in any case. Our own little mountain might be one of the most beautiful parts of British Columbia, but the average temperatures in the Sonoran Desert in March are usually about the same as we get at home in July, or even August – under whatever passes for 'normal weather conditions' these days."

Bud winked. "There'll be air conditioning, right? We'll be fine."

"You will. You don't mind the heat at all – you kept saying so in Jamaica last year. All the time."

Bud wriggled. "I was thinking more about you. You...well, you mentioned quite often how you found the nights there a bit sweaty."

I patted his hand. "Sorry, I did, didn't I? It was the humidity. And the flashes. The combination. I've been okay the past couple of weeks as far as the night sweats go, and you know what they say about the desert – 'it's a dry heat' – so I should be fine. Besides, I'm sure there'll be air conditioning, as you say; Serendipity told me no expense was spared when they built the Desert Gem. Didn't have to, because when the bloke who started up the whole Faceting thing died, it turned out he was rolling in money, and his wife and children invested all of it into this enterprise. Did it in record time, too, apparently. Poor thing popped his clogs last year, and the place opened a few months ago. Serendipity's restaurant is the final piece of the jigsaw; had to wait for some special equipment to arrive for the kitchen. It's her father's gift, and he insisted on the very best."

Bud leaned close. "Yes, he's quite the character is Sammy Soul. Here's to him!" He raised his glass. "I tell you what, I could get used to this private jet thing. We're being treated like royalty."

"You know what Sammy's like – once he makes up his mind about something, there's no stopping him. And the texts I've been getting from Suzie – when I can read them – have been gushing."

Bud chuckled. "If Suzie Soul still puts away the booze like she did when we got to know her, I'm amazed she can manage to text at all. I bet she thumb-bumbles all the time."

I grinned and replied, "Yes, that probably explains all the gobbledegook." I sighed. "I know what it's like to live with an alcoholic – all those years with Angus. It's so difficult. Having to watch every word. Not step out of line. Never cause a fuss. Be aware of their mood."

Bud reached across the aisle and squeezed my shoulder. "I know you had a tough time of it with Angus, but not everyone's a violent, controlling drunk. We both know Suzie's got one heck of a temper, but she never seemed to be driven by anger, which is a different thing altogether. But this restaurant of Serendipity's won't be dry, will it? Would a restaurant without alcohol even work?" Bud looked a little alarmed; he enjoys the odd beer, or glass of wine – or three – like me.

I grinned. "Don't panic – Serendipity's working with some local Arizona wineries; needless to say, her father knows most of the people who own vineyards in the area, being the owner of one back in British Columbia himself."

Bud nodded. "Yeah, we found out just how small that world is when we were looking into Annette Newman's death, didn't we? I guess what was true in Kelowna will be true here, too. Though I've got to admit, I didn't imagine the Arizona desert would be a great place to grow grapes."

"There's a good number of vineyards; in fact, there are three main wine-growing areas, and we'll pass through one of them – the Verde Valley – on the way to the place where we'll be staying. Though, honestly, I'm pleased we've decided to continue north after we leave Serendipity to see some of the spectacular landscapes. It'll be fun to visit places in real life we've only seen on film."

"That scene in *Forrest Gump* when he decides to stop walking? Yeah, it'll be great to see those sandstone buttes for real. Better than a winery, I reckon." Bud glanced around, and – despite the fact the six other seats were unoccupied – whispered, "Sipping champagne on a private jet, all paid for by a rock star I used to idolize…it's quite amazing the way some of our adventures play out, right? The unreal made real. But no corpses this time, Cait, okay?" Bud suddenly sounded grim.

I poked out my tongue. "It's not my fault, you know. I'm not the one doing the killing. It's just…well, sometimes we're stuck with something happening that we can't ignore…"

"…and sometimes you spot something you can't let go of."

"I usually like it when you finish my sentences, Husband. *Usually.*"

We squeezed hands, sipped champagne, and I was just envisaging what the sunset might look like in the desert when I heard a loud pinging coming from my pocket.

Bud looked surprised. "Was that your phone?"

The ever-helpful Mike had told us how to access the in-flight satellite Wi-Fi when we'd boarded; I hadn't expected anyone to get in touch with me while we were in the air, but it had been such a novelty I couldn't resist connecting. All of which meant I was able to tell Bud, "It's a text from Serendipity. Apparently, it won't be KSue meeting us tomorrow – so that really does seem to be her name – but someone called Norman instead."

Bud shrugged. "Okay. Good to know, I guess." He polished off his champagne.

I cleared my throat. "The reason there's been a switch could be a bit of a problem, though."

Bud put down his glass and turned to face me. His eyebrows arched in query. "Which is?"

I decided it was best to read Serendipity's text aloud:

> KSue in bits. Can't come. Found Linda dead. Lot going on here. So sad. Norman will meet you, not KSue. Adorable man. Timid. I'll see you here as planned. Enjoy Taliesin West. Don't worry. Opening is a go. No reason you can't stay at Desert Gem – not a crime scene! See you soon.

The expression on Bud's face was one of dread. "Linda is dead? Who's Linda?"

"One of the founders of the Faceting for Life movement. She and her husband set it up between them."

Bud's tone was grim. "A suspicious death before we've even got there?"

"Come on, Bud, nothing in that text screams 'suspicious death'. Look, I'm a professor of criminal psychology and you're a retired cop, so we're both almost bound to think the worst of a situation like this...but let's not get ahead of ourselves, okay? This is probably a perfectly natural death. Sad? Absolutely. But it's nothing for us to be concerned about."

He shrugged. "I don't suppose they'd turn this plane around if we asked, would they? No? Ah, well then, on we go."

I called, "Ready for a top up out here, please, Mike."

Arrival And Departure

Our arrival in Phoenix was weird; apparently, yet another advantage of flying in a private jet is that you get to use an airport's secret spaces and hidden routes to help you reach your limousine, so you're through, out, and whisked off without having to mix with more than a dozen people – which was a real treat. We settled into our delightful suite at the swanky hotel Serendipity and her parents had arranged for us, and unpacked the surprising number of things we'd need for our one-night stay. Despite the fact we'd been sitting in the lap of luxury all day, we both decided we'd like to put our feet up for a bit; there's nothing quite like being propped up on a hotel bed late in the afternoon, watching TV, seeing the sun go down, and knowing you haven't a single responsibility to fulfill for over a week – though Bud had texted Jack to make sure Marty had settled in, and was being a good boy. He had, and was.

Eventually we made our way down to dinner; Bud and I chattered happily as we surrendered ourselves to an admittedly over-indulgent meal of mouth-watering buttermilk fried mushrooms, luxurious duck and goat cheese enchiladas, and delicious smoked brisket tacos, which were much juicier than I'd expected – leading to a bit of a kerfuffle when I managed to dribble all over my bosom. The annoyance I felt about the greasy stain I'd made on my blouse had passed by the time we agreed to share a slice of moist, yielding cheesecake, and some not-too-sweet cherry bread pudding, served with glistening, rich chocolate ice cream. It was a more than hearty meal, absolutely in line with the Wild West inspired décor of the restaurant, and the "cowboy cuisine" theme of the menu. We both knew that a stroll before bed would give us a chance to let it all settle, besides, it was a delight to wander the downtown streets needing no more than a wrap over my bare arms. We passed enough people as we wandered to easily spot those – like us – for whom the temperature was wonderfully balmy, as well as locals who seemed to be bundled up well enough to overnight at the base camp on Everest.

Finally back in our sumptuous room, we flopped into bed, with me having made sure to put the Tums on the bathroom counter. Just as I was dropping off, my phone started to buzz. I debated ignoring it, but gave in, put the lamp on and read the text, which was from Serendipity.

> **Pushing back opening. Don't panic! Norman will meet you as planned tomorrow. Linda's death has affected us all in unexpected ways. Just wanted you to know. See you soon, Sx**

Bud was snoring beside me, and there seemed little point in waking him. I texted back that we'd be happy to fall in with whatever plans needed to be made, or changed, but turned off the lamp feeling a little less comfortable than I had. I couldn't help but wonder what Serendipity had meant by Linda's death having made an unexpected impact. I wasn't sure of the closeness of the relationship between Serendipity and Linda – I'd sort of assumed that, as the leader of the entire Faceting for Life movement, Linda would be a somewhat distant figure. But, possibly, if she'd been the one to give the green light for the restaurant, she and Serendipity had been closer than I'd imagined. Or maybe not, given that Serendipity hadn't initially foreseen the need to postpone her opening.

Bud stirred, shifted about a bit, then resumed normal snoring service. What he'd said at dinner had been right – the day had possessed a dreamlike quality, as though we'd been living the lives of other people. Rich people. And it had been a real eye-opener; how different the world of travel must be for those with unlimited budgets. I drifted off to sleep, where I enjoyed private islands, butlers, and a splendid room at a "money is no object" boutique resort in the Sonoran Desert, where – at least in my dreams – they brought me breakfast in bed, with a view of a perfect sunrise from our secluded quarters.

In the morning, the idea of breakfast in bed lingered, so we ordered room service. I've never been keen on actually eating *in* bed – you're bound to get crumbs on the pillows and sheets, which is a right old fiddle-faddle – so was delighted that our suite was sufficiently spacious to allow us to eat our perfectly grilled steaks and soft-poached eggs in comfort, at a proper dining table. I wolfed down two pieces of toast as well, with a slathering of raspberry jam, and a smear of guilt. And the coffee was strong, almost smoky, and plentiful. It was a wonderful breakfast, and I was almost glad we had to get our act together to leave the room before ten, because I'd eaten so much that I could have been tempted to go right back to bed for a nap otherwise, and I'd have missed the rest of the day altogether.

We checked out on the phone and took our luggage down to the massive reception lounge, where we felt a bit lost. Serendipity's only description of the person who was due to meet us was that Norman was "timid". I looked around for someone hiding in a corner, or cowering behind a column, then glimpsed a piece of cardboard being waved in the air with "MORGAN" written on it in big letters. I grabbed Bud, and we were off.

It turned out that the person holding the cardboard was about Bud's height – so around five eight or so – and about the same age – certainly in his late fifties. But the similarities stopped there: Bud was sporting smart navy shorts – he'd slathered his legs with sunblock before we'd left the room – and a pale-blue, short-sleeved linen shirt, which matched his eyes. Norman was dressed entirely in what looked to be home-dyed, ruby-red, un-ironed cotton – his bottom half swaddled in loosely-formed pants, topped with a massive collarless shirt that all but drowned him. His outfit hinted at origins somewhere on the Indian sub-continent, but I wasn't convinced that was intentional. He smelled good though – sandalwood, with a tang of musk, almost beachy – and his beard was long and snowy, with a row of multicolored elastic bands bunching it along its length, just like his ponytail.

"Hello, I'm Cait, this is Bud," I said as I stuck out my hand.

Norman looked at it with great suspicion, then grabbed it and waggled it up and down. "And I'm Norman. Norman McGlynn. Pleased to meet you. How thoughtful of you to wear every color all at once. Highly respectful, thank you."

I looked down at my rainbow-hued stripy pants and top, which I'd chosen because they were jolly, and suitable for the weather. I wasn't sure how my choice had been "respectful" but smiled as though I were graciously accepting a compliment.

Norman continued, "Serendipity sent me. KSue couldn't come. She's real upset about Linda." Given his words, I found it peculiar that his expression was joyous. *Odd.*

"We were terribly sorry to hear about Linda. Did you know her well?" I summoned my most sympathetic smile, and Bud nodded, mirroring my concerned look.

"Know her? Linda?" The question seemed to baffle Norman to such an extent that he said nothing for at least thirty long seconds. His eyes darted, and he shifted his weight from foot to foot. Finally, he said, "I'm not sure Linda was knowable. Certainly she's been my inspiration for almost a decade, and I have spent many months at both the original Gem, in Sedona, and the new Desert Gem. Indeed, my wife and I have been living there since it was able to accommodate us. But *know* Linda? Insofar as one can know the moon or the stars, I suppose I did. She was an incandescent light, illuminating the way for so many, allowing us to navigate the treacherous landscape that surrounds us all, helping us find the path we were always meant to take, that leads toward our true destination. I shall miss her presence on this plane dreadfully, though I have no doubt she'll find a way to return to us…maybe as her beloved husband Demetrius has done, since he moved on. Zara, their daughter, is now his channel, you see…so maybe their son, Oscar, will take on the same role for his mother."

I heard Bud stop breathing about halfway through Norman's response, so nudged him to make him start again. His shoulders drooped, then he smiled a too-broad smile; I wondered how much of Norman's earnest tone he'd be able to stomach before he burst.

"So sorry for your loss," was all Bud managed. We all remained where we were – still and silent – for a moment or two. Eventually Bud added, "I'm not sure how long it's going to take us to get to Taliesin West, but we have a tour booked for eleven, and…" He looked at his watch.

Norman glanced at the large piece of cardboard in his hand, then helplessly scanned the lounge. He nodded, folded the cardboard into the smallest square it would make, and said, "But of course. Yes, we should really get going. My wife's come with me – I hope you don't mind. We left the Desert Gem before dawn, you see, and she knows I don't like to drive in the dark, so…"

We followed Norman toward the massive glass doors which slid open as we approached, startling him; Bud and I managed to keep our response to an exchange of an eye roll, and two firmly affixed smiles. Outside was a woman who looked almost exactly the same as Norman – minus the beard, plus a pair of truly rose-tinted sunglasses – holding open the door of a gleaming red SUV. With our bags safely stowed in the rear. Bud and I settled into the back seats, and we were off.

Norman was driving, and his wife turned toward Bud and myself as much as was possible. She beamed and waved at us, then announced in a melodious voice, "Hello fellow travelers, I'm Elizabeth, Norman's wife." She laughed explosively. "Saying that never gets old. Love him to bits, I do...don't I, Norman?"

"You do, Elizabeth, indeed you do. And I you. As much, if not more."

I heard the air escaping from Bud's nose in the way it does when he's in a situation where he can't sigh with resignation, so realized I'd better lead the conversation.

"Lovely to meet you Elizabeth, though of course we wish it was under happier circumstances." I nudged Bud's knee with mine.

"Yes, so sorry to hear the news about your friend...I mean your...I mean Linda." Bud's tone suggested genuine condolences, even if he was clearly still struggling with Norman's earlier assessment of his relationship with the recently deceased woman.

Elizabeth turned to face the road ahead, pulled down her sun visor and moved it around so she could see us in its mirror. "Linda? Gone? She won't be gone for long. Not Linda. That woman was as ready to come back as it is for a person to be. I don't know how she'll return, but she will. In her heart she's bound to Estsanatlehi, which means she can change, and renew. Linda is the Turquoise Woman, personified. We'll connect with her again very soon, I have no doubt of that."

"Estalehani?" Bud sounded puzzled.

Elizabeth roared with laughter. "Close, but no cigar. Good try though, Bud. Est-san-atl-ehi. Always break up unfamiliar words into smaller parts. Makes them easier to say, spell, and write. Navajo Goddess. Some say she created humans, others that she had twin sons by her lover, the Sun, that she lived in a house made of turquoise taken from the Pacific. Linda Karaplis was a devotee. In many ways."

"Elizabeth has spent many hours, over the years, helping those who come to literacy later in life," said Norman. I could hear pride in his voice. "Does a lot for those to whom the education system hasn't been as helpful as it might. Knows a great deal about many, many subjects. A wise woman."

"And you've created things with your hands that we've sold to raise funds to buy the supplies I need to be able to follow my path – so don't go selling yourself short, Norman McGlynn." Elizabeth glanced around. "We're a team, you see, Cait, Bud. Folks these days don't seem to understand what that means."

"Common goals, different skills," I said.

"Same end, different means – we get it," added Bud.

Elizabeth adjusted her mirror and chuckled. "Good for you," she said quietly.

"You're a teacher, Elizabeth?" I thought I'd exercise my small-talk skills.

More laughing. "It's something I took up in my retirement."

"And what line of work did you retire from?" I poked Bud who was zoning out, and he perked up a bit when I made join-the-conversation eyes at him.

Elizabeth replied, "Banking. Many years in banking." She made it sound like a life sentence.

"Did you two meet at work?" Bud was at least pretending to be interested.

Norman and Elizabeth glanced at each other. "We did," replied Norman, returning his eyes to the road.

"Were you both at the same branch, or at a big HQ type thing?" It sounded as though Bud was scrabbling around at the bottom of a very deep barrel for questions.

"We were both cubicle dwellers," replied Elizabeth, implying solitary confinement, then added, "You two been to Taliesin West before?"

I was surprised she'd changed the topic so swiftly. "No. But I've wanted to go for years."

"You'll love it or hate it. One or the other. Might find it surprising, though. We did the first time we went, didn't we, Norman?"

Norman nodded. "Not at all what I'd expected. But inspiring in so many ways."

"How do you mean?" Bud was living dangerously by asking such an open-ended question.

Elizabeth replied, "Norman's good with his hands, like I said, and always has been. Can build anything."

"But not fine work," added Norman.

"We're not building a piano," chorused the couple, then they both laughed heartily, and joyfully.

Once they'd recovered, Elizabeth said, "You'll have to forgive us...we have our little ways. Norman likes to remind himself, and me, that whatever he's building won't have the precision required of a piano."

"And that's why Taliesin West inspired me," said Norman, "because there are more non-pianos there than you might expect. If Frank Lloyd Wright could get away with using less than perfect parts that still make up a wonderful, fabulous, awe-inspiring whole, then there's hope for all of us."

"Marvellous use of color at the place," said Elizabeth. "The man certainly looked at the landscape surrounding him before he chose his palette. But you'll make up your own minds, I dare say. Serendipity hasn't told us much about you two, but I can see you're both quite certain of who you are. 'Know thyself' was carved into the rock at Delphi. Important thing that – knowing who you truly are. It's why we Facet. Facet and Face It."

"I couldn't agree more," was out of my lips before I could stop myself. "At least, the bit about knowing oneself. My life's work has been all about considering the ways in which people don't really know themselves, or even those around them…don't really understand the consequences of their actions, or inaction."

Elizabeth half-turned. "Psychologist?"

I nodded. "Yes."

Elizabeth said, "The search for a deeper understanding of the human psyche is a valiant one. That's why I help folks to read – it's the only possible path to real enlightenment. We don't stand a chance of understanding ourselves, or anyone else, unless we understand the world in which we exist, and the best way to do that is to be able to learn. And that means you gotta read. The writing bit is useful, too, of course."

"Of course," I replied. "Good for you for offering help to those who need it."

Elizabeth waved a hand. "It's no sacrifice; I do it because I enjoy it. I cannot imagine anything more rewarding, or satisfying, than helping people to learn to read and write."

"And speak, and listen," piped up Norman. "Elizabeth has been instrumental in designing our talking, listening, writing, and distillation therapies. Zara has found her insights incredibly valuable, and we've all benefitted. Myself included." I noticed that Norman squared his shoulders and adjusted his grip on the steering wheel as he spoke. "I feel I'm a little more assertive than I used to be."

Elizabeth touched her husband tenderly on the arm. "Therapies *and* rubies…don't forget the power of the stones." She glanced at us in her mirror. "We've been wearing ruby red for a couple of months now, and both of us have invested in some rubies to carry with us at all times. Their power, and even the power of their color, influences our energy levels, allowing Norman to move toward being more courageous. And rubies are renowned for keeping travelers safe – so we'll all benefit from that property, since we're taking this journey together."

"Excellent," said Bud. "We could have done with a few rubies dotted around the airplane that brought us here. Terrible flight, wasn't it, Cait?"

I agreed.

"Well, you landed safely enough, even if there was sad news to greet you," replied Elizabeth. "But listen, we're only about fifteen minutes away and I don't want you to miss the landscape by having to natter with me all the time. Take it all in. Quite something, right?"

"We're certainly not in Canada anymore," replied Bud.

"Quite different to our home, halfway up a little mountain in British Columbia," I added. "The predominant color there is green – all the trees, you know. This landscape is anything but. Though I'm surprised to see how many of the homes not only have pools, but also what appear to be large areas of grass. Is that real grass? Or do the locals use the fake type, so it doesn't need to be watered?"

Elizabeth glanced out of her window. "A bit of both. Unsustainable. Totally unsustainable. But no one will do anything about it – not the ones who could, in any case. We do what we can, don't we Norman? As did poor Linda. Her guidance will be sorely missed."

"Until she starts to speak to us again, like Demetrius does," added Norman.

Elizabeth nodded. "Yes, until then."

Bud and I gazed out of our respective windows and I marveled at how densely suburban our surroundings were. I didn't feel as though we'd really left Phoenix, and yet we were almost at Frank Lloyd Wright's jewel "in the desert". Clearly there were desert mountains surrounding us – but everywhere else were homes and busy roads; it wasn't at all what I'd expected.

Finally, I could see we were driving along Frank Lloyd Wright Boulevard – which bode well – then we turned onto Taliesin Drive. I felt the excitement in my tummy. I was going to see the place I'd read about for so long.

I squeezed Bud's hand, and we shared a smile; mine was a little broader than his, but he puckered his lips, blew me a kiss, then whispered, "You'll love it, I'm sure."

Getting out of the car was a bit of a shock to the system; it wasn't even eleven o'clock, but the sun was high, the sky clear, and it was already hot. The dust we'd disturbed in the parking lot hung in the air, not seeming to have any desire to sink to the ground.

"Just wander up that way," said Elizabeth pointing through her open window, "there'll be signs telling you what to do. We'll leave you now, and we'll be back later. Gotta go feed this beast; there are charging stations at Northside, not far away. I suggest you eat here; we'll eat there. If we leave around two-thirty we should be delivering you into Serendipity's hands by five, at the latest. Sound good?"

Bud and I nodded, and we headed off in the direction Elizabeth had indicated. We were finally on our adventure alone, and it felt good.

Desert Oasis

Our guide for the tour was named Isaac, and he bubbled with enthusiasm as he greeted us and the rest of our group. I marvelled at the emerald grass and turquoise waters in front of the main buildings, could see the inspiration for the rust-colored paint on the wooden structures in the landscape surrounding the site, and was thrilled to be able to get my first close-up view of a saguaro cactus in the wild. It was massive.

"I wouldn't fancy that toppling over onto me," said Bud as we stared up at the monster. "Gotta weigh a ton. And those spines? Ouch. What do you reckon? Thirty feet tall?"

"I wouldn't even fancy it falling on a house," I replied. "Probably thirty feet, yes, and about fifteen wide. I love the arms. And look at that knobby bit on top, at the side – it looks like it's growing a second head. Plants are amazing, aren't they? All so different...and yet all magnificent, in their way. I'm glad we got to see this sitting in its natural landscape; at least we've escaped all the houses down below us."

"Good thing, that," replied Bud, as our group straggled toward the first building we were due to enter, "I was beginning to wonder if we'd get to see any actual desert. I'd expected Scottsdale to feel as though it were separate from Phoenix, but the drive made me realize it's not. I hope the place we're staying at is a bit more like this, and a bit less like the suburban wasteland we drove through. If anywhere else could be like this."

"Oh bother." I scrabbled in my bag for my phone which was pinging away.

"Everything alright back home? Any problems with Marty? Who is it?" Bud looked concerned.

"I'm sure it is. I'm sure he's fine. This is from Serendipity. It's a bit garbled." I read out the text:

Chaotic. O gone. In mountains? Searching. Bad. Come asap xo.

"'O gone'? What's that mean?" Bud sounded anxious.

"Maybe Oscar – Linda's son. Gone missing? Died too? No idea."

Bud sighed. "If we go with your first suggestion, which I kinda prefer, then that's a dead body *and* a missing person, so far."

We both sagged a bit, then I typed: "Sorry. See you later" and put my phone away.

"Come on, they're leaving us behind." Isaac was beckoning to us, and I realized only Bud and I were still taking in the overall beauty of the main facade. "I won't let this take the shine off our visit here," I said, as we cantered to join our group.

I had a little word with myself as we caught our breath and stepped under an awning to grab a bit of shade, then enjoyed being told about Wright's design ethos and choices, his hopes and plans for Taliesin West, how they were challenged, revitalized, and changed – and how he'd used local workers and artisans to make his dreams a reality. We ooh-ed and ah-eh at the public and private spaces, though I especially adored the bathroom he'd designed for his personal use, which was a symphony of function meeting form – a simple, ribbed, stainless-steel box set within rugged rocks. Exquisite.

Finally, our tour was over, and we ambled around the little shop, where I gave into temptation and bought a set of four coasters – which I managed to convince myself would be useful at home and in my office. Each displayed Frank Lloyd Wright's Organic Commandment: Love is the virtue of the heart; Sincerity the virtue of the mind; Courage the virtue of the spirit; Decision the virtue of the will.

As we sat under canvas awnings, nibbling on a salad, I wanted to say so much about how I felt about actually being there, but decided to open with: "What was your favorite part?"

Bud smiled. "The look on your face as you walked around." I grasped his hand. "Oh, look…you put down your fork, I must have touched a nerve." He grinned, then reached over and kissed me on the cheek. "What was *your* favorite bit?"

"Lots: his bathroom; the way you could actually see how he'd developed his ideas and their realization over twenty years; the way he played with light, water, rock, space, and the relationships they have with each other. It must be wonderful to be here for twenty-four hours and see how those relationships change. But the thing I wasn't prepared for was how I would feel about glimpsing all the photographs of the man himself."

"Because he reminds you of your father?"

I nodded. "Yes, I know I've commented upon that before, but to walk into a room and see that profile, that mouth – it was weird. To be honest, if you put Dad and him next to each other I dare say not many people would see the similarity – but there's something about him that strikes a chord. And that touched me in unexpected ways today."

Bud squeezed my hand again before returning his attention to his lunch. "I hope it didn't make you feel too sad."

"No, not too bad. I miss Dad, and Mum, of course. I think he'd have adored the chance to come here. Maybe Mum not so much, especially given the heat. But they're gone, and have been for quite some time…so it's a gentler sadness now than it might have been a decade ago."

"I know how fortunate I am that my mom and dad are still alive, but I understand what you mean about grief. It mellows a little, with time, but it's unbelievably painful at first. I'd have done almost anything to somehow rid myself of the desperation I felt when Jan was killed. When they say grief is the pits, it's because that's exactly where you are with it – in a deep, dark pit, with no way to climb out…except a bit at a time, heading for the light of consolation."

I squeezed his hand. "That's an eloquent way to speak about loss."

Bud chuckled, "What – you mean 'for me'?" I shook my head. Bud winked and said, "Not related to your father, was he? Frank Lloyd Wright, I mean."

I picked up on his change of tone, and decided to follow his lead. "I don't think so. I know he got the 'Lloyd' from his Welsh mother – and he certainly cherished his Welsh heritage, as witnessed by the fact he used the name of the Welsh mythical character whose name means 'shining brow' for both his original Taliesin home, and this one. But he was also a man who was determined to develop a truly American form of architecture, and, though I know he travelled extensively, I don't think he managed any procreation in Wales…though I wouldn't have put it past him."

Bud nodded. "Yes, he had quite the life."

"And he must have been incredibly charismatic; he managed to get so many people to do his bidding. Do you think – as Isaac suggested – that was the Welsh in him?" I winked, and pushed away my empty plate.

"Undoubtedly, Wife," replied Bud with a grin. "Come on, just time for a bathroom break before we're on our merry way," he added, looking at his watch. "I just hope the McGlynns don't try to talk us into joining their movement while they're driving us to meet Serendipity."

"Elizabeth's too sensible, and Norman wouldn't say boo to a goose."

Bud stood. "True. Though it's early days yet – there'll be lots more of them where we're staying. They might only let out the ones who appear to be acceptable to society."

I also stood. "The way Frank Lloyd Wright inspired people, took them along with him on his sometimes mad, and usually outrageous, journeys toward new architectural and design solutions? That's the sort of thing Linda and Demetrius Karaplis must have done when they established their Faceting movement; they, too, must have been charismatic. It's a shame they're both dead, because folks who have that ability are always fascinating to meet, listen to, and watch. You've met them, I'm sure – though you're more likely to have met the criminal ones. I know I have."

Bud nodded as we moved outside, the heat of the sun shocking us both, "I have, though not as many as you might think. What inspires most criminals isn't another person with a big, life-changing idea – it's more likely to be their own greed, anger, or lust."

"But that's the thing, Bud, these charismatics tune into that, and exploit it. Even the venerable Mr. Wright would have used his clients' desire to be highly thought of within their community to get them to loosen their purse strings and spend more for the best – in other words, him. He, like those of his ilk, would have possessed a natural ability to home in on a person's deepest desires to be able to get what *he* wanted – even if they also got what *they* wanted, too. Convincing a person of a mutually beneficial outcome is what charismatic individuals are able to do: they – the inspirers with charm – get what they want, whatever that might be, and I believe in Wright's case that was the opportunity to bring his design vision into being using other people's money. Of course, it only works if the person who's been inspired believes they were right to do what they did, because they're also fulfilled in some way – feeling good about the outcome."

"True," said Bud as we finally returned to the front of the main buildings, taking the chance to soak in the entire vista for one last time.

"There they are. Yoo-hoo, Cait, Bud!"

We looked toward the parking area, and spotted Elizabeth and Norman, their ruby garb glowing in the sunlight, garnering more than a few sideways looks from the people milling about close by. We waved back, and headed toward them.

"I wonder if they've heard from Serendipity, too?" I said as we approached. The anxiety etched on their faces suggested they knew something was amiss.

"Oh good, now we can get going," said Elizabeth, grabbing my arm. "I'm going to drive because Norman doesn't like to put his foot down. I don't want to alarm you, but we've received word from the Desert Gem that there's been a bit of…well, let's just say there've been some unusual goings-on and they want us back as soon as possible, so we can help out."

"You mean with the search for 'O' – who I assume is Oscar Karaplis?" Bud sounded grim.

Both Elizabeth and Norman looked surprised. "Did Serendipity manage to text you?" Elizabeth herded me as we jogged along. "Good for her."

"Yes," I replied, as we got into the SUV. "Her text suggested that things were a bit chaotic there."

We all buckled up, and Elizabeth exited the parking lot as fast as she dared – given the number of folks ambling about the place, and the amount of dust our wheels kicked up. She stamped on the brakes as a couple scuttled in front of us. "Oscar's completely disappeared. He always was a bit off, if you ask me," she snapped, glaring at the hapless pedestrians. "Weak. Rudderless. Linda doted on him, which was odd, and annoying."

Norman said, "Oh I wouldn't say that. I'm very worried about him. The desert's not a place to go wandering about, you need to be on full alert – real treacherous if you're not paying attention. There are so many dangerous creatures out there: Gila monsters, scorpions, and rattlers."

"Oh my," I said. Norman had made it sound as though the landscape was overrun with deadly creatures.

Bud cleared his throat rather dramatically. "The deceased was this Oscar's mother, right? And we've been given the impression that her death was unexpected. The boy might have gone somewhere to do a bit of private grieving."

Elizabeth took her eyes off the road for long enough to give Bud a venomous glare in the rear-view mirror. "And this is the voice of experience speaking? You don't really know the people involved, do you? Maybe you'd better wait until you've met them all. Your wife might be a psychologist, but that doesn't mean you've picked up all her hard-earned knowledge by osmosis."

I was quite taken aback by Elizabeth's acid tone, but knew Bud would cope.

He replied courteously, but firmly, "I know we've only just met, and of course we don't know each other at all well, and you're also right when you say I don't know any of the people involved. But I do have over thirty years working in law enforcement under my belt, and I've seen a good number of people trying to come to terms with news of an unexpected death, so I guess I have a right to use that experience to form my opinions."

Both Norman and Elizabeth exclaimed, "You're a cop?" Their tone suggested this wasn't a good thing.

Bud replied evenly, "Retired now. Trained by the Royal Canadian Mounted Police, Vancouver cop, detective, homicide specialist, then onto a few other areas."

Norman giggled. "Oh Elizabeth, look at us, we're driving a cop around. Who'd have thought it? Us with a cop!"

The belly laugh they shared allowed Bud and I to exchange a look that told me he was thinking the same as me: the McGlynns' reaction to discovering his professional background wasn't what one might call "normal". As our journey continued in silence, and I watched the terrain become more barren, with fewer and fewer man-made structures, I couldn't help but wonder exactly how Linda Karaplis had died – and why Bud's career had proved so seemingly entertaining for the couple transporting us to our ultimate destination. As we drove further into the wilderness, the trees seemed to be struggling, and the scrubby hillsides looked so much less spectacular than the red-soiled areas dotted with magnificent buttes that I longed to see. Yes, Taliesin West had surpassed my hopes and expectations – but I had a dreadful feeling that the remainder of our time in Arizona wasn't going to be quite what I'd hoped.

Rustic Elegance

The first sight I caught of Serendipity Soul's restaurant was a glint, which grew to be a glare, which ended up being a blinding light. The sun was catching the bevels on what – oddly – turned out to be leaded windows set into the strangely unprepossessing structure which, if I hadn't known any better, screamed "shack in the woods" rather than "oasis in the desert". It was surrounded by a surprising number of trees, though they thinned out beyond the immediate area, being replaced by much more exotic flora, and, yes, on the shoulder of a hillside beyond, there was at least one saguaro cactus standing stark against the sky – for which I was immensely grateful.

"Are we there yet?" Bud whispered in my ear with a smirk as we unbuckled and swung our legs out of the SUV. It was good to unfold.

Almost before my feet touched the ground, a familiar figure clad in somewhat besmirched chef whites was running out of the front doors of the building, arms outstretched. Serendipity Soul's brunette hair was shorter than it had been when we'd last seen her, and she was a little more rounded – which suited her.

"Incoming," warned Bud, but he needn't have bothered, because Serendipity flung her arms around Elizabeth, not me, and they held each other, swaying, for at least a full minute. They didn't speak. The process was then repeated between Serendipity and Norman. Still no words had been exchanged. Then all three drew back from each other and bowed at the waist. Bud cleared his throat quietly.

"Not a word," I warned under my breath.

Finally turning her attention to us, Serendipity's greeting was a tight embrace, first for me, then Bud. I was glad that our hugs didn't last as long as the ones she'd given the McGlynns, but, even so, Bud's eyes as he stared at me over Serendipity's shoulder were wide with unease. I hoped this wasn't a routine that would be constantly repeated, though feared it might. Serendipity drew back from us both and bowed; Bud and I exchanged a glance and mirrored her action – it seemed the respectful thing to do.

Our hostess laughed. "No need for you to do that, it's just what we do. But if you want to, that's fine, too. Bowing shows we respect the person we're greeting. The hug? That's so we speak with our body of our friendship for the person, rather than having to use words. It lasts at least one minute, so there's enough time to feel the other person's heart beating, and get to know how they smell, and feel all over. It allows us to become comfortable with the other person's presence, and them with ours, so that when we step away we're already bonded." Serendipity beamed as she spoke, and Elizabeth and Norman did the same.

"I didn't greet you like that at the hotel because…" Norman shuffled. "Well, it's a bit much if you don't know what's happening, or why; I didn't want to overwhelm you, you know?" He blushed, the pink of his cheeks enriched by the ruby of his shirt.

"Serendipity did a good job of explaining," said Elizabeth briskly, "now come on, tell us what's going on. We want the full story. And did you know Bud used to be a cop?"

Serendipity looked puzzled. "Of course I did. That's how we met – Bud was investigating the death of one of my neighbors back in Canada. I told you that." She paused, then added, "Well, I'm pretty sure I told you. In any case he's retired, right, Bud?"

It was Bud's turn to wrinkle his brow. "I'm a retired Canadian detective visiting the United States of America on vacation; I can't imagine why Norman and Elizabeth would have to worry about that…unless there's something about which they'd like to inform me, that they think I should know."

Norman and Elizabeth's faces split into broad smiles, and they both laughed heartily. "Nothing at all. How about we all get inside the restaurant, and you fill us in, Serendipity?"

The aroma of something spicy hung in the air as we entered the vestibule of the empty building, and my tummy rumbled. Loudly. It proved to be a useful ice-breaker.

"Come on, Cait, Bud, let's get you something to drink and eat," said Serendipity. "How about you pick out a couple of beers for yourselves from the selection in the cooler; a lot of them are locally made, and the labels are pretty good at explaining the type of beer, and where they come from. I'll rustle up a few bowls of posole. Will you stay?" Serendipity was now addressing Elizabeth and Norman.

"We should help with the search for Oscar." Elizabeth was all business.

Serendipity replied, "They're on their way back down from the hills. Should all be here in less than an hour, before the light's gone. I stayed to cook up a big batch of posole and I've got frybread ready to go. I thought the best way I could help was to be able to feed everyone when they were done, so that no one else had to stay to prepare a meal at the refectory. I suggest you four dig in before this place is full."

I looked around the restaurant and calculated there was seating for around forty people. I also noted the tremendous effort that had been put into making the place look as though it had been flung together: the mismatched chairs and tables, the eclectic artwork, the pseudo-antique farmhouse feel – I reckoned it had been created on a big budget by someone with an impeccable eye for design. Rather than comment on our surroundings, I couldn't help but ask, "Has Oscar been seen at all since his mother's death?"

Serendipity turned as she headed toward the swing doors, which I suspected must lead to the kitchen. "Not since a few hours after it was discovered she had passed."

Elizabeth motioned in Bud's direction. "The cop here thinks he's run off to grieve."

Serendipity hovered uncertainly. "It must be devastating to lose a parent, so he's bound to be sad, of course. But it could have been a lot worse – she died in her sleep, peacefully, so he had no cause for concern on that front. The only odd thing that KSue mentioned was that Linda was fully clothed, and everyone here knows how unusual that is."

"That's real strange," said Norman. In response to my raised eyebrows he added, "Linda always slept naked. Did it her entire life. Very proud of the fact. Why she'd be in her bed wearing clothes is a real mystery."

Elizabeth gave Bud a sideways glance and said quietly, "But still nothing to worry about that would need a cop to get involved."

Bud and I pretended to give our full attention to the dizzying array of bottled beers on offer. As we read labels aloud, pointing at novelty designs and witty names, I whispered, "If all they've got to go on is the fact the woman didn't undress before she went to bed, then it really doesn't sound as though there's anything suspicious about her death after all, and I reckon you're right – grieving son gone walkabout."

Serendipity emerged through the kitchen's swing doors, then scooted to the massive serving hatch behind the counter, where she'd pushed through some steaming bowls. She ushered us all to a table beside floor-to-ceiling windows at the rear of the building where there was a delightful view across a wide deck down into a little valley, as well as across the tops of the surrounding, slightly lower, peaks; the restaurant was perched on the shoulder of a higher hill offering a wonderful vista to the west we hadn't been able to see from the parking area.

As we all settled to our meal of what was – essentially – a hearty meat and vegetable soup, Serendipity stared intently at the sky. The sun had already dipped below the hilltops, their outlines sharpened by the changing light, transformed into mauve silhouettes.

She sighed. "This is such a beautiful place, especially at this time of day. Sunset is so…magical. It allows you to believe there really is a space between worlds, where anything is possible."

"Maybe Linda has already begun the journey to return to us," said Norman quietly, then he glanced at his wife, who was chewing.

"This is delicious," said Bud. "What's in it?"

Serendipity turned her attention to him and said, "*Chiles*, of course." She smiled at her Spanish pronunciation, then continued, "Pork, vegetables, and hominy. It's my interpretation of a Navajo recipe, taking the original ingredients and injecting a bit of modern elegance, without losing the original rustic charm – an example of the sort of menu I'll be offering here."

"Just like the décor," I replied.

"Exactly," said Serendipity, obviously delighted that I'd noticed.

"It's delicious," said Bud with surprising enthusiasm, "but what's hominy? Is it this lumpy stuff?"

Serendipity smiled. "Yes, it's the lumpy stuff. It's a sort of maize, prepared in a specific way to make it edible. It's not like the sweetcorn we have back in British Columbia – this stuff puffs up when it's treated, then it's used as an ingredient, or it's ground to make meal, which some use as a thickener, or for grits. I soaked it last night, thinking I'd be using it for the dinner I'd originally planned for this evening. At least it was ready, so I could use it for this; it takes hours to prepare, and the posole itself also takes a fair amount of time, though I dare say you'll be pleased to hear that I used pork tenderloin, rather than boiling the meat off a couple of pigs' heads."

Bud gulped and replied, "Yeah, have to say that sounds better. And the sauce, or liquid, you know, is so tasty. I can really taste the *chiles*, but it's not too hot at all."

"Not a fan of spicy food?" Elizabeth's tone carried an edge.

"If the heat's too intense that's all I can taste. Great job, Serendipity." Bud's well-earned praise was accepted graciously by our hostess.

"I bet everyone will be happy to tuck into this when they come down from the hills. Do you think that's really where Oscar's gone? That he's just wandered off into the desert, somewhere?" Norman had almost emptied his bowl.

Our hostess shook her head. "No idea. He was nowhere to be found this morning. He was here when Linda's body was discovered yesterday, but no one seems to have seen him since dark time."

"Dark time?" I had to ask what she meant, because it was such an odd turn of phrase.

"Lights out, I guess you'd call it…not that there are many lights to be turned off," replied Elizabeth brightly. "Part of our dark skies decision." Elizabeth glanced at Serendipity as she spoke. They didn't make eye contact.

Serendipity pushed away her bowl, untouched. "A vote was taken, and it was agreed that all non-natural lighting would be turned off at sunset. After that, only firelight, candles, or oil lamps are acceptable forms of illumination. That's why every table here has an oil lamp. Castor oil, or olive oil, of course, not paraffin-based. And any electricity used here is generated by our solar farm. We manage quite well."

"I didn't know you could use those oils in lamps," said Bud.

Our hostess nodded. "Both are truly sustainable fuels. We get the extra virgin olive oil I use in the kitchen and the low grade we use in the lamps from the same supplier in-state; olives grow well here in the desert – in fact, they need to be a bit stressed to crop well. Olive oil is one of the earliest forms of lamplight, and castor oil is available because – again – the plants grow well here. All the necessities of life."

"And you've got the technical necessities, too, like cellphone reception," I said, sitting back in my seat, my tummy relishing the warmth of the posole. "You're obviously able to text, and phone."

The three residents laughed. "I'm afraid that's a bit of a problem. Unreliable. Best place is outside, of course, but then you need all the stars to align." Norman was still chuckling.

"My husband doesn't mean that literally," said Elizabeth, "but it's all a bit hit and miss. The further up you go, the better the reception…or the further down toward civilization you travel."

"I had to walk about half a mile to get my last text through to you," added Serendipity, "but often I'll type a whole bunch before I go down the road in the truck to get supplies, then send them all at once. It's a bit different for me, though, because I leave the place quite often. People who are living here, working on their personal development or on one of our projects, like Elizabeth and Norman, don't seem to mind though, do you?"

Both shook their heads. "It's one of the best things about the place; as soon as you realize it's possible to untether yourself from the rest of the world just by putting your phone in a drawer and forgetting it's there, the better you're able to focus on what really matters. Disconnect to reconnect. Facet and Face It, right?" Elizabeth beamed a beatific smile at her husband, then at Bud and me.

"But I can use Wi-Fi here, right?" I asked. Another gale of laughter ensued.

"None here – another vote," said Serendipity, nibbling her lip.

"Looks like that laptop you dragged along will be doing a job of work as a paperweight this week," said Bud, winking. He can't understand why I always take it everywhere with me; he's even been so bold as to refer to it as a fetish, which I've always thought an uncalled-for assessment of my positive feelings toward it.

Now a little concerned about our lack of connectivity, I pressed, "So where would I go to get a good cell signal, if I really needed one?"

All three waved their arms in different directions. "The signal's all around, you just have to catch it," said Norman, somewhat unhelpfully.

The door opened and a rather striking-looking woman poked her head inside. "Am I the first?"

Serendipity rose. "Come on in, Barbara. You are, but we've been expecting you. Any luck?"

The woman opened the door wide and removed her dusty boots, placing them in the outer entryway. She was wearing the same balloon-form cotton clothing as Elizabeth and Norman, but her outfit was a deep purple, like her short, wiry hair.

"Barbara is one of our wisest elders," said Norman quietly. "She has a wonderful way with words. An excellent communicator. Sometimes I wish I had the courage to speak up, like she does, but…" He fell silent.

As Barbara approached, I could tell she was nearer seventy than sixty, though her brisk movements suggested a high level of fitness and mobility. "He's nowhere to be found. Looked high and low, we have." She spoke with a broad South African accent. "If he's decided to hide out, we'll never find him."

Bud and I had nothing to offer on the matter, but the three others at the table who knew Oscar Karaplis personally nodded sagely as they all rose, and the hugging and bowing thing took place between them and Barbara. It took a while; I wondered how long group get-togethers would take before they even got going.

"How old is Oscar?" I asked when everyone had taken a seat. "I mean – could he fend for himself overnight, in the wilderness?"

"He's almost forty, so he should be able to," replied Barbara. "Besides, he's often out there, roaming about. Knows how to handle himself in the desert, does Oscar. Me? If I stray from the paths I get all turned around – those cholla bushes mean you have to weave around them, then you don't know which way you wanted to go in the first place. Him? He's like a...I don't know – whatever sort of creature doesn't get turned around in the desert."

I replied, "I had no idea how old Linda's children were. Nor Linda, for that matter."

Serendipity smiled sadly, "Linda recently marked her seventieth journey around the sun, and we all celebrated with her. Oscar's almost forty, but Zara's not yet thirty; she was a late blessing for Linda and Demetrius."

"And it was her arrival that inspired them to begin a life of Faceting," said Norman, smiling. Beaming.

Oh gracious, this is getting old already – is everyone going to be hugging and grinning all week? was what I thought; "How interesting," was what I said.

Serendipity offered, "I'll fetch some posole, okay?"

"Great, thanks," replied Barbara, as Serendipity cleared away our dishes.

"This one –" Elizabeth stuck a thumb in Bud's direction – "is a cop and he thinks Oscar's gone off for a good old cry. But

Serendipity says KSue told him Linda went peacefully. Though who knows what that means."

Barbara rolled her eyes. "Yes, KSue Henritze is, indeed, vagueness personified. Always muddled that one. No idea why. I mean, I think it's excellent that she's working on herself, but if she keeps thinking she's dumb, and telling everyone she's dumb, then she'll always be dumb. No way out of that one."

"She has a good heart," said Norman, "kindest woman you could wish to meet."

Barbara nodded. "She is, but she's not the best person to find a dead body and to be able to tell anyone about what she found. If it hadn't been for Don finding her crying in the plaza, who knows how long it would have taken her to even tell anyone Linda had passed. Just as well they got to her when they did, or the body would have started to stink. The ice is helping, alright, but it'll be good to get her in the ground."

I didn't understand. "You mean Linda's body is still here? At the Desert Gem? They didn't take it away?"

The rest of the group looked confused. Barbara asked, "Who would take her away? To where? Who's 'they'?"

Bud replied, "The cops? The ambulance? The medical examiner's office?"

Barbara shook her head and appeared to bat Bud's words away with her hands. "She's still at her place, where she died. In her bathtub, on ice. I think it was Frank who stayed behind to keep topping it up through the day," said Barbara. "Why would anyone have called the cops?"

Bud and I exchanged a stunned look. "She hasn't been examined? Doesn't anyone know how the woman actually died? There'll need to be an investigation." I could tell Bud was working hard to sound civil.

"No worries," replied Barbara brightly, "Dr. Nderu will be up from Phoenix in the morning and he'll take a good look at her then, sign the death certificate, and sort out the registration of the death etcetera. He's one of us and always does it for us. Her funeral will be held here – where she'd have wanted to stay – tomorrow, at sunset. It'll be a great way to mark the end of Linda's life." She paused as Serendipity placed a bowl on the table in front of her. "Thanks for this, I need it."

Barbara wasted no time tucking into her soup as I said, "But surely you can't just bury someone's body wherever you like – can you?"

Serendipity hovered beside us. "Yes, it's legal in Arizona. With all the medical side of things sorted, and the paperwork filed, you can inter a person without using a funeral director; there are already some Facetors buried in a little plot just over the hill. They died here and, of course, wanted to stay. Linda got the clearance for there to be a designated burial ground here; all you have to do is make sure it's noted and marked on maps. It's so sad – both the founders and most of the earliest members are gone now. They put their everything into creating the movement, then getting this place built, now they've all passed on, mostly since the Desert Gem opened its doors, though it's still not fully functioning, yet. You're the very first outsiders to visit. So sad they didn't have more time to be able to see how we're starting to flourish. But you know what? At least they were all delighted to know that Demetrius had found his way back to us."

"Maybe they're all trying to pierce the veil themselves but don't have the strength Demetrius had," said Norman sadly. "But he was the first to pass, I guess."

Barbara paused eating, her spoon mid-air. "That's because of the bond between the father and the daughter – and that Delphic blood he brought from Greece with him. Good for Zara, I say – she's changed the way so many of us see things. Sometimes it takes the young ones to make us reconsider our way of thinking."

"But, Barbara, *Demetrius* is the one doing that," replied Elizabeth. "He's the one speaking through Zara. It's his knowledge of what's beyond that we're learning from, not Zara herself. I mean, what would she know? At her age you don't even know the questions that matter, let alone the answers. No, it's Demetrius who's leading us to a brighter, better place, not Zara, and don't you forget that. That's the only reason we're all taking on board the new thinking – because it's coming from beyond, not this plane."

Norman nodded slowly. "Exactly, my dear. Exactly. Demetrius has seen the light, has walked into it, and is exploring what's beyond…and he's using Zara to pass that knowledge to us." He paused and looked at Bud and me intently. "This is the most exciting time of my life, you know. I feel I'm so close to developing the confidence I've always lacked – and it's Demetrius, through Zara, who's helping me. Of course, not in quite the way I'd imagined, but, nonetheless, I am making progress, aren't I, dear?"

Elizabeth's smile and tone were tinged with what I judged to be a hint of frost, if not ice. "You sure are, Norman."

At that point a figure encased in dirty gray robes, sporting a deeply-tanned head with a horseshoe of sandy hair, all but fell through the double doors. The man gasped, "They've found him. I said I'd let you know."

We all leapt up, and the grubby person was peppered with questions.

"Is he okay?"

"Where was he?"

"Who found him?"

"Is he alright?"

"Why did he leave?"

"No. On the far ridge of Lump Hill. Ambroise. No. No idea." The answers gushed out in the right order; I was impressed.

"Ambroise found him? Oh good, he's been so anxious about Oscar – they're such good friends," said Serendipity. "But what do you mean, Don? Oscar's *not* alright? Is he hurt? Broken bones? Does he need a healer, or a hospital?"

Don had finally caught his breath. "Beyond both. Crossed over. Broken neck. Like a bird. Ambroise said a fall. They're carrying the body back to the main compound. We can meet them there."

The desire to leave the restaurant immediately was obvious, so Bud and I followed as we all left and stepped outside, where the dying sun glowed behind the inky hilltops, the sky was an infinite number of colors, wreathed with skeins of cloud, and dotted in its darkest parts with a few glinting stars. Bud reached for my hand, and I for his as we walked behind the group of Facetors, all of whom had become silent.

"I guess they'll have to call the cops now," said Bud quietly.

"Welcome to the Desert Gem – an oasis of tranquility in the magnificent Sonoran Desert," I replied.

Unknowable Knowledge

It was almost completely dark as we trooped our way toward what looked like the middle of nowhere; I hadn't seen any structures beyond the restaurant when we'd arrived, and we were following an almost-invisible trail to an unknown destination; I felt quite disoriented. As we walked in silence, I suspected Elizabeth might suggest this as analogous to a life journey, then wondered if I thought of it that way, too. When we picture our lives in the future, we do so within the framework of reference we possess at that time, so the vision I'd had of living and working in Cambridge, teaching and researching there as a professor of criminal psychology, with visits to see Mum and Dad in Swansea, hadn't been one with limited horizons, it had been what I'd truly wanted for myself at that time. But then there'd been Angus, and the damage he'd done to me both physically and mentally, and his death – followed by all the false accusations that had swirled around about my involvement in his demise. Had I run away to Canada? Yes. But, as it turned out, that was where my future had been waiting for me. Had something unknown steered me there? I squared my shoulders – then that would mean that Bud's wife's tragic death was part of some great plan, and that hardly seemed fair to Jan, or even Bud, who I knew still mourned her loss every day.

"Penny for them," said Bud, squeezing my hand.

I decided I should be completely honest, but spoke quietly.

When I'd finished, Bud let go of my hand and placed his arm around my shoulders. "You're right, I do think about Jan every day, and I make sure I celebrate at least one happy memory of the times we shared, to offset the anger I still feel about her being murdered. Then I think of us, and of you, and I'm filled with gratitude that we found each other. What we have doesn't diminish what Jan and I had, and the time I had with her isn't something I compare with our relationship. Two entirely different things. I miss her, and still grieve for her, but in a way that doesn't mean I yearn for her. She and I had what we had, and now you and I have what we have. Thank you for understanding that."

I smiled up at him. "We've only been here a couple of hours and listen to us…maybe there really is something about this place that encourages a person to look inside themself. Frankly, I'm not usually given to self-reflection, or analysis."

"Really? Oh, I hadn't noticed. Hey, Facet and Face It," whispered Bud wickedly. "But let's not drink the Kool-Aid tonight…let's see what the others are like first, eh?"

We rounded a bend on the so-called path, that must have been rising imperceptibly as we walked, then there it was: a long, blank structure with fire bowls dotted along its top. As we got closer, I could tell it was a wall, rather than a building, and we were heading toward an opening in it. The top of the structure was illuminated by the dancing flames, and I could see it was rounded, organic-looking, and smooth. It looked as though the traditional farmhouse-style used for Serendipity's restaurant had been a design decision made by a different person, because we were clearly approaching a place where the pueblo revival architectural style had been used. I was delighted; I hadn't seen any photos of where we were going to be staying, and knew I'd be entranced by this unique experience.

As we passed beneath an arch with a round-shouldered top, I was blown away; it was almost as though we'd stepped back in time. A collection of small adobe pueblo dwellings, the same color and texture as the soil and terrain we'd passed through on our journey, sat within the shelter of the wall, all illuminated by fire bowls on their roofs. I counted about twenty such places surrounding a plaza, at the center of which stood a large edifice where an outer ring of gently bubbling water surrounded an inner ring of dancing flames, within – and above – which rose an earth-colored sculpture of something writhing and organic, almost like the branches of a tree or the tentacles of an octopus, which opened toward the sky and the stars, seeming to hold them in its embrace. It was impressive.

"Oh, nice," whispered Bud.

"Isn't it," I replied softly; it seemed to be the sort of place where one should always speak quietly, so as not to shatter the tranquility.

A disturbance made us all turn, and a group of four young people, clad in the same gray outfits as Don, entered beneath the arch, carrying the weight of what I assumed was Oscar's body wrapped in some sort of sheeting, secured with ropes. Our group drew back, with our heads bowed, as the corpse-bearers passed us and disappeared into one of the distant buildings.

They were followed into the compound by stragglers, who all looked tired and dusty. In their midst was the only person who appeared fresh: dressed in spotless white, a tall young woman with jet-black hair walked with her head held high, her expression neither happy, nor sad. As she approached the circle of fire, her eyes gleamed; a large jewel glinted on her chest as she moved.

Serendipity rushed toward the young woman. "Oh Zara," escaped from her lips as a whisper.

The women held each other for what seemed like a very long time indeed, then drew back and bowed deeply. I held back a sigh of annoyance, because my irritation with what I felt to be an unnecessarily elaborate form of greeting seemed petty under the circumstances. Indeed, as Zara was held in turn by Elizabeth, then Barbara, Don, and Norman, I could see the comfort each person took from the lengthy physical contact; their body language clearly spoke of decreased levels of anxiety after the hugging. I admitted to myself that, psychologically speaking, the entire silent-hug-greeting thing had merit.

I also wondered if that was why everyone I'd been close to so far smelled so delightful; even Barbara had barrelled into the restaurant in a swirl of beachy-freshness, despite the fact she'd been scrabbling about on a desert hillside for hours. The tragic deaths notwithstanding, I was finding my trip to be full of fascinating observations, and there were so many questions I wanted to ask...though I knew they'd have to wait. I watched with interest as Serendipity hugged a tall man with raven hair; she'd mentioned someone named Ambroise frequently in her texts, though she'd never been specific about the nature of their relationship. I suspected this was he; they held each other throughout the entire time Zara was being hugged by all the others.

Before Zara left us, to follow the rest of the group toward the building where her brother's body had been taken, she bowed toward Bud and me and said, "We shall connect later, when the time is right." Her voice was low, her tone somber, her gaze sad – and she was close enough for me to smell lemon, with a musky undertone. Her carriage as she moved away was stately, bordering on the ethereal; I judged her to be holding back her emotions at her brother's tragic death.

As the rest of the group followed Zara, Serendipity introduced us to Ambroise, who was as tall, dark, and handsome as she'd mentioned in her texts and emails to me. He seemed affable enough, though excusably distracted, having been the person to discover Oscar's remains after many hours of searching. He didn't hug either of us, but bowed, saying, "Serendipity has told me how you once saved her. We all owe you a debt of gratitude, because you were saving her not only for her parents, who love her a great deal, but also for all of us." He bowed again and flashed a smile that hinted at being a little cheeky; I didn't know quite what to say.

Bud replied, "Anyone would have done the same; no one deserves to have their life taken from them."

"Indeed, you have my complete support for that statement, especially given what I have just witnessed," replied Ambroise. His French accent was enchanting; clearly his English was excellent, and he had an air about him of timelessness, his wavy hair curled around his square jaw, and his muscular frame was just discernable despite the baggy garments he was wearing; in his case they were dark blue, which seemed a drab choice, given the rainbow hues chosen by the other Facetors we'd met.

Serendipity looked up at his grubby face; he was a head taller than her. "You poor thing. I know how close you two were. It must have given you a shock to find Oscar like that. Don told us he'd broken his neck. Had he fallen?"

Ambroise shook his head, sadly, and shrugged. "It appeared this way." His eyes filled with tears. "He had cuts on his arms and face, and he was grubby, his clothes torn. It looked...maybe...as though he had tumbled. Maybe he slipped? I do not know. In any case, whatever it was must have happened some time before I found him. His body was...stiff." He shook his head, as if to rid himself of the enormity of what he'd seen.

"That suggests he died somewhere between two and twelve hours before you found him," said Bud. "When was that, exactly?"

Ambroise looked surprised. "I cannot be certain of this. I sat with him, thinking about the journey he was undertaking on another plane, for some time. I had my cellphone with me – we all did, so we could at least try to communicate with each other

– and it told me it was 5.23 p.m. when I started texting the others, telling them where we were."

"And when exactly was he last seen alive by anyone?" asked Bud.

Serendipity and Ambroise exchanged a puzzled glance. She said, "There's no need to worry about all that, Bud. You can stand down – no investigation is needed. Poor Oscar must have gone off into the wilderness to grieve his mother's loss, as you suggested, and fallen. It's just a terrible accident."

This time it was Bud and I who exchanged a concerned look. "But you'll be contacting the authorities about this, won't you? Or someone will. There'll need to be a formal investigation." Bud's tone was firm.

"I don't see why," said Serendipity. "We know why he's dead. Ambroise just told us."

"Nevertheless…" Bud was issuing a warning.

Our backgrounds, and our time together, mean Bud and I tend to think that two deaths in one family, within a couple of days, must be suspicious. In this instance we really had nothing to go on, of course, except the belief I knew we shared that, while coincidences do occasionally happen, they are often an illusion, masking links between occurrences that have been manipulated by an unseen hand. And usually a criminal one, in our experience.

"Ambroise, we should join them at Oscar's," said Serendipity quietly. "I know this is all very awkward," she addressed Bud and me, "but would it be okay if I just showed you to your quarters, and we sort your luggage later? You could at least check the place out, use the bathroom to freshen up, that sort of thing. I dare say Zara will want to make a plan for a double interment of her mother and brother tomorrow, and Doc Nderu will be here in the morning anyway – so I guess they'll put Oscar on ice until then, too…which means they'll need a lot more ice. Just as well Dad insisted upon my getting that massive icemaker. Who knew this was the sort of use it would be put to just a few days after it was installed?"

"We face the unknown every day when we wake, and every night when we sleep," said Ambroise, dreamily. "This is the wonder, and the challenge, of life. It is why we all Facet and Face It."

Serendipity beamed at him. "I agree. Of course. But, for now, let's get Cait and Bud settled in, so they can have some alone time, while we attend to…well, everything that needs attending to. Come on, I'll show you the way."

As we followed our hostess, Bud whispered, "I don't like this at all, Cait. It's got to be a legal requirement to report a death…two deaths. Why haven't they?"

"I'm uneasy about it, too, but what can we do? There's no cell reception, we're basically incommunicado, so our options are limited, to say the least. But, if there's a doctor coming in the morning, maybe we can urge him to contact the authorities? Even if he's a Facetor himself, I bet he'll want to hang onto his licence to practice."

"You're right," replied Bud, his voice heavy with resignation. "We'll tackle it in the morning – so let's try to forget it for tonight…if that's possible."

"Here we are," called Serendipity brightly. "Your home away from home for the next week."

Unsettled Settling

I was thrilled that the unprepossessing building was fitted out like a luxury hotel suite, but with character. The bathroom – which was my first port of call – was elegantly appointed with a large, stone-tiled walk-in shower, a space-age loo, and a basin carved into some sort of rock surrounded by any number of toiletries.

When I joined Bud in the main room, he'd already taken off his shoes and had flopped onto the oversized sofa. As I entered, he leapt up and said, "Oh good," then disappeared into the bathroom.

I gave my attention to our temporary home: the terracotta-colored Saltillo tiles on the floor played well against the walls which were smooth, whitewashed, and curved, without a right-angle in sight. Dark wooden log beams running across the ceiling gave the place a coziness, as did the rounded belly of the fireplace opposite the foot of the bed. The dark-wood theme was continued by the two ceiling fans, and the deeply carved wooden furnishings matched the style of the heavy door through which we'd entered, as well as the one behind which Bud was now…well, doing whatever he was doing. Small windows high up in three of the walls meant I felt as though I was being hugged by the room, but the fourth wall housed wide French doors, which showed me nothing but blackness beyond. I opened them out onto a small patio, where the tile continued, and could see that the dwelling had – essentially – its own enclosed little courtyard, with what I worked out was the massive wall surrounding the entire development serving as a backdrop for a bubbling fountain, wonderful desert planting, and inviting lounge chairs.

The overall impression was of good quality natural materials having been used by top-notch craftspeople to create a luxurious cocoon of comfort, where one could truly relax. The one noticeable omission was a television, which gave me a little pang of sadness, because an indulgence of mine when I travel is to watch local TV stations, largely to enjoy the commercials, which usually offer a great way of coming to understand an area – almost better than the local news coverage. Setting aside that thought for a moment, I realized I had a more pressing need, and hunted about for somewhere to charge my phone which – although I'd been warned there would be no signal – I still always like to know will have enough juice to meet my needs, whatever they might be, whenever they arise.

I found a power point in the base of what otherwise looked like an antique glazed pot serving as a lamp base on the bedside table, scrabbled around in my giant handbag for my charger, and plugged in. I checked the room for other "modern day" touches and found a little booklet on a small round table tucked into a curvaceous corner that listed what could be found where. I read with some amusement that I could look forward to being able to use a "salon quality" hairdryer in the bathroom, a "professional quality" steam-iron and board could be found in the closet, and we even had access to a "high security" safe tucked into one of the nightstands. All the mod-cons! There was also an entry about a satellite phone being available in the office, if it was needed. Which was good to know; remote is good, completely cut off from the outside world less so.

I pulled open a map of the entire Desert Gem site; it was clear we'd only seen a fraction of the whole, and I was able to finally work out the spatial relationship between Serendipity's restaurant and the walled compound: they sat beside each other, though a little distance apart, with the fire-bowl-topped wall forming what looked like a horseshoe with all the dwellings encircled by it. The part that was open faced away from the restaurant and allowed access to parts of the overall facility that appeared to sit within in the desert itself. I noted the solar farm to which Serendipity had referred, there was a waste-water treatment area, a bio-digester, gardens, a rather weird-looking pool, an administrative building, an amphitheater, something called a communications hub, and a refectory. Other features had dotted outlines but no names – I guessed they might represent phases of future development.

Bud's head emerged from the bathroom. "My legs feel yucky and sticky – all that sunblock and dust, I guess. I'm gonna take a quick shower – I know we haven't got any of our stuff yet, but I found everything I need in here to allow me to feel fresher, despite the fact I can't change my shirt. There's even a bit of rock to rub all over your armpits to act as a deodorant, so I'll give that a go. Won't be long." I nodded, and he disappeared again.

I picked up a book from the bedside table because the cover intrigued me: it was embossed with an iridescent line illustration of what was obviously a multi-faceted gem – the logo of the Faceting for Life movement. There was no title, nor the name of an author, but there was a seemingly endless table of contents, and the book ran to about a hundred pages. It was an "introductory" text giving an overview of the movement so, of course, I sat on the edge of the bed and read it.

Bud came out of the bathroom about ten minutes later and he was, indeed, looking much better for having freshened up. His hair was still wet; I imagined he'd decided against using the hair dryer, however superior its quality, preferring to allow the dampness to help keep him cool.

"I can't see us needing to use that," he said, nodding toward the fireplace.

"You're right, I'm quite warm enough in here, and there isn't any visible form of air conditioning in the place, beyond those fans. That's as fast as I can make them go – but I've also opened the little windows up there, and the French doors, which helps. I dare say we'll acclimatize. For those who are here in the depths of winter, I bet the nights can feel quite chilly, so maybe it'll get some use, at some point."

"Probably, though it's hard to imagine." Bud plopped onto the sofa, then stood up again and added, "How about we sit out there, on those lounge chairs, under the stars? Let's turn out the lights in here…I'm not even sure we should have turned them on, given what Serendipity said about 'dark time'."

We switched off the lights after I'd lit one of the small oil lamps that were dotted about the place, then went outside. The chairs were comfy, and the babbling of the little fountain was soothing. The darkness enveloped us, and the sounds of nature gradually came into focus. We sat in silence for a few moments, sharing a smile as we heard the familiar sound of a pack of coyotes somewhere in the distance.

"Amazing that we hear the same thing back home," said Bud quietly.

I nodded. "There are so many differences here, and yet so many similarities: the howling of the coyotes and the calls of the frogs…if that's what those screechy sounds really are; the forests of cacti that take hundreds of years to reach maturity, like the cedars where we live…and the silence, when you have the chance to enjoy it."

"It smells different though, doesn't it?"

I nodded. "At home the night smells fresh, and there's always moisture in the air. This air is arid, and it smells old, and a little musty."

"So, what's next?" Bud was still speaking softly – it seemed the right thing to do, given our surroundings. *"Persona non grata* at the gathering around the corpses of Linda and her son, I guess. That's all a bit…well, I don't even know what to say, to be honest, other than that someone should have called the cops."

We exchanged a weary smile. "There's so much I want to say, but daren't, because I know we're both dreading the same thing – unexplained deaths we're both going to want to have explained, right?" Bud nodded. I continued, "Well, until we have the chance to find out more on that front, I can at least report that I've discovered a fair bit about how the Faceting movement has changed in the past year or so, since the death of Demetrius Karaplis. I found a book and speed-read it. Want the *Coles Notes* version?"

Bud sighed and smiled. "Go on then, I can tell you're dying to share."

I was. "So, when we met Serendipity, and the Jacksons, in Kelowna three years ago, they told us a little about it. Remember that pamphlet they gave us?" Bud shrugged, and looked vague. "Well, it all seemed terribly innocent, and maybe even a bit naively batty, back then, but it appears that since Demetrius has 'passed to another plane' he's taken it upon himself to speak through his daughter Zara to lead the movement in a slightly different direction."

"Do tell," said Bud, looking irritatingly patronising. Then he winked, so I pressed on, smiling sweetly.

"Quick refresher: back then, the Facetors followed a behavioural pattern focused on what they called the fourteen Critical Facets, which they believed needed to be attended to every day in a conscious way. The Facets were – and still are, by the way – playing, achieving, developing, creating, loving, connecting, giving, relaxing, organizing, spiritualizing, vitalizing, indulging, dreaming, and laughing. The core belief of the movement was that by attending to each Facet every day, the followers would become at one with the whole cosmos – and the best version of themselves. Remember Lizzie Jackson?"

"How could I forget her?" Bud rolled his eyes.

"Well, she called it 'buffing' – attending to each facet. But, at that time, there was no real direction given for the specific type of attention that should be given to each facet. So, for example, each Facetor would decide for themselves who they would give to, and what they would give them, to attend to the 'giving' facet. If you recall – or maybe you weren't there when she told me – Lizzie Jackson would give free Tarot readings to fulfill her 'giving' activities, but I dare say she could just as well have knitted pairs of socks and gifted them to people, had she been a keen knitter. It might be that's what the McGlynns have been doing in terms of raising funds to help with adult literacy, for example."

"Okay, so there were some loose rules, and individuals followed them in their own way, for their own betterment, and doing other people a few favors along the way?"

I nodded. "But, since Demetrius died, the framework for the Facetors has become much more complex, and the element of 'spiritualizing' has taken the lead. It seems that his death taught Demetrius that this was where the movement was lacking, and he's now telling the Facetors, through Zara, what he's discovered."

Bud scratched his head. "And how exactly does he speak through his daughter? And, no, I cannot believe I'm asking that question."

"Ah, now that's not dealt with in the book I read – however, you'll be pleased to know that for $49.99 you can buy another book that will explain all that. In detail. Oh, and there are sixty-three other volumes, each at $49.99, which are also available for purchase, that promise access to the deeper insights that one slim tome cannot begin to cover." Bud's eyebrows rose. "But – and here's the stinger – there are *more* books that aren't available to everyone. You only get to know the titles, and get the secret codes to release them for sale, once you achieve a certain level within the movement. And that's another big shift in the whole thing – the idea of a hierarchy. Prior to Demetrius's death it was all pretty much a flat structure, with him and his wife Linda acknowledged as the architects of the movement, and its *de facto* leaders, but – other than their original small, cooperative store at the Gem in Sedona – that was about it as far as their 'organization' went. Now, it seems, there's a complex set-up, and the Facetors' online presence is quite something. I won't bore you with all the ins and outs – because your expression's telling me that's not what you want –" Bud smiled, and blew me a kiss – "but suffice to say it seems to me that you need to spend a *lot* of money on books you have to study, then you pay to get tested on the knowledge you've acquired to pass some sort of exam, then you get to move up a level, where you're able to access the next set of books, which you have to buy to be able to study, to get tested on to pass another exam that lets you move up again, and so on."

Bud shook his head. "And how many levels are there? Oh no, let me guess…fourteen? Like the facets."

"Clever boy!" I reached over and patted his hand.

"So what you're saying is that Faceting for Life has become what – just some sort of money-making machine based upon selling books, and passing exams?"

"Oh no, hang on, it's not just books: you 'can' – by which I mean 'really should', or 'must' – subscribe to an online podcast channel which lets you listen to Zara speaking – passing on her father's wisdom from the next plane. Also, there are any number of 'journey supporting' goods and services available for purchase via what is clearly a pretty comprehensive online store, as well as lectures and workshops you can buy into. There are even cruises, if you can believe it. They take over a cruise ship and you all get together tootling around the Caribbean for a week developing yourself up the hierarchy, hoping all the time that you achieve a high enough level – or show enough potential – to be invited here, to the Desert Gem, which is, apparently, something Facetors around the world would give most of their bank balance, if not their right arm, to do. Who knew we were so fortunate to be here?"

"Not me, for one," said Bud.

"And not me, for two. It's clear that the Faceting for Life movement is not what it once was. It's…well, it sounds a bit fishy to me, though, if I'm being totally honest, it's really quite clever, too. They don't seem to be breaking the law, and someone, somewhere, has put their finger on an almost perfect way to suck cash out of people's pockets, and for them to be smiling when they hand it over. They're tapping into the need we humans have to believe there are answers to all our personal and spiritual questions…and promise those answers if one 'invests' in developing one's skills as a Facetor."

Bud stretched. "If people are paying to listen to what a dead person is 'saying', I'd have thought that would amount to fraud. If I had anything to do with it, I'd certainly be investigating. I tell you what though, Wife, I find it hard to believe that Serendipity's mixed up in all this. I kinda got it that she'd be into the overall thing as you say it used to be, because I think we can both understand she must have had a bit of an unstable upbringing, given the fondness Sammy and Suzie Soul had – and still have – for all sorts of consciousness-altering substances; the Faceting framework, as you explained it used to be, would probably offer comfort, and some sort of structure, for a person finding themselves in that sort of set-up…but she always struck me as pretty level-headed, in spite of her parents, to be honest. By the way – who's that guy she was hugging for ages earlier on, and what happened to Raj Pinder? I though they were an item. They were when we left them in Kelowna."

"She and Raj split about a year after we met them; he was sucked into the world of business with an entire winery to run, and she wanted to develop her chef skills, so travelled around Europe for a while, cooking as she went. I suspect Sammy and Suzie bankrolled her journey of discovery. That's Ambroise Beausoleil we saw tonight. She mentioned him to me in her texts and emails. He's from France, near Caen, but they didn't meet there – they met at a Mexican resort called Puerto Peñasco, which I understand is a really popular place to visit if you live in Arizona. Serendipity and Zara had struck up a friendship online, it seems, and she joined the Karaplis siblings for a short holiday in the sun. She met Ambroise there. All I really know is that he's French, an engineer, and – by the looks of it – she's besotted with him, though she's never said so, outright, when she's mentioned him to me. I'd say he's about five years older than her, in his early forties. What do you reckon?"

Bud shrugged. "I guess. My main impression of the guy was that he'd experienced a traumatic situation, finding his friend dead like that, and was working hard to keep it together. They look well enough matched, I guess, but that's nothing to go on really, is it? But why would she be involved with something that sounds so – as you so elegantly put it – fishy? Not that Ambroise character, the Facetors."

I gave it some thought. "I don't know. If all Serendipity wanted was to own her own restaurant – one that wasn't attached to her father's winery and golf course in Kelowna – then I reckon Sammy and Suzie would have backed her wherever she wanted to have it. To say they're not short of a bob or two is putting it mildly. But here? Almost literally in the middle of nowhere? No, I can't say why she's doing what she's doing…unless she feels truly connected to the Faceting way of life. Maybe she was searching for a spiritual meaning and has found it in all the newer stuff that Zara's been talking about? As I said, the little book I read didn't give away too much – though it spoke at length about the 'mysteries' that would be 'revealed' to a person moving into the lifestyle, and up the food chain."

A scream startled us both. We sat up, like meerkats, and looked around our little courtyard as though there might be some clue as to where the sound came from. Of course, there wasn't.

"Should we?" Bud's expression was pained.

I stood. "We should. Because we both want to know what on earth is going on, don't we?"

"Maybe it's 'need', rather than 'want', but you're right, Wife, we do."

Foolishly Insightful

We emerged into the main plaza, but there was no one to be seen. The screaming had morphed into something different; a single wail sliced through the silence of the night, full of agony, and despair. It was chilling. We followed the troubling sound, moving away from the blazing circle in the plaza, our path lit by the fire bowls atop each dwelling. We walked into what was a sort of street, or at least a double row of little adobe structures like ours, until we saw a crowd surrounding a figure writhing on the dusty ground. It appeared to be a woman, and not a young one. I could make out that she was dressed in dark green, and extremely grubby. No one moved to help or comfort her as she wailed and beat the ground with her fists. We hung back, hovering outside the encircling group, watching with concern as she seemed to wear herself out, then lay still and silent.

Serendipity's chef's whites glowed in the firelight as she stepped toward the figure. The woman in the dirt raised her head and screamed, "You believe me, don't you? It's not right, I tell you. It's wrong. All wrong!" She started to pound the earth again, and Serendipity was joined by Ambroise. They bent down to help the woman to her feet, brushing down her garments as she stood stock still, wild-eyed. The figures of the surrounding group grasped each others' hands and shuffled toward her. A sound like the hissing of a thousand snakes rose from them, but I realized they were all quietly chanting, "Facet and Face It, Facet and Face It." Then they began to sway in unison.

I turned to Bud. "Umm...I don't like how this all...feels."

He sounded grim when he replied, "Nor do I, Cait. Nor do I." Without hesitation he strode forward, pulling apart the hands of a couple of the people in the circle, and joined Serendipity and Ambroise, who looked completely taken aback when he approached and said loudly, "Here, let me help."

The hissing stopped abruptly, which was almost more eerie. I followed Bud's lead and joined the foursome at the centre of the group. "Yes, come along – how about a nice cup of tea? I bet Serendipity could rustle one up, couldn't you?"

Serendipity looked at me as though I were speaking a language she had to mentally translate. "Tea? Tea? Oh yes, of course I could. Let's take KSue to the refectory, there'll be some there, I'm sure."

"It's KSue – right? Can you walk?" Bud sounded concerned as he tried to gain the attention of the short, spare woman. Her face was wizened, and caked with tear-streaked dust. She looked to be somewhere in her sixties, and her short, straw-like hair was sticking out in all directions.

KSue looked up at Bud with a dazed expression – she couldn't have been more than five feet tall – then smiled, hesitantly. "I think I can manage, but I'll lean on you, thanks." She sounded hoarse.

Bud stuck out his arm to support her and said, "Lead the way, Serendipity."

As we followed Serendipity, the encircling crowd parted. I studied as many of its members as possible as we passed by; most were of indeterminate gender, all wearing the shapeless garb I realized was the norm for the Facetors, in a variety of colors. Eyes glowed, reflecting the flames that danced upon the rooftops, and my overwhelming impression was that every face bore a similar expression: one of mistrust and curiosity, laced with fear. I was extremely relieved to note that no one followed us.

We walked beyond the point where there were houses, turned a corner, and the night enveloped us. I stuck my hand into my pocket, but realized I'd left my phone charging in our room, so I had no access to a handy-dandy flashlight. We all slowed as our eyes adjusted; the coyotes Bud and I had heard earlier sounded as though they were moving further away, across the desert, and I noticed there wasn't a single frog calling any more. Not even the crowd we'd left behind made any noise.

KSue sobbed, "I'll be glad to sit down."

"Nearly there. I'll open up," replied Serendipity.

A large black mass loomed up in front of us, and Serendipity left our little group, opened a door, and we saw the light from an oil lamp sputter into life. I felt an unexpected wave of relief wash over me. *Pull yourself together, Cait,* was what I thought; "Let's get you settled with a nice, sugary drink, KSue," was what I said.

We entered what turned out to be a large, barn-like building, fitted out with long, wooden tables and benches. There was an area obviously designed for serving food and drink set to one side – its stainless-steel finish gleamed in the lamplight.

Bud pulled out a bench for KSue to perch upon, and I joined Ambroise in lighting a few more oil lamps. Serendipity had disappeared into what I guessed was the kitchen, where I heard her clattering about, and the sound of running water; I hoped she was filling a kettle.

We'd fussed over KSue for a couple of minutes when Serendipity emerged. "What sort of tea would you like, KSue?"

"Bourbon."

"Pardon?"

"Have you got any Bourbon back there? Or Scotch? Any hard liquor at all?" KSue's voice was rough, and surprisingly deep, considering her small frame. "Now's not a time for tea, believe me."

Serendipity looked at Ambroise, who shrugged, then she disappeared again, re-emerging with a bottle of brandy in one hand, and five glasses in the other; I was glad to see that years of working in the hospitality industry had paid off so usefully.

We huddled at the end of the table with Bud and me facing KSue, Ambroise, and Serendipity. She poured, and we all drank. In silence.

A million questions were popping like fireworks inside my head, but Bud's hand on my knee helped me hold back; I could tell that the woman who'd found one of her oldest friends dead the previous day needed a little time to compose herself, so I put all my effort into sipping my brandy slowly – because, between us, we'd emptied the bottle.

"I'm sorry it's not very good," said Serendipity apologetically. "It's only cooking brandy, not the decent stuff." I was surprised that such a spartan eatery had any sort of brandy available at all.

"It's just what the doctor ordered," said KSue, sounding a little stronger. She'd polished off her drink and placed the glass carefully on the rough-hewn tabletop. "One's enough though. Haven't touched the stuff in years. It'll probably go straight to my head. Not that that would be a bad thing. No idea how I'll sleep tonight – or ever again, come to that. Certainly didn't sleep a wink last night, that's for sure."

Bud's tone was gentle, reassuring. "Hello, KSue, I'm Bud Anderson, and this is my wife Cait Morgan. I wish we were meeting under different circumstances, but here we all are anyway. Now tell us, what it is about your friend's death that's troubling you so deeply?"

KSue stared into her empty glass, rolling it between her little hands as though it were the Holy Grail. "Oh, you'll think I'm being silly. Everyone else does. And I can be, sometimes. Well, quite often, I guess. You see I'm just not clever enough to know what's wrong, but I know that something's not right. But when you don't have the words to explain what you mean people can sure get angry with a person, and then I get flustered, and then…well, it just makes me worse. I've been at it all day; I've attended to every Facet, and I'm still no closer to understanding…no closer to being able to put it into words."

Ambroise and Serendipity exchanged a worried glance, but Bud reached out toward KSue and lay his palms flat on the table. "Don't worry if the words are the right ones or the wrong ones, just explain how you feel, and tell us – if you can – what it is that's made you feel that way."

KSue's expression suggested Bud might actually be riding a white horse and clad in armor. She beamed, as a small child might. "Thank you. It's Linda, you see. She just shouldn't be dead. It's wrong. Absolutely unexpected. Of course I'm upset because she's gone, I know that's natural. But all everyone keeps saying is that she'll return. Which I believe she will. But the fact remains she shouldn't be dead. No one listened to me when I said that. Everyone seems to have accepted it, and they're moving on, ready to find her when she renews. But she shouldn't have to. She shouldn't be dead. Not like that."

I smiled and said, "Can you explain exactly what happened when you found her? Did she look as though she'd fallen, for example?"

"Not a mark on her. Lying on her bed, fully dressed."

"On, or in the bed?" I thought it might be important.

"On. The bed was made up, not open like it would be when you get out of it. Or into it."

I nodded. "That's useful to know. Now, like Bud said, maybe we can try to understand what it was that made you feel her death shouldn't have happened. So, was there anything in particular that seemed odd, or unusual about her when you found her?"

"She had all her clothes on, and had her arms crossed. She looked so…peaceful. So, no, nothing unusual." KSue paused, and smiled. "It was the sort of look she used to have on her face when she'd lie in the sun, after swimming. I could only ever manage ten lengths, but Linda could do fifty. And she did. Every day. It's a big pool. Long and thin. It's there to allow for exercise, and contemplation, of course. Demetrius wanted it that way. And that's how I know she couldn't have just up and died. She was strong, considering. It's all wrong, And I said so. She wasn't the sort of woman to just lie down and die. It's not *normal,* right?"

Bud and I looked at each other, then at Serendipity and Ambroise, who appeared to be studying the grain of the tabletop.

Bud replied, "It's certainly unusual for a person who dies…unexpectedly to present as someone who intentionally lay down to die, in the way you describe. Did Linda look…relaxed? Prepared for death?"

"She was smiling."

Bud pressed. "Like this?" He closed his eyes and smiled. "Or like this?" He grimaced, gritting his teeth.

"Neither. But I can't explain…not smiling exactly…oh, I don't know…I'm so stupid." KSue was starting to blub again.

Bud tutted, and smiled. "No, you're not. You're upset, and that's perfectly natural. Most people go through their entire life never seeing a dead body, so it's totally to be expected that you wouldn't know how to describe it. Don't worry, we'll take it one step at a time. Now, tell me, were Linda's hands crossed on her chest like this, or more casually?" Once again Bud showed KSue what he meant. He was leading her gently.

KSue gave the question some thought, then said, "Hang on, I can't remember. Let me check." She fished about in her voluminous trousers and pulled out a cellphone. She proceeded to click and scroll, then pointed the screen at Bud. "Crossed, see?"

"You took photos?" I sounded as surprised as I felt.

"Of course. I took lots." KSue was indignant.

And you didn't think to mention it sooner? was what I thought; "They could be very helpful in allowing us to maybe understand the source of your unease," was what I said.

Since KSue had passed her phone to Bud, only he and I could see the screen easily; Serendipity and Ambroise leaned forward as far as they could, but it was impossible for us to all see it at once, so Bud and I went first.

The photographs looked as though they'd been taken by someone in the middle of a thunderstorm, during an earthquake; some were blurred, some just the white of a flash, fingers appeared in front of the lens on occasion, and parts of Linda's body were sometimes so large they were out of focus or had been lopped out of the shot altogether. By scrolling through thirty or forty photos we got a good idea of the overall situation. There was no doubt that Linda Karaplis looked peaceful: her hands were crossed on her chest; her expression not one of happiness, but more of simple repose. As KSue had said, she was fully clothed in a turquoise dress matched with what appeared to be embellished turquoise slippers, and she was wearing what I would have classified as a great deal of silver and turquoise jewelry. I wondered if that had been normal for the woman.

There were some obvious questions, so I decided I should ask them. "You knew Linda well, KSue. Did she say or do anything in the days before her death that might have suggested she intended to take her own life?"

KSue's answer was immediate. "No. She knew life on this plane was a gift, a chance to become the best person one could. She wouldn't have shortened her time here."

I pressed. "So you didn't find a note, or anything like that?"

"Why would she write a note?" KSue sounded as though I was asking an incredibly stupid question.

I sighed and returned my attention to KSue's phone. The photographs that followed were of Linda Karaplis alive, laughing in the sunlight beside the large structure at the center of the plaza, dipping her hands playfully in the bubbling ring of water; they showed her to be a large, vivacious woman, wearing a flowing turquoise dress.

"When were these taken?" I asked.

I showed KSue the photos in question.

She looked blankly at her phone. "No idea. Last week? A couple of days ago? I'm not good with time."

Bud fiddled about and accessed the data relating to the photos. "They were taken less than twenty-four hours before those showing her…remains."

I scrolled on. Interspersed with "studies" of blurry saguaro, close-ups of spiny cholla, glorious sunsets and sunrises, and quite a lot of pictures of fingertips, walls and floors, there were photos of Linda showing her from every angle, in every possible situation: eating, drinking, swimming, standing, sitting, laughing, crying, dancing, and even – oddly – sleeping. In each photo her hair was the same suspiciously perfect, lustrous turquoise bob, but there was nothing fake about her blue eyes, which sparkled. It seemed that every item of clothing Linda owned was turquoise, and she was invariably bedecked with silver-mounted turquoise jewelry, the most remarkable aspect of which was that she wore a turquoise ring not only on every finger and both thumbs, but also on each of her ten toes. As someone who can't even wear flip-flops with a toe-post, I couldn't imagine how uncomfortable ten toe rings must have been; it obviously impeded her ability to wear shoes, because she was barefoot in every single shot, which also allowed me to see that the actual skin of her feet was turquoise, which was puzzling. Tattooed? Dyed? I realized that what I'd assumed to be slippers in the photographs of her corpse were, in fact, her bare, bejewelled, feet.

I said nothing, but looked at KSue with the suspicion that she'd possibly felt more than friendship toward the dead woman; though none of the photographs overtly suggested any type of relationship beyond that, they were the sort of candid shots that one person captures of another so they can look at them – possibly longingly – at another time.

I eventually held the screen toward KSue, Serendipity, and Ambroise. "When was this taken, please? I mean, what were the circumstances?" The photograph I was interested in showed Linda holding hands with Zara on one side, and a man I guessed was her now-late son, Oscar, on the other; both children had jet-black hair, piercing blue eyes, and were smiling joyously. They were standing beside the magnificent centerpiece of the plaza, but it was the only thing to be seen – there were no other structures, of any sort.

"That was about nine months ago," said Serendipity. "We were all here that day, weren't we? All three of us." Ambroise and KSue nodded. She continued, "It was the ceremony to dedicate the site to Faceting. The four elements are represented by the structure you see, the one that's in the center of the plaza, and it was the first thing built here. Once that was completed, and the blessings were carried out, then the rest of the project got underway."

Ambroise spoke quietly. "That was an extraordinary day – so special…full of promise."

"Nine months, like a baby," said KSue quietly. "You know – until you give birth. That was what Demetrius and Linda wanted, and Zara and Oscar, too, of course. Well, they usually wanted what their parents wanted. Nowadays, in any case. They didn't used to when they were younger, of course; then they both rebelled against the movement, in their own ways, but Linda always had faith they'd return to the true path, and they did. I mean, look at Zara now. Where would we be without her? If it wasn't for her, we'd be…well, we wouldn't be here, that's for sure."

Serendipity shifted on the bench. "Well, I'm not certain that's quite the case, KSue. Zara told me that Linda was the moving force behind the Desert Gem. Which isn't to say that I think Zara and Oscar were against it, but it was Linda who led us here."

"No, it wasn't Linda," replied KSue firmly. "Demetrius left his money so that each of them got one third. Oscar and Zara said they'd go ahead with this place using just their two thirds even if Linda didn't get involved. They were the ones who got the whole thing off the ground." KSue giggled. "What I mean is they bought the land, and got the elemental edifice built, and it was only then that Linda got on board. I was there the day she changed her mind. And even then she only agreed because Demetrius made it clear it was what he wanted her to do."

"Demetrius was dead by then – so he spoke to Linda through Zara?" Bud managed to sound interested, rather than incredulous.

KSue nodded. "Yes, he'd crossed."

Serendipity shrugged and threw me a glance which told me she thought KSue had it all wrong.

"That was the first time I saw Zara channelling Demetrius." KSue clapped her hands. "Oh, she was impressive. And when Demetrius spoke, I knew it was him right away, and then he proved it."

I was intrigued. "Really? How did he prove it was him?"

Even in the flickering lamplight I could tell KSue was blushing. "He and I had a bit of a run-in over him forgetting

Linda's birthday one year. Zara was only four or five at the time, and Oscar had already left home. Demetrius reminded me of it through Zara. And no one knew about it but we two. You see, we both promised we'd never tell a soul because we knew it would hurt Linda if she found out we'd fought about something to do with her. That wouldn't be at all fair to Linda. But Demetrius mentioned it through Zara that day, so I knew it was really him." She smiled a little. "Even then he didn't say exactly what we'd argued about. He still wanted to protect Linda's feelings, even from the other plane."

"And he went on to tell Linda that he wanted her to support this development?" Bud leaned forward a little.

KSue nodded, then giggled, in her nervous schoolgirl way. "It was the day everything changed for Linda. She'd been devastated by his death; grief had completely overwhelmed her. If I'm honest – which I always try to be – I was worried about her…about what she might do, to stop hurting so much. But then…then he spoke to her, explained to her about the other plane, and how he'd crossed – and she was so happy. For the first time since he'd gone, she was full of joy. She was so excited to be back in touch with him. He told her this was where her path had been leading, and that she'd find fulfillment here. It was also the day he told her how he wanted the place designed – in general, not in detail. He spoke to her a lot about it after that. Linda told me all about their conversations, of course. We didn't have any secrets." KSue's eyes filled with tears, "Except about the birthday party that didn't happen, and the pact Demetrius and I swore about that."

Ambroise shifted, looking uncomfortable, and I realized my bottom was numb; the benches hadn't been designed for long, lingering meals, it seemed, nor for heart-to-hearts about the death of a loved one.

KSue stifled a yawn. "I knew that stuff would go to my head. I'm a bit sleepy now; if I go to bed soon, I might catch up on all the sleep I didn't have last night. But first – please tell me you understand what I mean? Linda looks...wrong...doesn't she?"

Bud tilted his head. "I'm no doctor, but I think it's a good thing there's one coming here in the morning. I believe someone who knows what they're doing should take a look at her remains. To be honest, there are any number of reasons why your friend might have suffered what you say was an unexpected death, but I have no idea why she was lying in a way that suggests she was prepared for it. I think, therefore, you have every right to feel that something's not right, KSue. And I think it's a good indication the police should be called."

The woman's smile was beatific as she looked at Bud. "Oh, I don't know about that...but thank you. Thank you for listening to me. For hearing me. For understanding me. No one ever seems to do that." Tears spilled from her eyes. "Except Linda. She always had time for me – allowed me to speak, and helped me find the words for what I really meant to say. She was...oh dear, whatever shall I do without her? It's like...like there's a big hole in my life where she once was, and I don't think any amount of Faceting will ever help." She covered her face with her hands, and sobbed.

Serendipity produced a ragged piece of fabric from her pocket and handed it to the grief-stricken woman. "Come along, let's get you to your bed, KSue. Maybe some sleep will help. You can't spend another night sitting on a bathroom floor beside Linda's body; you need comfort, and rest."

KSue gazed at Bud and said, "May I take your arm again?" Bud nodded, and we walked out into the darkness.

Too Much, And Not Enough

When we got back to our quarters, having delivered KSue safely to hers, our bags had arrived; we had no idea who'd dropped them off, but both Bud and I were too tired to care. To say it had been a long, and exhaustingly weird day, would have been an understatement of gargantuan proportions, but I said it anyway. Bud agreed, then we both flopped onto the bed.

"No wonder there's no telly – if the few hours we've been here are anything to go by, no one would have time to turn one on, let alone watch an entire show." I meant it. I felt as though my brain had been fried. I realized, only too quickly, that the heat I felt wasn't because we'd been gadding about in the desert, but because I was starting to have a hot flash.

Bud made sympathetic grunts and suggested I took a cool shower. I knew it was a good idea really, but the bed was so comfy, and I felt so pooped, that I went through a long conversation with myself before I struggled to my feet to hit the bathroom.

"I'll just wait here," said Bud.

"You could unpack a bit," I suggested.

"Sure, I'll do that. Enjoy your splish splash."

I did. And I enjoyed the plush, ethically sourced towels, and the exotic yet sustainably produced toiletries, all in compostable packaging. I even went so far as to treat myself to the use of the hairdryer, and although I couldn't attest to its similarity to anything that might be used in a salon – not having been to the hairdressers' for decades – it was certainly powerful, had several settings, and dried my hair more quickly than the one at home.

I emerged feeling much fresher, swaddled in a waffly robe. "Have you got our stuff out yet? I could do with my toothbrush, please." Bud was snoring, and the bags were untouched. He looked so peaceful; his silvery hair was curled at his neck, his shirt looked as though he'd slept in it for longer than he had, and his breathing was deep and regular, if somewhat reminiscent of a steam train. I didn't have the heart to wake him, but I did grab my phone to take a picture. I sometimes sit and visualize his hands when he sleeps, curled like otter paws on his chest, rising and falling, and my eidetic memory means I don't really need photographs to be able to examine the details of the way his eyes crinkle and his nose twitches, but at least I'd have evidence that he'd napped, if challenged. He made truffling noises and his eyes peeled open. They were a little bloodshot.

"Sorry, must have dropped off for a sec."

I sat on the edge of the bed and held his hand. "You were out for a bit longer than that, I think, but look, let's not worry about the bags tonight, let's just get into bed and get some sleep. We're both wiped out."

"Sure. Good idea."

I got into bed as he headed to the bathroom, then he joined me, and I blew out the oil lamp. Our room was truly dark, which is something we're used to because our own home is so remote, and it was good to be able to listen again to the sounds outside, beyond the wall surrounding the camp. I felt my body relax.

Of course, it didn't last. I was still lying there an hour later, but with my eyes squeezed shut, searching for sleep. I've learned that when my mind's working away nineteen to the dozen I stand about as much chance of sleeping as I do of being able to surf, which – for a non-swimmer like me – always looks like assault and battery by a wave. I sat up as carefully as I could, not wanting to disturb Bud who was – for once – not snoring at all.

I padded out to the patio, and pushed the doors closed a little – I was relieved they didn't squeak – then sat on a lounger. The stars were magnificent, the air less musty than it had been earlier in the evening, and although noises were coming from the desert, I wasn't sure what I was hearing. The waffly robe was just the right weight for the temperature; I was comfy, and it was peaceful…so I hoped I'd find sleep right there. But, instead, I kept seeing KSue's face contorted with grief and anger, the photos of Linda Karaplis lying dead on her bed, and the expressions of the people who'd made me feel distinctly uneasy as they'd encircled poor KSue, shuffling, swaying, and chanting.

I sat up and focused on all the facts as we knew them. There was no question that a dead woman found in her bed as Linda had been, her son breaking his neck within twenty-four hours, her daughter speaking on behalf of her late father, and a group of followers who seemed more than a little sinister was a scenario that would make anyone feel uncomfortable. And I did. But…what could, or should, Bud and I do about it all?

We had no idea why Linda Karaplis had looked the way she had, though – of course – she might have been expecting her death because she'd caused it herself, despite KSue's assertions to the contrary. Until we could get some medical insight, we weren't likely to be able to work out the answer to that question. And, if her son had simply been out in the desert seeking solitude in his grief, why on earth should I imagine anything other than a tragic accident had befallen him? Was I making mountains out of molehills? Was I off-kilter because…well, because of my academic interest in all things criminal?

However, I reasoned that even if I was letting my imagination run away with me, there was one thing I was certain of: the Faceting movement was headed in a direction that differed significantly from its original purpose, and while I was trying my best to not label it an exploitative cult, it was taking some doing.

But then – what about Serendipity? She wasn't the cult type. I shuffled my bottom until I was upright, but comfy, and focused on recalling everything I'd ever read, or viewed, about cults, and the psychology behind them.

I closed my eyes to the point where everything goes fuzzy, and started to hum, because that helps me recollect whatever it is I need to revisit; having an eidetic memory is something I've learned to live with and use, but – despite the fact I've read up on everything that's ever been published about it – all I really know is that, for each person who possesses it, it's always experienced in a slightly different way. The thing is, most people who have it don't even know they do until they've already developed ways to cope with it. I didn't realize until I was almost in my teens that I was different from my friends, not because they all had appalling memories, but because I had a strange one, which was when I stopped talking about it – I was beginning to become an object of ridicule, and folks started to give me sideways looks in the hallways at school.

As I sat and hummed, I mentally scrolled through pages and screens full of information, diagrams, histories, insignia and symbols, and interviews with those who'd left cults, as well as those who still belonged and believed, giving first-hand accounts of many, different, "one true path" belief systems.

I opened my eyes – and there was Bud. He was scratching his head, and looked utterly dishevelled. "Have you any idea how loudly you were humming?" He sounded a bit crotchety.

I slapped my most winning smile on my face. "Sorry?"

Bud shrugged. "Ah well, I'm up now – so, tell me, what have you been sitting here recollecting?"

I explained as his eyebrows rose toward his hairline. I concluded with: "I couldn't sleep."

"And now, nor can I," he began, then smiled and asked, "and what's the summary of your findings?"

"You really want to know?" He nodded. I patted the arm of the lounger beside mine. "Okay, but bear in mind my insights only go as far as my research allows, and I have read with breadth, but not great depth. This was an interest of mine stemming from agreeing to help a colleague with a paper – but then I went to Budapest, and you know how all that turned out, so I didn't move forward with the cult stuff. But, based upon my research back then, I can say – in general terms – that most cults are usually formed by those who exploit the need felt by so many to believe in the ability of a 'chosen one' to lead them, by a specifically defined path, to a place – maybe spiritual or physical, or even both – where they will find the answers to all the questions they have about the purpose of their life. Also, quite often, the promise of some sort of paradisical place, or more nebulous ultimate joy, is also offered by these charismatic individuals. You see, the desire to know the answer to 'Why am I here?' has existed for as long as humankind itself. Some join cults where they come to believe their purpose is to act in a certain way during this lifetime because it's all they have – that they can, in fact, not only gain a true understanding of their purpose, but can also both create and delight in a paradise here on earth. Others join cults where they are taught that how they behave during this lifetime will determine what happens to them after death, even to the extent that it influences how they will live their next life, here on earth."

Bud sat back on the lounger he'd been perching on. "So there are cults where there's no actual 'good stuff' until you're dead? Just…what?…a lot of rules to follow?"

"Yes, many cults focus on what's beyond this life as a way to encourage their members to undertake certain tasks, or follow a particular lifestyle, with the promise of rewards at some point in the future. By far the best way to prevent followers from being able to realize that the promised benefits will never be theirs is to make sure they believe they'll only get what they want after this life is over."

Bud scratched his head. "But why? I mean…what's missing from the lives these people led before they joined these cults that the cults give them? If there's nothing concrete, so to speak."

"Again, there are some commonalities, but it's dangerous to generalize, and it really depends on the cult, too. But let's just say that many who join cults say that – until they did – they'd felt lost and alone in the world. The cult offers them their first recognizable experience of being valued, of having a productive role, being praised, or of being loved. Even individuals who come from what society would label as 'happy, stable families', where one might expect them to have already experienced those things in their prior life, claim they feel their fellow members of the cult are more like 'real family', because of the values and life journey they share."

"So all cults are preying on the weak?"

"Oh Bud, that's a big question, with an incredibly long answer – because what some might perceive as weakness, others see as a simple lack of desire to value goals society has deemed desirable. Underachievement at school, for example, is generally agreed to be a problem for a child – they're seen as a failure. But there's a great deal of research which suggests that common Western academic frameworks are far from ideal for many individuals, having been created to serve societal needs for a productive workforce rather than the needs of true, rounded human development. Indeed, there are a lot of sought-after alternative educational offerings which promise to develop the whole person, while also attending to the basic needs of teaching reading, writing, and mathematics, but then allowing the child to use those tools to explore the world in the way *they* choose, rather than forcing them to follow curricular designed by what some say is an outdated, hierarchical education system."

Bud looked thoughtful. "They have that open air school near us, back home, don't they? I know there's a wait list for the place, and the kids there don't seem to mind being outside in all weathers, using nature as their classroom, and as a teaching tool, too." He smiled. "I guess they turn out to be the hardy ones."

"Hardier than me, in any case." I smiled. "The other aspect most cults have in common is the need to keep their devotees following their rules, and thereby their leaders. It fascinates me that one of the things many of the interviews with cult members highlighted was their deeply-held belief that they were achieving the best possible form of 'freedom' by following sometimes complex, and some might even say baffling, sets of restrictive practices – many of which went beyond the behavioral, extending to the psychological, with devotees truly believing that to merely *think* in a certain way was bad. Alongside that, a frequently-used device is to promise all sorts of ills befalling those who stray from the cult's path in some way. Interestingly, another commonality is that it's usually not the cult leader who metes out the punishment, but the other devotees themselves – the pack choosing to maintain its equilibrium by controlling, or 're-educating', those who don't conform. It's a great way to allow those who *do* follow the letter of the cult's law to continue to feel special, and chosen. But – and this is my problem – I can't quite see the point of the Faceting for Life movement, and that bothers me."

Bud smiled. "Other than making a fortune by forcing people to pay through the nose to access information online, or in books, that they need to study to be able to move up a level? Maybe this is one of those situations where it's more about an expensive carrot, rather than a stick?"

"Yes, maybe."

Bud stood and stretched. "So, we know it's some sort of money-making racket, which might be benign, but you're going to want to do at least some investigating into the Faceting movement – if only so you can work out its direction, and any other purposes, right?"

I also stood, because I knew I should head to bed. "Yes. You see, what I don't really understand is why Zara would be speaking on behalf of her father. Maybe when he died she felt the 'family business' would falter? But it really wasn't even a 'business' at that time. And let's not forget that it sounds as though all the early members, as well as the two founders, are now dead. And – with the exception of Demetrius – they've all died since the Desert Gem has been built. But…why?"

"Cait…"

"Okay, okay…I have absolutely no reason to suspect that the others who've died didn't just drop off their perches quite naturally. I…we…don't know anything about how they died, or how old, or unhealthy, any of them were, or if they fell off a roof, got hit by a car, or had a massive cactus land on them. I'm apparently incapable of stopping myself from seeing warped psyches all over the place. But…not everyone we meet is a killer. Not everyone who dies has been murdered. Got it, Husband, got it!"

Bud smiled. "Good. Now, come on, it's very late, Wife. You'll be a wreck in the morning. Come back to bed. Let's talk some more in daylight."

I knew he was right, so padded back to the no-doubt ethically sourced sheets, let my head sink into the pillow and…

Abnormally Normal

Knocking woke me. I sat up to see Bud pushing a little cart to the foot of our bed; he was dressed, and looking fresh and ready to go.

"Breakfast is served, m'lady." He bowed and pulled lids off platters of golden, glistening scrambled eggs mounded upon what appeared to be sourdough toast, and some massive muffins, that looked as though they might contain chocolate chips.

I perked up immediately. "Did they just guess this is what we'd want? Or did you...?"

"Nothing to do with me, a guy just brought it to the door. There's a note." He opened a folded piece of paper and read: "'Wanted you to have a delicious start to the day. Hope I made some good choices. Please come by the restaurant when you can. Serendipity.'"

"What time is it?"

"Half nine."

I sat bolt upright. "Oh no, I hadn't meant to sleep for so long."

"You know we're on vacation, right? Relax, we don't have a schedule. We'll have this, you can hit the shower, then we'll amble down to Serendipity's place. I've even unpacked." Bud proudly pulled open the closet door to reveal our clothes, all neatly hung up. "Your toilet bag's in the bathroom. Goodness knows what's in it; it weighs a ton, and – whatever it is – someone should tell you that you look fine as you are. And that's me...telling you. Now, come on, where do you want this?"

Bud pulled a couple of chairs to the foot of the bed, and we managed to fit the trolley between us, using it as a table. The eggs were delicious – buttery, cheesy, and spiked with slivers of *chile* and fire-roasted peppers – and the muffins were dense and moist, almost like brownies. After a couple of mugs of rich, silky coffee to wash it all down, I was into and out of the bathroom in record time, and decided to wear my sky-blue two-piece with my blue-and-white checked overthingy – which I hoped would waft around me making a nice breeze. I also pulled on the white spudgy shoes that mean I feel like I'm walking on air, even when my feet get hot, or the ground's a bit uneven – which it certainly was between Serendipity's restaurant and the main compound.

When we left our little house, the plaza was deserted. Since we had no idea where everyone was, and decided we couldn't even begin to guess, we did as our hostess had asked, and presented ourselves at her place of work.

Serendipity greeted us with a long hug each, and offered a jug of juice. It looked like green slime, so I passed, as did Bud, though he did a much better job of it than me; he rubbed his tummy and said, "Thanks, but no thanks. That lovely breakfast you organized for us filled me up."

Serendipity smiled. "My pleasure. You're the first guests we've had here who aren't Facetors, so we'd talked about it ahead of time and thought it best if you had the opportunity to breakfast in private rather than having to make your way to the refectory, where it's a communal experience. Besides, you don't have to follow our timetable – the breakfast is all cleared away by seven, so you'd have missed it in any case. Lunch will be served any time now," she looked at her watch, "and the final meal of the day has to be finished long enough before sunset for all the clean-up to be completed before the last rays of light leave the sky."

Serendipity's voice had taken on a bit of a sing-songy tone, and she was staring out of the window toward the valley below as she spoke. I seemed to break whatever spell she was under when I said, "Gosh, that sounds quite regimented."

She smiled. "It's a rhythm, and if we're all going to work well as an entity, we need a rhythm."

I couldn't help but suspect these were not Serendipity's own words, and felt a prickle of unease.

Bud asked, "Did you have anything in mind for us today? Or are all plans on hold until the doctor has arrived, and decisions can be made?"

Our hostess sat beside us. "Doc Nderu is here already, over at Linda's dig. That's what we call our little dwellings – our digs."

I smiled. "That's quite a British term. When I was growing up, we had lodgers, and they referred to our back bedroom as their digs – it was the first time I'd heard it; they were university students."

Serendipity looked bemused. "Really? Oh no, it's not meant that way here – our dig is where we consider the work we're doing on each of our Facets, and what progress we're making. Where we dig deep inside us, to bring forth the gem that's hidden within."

I could see Bud's back stiffen as she spoke, but he didn't join our conversation.

"Ah, interesting. So…um…will Dr. Nderu be making a determination of the cause of death for both mother and son?" It was what I really wanted to know, so thought I might as well just ask.

Serendipity shrugged. "I guess. Ambroise was keen to know that too, so he went over when the doctor's car passed here. If you're interested, you should go too. No one would mind. Maybe KSue would be pleased to see you, Bud, and I know she'll be there. I would think everyone else will be in the refectory by now."

I was puzzled. "People will just get on with their normal day?"

Another shrug. "Sure, why not? Everyone has duties, and they need time to continue their personal development, too. We're only talking about the physical casings that are left behind, after all; we'll hear from Linda again when she wants to get in touch – though, of course, with Oscar gone too, it'll be interesting to see who she chooses to speak for her, and when. We're still waiting for the other elders who passed over to make their way back to us. It can take time, Demetrius said; it even took him a couple of months and he was by far the most developed of all of us."

I decided to go for it. "You've been part of this movement for – what – about five years now?" Serendipity nodded and beamed. "So...you must have seen a lot of changes since Demetrius died. Do you think they're good changes?"

She took a sip of green slime and replied, "You're right, there've been quite a few, but we needed structure. You see, when I began Faceting, there wasn't really anything to join up to...no framework for connecting with other Facetors; I was lucky that I had Lizzie and Grant Jackson living close by in Kelowna to be able to work with. But, back then, it really wasn't much more than an idea, a mindset...a self-determined process with no real purpose, other than a general feeling of well-being. Of course there was the Gem, but even that was more of a spot to allow informal gatherings, stock up on a few Faceting-related supplies, and that was it. Now? Oh Cait, it's so much better. We've all got direction. We know about the other plane, so there's the comfort of understanding all about that, too. I finally have a purpose."

"And what is that purpose?" I couldn't wait to know.

Serendipity put down her tumbler. "Well, I'm on the journey to discovering that, and I'm doing quite well. You see, until I came here – and I've been here since the original blessings, as you know – well, until then, I wasn't even really on a journey…just puttering about in my own little world. Well, now I have a framework, a new lens through which I view my life, my Faceting, and my journey. I'm getting much, much better at my talking and writing therapies…and I'm becoming more attuned as a listener – though my distillation needs a bit more effort."

I looked at Bud, and we both shrugged. "Elizabeth mentioned something general about being involved with helping set up such activities, but we're not familiar with those parts of Faceting," I said. "There was a slim volume in our…dig…which explained the basics, but it didn't mention any of that."

Serendipity nibbled her lip thoughtfully. "Ah, yes, of course…you don't get to learn about those therapies until you enter the movement. You're…umm…you're not thinking of joining us, either of you?" Bud and I didn't even need to glance at each other before we both shook our heads.

"Not my cup of tea," I said.

"Me neither," agreed Bud.

Tapping one finger on the table, Serendipity gazed deeply into my eyes, then Bud's. She shrugged. "Oh well, it won't hurt to tell you, in confidence, I'm sure, especially since Elizabeth has already mentioned them. We practice a series of linked therapies, so we can develop our potential. We talk to each other, in pairs or groups, but we don't just chatter idly, we speak with intent. It's a part of how we attend to the Facets of giving, and connecting…as well as dreaming, because we're also encouraged to talk about what we dream of for ourselves, and others. We explain situations that have helped us learn something about ourselves, others, or the world around us – joyful learning, and even painful learning." Serendipity paused, and added, "I guess you guys would know all about painful learning."

"Learning is learning," said Bud, sounding sage.

Serendipity continued, "We also practice a listening therapy, to learn from the wisdom others are sharing; but we mustn't just listen, we must listen with intent, and truly hear what's being communicated. Then our task is to comprehend what we've heard, which we do by using a writing therapy; at the end of every day, after dinner, we all retire to our dig and write down what we've heard and learned that day…page, after page, after page…just letting the words flow through us, then we place all our pages into a receptacle built into the wall above our bed, where they rest overnight. Our contemplative therapy before sleep is to consider the words on that paper resting above our heads, and to distil what we've experienced that day into an essence we can apply to our own lives. In the morning we throw all our pages into the fire in the plaza, at dawn."

"So this isn't something that Facetors who live elsewhere can do?" I was curious about this ritual.

Serendipity smiled. "We're the lucky ones – we get to do it all in real life, but there's a digital fire on the app, so you type in all your notes from the day there, then it gets consumed by digital fire at dawn, wherever in the world you are."

"There's a Faceting app?" Bud sounded incredulous.

Serendipity chuckled. "There's always an app these days, Bud. But, yes – in fact the app pre-dates the ability anyone had to carry out the ritual here. And the wonderful thing is – and I know, because I used the app before this place opened – it doesn't matter if the fire is real or virtual; when the notes have burned, they're gone…and so is the weight of the words. All that's left is their meaning, and their lessons…that *essence*. And that's my downfall, you see – it's taken me quite some time to feel comfortable about opening up to other people about what my life's been like, especially about when I was little, given my parents' lifestyles – you know, the drugs, the open marriage and all that?" Bud and I nodded. "But once you let go, it gets easier, as long as you stick at it, and keep doing it. But the distillation of what I've heard and learned from others, so I can apply it to my own life? That's a challenge. Though I must tell you that my process has shown me how much I learned from you both, in Kelowna."

I was puzzled. "Like what?"

Serendipity stared directly into Bud's eyes. "From you," she began, "I learned how true respect looks, and works. The way you supported Cait as she did what she did – even though I know it was very early days for you as a couple – was a real lesson. Sadly, my parents spent so much time being angry at what the other was doing in their lives I'd never had the chance to see what a truly supportive relationship looked like."

Bud flushed. "Thank you."

Next she turned her attention to me. "And from you I learned how to be utterly dedicated to seeking the truth, and bringing it into the light. You were amazing, even when you were injured. You just didn't stop, and you made us all see someone we thought we knew as they truly were, not as we all thought they were."

I shuffled my bottom on the chair, feeling a little uneasy; I'm just not used to being complimented, so I'm never quite sure how to react. "I'm glad you feel that way," was the best I could muster.

Serendipity studied the table, then her fingernails. "You won't tell anyone what I've said, will you? Not even Ambroise. He's…well, he's so much better at it all than I am, you see. He's already progressed through many levels. He's utterly dedicated to his Faceting journey, and so good at following all the rules; this knowledge about the special therapies isn't really meant for anyone who hasn't committed to becoming a Facetor, so I don't want him to think I've broken a trust by telling you."

Bud smiled at our hostess and replied, "You obviously know you can count on us."

She stood and rolled up her sleeves, her eyes darting. "I'm so sorry, I must get on, now. The burials will be at sunset, and all are welcome. Dinner will be served in the refectory before that, of course, but you might prefer to dine here, with me and Ambroise. He's preparing our meal tonight – a simple one, but he's extremely talented in the kitchen. He learned from his mother; it was only ever the two of them because his father was never a part of their lives, and he was her shadow in the kitchen. We'll have our gala dinner tomorrow night; I hope you don't mind the delays."

Bud also rose. "Of course we don't. We're just honored to be here at all – and we'd love to dine with you and Ambroise this evening. What time?"

"Around five, I'd say. Then we can join the group for the interments."

"Excellent," replied Bud, nudging my foot with his. "We're going to take ourselves off to see if KSue needs any support now." He spoke briskly. "And you think she'll be at Linda's dig? Where would we find that?"

"It's about halfway along the double row of digs that lead from the plaza to the refectory, where KSue was thrashing about last night. I'm sure she'll be delighted to see you. Thanks for stepping up, Bud, Cait. I'll be here all day if you need me – there are lots of last-minute details to finalize even though we're opening late, because…well, never mind my problems, they're mine, not yours. Lovely to see you – and I'm already looking forward to dining with you later."

We left with a wave, and I saw Serendipity's brow furrow as she pulled out her phone, and stared at it. We both popped our sunglasses on, and I was delighted to feel a slight breeze.

"They might think there'll be burials tonight, but my money's on the doctor putting a stop to that. There'll need to be a follow-up investigation into at least Oscar's death, I'm sure." Bud sighed, sounding annoyed. "The whole Faceting thing still sounds a bit…well, woolly, to me, and yet sort of prescriptive," he added. "What do you think?"

I considered my answer. "I'll admit that last night, with that group of people all hissing and swaying in the darkness, I felt somewhat intimidated, and was ready to label the movement as some sort of sinister cult. But, to be honest, what Serendipity just explained sounds more like a self-help group for those seeking personal development. It's actually quite healthy to speak about life experiences and lessons learned – because talking can allow the speaker to gain an even better understanding of what they really have learned, how they learned it, and how that learning might be applied to other areas of their life. Indeed, group therapy works on a similar basis – it's hardly new, and not at all worrisome. The writing bit? Well, if you talk to people who consistently keep journals, they'll tell you all about the therapeutic quality of regular, thoughtful writing…so there's that. Then the burning of the written words? Again, not an unusual way to rid oneself – with ceremony – of something that could otherwise weigh one down. No, I'm not seeing anything dreadfully malign in what Serendipity explained, just a somewhat original way of linking it all together – the idea being the overall positive development of the Facetors."

Bud nodded. "Sounds about right: mainly harmless, but a bit self-indulgent."

I stopped strolling. "Oh, come on now, Bud, you know as well as I do that many people, from all walks of life, could –

whether they know it or not – do with a bit more insight, and feeling of fulfillment. I don't think for one minute we're going to meet a group of people here who are a representative cross-section of society – after all, as we know, just the books you have to read to even belong cost a pretty penny. But, you know what? If they're all here looking for answers, for purpose, rather than taking out their anger and frustration on the rest of the world, then what's the harm? They might spend just as much of their money on various forms of self-medication, or even self-destruction."

We strolled on. "Fair enough," replied Bud, "unless the recent deaths here suggest that someone's got it in for the folks at the top of the pile, and the entire set-up isn't as innocent as this lifestyle sounds."

"Now who's seeing mass murderers at every turn?" I gave him a loving shove. "Anyway…we're off to see the doctor, to find out whatever we can to put our minds at rest about how Linda Karaplis died…and maybe even solve the puzzle about why she looked as though she lay down and waited for death to find her."

"Indeed, we are, Wife, indeed we are. On we go."

The Clean-Shaven Bearded Man

By the time we reached the compound walls, I was glad my arms and legs were covered, because I might have burned a little otherwise; just walking to and from the restaurant had taken more than half an hour, the sun was hot, and there wasn't a cloud in the sky.

KSue was sitting on a rock outside one of the digs, so we guessed that was where Linda's remains, and the doctor, were to be found. She leaped up when she spotted us and crossed the plaza to greet us – thankfully with just a bow.

"I knew you'd come," she said. "I asked Dr. Nderu to wait to start his examination, because I thought you'd like to be there, but he had to get started, so he went and did Oscar first. He got here about ten minutes ago. Shall we go inside?"

I hadn't expected we'd be invited to join either of the examinations, but we both followed KSue without anything but an immediate acceptance of her invitation.

KSue chattered on, "He's such a lovely man, and quite good looking, some say. Not really my type. But the funny thing? His name means 'bearded man' but he's hardly got a hair on his head, let alone a beard. So funny. But, as I say, lovely man. I met him some years ago when he first visited the Gem, in Sedona. His wife makes beaded necklaces, and she became one of the sellers at the marketplace there. Lovely woman."

As KSue nattered, I took in our first sight of Linda Karaplis's dig. It was almost exactly the same as our own, with the exception of the fact that it had been personally decorated by the woman herself, whereas ours had been designed to house guests. At least, I guessed the décor was Linda's choice because almost everything was turquoise – either in color, or actually made of, or encrusted with, turquoise stone. Like our dig, the place was cool, but this one was also dimmer, because all the windows, and the doors to the patio, were covered with turquoise chiffon curtains. I wasn't surprised when KSue led us to the bathroom, but what did take me aback a bit was the fact that Ambroise, Zara, and Dr. Nderu were already in there – as was Linda's body, which I'd expected, of course. There didn't seem to be the remotest possibility of even KSue fitting into the small space, let alone Bud and me.

Ambroise came out to greet us, with the inevitable hug for KSue, while Zara didn't even acknowledge our arrival, which I felt was understandable, given the fact she was attending to her mother's remains. It appeared the doctor was well into, or had even completed, his examination; he knelt in the corner, writing something on a pad in a large binder he'd placed on top of the toilet.

He looked up and said, "Ah, KSue, there you are. I know you found the body, so I have some questions for you, to help me complete my paperwork – but maybe we could move into the other room? It's more commodious." His voice was deep, and he spoke slowly; all in all, his delivery reminded me of John Wayne.

The doctor was dressed in non-Faceting clothes – a baby-blue cowboy-style shirt above well-worn jeans. He had a broad smile, fabulous teeth, and – as KSue had said – not a single hair on his head. It was hard to decide how old he was, but I guessed at somewhere in his forties. Or maybe his fifties. As he unfolded and stood, I realized he was well over six feet tall.

We all scuttled into the main room, where KSue perched on a chair, as did Zara, while Bud, Ambroise, Dr. Nderu and I stood in an awkward line in front of the fireplace. None of us went anywhere near the bed.

"This is where you found Linda?" The doctor pointed to the mounded bedding as he spoke.

KSue nodded.

"And when was that?"

KSue looked at Bud as though she were drowning, and he was holding a lifeline. "I…I'm not sure," she stammered.

"You said around eight," said Zara flatly. "Though you didn't fetch anyone until well after lunch – around two."

"Is that correct?" The doctor sounded concerned.

KSue nodded. "I came to fetch her to go swimming, and when I got here she was clearly quite dead…but I didn't want to leave her, and I thought…well, I know it sounds foolish…but I thought that if I didn't tell anyone, then…oh, I don't know…" KSue finally stopped talking.

Bud came to her rescue. "Did you feel that if you didn't tell anyone, then it might not 'become real'?"

KSue exploded with relief. "Exactly – if I just stayed with her and talked to her, then I could hang onto the belief that she wasn't really dead at all." She smiled, looking older at that moment than her years. "Thank you for hearing me, and understanding. It means a great deal."

Bud stretched out his hand and said, "You must be Dr. Nderu; I'm Bud Anderson, and this is my wife, Professor Cait Morgan. We both have backgrounds in homicide investigations, and I just wanted to mention – in case you're not as familiar with the phenomenon yourself – that it's not unnatural for those who discover an unexpected death to have the reaction KSue just explained. A sense of unreality; they know the person's dead but feel that – somehow – until they share that news, the person is still 'with them'."

Dr. Nderu smiled broadly, showing how very many teeth he had, as he shook Bud's hand, then mine. "Thanks for that. I'm not unfamiliar with the reaction you describe, though I've found it tends to happen more frequently with family members, rather than between friends."

KSue gushed, "But Linda and I *were* family. We loved each other like sisters, and we've felt that way for decades."

Zara shifted in her chair. "But you weren't sisters, were you, KSue? Linda was my mother. You should have told me about her death as soon as you found her. I could have attended to her passage myself, as I am certain she'd have wanted." Her tone suggested she was trying to rein in tears. "I would have valued that time with her myself."

KSue began to blub. "I'm so sorry, Zara, I've said I'm sorry over and over…but I can't go back and fix it now. I did what I did. It's not as though it'll ever happen to me again, so there's no point saying I'll do it better next time, because there won't be one…but…oh, you know what I mean. I wish now that I'd come to find you sooner, but I didn't because…"

Zara shook her head sadly. "Because you wanted time to be alone with her, to say goodbye to her, to comfort her as she passed on – as did I." She paused, sighed, and stared at her feet. "But all I got was my mother's empty shell already dumped into a bath full of ice, instead of having the chance to see her resting where she died." The young woman's eyes filled with tears as she looked up at KSue and added, "I don't expect any of you to understand, but it would have made a great difference to me to have seen Mother in repose, instead of having already been – literally – manhandled into a bathroom." She tried to swallow her tears, but failed.

KSue sobbed and pulled a large square of ragged cloth from her pocket. Bud reached down and rubbed her small shoulder, an act which KSue's expression told me she found to be a great comfort.

Zara stood, trembling a little I noticed, and Ambroise stepped back, deferentially, to allow her to move from her seat. She unhooked her long black hair from behind her ears, allowing it to fall upon her white-silk encased shoulders. She took a deep breath, visibly composed herself, and said sadly, "I shall retire until the interment. I do not wish to be disturbed. I need to connect with Demetrius. Facet and Face It." She bowed deeply, then left the room. Ambroise followed her; I wasn't sure why, given that she'd said she wanted to be alone with her dead father.

Dr. Nderu bowed toward Zara's receding figure, then addressed us. "In that case, I'll head off to the refectory to see if there's any lunch available."

"Have you finished with KSue?" I couldn't believe he was.

He smiled. "Yes, I just wanted to note the times involved, thank you."

"Have you contacted local law enforcement?" Bud sounded anxious.

"I don't believe that's necessary. I have my findings." Dr. Nderu's reply was polite, but firm.

A vein pulsed in Bud's neck. "But surely it's a legal requirement to advise them of what's gone on here."

The doctor shook his head. "We do things a little different around here. My paperwork will be sufficient."

Bud literally bit his lip. His nostrils flared.

"Will you stay for the interment?" I asked, as calmly as I could.

The doctor shook his head. "No, I'll get back to Phoenix to organize all the paperwork."

"May we know the exact causes of death you've noted for both Linda and Oscar?" Bud was working hard to keep his frustration in check.

The doctor shrugged. "Sure, they'll be a matter of public record by the end of the day. Oscar suffered a broken neck. Death would have been instantaneous. Pretty straightforward. Looked as though he'd been running about in the desert for some time – good number of lacerations, and he even had some cactus spines sticking into his flesh. Cholla. Then? Well, my guess would be that he fell for some reason; cuts, fresh bruises, bump on the front of the head making a gash, and a broken neck."

"So he could have been badly beaten – by a person, or persons, unknown – then thrown to his death." Bud's tone was grim.

Dr. Nderu shook his head. "Not in my professional opinion. And, also in my professional opinion, Linda died of a heart attack."

"Precipitated by?" Bud spoke quietly.

"Hmm…a number of possibilities."

Bud reacted swiftly. "Were you aware of any ongoing health issues that might have contributed to her demise?"

The doctor shuffled, and I noticed how very large his cowboy boots were. "I don't feel comfortable discussing that with someone from outside the family." Dr. Nderu sucked his bottom lip. "Linda had been my patient for some little time. Sure, she had a physician when she was in Sedona, but he retired, and when she moved here she asked if I'd take her on. Her last doctor was a Facetor, as am I, and she wanted continuity; it helps if we understand that aspect of a patient's life. Linda wasn't a woman who took life for granted; she wrung every drop out of each moment."

"Oh, she did," shouted KSue joyfully. "She was an inspiration in every way. Even after she got sick, she managed to have more energy than me, and I've never had a day of sickness in my life."

"Linda was suffering from an illness?" I asked.

Dr. Nderu glanced sideways at KSue before replying. "As her physician I must respect my patient's request that I speak to no one about the condition of her health."

"She wore a wig, didn't she?" I observed.

"How did you know that?" KSue sounded amazed.

"In all the photos you showed us of Linda, her hair was immaculate, and it never changed, at all. I suspected a wig immediately. Was she receiving some sort of medication or treatment that meant she'd lost her hair?"

"She had alopecia and rheumatoid arthritis, but she didn't take any meds...wouldn't touch them," said KSue with vehemence.

"Is that so, doctor?" Bud spoke quietly.

Dr. Nderu shook his head. "I can't say."

KSue sighed. "Linda was amazing – managed to keep her body moving when I could tell she was in agony. And her hair? It began to fall out not long after they started to build this place. Never grew back properly – it was all just patches. She hated it, but refused to be ruled by it. She had a couple of wigs made, both the same as each other. They were just wonderful...so shiny. One of them she mainly kept for swimming, because she liked the feeling of the water running off the hair onto her shoulders as it dried. Though she did admit they got a bit hot in the summer."

"But you don't think an autopsy is indicated, doctor?" Bud pressed.

Dr. Nderu adopted a more confident stance. "In our world of Faceting, we believe that the spirit crosses onto another plane when the body no longer houses it, but we also believe that the spirit cannot find its way back to those it wants to connect with on this plane until its earthly husk has begun to return to the elements. The more of the husk that's returned, the easier it is for the spirit to cross. Obviously, the desire to quickly inter Linda's remains, and those of Oscar, too, of course, is keenly felt by their only remaining family member – Zara – who is understandably anxious to have the chance to reconnect with her mother and brother, in the same way she has done with her father. Demetrius was cremated, but, since Linda and Oscar are to be buried, it's important that this is done as soon as possible."

Bud's hand began to burrow through his hair – which always tells me he's deeply concerned about something. In this instance I knew exactly what was bothering him.

He paced about the ornate room, then turned to Dr. Nderu and addressed the man using his most professional tone. "I understand your connection with the movement and the family, doctor, but what I cannot grasp is your reluctance to request the involvement of the authorities, and an autopsy." He held up his hand to suggest the doctor shouldn't speak. "I am not for one moment suggesting that your professional ability is less than it should be; if you say that a heart attack is what killed Linda Karaplis, then I take your word for that. And, despite the fact you cannot confirm or deny that the deceased's health had been significantly compromised by illness, that still doesn't explain the specific circumstances of her death."

The doctor looked puzzled. "I don't understand what you mean. What 'circumstances'? Linda was found dead in bed. At least –" he looked at KSue – "that's what I was told on the phone last evening. You found her in bed, didn't you?"

KSue nodded. "Yes, but she wasn't in bed, she was on the bed."

Dr. Nderu's brow furrowed more deeply. "I can't see how that makes a difference."

"And her arms were crossed on her chest," I added.

The doctor seemed surprised, but rallied and said, "Like this?" He placed his arms exactly the way Linda's had been.

I was on full alert. "That means something to you, doesn't it?"

Dr. Nderu said nothing, but sat down and held his head in his massive hands. "Without wanting to disrespect my late-patient's desire for privacy, I feel I can at least tell you that Linda believed in a holistic approach to life, and health. As such, she was familiar with the practices of Ayurveda, an alternative medical system with its roots in the Indian subcontinent. She carried out research when she was…diagnosed with a serious and painful condition, a few years ago. She declined the medications offered by Western medicine, preferring to follow her own treatment regimen." He finally lifted his head. "I believe she was using natural remedies to help manage a range of symptoms from lack of sleep, to poor appetite and digestion, as well as for pain management, and an overall boosting of her immune system. Linda had accepted that she would live in pain, but did what she felt was right to be able to enjoy her time on this plane as much as possible. However, I can't rule out the possibility that she might have used a larger dose of one of her remedies to leave behind a body that was no longer serving her well."

I turned to KSue. "Are you certain Linda didn't mention anything to you about taking her own life?"

KSue's mouth hung open. She shook her head, her eyes wide. "You asked me that before. I said no then, and I'll say no now. Linda wouldn't have ended her own life prematurely."

"And it wasn't you who placed her hands on her chest like that?" Bud's voice had a slight edge.

KSue looked tearful. "I found her just the way she looked in the photos. I told you that. I believed you'd heard me and understood that I was speaking truthfully. I just sat beside her, that's all."

The doctor was looking grim, and puzzled.

"What's wrong?" I asked him.

He shook his head. "The others all told me I'd be needed, but Linda didn't. That's...odd."

Bud's head-scratching was threatening to draw blood. He snapped at the doctor, "What do you mean?"

Dr. Nderu took a moment to gather his thoughts – weighing his answer, I reckoned. "Prior to today, I have attended here four times to examine human remains, and complete the appropriate paperwork. In each case the deceased presented in the same way as you tell me Linda was found: in repose, arms crossed, fully dressed, and lying on top of their bed. In each case I attended within a couple of hours of their passing, because I'd been able to plan ahead."

I shook my head. "That makes no sense. What do you mean by 'plan ahead'?"

The doctor looked resigned. "In each case I had been warned to expect a death. And those deaths occurred, as I had been told they would."

Bud and I managed a sideways glance. Bud said, "You mean a series of suicides?"

The physician held up his hands as though to push away the idea. "Absolutely not, they were natural ends to wonderful, well-lived lives."

"That you knew about in advance?" I couldn't believe I had to clarify the point.

"Indeed."

KSue surprised us by nodding. "I knew about three of them, but not the other one."

I was beginning to think I was losing my mind. "Who told you that these people were going to die – and how long before their deaths were you alerted? Did they tell you themselves?" I tried my best to remain calm.

Dr. Nderu looked surprised. "They told me, but it was Demetrius who told them, of course. The amount of warning varied, from a couple of days to a week, in one case." He spoke as though this were the most natural thing in the world.

I could tell Bud was working as hard me to retain his civility. "I understand you have certain beliefs about the way your dead founder has been able to speak through his daughter since he 'passed over', so – to be clear – are you, in fact, telling us that Zara Karaplis told four people they were going to die?"

"She told us all," said KSue. "Well, she told us about three, in open sessions, when she was channelling. I guess she must have told the other one directly."

Bud was close to the edge. "And you don't see that as 'suspicious' in any way? How did they all die? One cause? Different causes? Were there autopsies carried out to discover the answer to those questions? Because, if you didn't request them, and yet signed all the death certificates, I think you'd be on incredibly shaky ground as far as both the law and the medical boards around here are concerned."

Dr. Nderu jumped up. "You have no idea what the human body, when controlled by a well-trained mind, is capable of. Many yogis and sadhus in India have been able to control their body's functioning with great accuracy and efficacy for centuries. The Western research fields of biofeedback methods, autonomic feedback, autogenic training – all these, as well as yoga – are studied by those at the highest levels of the Faceting movement, and stopping their own hearts could have been within the capabilities of all those who have passed."

I tried to sigh away my frustration. "But if you haven't requested any autopsies, you don't actually have any idea what's killed all these people, do you? Their hearts stopped beating – that's all you have, which is ultimately the cause of death for everyone. The question is: what made their hearts stop beating?

You have no idea. Right? You cannot seriously believe they all just laid down and...died."

"I have faith that it was their intention to leave this plane. Their passing was foretold, allowing them enough time to put their affairs in order, make their farewells, and prepare for what was to come." The doctor was sounding less like a medical professional and more like an unquestioning devotee. I could feel the anger in the pit of my stomach. He continued, "If they were not capable of being able to shut down their bodies, then what business is it of mine if they used an aid to smooth their journey? There are many plants available which could prove effective in such cases. And easing one's own path is not illegal."

Bud sounded alarmingly calm and quiet when he spoke; I know from my experience of having watched him interviewing murder suspects that he's at his most dangerous when he's sounding his most reasonable. "So, setting aside your flagrant disregard for the law of the land, and your profession's codes of conduct, for one moment, and assuming that the previous deaths – which were predicted – might have been suicides, are we to understand that the death of Linda Karaplis is not one to which you were alerted?"

The doctor sighed heavily. "As you say. It was a shock."

"Exactly!" KSue sounded vindicated – though I couldn't help but wonder why she hadn't told us about previous deaths having been announced, and Linda's not. She cried, "I told you it was all wrong. If Demetrius had known about *anyone* being due to pass, then *surely* he'd have known about Linda? And I'm certain he'd have told Zara about it."

Bud opened his mouth, but I jumped in. "Are you certain that he didn't? If Zara only made three public announcements, keeping the news of another imminent death 'private', might she have done the same with her mother?"

KSue's brow furrowed. "Oh, I didn't think of that. But I don't think so. I truly believe Linda would have said a proper goodbye to me if she'd known. And…" Her face lit up. "And Zara would have been with her mother, wouldn't she? She was shocked when she found out she was dead, as was Oscar. If Zara had been told by Demetrius that her mother was about to die, she'd have shared that information with her mother *and* her brother, I'm certain of that. And Linda would have told me."

"If Linda *had* told you that Demetrius had predicted her imminent death, would you have tried to stop her dying?" I thought I knew the answer.

"Oh no, not if it was her time." KSue had surprised me again.

Bud scrubbed at his face. "Doctor, my profession for many years has been to investigate suspicious and unlawful deaths, and I am in no doubt that the series of events you have described falls under at least one of those headings. So, let me ask you this: do your beliefs lead you to understand that Linda is still, wherever she might be, somehow aware of what's happening to her earthly remains?" Both Nderu and KSue nodded. "So don't you think she'd be pleased that you cared about her enough to find out how she died?" The body language of both KSue and the doctor told me they were unsure. Bud pressed. "Are you telling me that my wife and I – strangers here – are the only ones who believe action should be taken on behalf of this woman?"

"I would be guided by Zara," said the doctor. "She's Linda's only surviving relative now, and I don't think she'd want to hold up the interment of her mother's body."

I said, "I have a suggestion." Everyone looked at me. "If we speak to Zara about this, telling her our concerns about Linda's unforeseen death, then maybe she'll understand, and request an autopsy herself."

The doctor looked relieved and headed for the door – a little too quickly. "Excellent idea, let's do that now."

KSue trotted after him. "But Zara said she was going to be connecting with Demetrius – she didn't want to be disturbed."

As we followed, Bud muttered, "Zara had better listen, and take action – or I might have to get in touch with the local authorities myself. This entire situation is ludicrous."

I stroked his back as we marched out into the sunlight – the difference in temperature was amazing, the heat quite taking my breath away. "Maybe Zara's just so grief-stricken that she hasn't worked out that there's anything to be worried about, yet," I said. "Benefit of the doubt, and all that."

Bud turned and stared at me. "Who are you, and what have you done with my wife? You not taking an opportunity to judge someone? Is that truly you, Cait Morgan?"

"Hardy, har, har! I'm making a huge effort these days to be less judgy, and more thinky. Doesn't it suit me?"

"If the change takes, I'll be impressed," said Bud, just as we stopped outside what I assumed was the door to Zara's dig, where we were greeted by Ambroise.

"You can't see Zara at the moment, she's channelling." He sounded...*proprietorial?*

"We must. It's about her mother's death," said Bud, his tone controlled, but insistent.

"It wasn't foretold, you see," chimed in KSue, "which is very odd, and I'm worried that maybe Linda's passing wasn't what she wanted."

Ambroise's hair gleamed in the sunlight, and his eyes narrowed. He nodded his head slowly, and his expression softened. "Ah, I understand. This is your concern." He laid his hand gently on KSue's shoulder, and patted it as they exchanged a sad glance. "Now that she is gone, I feel I can tell you that, a few days ago, Linda was told she would die, within the week, by Demetrius. They spoke about it at length. She was not unhappy about it, though she was not sure how she would choose to pass.

I do not know what she decided, but I know she was considering several…alternatives. She asked that no one, not even Oscar, be told about it."

KSue's eyes filled with tears. "Oh no. Poor Linda! She didn't want *me* to know?" She stared up at Ambroise's sympathetic face as a fat tear rolled down her cheek. "So how do *you* know?" She sounded more puzzled than cross.

Ambroise smiled sadly. "I am able to help Zara achieve the state where she can channel more easily – without it being so exhausting. You know this, KSue. Demetrius spoke about Linda's passing before I had time to leave the channelling chamber."

Both Nderu and KSue nodded, clearly accepting Ambroise's explanation.

"So you're telling us that Zara knew, you knew, and Linda knew, but that was it?" Bud sounded professional, curt.

Ambroise nodded. "It was what Linda wanted. We respected her wish."

I had to ask, "And did Demetrius tell Linda exactly when she would die?"

Ambroise shook his head, his eyes wide, and sad. "He did not, which is sometimes how it goes. He said within a week, but it was, as we now know, less than that. Zara had wanted to be with her mother when she passed. It has upset her greatly that she missed the opportunity to be connected to her mother at the critical moment. Had she been there, she could have helped Linda find her way back to us more easily."

I dared, "Do you believe that Linda took her own life, to fall in line with what Zara told her Demetrius had said?"

Ambroise bowed his head and spoke softly. "This I do not know, for certain. Linda was an incredibly strong woman – I admired her spirit enormously. She might have decided that she wanted her passing to take place when she chose, in a manner she selected for herself. But I have no real knowledge of that."

"The doctor needs to sign a legal document explaining the reason why she died," said Bud. He stared hard at Nderu, then added, "And that means beyond the fact that her heart stopped beating. There should be an autopsy to establish the facts."

Ambroise looked deeply puzzled. "An autopsy? But why? It was her time. She was ready to die. What purpose is served by cutting her open to find out what method she used to achieve that…if she did."

"It's the law," said Bud. "And it also applies to Oscar."

Ambroise replied with a shrug. "Sometimes the law is not…helpful."

"Zara could – and I believe should – request an autopsy, for both her mother and her brother." Bud's tone was steely.

"Dr. Nderu, do you believe this is necessary?" Ambroise smiled at the doctor, who looked as though he'd rather be anywhere else in the world.

Before he had a chance to answer, Zara appeared at the door. "Something's amiss. There are unpleasant vibrations."

You're not kidding, was what I thought; "Bud and I think autopsies should be performed on the remains of both your mother and brother, to better understand the exact causes of their deaths," was what I said.

Zara blinked, but her expression didn't change; she turned to face Ambroise. "What's been spoken of here?"

"I have told everyone how I found Oscar, who had fallen. Now I have also told these people how Demetrius informed your mother that she would soon join him on the other side. There is a suggestion that an autopsy would discover if she eased her own passage, and if so, how." Ambroise's succinct summation was impressive.

Zara smiled, sadly. "I see." She turned to Dr. Nderu. "I'm so sorry that you have been put in such a difficult position by our guests, doctor. I believe my brother died as the result of a fall – most likely in the dark of the night, a dangerous time in the desert. Ambroise has explained how he found Oscar, and I have no reason to doubt his, and your, findings in that respect. It is a terrible loss, but I truly believe his death was a tragic accident." She sighed, and I was – once again – impressed by the immense maturity being displayed by this still-young woman. "As for my mother? Following the news my father gave me, she and I discussed the possibility that she would take her own life, on her own terms. She informed me that she planned to do that by ingesting a lethal amount of a natural poison. I understood her decision. Does my having told you this mean that an autopsy can be avoided, because you now know her exact cause of death?"

Dr. Nderu looked down at Zara's small, white-gowned figure, and replied somberly, "Do you know which poison?"

"I do. Datura. She grew it in her personal garden. She had been using it to manage her symptoms. She knew exactly how much to take to allow for its medicinal properties to be effective, and exactly how much to take for it to prove fatal." Zara's face shone in the sunlight as a small, sad smile curled her lips. "She thought it a most beautiful plant."

KSue blurted out, "But why didn't she tell me?"

Zara tilted her head and smiled at KSue. "She didn't want you to suffer. You were very dear to her." Zara's tone was soft; it dripped like honey, salving KSue's distress.

"But she didn't tell you about the planned timing of her death, did she, Zara?" Bud's tone wasn't sharp, but grave. "Your mother chose to not have you with her when she passed. Why do you think she did that?"

The significance of Bud's statement wasn't lost upon the young woman – for all her self-control her micro-expressions gave away that much. Her reply was smooth, however. "That will always be a great regret, but I know she will return, renewed, and then I shall be able to tell her that I forgive her for that choice."

Ambroise, KSue, and Nderu all bowed their heads, and Zara focused on Bud and me. "I believe you have no reason for concern. My brother's death was an accident. My mother's passing was hers to plan, and make happen. We shall bury them at sunset, and they will begin their journeys back to us. Of course, all – even guests – are welcome to attend the ceremony. Now, I shall retire."

Zara left us, and Dr. Nderu beamed. "I shall complete the paperwork back at my office," he said, and all but ran toward the main plaza.

"And this is the end of it," said Ambroise as he hugged KSue.

Bud and I headed back to our dig. As we walked, Bud said, "I don't like this one little bit, Wife."

"Nor do I, Husband."

Baffling Enlightenment

When we were alone again, Bud paced around our room, muttering. I knew better than to try to engage him in conversation, so allowed him to let off some steam while I hit the bathroom, and ran some cool water over my wrists; we'd been baking in the sun for an age.

When I returned, Bud was swearing at his phone. "No signal," he said. "Of course!"

"Who did you want to call?"

"I don't know anyone in law enforcement down here, but I thought someone back home might rustle up a name or two for me," he said, glaring at the useless block of plastic in his hand. "but even calling 911 would be better than nothing."

I knew it was my turn to be the voice of reason. "The doctor's going to record Linda's death as suicide, based upon a statement by the daughter of the deceased; Oscar's death will be listed as an accident, and they have a legal burial ground right here. I really don't think there's any more we can do. We made our opinions known, but Zara has made her decision clear."

"But it's not just about Linda and Oscar." Frustration in every word.

"I know, it's all the others, too. Neither of us believes for one minute that the voice of a dead man is predicting death from beyond the grave, which means Zara is the one doing the predicting – and these people have such faith in her, and in what they're being told, that they've all just decided to end their lives to fit in with her predictions."

"Exactly."

"Which means that Zara Karaplis is, essentially, a mass murderer, even if 'all she's done' is predict a handful of suicides."

"Exactly."

"I love it when you agree with me."

"What?" Bud looked puzzled – distracted – then smiled. "Yes, Wife, you've summed it all up very nicely." He stopped pacing. "She doesn't look like a serial killer, does she?"

"They don't all look the same, Bud."

"I know, I know – but you know what I mean."

"I do. But she's fascinating, isn't she? For a woman still only in her late twenties to possess the gravitas she does is quite something. I think of some of my students, the grad students especially, who are the same age as her, and they're still trying to find out who they are and what they want to do in life. Zara seems so very self-possessed, at peace with herself, and the world. She's got an incredible ability to convey a depth of emotional connection without doing much at all. I'd put money on her having spent much of her early life with adults, rather than with children of her own age; she projects the qualities of what some call an 'old soul'. Quite entrancing, in a strange way. But, since she's the one who's doing all the pronouncing about deaths to come – even her own mother's – she'd need to be that unique for her words to have the impact they do. But, even though she's observably dynamic, what I'm struggling with is understanding why on earth she'd be doing it. My favorite question."

Bud slumped onto the sofa. "I wasn't looking forward to coming here, you know that." I nodded. "But I never for one moment thought it would be…like this. They're all nuts."

I joined Bud. "As a professor of criminal psychology, I feel it my duty to point out that's not a technical term. You know that, right?" Bud nodded. "But I'll grant you there's a communal mindset here that's quite specific to this group, and the belief that Demetrius is speaking through Zara really does seem to have…well, I would say it's enthralled people, in the true sense of the word."

Bud sat up and started his head-scratching thing. "I understand what you mean about Zara and the way she's got a certain aura about her – and I almost hate myself for using that word. She projects…oh, I don't know, I can't give it a name. But the way she glanced up at me when she was kneeling on that bathroom floor beside her mother's body made me – *me* – believe she knew something I didn't, which was unnerving. But what I cannot wrap my head around is why several people would kill themselves just because of what some young woman tells them a dead man has 'told her'."

I gave the matter some serious consideration. "In order to hold that much sway over people, and even given her unusual personality, Zara must have to 'prove' to those listening to her that she's speaking for Demetrius."

"Like the way KSue said Demetrius proved it was him? That thing about an argument only the two of them knew about?"

"Yes, like that."

Bud stood up and started pacing again. "But how? I mean it's a given that it's not Demetrius doing the talking, so how does Zara have the knowledge – the insights – to convince people it really is him? Like, how did Zara know about an argument that took place between Demetrius and KSue when she was just a little kid?"

"Remember what KSue said…exactly?"

Bud shrugged. "Remind me."

"She said, 'Demetrius mentioned it through Zara that day, so I knew it was really him. Even then he didn't say exactly what we'd argued about. He still wanted to protect Linda's feelings, even from the other plane.' Now it could be that Demetrius and KSue argued in front of the four- or five-year-old Zara, or somewhere where she could overhear, or see, them. The mind of a child is a wonderful thing – it grabs and retains all sorts of stimuli; Zara might have remembered that her father and KSue had a blazing row many years ago, even if she didn't know what it was about…so the topic of the forgotten birthday wasn't mentioned specifically by 'Demetrius' not because he wanted to 'protect' his widow's feelings, but because Zara never knew what it was all about in the first place."

Bud's expression softened as he nodded slowly. "Yes, I can see that being a reasonable explanation. So do you think Zara has similar insights into the lives of all those people she's convinced to kill themselves? 'Proofs', if you like."

I shrugged. "Maybe, though I don't know how. Possibly, if the people who pre-deceased Linda were all the earliest members as Serendipity said they were, they'd all also have been a part of Zara's life since she was young. Maybe she knew a great deal more about them than they'd have imagined; adults often don't notice that a child is lurking – and this lot do seem to be more than a little self-absorbed."

Bud rolled his eyes. "You're not kidding. I know we were talking last night about how good it is for people to seek out happiness through self-awareness, but there's a normal level of self-analysis, and then there's this bunch."

I had to agree, then added, "Do you think we should find out more about the other people who died here? And – I hate to add this to the mix – why do you think Oscar took himself off running about the desert after his mother's death, as Dr. Nderu's examination of him suggested."

Bud let out a wry chuckle. "Who knows – though running away seems appealing at the moment."

I checked my watch. "There'll be no running for us – we're due to be having dinner with Serendipity and Ambroise in an hour. Besides, we don't have a car."

"Trust me – if we needed to get away from here, I'd find a vehicle somewhere we could use."

It was my turn to laugh. "Car theft? You?"

Bud looked worn out, but managed a twinkle. "I've learned a thing or two from some of the best – or maybe that should be some of the worst – in the business, over the years. Who knows – all that knowledge might come in handy one day."

"Well, not today. We've got a dinner and a double funeral to attend. And while for once we believe we know who is doing what, to whom – we both know we want to work out *how* Zara is able to convince people that Demetrius has returned…and *why* she'd bother. I mean – why would she want all those people dead…including her own mother? It's baffling. To be honest, we could do worse than try our luck talking to Ambroise; if he's the one Zara turns to for help with her channelling, then maybe he knows more than he's said…or even more than he thinks he does. At least now we've got an idea of what we're trying to find out, right?"

Bud looked distracted. "A framework for our investigation into five – or six, if you count Oscar – deaths? Yes, you're right, we do. So often we're trying to work out who has ended another person's life; this time we're looking for something quite different…an understanding of how a person is able to convince people that a dead man is telling them to kill themselves. Weird, right?"

"That's a word we could apply to so many aspects of our time here so far," I replied. "Oh, and by the way…bagsy the bathroom first."

"You're welcome to it," called Bud as I headed off.

As I tried to make my hair look presentable, I wondered what would be a good wardrobe decision for an intimate dinner followed by a double interment. I hadn't packed anything black for the trip, not imagining I'd need it, which is so unlike me as to be remarkable. That would teach me!

Helpful Mishap

Plodding along the uneven path down the hill toward Serendipity's, I dared to raise my eyes from the rubble beneath my feet and took in my surroundings with a bit more attention. The air was heavy and oppressive, and I could see clouds gathering in the distance – they looked ominous enough to make me square my shoulders and wonder just how much rain fell in this particular part of the desert, and when.

There were no lights showing at the restaurant when we arrived, and I was surprised we weren't greeted by any wonderful aromas – a bit disappointed, too. We wandered into the seating area, but the place was empty. A crash in the kitchen gave us both a fright, and we headed to the swing doors, peering in – in case we were needed. Serendipity was bending to pick up several stainless-steel bowls that had taken a tumble, while Ambroise stood at the counter chopping something green, as though his life depended upon it. We pushed open the doors and said, "Hello," in unison. They both turned to face us, looking surprised.

"*Zut!*" Ambroise's shout grabbed Serendipity's attention.

She rose and ran to his side. "Oh no, look what you've done!"

Ambroise immediately dropped his knife and stuck his arm up in the air. "It is not deep, just a lot of blood," he said calmly.

Bud and I rushed in, apologizing, and asking if we could help. Ambroise ran water over his hand, and Serendipity examined the small but bloody gash on his left forefinger.

"Sit down, hold it up, support it, be patient. You won't need stitches, but I'll finish the prep." Serendipity's voice was calm.

She looked at us. "I'm on-site first-aider. Won't be a second…off to get my bag of tricks."

I felt dreadful, and Bud's expression told me he shared my guilt; it was our entrance that had caused the accident. We could do no more than offer to help in any way possible. As our hostess returned with what was essentially a small suitcase full of first-aid supplies, both Ambroise and Serendipity brushed off the cut as nothing to worry about – something those who work in kitchens are used to dealing with. After a few minutes, we ended up sitting at a table beside the large windows at the rear of the restaurant with Ambroise, his left hand supported on his right shoulder by a sling.

Heading back to the kitchen, Serendipity called, "I'll finish up out here – it's just *quesadilla* and salad, but I promise there'll be no blood in the dressing." She laughed as the doors swung closed behind her.

Ambroise really didn't seem overly concerned about his hand, so I thought it best to do what Bud and I had agreed, and ask some leading questions; at least his injury meant he was more or less trapped with us.

I opened with some general observations about how delightful the restaurant was, and how interesting it had been to find out a little more about Faceting, but led the conversation as quickly as I could to the topic of Zara's channelling. "It must be quite something to see," I said. "But, following on from what you said earlier, how exactly do you help Zara do it?"

Ambroise didn't flinch. "I sing to her."

"Pardon?" I hadn't been expecting that.

"My mother was a trained singer who performed as a soloist with many local choirs, and she taught me how to project and control my voice. This means I can sing notes for a long time; their vibrations soothe Zara, and she is better able to enter the place in her mind where her father connects with her."

"So the resonance of your voice helps her 'tune into' her father's messages?" Bud sounded skeptical.

It was clear from the shift in Ambroise's demeanor that he'd picked up on Bud's tone. "Vibrations are important in all parts of life. As an engineer I discovered this; allowances have to be made for all sorts of vibrations – they can be very destructive."

Bud nodded. "We live in a part of the world where a lot of the older buildings have had to be upgraded to allow for the threat of seismic events," he said, "but I don't have the background to understand how smaller vibrations might affect a building's integrity. Is that something engineers spend a lot of time researching?"

Ambroise settled back in his seat. "It is. If one is constructing a bridge, for example, the traffic will cause vibrations, as will the wind, and so forth. Indeed, there are many meanings of the word 'vibration' for the engineer. But, beyond that, I mean that every living thing vibrates, all the time. It is the nature of life, of the cosmos. Even things which some people believe have no life – like rocks, and stones – have a frequency, a movement within themselves. This is the power of vibration. And it is why we can live in greater harmony with our surroundings once we are attuned to them."

"Like the 'om' thing in meditation?" Bud sounded truly curious.

Ambroise smiled. "Like this, yes. The resonance of the sound within the body allows for a meditative state to be reached, and it is similar when I sing to Zara."

"It must have been a bit of a shock for you if Demetrius arrived more quickly than expected and Zara blurted out that Linda was about to die," I said. I was interested in the conversation about vibrations, because I'm well aware of how humming aids my own process of recollection, but wanted to get to the heart of what we'd agreed we needed to ask about.

Ambroise's chin tilted up as he replied, "It was. I usually have time to withdraw before Demetrius talks about…meaningful matters like this."

"A difficult prediction for Zara to deliver, I'd have thought," said Bud, following my lead.

Ambroise's shoulders suddenly became very French, rising a good six inches. "She sometimes does not grasp the true nature of what she says until she has spoken it aloud, so, yes, she seemed shocked to hear herself tell her mother she would soon be leaving this plane. But she's dedicated herself to passing on her father's words and wishes, so has become used to speaking that which is not something with which she is familiar."

"Linda was there when Demetrius predicted her death…she heard the news first-hand, as Zara spoke it?" I was keen to clarify that point.

Ambroise nodded.

"And how did she take it?" I couldn't imagine how that would feel.

"I was retiring from the chamber by then, I did not see her face, but heard her say, 'Good, I am glad', so I believe she took it well."

I allowed my amazement to show. "I see."

Ambroise said, "I am glad you do, because I must admit I do not. It seems strange to me that people are prepared to leave this plane. I enjoy my time here, and endeavor to make the most of it. It would be difficult for me to leave, when there is so much I have yet to do."

I decided to dig a bit deeper. "What plans do you have?"

Ambroise leaned forward, and his face gathered into an earnest expression. "I am developing my Faceting skills every day, in every way – but I am anxious to reach my goal of true enlightenment. Only then, when I am able to achieve cosmic connection, shall I feel fulfillment."

"But, surely, as an engineer, you're more concerned with the physical than the metaphysical," I blurted out.

He made one of those downward-smiling faces at which only the French truly excel. "They are both parts of the same thing. It is impossible to comprehend one without the other. My academic and professional experience have taught me a great deal about the physical, but I never attended to my spiritual side. This was not beneficial for my being. My mother was a good woman, but she was not a spiritual person. I am now focused upon that part of my life. I need to do this, in order to reach my desired goal."

"And what's that, exactly?" Bud was trying to sound non-patronising, but failing.

Ambroise sat back in his chair and took a deep breath. "Freedom, in the truest sense of the word. If we are truly enlightened, we realize how little we need in the physical world. This is my goal: to possess nothing, and for even that to be more than I need."

I was just about to comment that Ambroise's words were somewhat opaque, when Serendipity emerged through the swing doors, placed a wide platter of greenery on the table and said, "Hang on now, Ambroise – don't go knocking the physical too much. If it wasn't for Dad's money I couldn't have afforded to move here, let alone set up this place, and you wouldn't have been able to pay to study to advance as far as you have within the movement." She placed her hand on his shoulder. "No, I'm not bringing up the question of money to annoy you, but you have to accept it's Dad's support of me, that I use to help you, that's made all this possible. The good old physical part of life – like money, somewhere to live, and food to eat – has to be attended to somehow, otherwise we aren't able to have time for the luxury of self-development. What do you think would happen if your monthly fees here weren't paid? You'd be out, whatever level you've managed to achieve."

She smiled, and returned to the kitchen, seemingly oblivious to the devastating blow she'd just dealt Ambroise's pride; he flushed and started to fuss with his sling – quite unnecessarily. I watched him intently – yes, he was embarrassed, but he was also…what? Angry? There was a flash of that, but, overall, he'd slunk back inside some sort of shell, from which he'd been happily emerging as he'd been chatting about his views on the cosmos. Now he'd rearranged his face to present a bland and pleasant persona again.

"This looks interesting," said Bud a little too brightly, staring at the salad. "What's in it?"

"No blood, I believe," said Ambroise, and forced a smile. "It's a selection of salad leaves, tomatoes, and shallots we grow here; the beans are white tepary beans – we grow those here, too, and they are a little sweet; there is also nopal – which is the pad of a cactus. There are no spines, they have been removed."

Bud tried to look enthusiastic, but I knew the idea of eating cactus wouldn't appeal to him at all.

"And here's the star of the meal," said Serendipity as she arrived with another platter. "Thanks to Ambroise's chopping skills – before his little accident – this quesadilla contains lots of tasty herbs that we grow on our own deck out there, as well as panela, which is a type of cheese that originated in Mexico, a bit like mozzarella. And there's shredded, roasted chicken, raised here at the Facetors' little farm. It had a happy and productive life."

Bud perked up at the thought of something he liked the sound of, and my mouth started watering, too. We all tucked in, grabbing a quarter each of the quesadilla, and selecting a portion of salad to accompany it on our plates. I noticed that Bud did his best to avoid the slices of cactus, which was a shame; they'd been marinated in an oil infused with a variety of herbs, so I couldn't be sure what flavor came from the cactus itself or from the dressing, but the overall experience was of a fresh taste and a slightly spongy texture. It was lovely – as was the quesadilla, which was thick, moist, luscious and terribly moreish.

Serendipity served us a wine from an Arizona vineyard: it was a greenish white, sparkled slightly, and was poured over frozen grapes – which was novel; its almost grassy flavor complemented the meal perfectly. It was hard to believe we were dining before attending a double interment, because the conversation wasn't about death or the dead people at all – instead it was about the landscape we were overlooking, the food we were eating, and the wine we were drinking. Ambroise appeared to emerge a little from his funk as we chatted, and he and Bud seemed to get along just fine, while Serendipity filled me in on how her parents were coping with having to break in the fourth head chef at their restaurant back in Canada since she'd left the place.

Having complimented Serendipity for the umpteenth time about her food, she got up and brought a copy of the menu, which we hadn't had a chance to see. Bud and I read through it; it was short, offered a variety to please most tastes, was entirely peanut-free – as befitting a chef who, as we'd discovered during our time in Kelowna, suffered from a serious peanut allergy – and sounded delicious.

"I see you've catered for vegetarians and vegans, as well as those who can't tolerate gluten," said Bud, acknowledging all the little symbols beside each item.

"And for omnivores, like you," said Serendipity, smiling. "Everything we serve is organic, of course, and is either grown or raised right here, or is supplied to us by foragers, farmers, or producers within Arizona. Everything has the smallest carbon footprint I can manage, and I've worked with local cooks and elders to make sure that any traditional foods I'm inspired by, or recipes I'm amending, aren't being used in a way that could be seen as either disrespectful, or as cultural appropriation. I hope I've done a good job."

I replied, "Well, as far as the cultural appropriation aspect is concerned, we're entirely the wrong people to ask, because that's a question you've already had answered by those who matter – the people from whose culture those ingredients and dishes arise. But I can tell you that – from my point of view at least – I could eat everything listed quite happily. Of course, then you'd have to roll me out of here straight to my bed. Congratulations – I'm sure it'll be well received, though" – I couldn't help but ask – "won't it be a difficult proposition – being all the way out here? It's a long drive from...well, anywhere, really."

Serendipity nodded. "I know what you mean, but destination dining is a real thing, and Arizona's full of foodies. Because there are guest residences at the Desert Gem, folks can choose to stay over, and we have a collection and delivery service, too – for people, not food. We offer to pick them up and take them home. Norman has spent months contacting drivers all over the state: we've now got access to owners of electric vehicles who will operate as a sort of contracted taxi service in each of their own local areas, so people can come, eat, drink, and get home safely, and in comfort. The drivers get their vehicles charged up for free while they're waiting here for their passengers, and they get fed, too. It's a win-win."

"But how do people book a table, or let you know they're coming, if the cellphone reception is as bad as you say it is? You don't have a landline all the way out here, do you?" I thought it was a sensible question.

Serendipity smiled. "I've negotiated a reasonable deal with the office at the Desert Gem. They have internet access there, using a satellite. They operate our booking service for us, and tell us what to expect. We pay them for their service."

Bud said, "You seem to have thought of everything."

Serendipity made googly eyes at Ambroise. "Not me, him. He's good at planning things."

Ambroise smiled, blushing slightly, and responded somewhat coyly, "It's like any engineering project; I consider the entire undertaking as a system that has many parts, then I put them together, using people with the appropriate expertise. That is all. I do not do it myself, but I can encourage people to do their part. But, since I am claiming to be the great planner, I have to say we should now bring this meal to an end, and begin our walk to the burial ground, or we shall be late."

The sun was already resting upon the hilltops, and I knew Ambroise was right, but I also knew I hadn't quite got all I wanted out of the pair, so I suggested, "Why don't Bud and Ambroise go ahead, and I'll stay here to help you, Serendipity – we can give Ambroise's poor, injured hand a break." I hoped it would give me a chance for a bit of a chat with our hostess, alone.

"Great idea," said Bud, following my lead. "Are you going to have to put that sling thing back on now, or is your hand alright?"

Ambroise examined his finger. "Hardly a scratch," he said, "and I shall be happy to walk ahead with Bud, if that suits you, Serendipity?"

"Sure, we'll see you there."

Once "the boys" had left, Serendipity and I carried the dirty dishes into what was an amazing kitchen, fitted out with some impressive equipment; I spotted a refrigerator bigger than my first flat, a freezer room, something that looked as though it had come from Cape Canaveral – but turned out to be an ice-maker – and ovens and grills of all sorts. Clearly Sammy Soul hadn't stinted when it came to setting up his daughter's restaurant. Even so, Serendipity didn't dump everything into one of the numerous dishwashers. Instead, I wiped as Serendipity washed.

"So...tell me about Ambroise," was my opening gambit.

"There's not much to tell," she replied.

"Oh, go on," I pressed, "your emails have told me some things, but now that I've met him – and have seen the two of you together – it seems you're quite keen on him. I'm not wrong, am I?"

Serendipity paused, a plate in her hand. "Oh Cait, I like him very much. Yes, that's true. Well, more than that, if I'm being honest – and I always try to be honest, and open. And...and I believe he feels the same way about me. But...well, I knew from quite soon after I met him that he'd made a promise to himself that means we can't have more than a friendship. So that's what we are: friends."

I was intrigued. "Come on, you can't say that much and no more. What do you mean, exactly?"

Serendipity put down the plate she'd been holding. "As I told you, Ambroise is totally dedicated to developing his Faceting abilities, but what I didn't say was that he's so focused he's taken an oath of celibacy, so that he has absolutely no distractions in his life, until he reaches true enlightenment."

"Celibacy? Who's he sworn the oath to?"

"Himself. It's something he takes extremely seriously. And I also know he's having to come to terms with some abandonment and trust issues, too."

I wondered how to respond. "I understand the trust issues, having suffered through a relationship where I was always being lied to, and taken for granted. But you seem to be very attached to him – even if there's no chance of more than a friendship between the two of you."

Serendipity picked up another dish. "We really have become very close during the past year, and our friendship is deeper than the one I had with Raj, to be honest. It really does make a difference when you get to know the truth of a person's soul before you move to the physical phase of the relationship."

"But you just told me Ambroise has sworn himself to celibacy. Will there even be a physical element?" I was confused.

Despite the fact we were completely alone, Serendipity whispered, "That's just it, you see…" She sounded excited, breathless, like a teen, not a woman in her late thirties. "He's told me he'd never imagined being able to trust someone the way he trusts me, and that if anyone could tempt him to break his vow it would be me." She beamed, her eyes twinkling. "Imagine *me* making someone feel that way. I've never thought of myself as particularly attractive or alluring, but Ambroise thinks I am. Tells me I am…all the time. He's struggling with it, of course, and I understand that; his vow was taken in true earnestness. But I just feel…oh, Cait, I feel so incredibly *special* that I've touched his soul that way. He's so drawn to me, Cait, that he sometimes has to stay away from me, or he'd just give in and break his vow right there and then." Her expression told me she'd like nothing more. "I really think he might be *the* one for me. We're connected in ways I never even imagined existed. It's…it's like being with someone who instinctively knows how I feel, and what I need. We're true soul mates, Cait. Of course the physical aspect is something I want – oh, I'm not going to deny that – but it puts it in perspective, doesn't it?"

I thought it best to not respond, largely because I knew Serendipity was on a cloud so high in the sky there'd be no reaching her, so I smiled, and we continued to clear away the last of the dinner things, then she made a circuit of the kitchen, flicking switches, and wiping down surfaces. Eventually we were ready to leave, and we headed up the hill, the setting sun behind us, the night closing in ahead.

"I hope it works out for you and Ambroise," I said quietly, as we climbed.

"So do I," whispered Serendipity. "We both try hard to not show our feelings when we're with other people, especially because everyone knows about Ambroise's vow, and neither of us want anyone to think he doesn't take it seriously. We don't spend an inordinate amount of time together either – it's critical that he spends time with other people, so no one guesses how he feels about me, you see, but I very much enjoy how connected I feel when we are together. It's like magic, Cait. Like the way you and Bud must have felt when you were first a couple."

I smiled, the remembrances of the first months Bud and I had dated flooding back. "Maybe, for us, it was a little different," I said.

"Because Bud's wife had been murdered?"

I nodded.

Serendipity replied, "I guess that is a big difference, but, like I said, Ambroise has some issues he has to tackle, which isn't the same thing at all, I know – but he's had to come to terms with his father abandoning him and his mother when he was a baby, then his mother died while he was still quite young – when he was studying at university. He told me he felt he should have been there for her instead of being off on his own…he had no idea she was as sick as she was. Her death came as a great shock to him – he only managed to be with her for a few hours before she passed. It's a lot for him to process. But he found Faceting, you see, and that was his salvation, so I really do understand his vow. And I think he might be my salvation, Cait. My chance, at last, to know what it's like to be with someone who's stable, and loving, and always there for me in every way. That's what I've been looking for, hoping for, my whole life. Yes, I thought that Raj and I could make a go of it – but my feelings toward Ambroise are so different, so…intense, that now I wonder what it was I even felt for Raj. Maybe it was a case of 'any port in a storm', and he was at hand. This is a different thing altogether. This is the real deal."

I wasn't old enough to be her mother – just about – and there isn't a maternal bone in my body, but I felt terribly sorry for Serendipity at that moment, and wished I had a magic wand I could wave to allow her to be as happy as she wanted – which I suppose is what all parents want for their children, in a way. Then, with an even heavier heart, I realized we were about to attend the burial of a mother and her son, to be overseen by the only remaining member of their family – a young woman who, rather worryingly, was indeed young enough to be my child.

I had to acknowledge I didn't feel the warmth, or even sympathy, toward Zara that I felt toward Serendipity, then told myself I hardly knew her, and that we'd not met under the most auspicious of circumstances – and I suspected her of some pretty dark deeds. All of which meant that, by the time I spotted Bud hovering at the edge of a circle of people all holding hands, swaying, and hiss-chanting, I was almost in the right frame of mind to face whatever might come – and the irony of the entire "Facet and Face It" thing wasn't lost on me at all.

Unearthly Burial

Serendipity waved as she left us and headed toward the crowd, while Bud and I held back a little, and grasped each other's hands; he gave mine a squeeze as he whispered, "Good heart-to-heart with our hostess?"

"Tell you later. Did you get anything interesting out of Ambroise?"

"I know a lot more now about how to calculate the amount of weight that can be borne by various materials than when we began our walk, so there's that." He flashed a grin. "Tell you later – it's fascinating stuff…at least, Ambroise seemed to think it all was; he gushed a lot about it all, and ended up sort of bounding along – like a puppy. But that was about it. Not as interesting as this set-up. Not making you feel nervous this time, are they?"

"Not at all – I'm interested to see how this all works."

The earthly remains of Oscar and Linda Karaplis were already set upon a raised platform each, neither in a casket, but shrouded; her in turquoise, him in gray. We were surrounded by folks dressed in a rainbow of colors, all muted in the darkness, but highlighted by the oil lamps everyone had placed on the ground in front of them. I was glad I'd decided to wear navy, as had Bud, because we really did fade into the night.

Barbara read a passage that spoke of moving between planes, and about how everything in the cosmos is made of the same matter, so we are all always part of it, whatever our current state of being – which went on a bit. Then Ambroise stepped forward and sang a song in a form of French that sounded archaic; he had an extraordinary voice – a true counter tenor, with a rounded tone. It was an absolute delight to hear the notes soar in the still of the night, with the stars glinting above us; it seemed as though even the desert creatures were listening, and I, along with everyone else, was entranced.

When he finished, he began to sing one continuous, sonorous note, and I literally felt it resonate inside my head – it was an extraordinary sensation. Then Zara began to sway, and I realized she was doing her channelling thing; I shuffled forward a little to try to get a better view of her and could see she was standing at the edge of the graves that had already been hacked into the stony ground, barefoot, swathed in white, with the jewel I'd seen her wearing the night before now clasped in her right hand, glinting in the light from the oil lamps by which she was surrounded.

"I am with you." The voice that came from Zara's mouth was her own, but a little deeper. Everyone was so quiet I could hear the wicks in the oil lamps sputtering and fizzing. "I must speak," the voice added.

We all waited. And waited.

"My wife and my son are here with me now. We shall rejoice. As should you."

There was a mass hissing of "Facet and Face It", then we waited again, in silence.

"KSue, you must not grieve for your friend, she is happy to be with me again."

A gasp from a small figure I could tell was KSue was followed by: "He spoke to me! To me!" KSue clearly felt this to be a great honor.

"My wife asks me to tell you she will return when she has renewed, and has recovered from her passing. She will choose the one who will speak for her, as my daughter speaks for me."

We all remained silent.

"We have outsiders with us, you must treat them kindly, welcome them. More will come. This is good. This is what we desire. Be mindful that both these outsiders have people who loved them who have passed and are now here, with me, so I know them better than you. Jan wishes to say she forgives you, Bud, and says that you must forgive yourself. She asks you to care well for Marty. Angus wishes me to tell you he asks for forgiveness for his poor treatment of you, and is pleased that you are now happy, Cait, and your parents send their unending love."

Bud and I turned toward each other, our mouths open.

"Now we must give the remains of my wife and child back to the earth. It is time."

As Bud and I watched, still stunned, the bodies were lowered into the waiting graves, then a huge cheering erupted, and every member of the encircling group picked up their oil lamp and threw it into one of the two gaping holes. Soon, both corpses were engulfed, flames shooting toward the stars, crackling and popping, illuminating the joyous faces of the Facetors, who were all hugging and cheering and swaying. The atmosphere had shifted; the flames gave the entire scene a Hellish aura, and I couldn't help but notice that some of the older men were giving some of the younger women "hugs" that seemed to be more than friendly.

I noticed, through the throng, that Zara looked to be physically drained, and was helped away from what was on the verge of becoming a melee by Norman, Elizabeth, and Barbara.

KSue ran toward us clapping her hands. "Demetrius spoke to me – did you hear that? And he spoke to you two, too. I can hardly believe it. Linda managed to get a message to me – and you must both be delighted to hear from your loved ones."

I grabbed KSue as the flames from some of the oil that hadn't quite made it into the graves came closer. "Careful, KSue, stand back. That could be dangerous."

She laughed, "No one ever gets hurt, don't be silly."

"This is normal?" Bud looked boggled.

"Oh yes – you see, private cremations aren't allowed in Arizona, just burials, but if we do this, then cover them over, no one knows any different – and they're able to start on their journey back to us much faster. Do you think there's a chance Linda will choose to speak through me? I do hope so, it would be wonderful to reconnect with her ."

"Maybe," was all I could muster.

A woman who looked to be in her early twenties – who'd just left the embrace of a man more than twice her age whose expression as he'd hugged her had seemed to be more of a leer than a smile – came and grabbed KSue, holding her for a long time; KSue beamed with silent glee.

Bud pulled my arm. "Let's go," he said.

We left the unsettling merriment behind us and made our way slowly toward the plaza. We didn't speak.

Back inside our dig, with a couple of oil lamps alight, and both of us perching on the edge of the bed, Bud said, "That was unexpected." He's quite adept at understating things.

"Do you mean the way the funeral party incinerated the corpses, or the fact that your dead wife and my dead ex-boyfriend – and my dead parents – chose to communicate with us?"

Bud stood and paced. "Both, of course." His head-scratching told me to wait – there would be more. There was. He turned to face me, and I could see anger glinting in his eyes. "I don't like Jan's memory being used like that. It's disgraceful. I hope you weren't too upset about Angus, and your mom and dad."

I patted the bed, and Bud sat beside me again, where I took his hand. "It threw me, alright, but didn't upset me."

He nodded. "Good, but before I say anything else, let's just get something straight: we're both one hundred percent certain that Zara isn't speaking on behalf of her dead father, right?"

I nodded, and allowed myself to smile as I replied, "One hundred percent. But the fact you even asked the question tells me how rattled you are. So, let's be realistic about all this – I believe the reason Zara picked on us tonight wasn't so that the Facetors would be more likely to accept us while we're here, but to show us – and her followers, of course – that she possesses knowledge about us that could, theoretically, only have been gleaned from an omniscient person on the other plane. She was very publicly displaying the fact that her communication with her dead father allows her to know everything about everyone – outsiders included. Imagine how powerful that must be, if you're a true devotee."

"But how *does* she know about Jan? About Angus?" Bud's voice had risen half an octave.

"Okay, let's work it through. Jan's death, and the way she died, was public knowledge – in the media for weeks. There was even a story about Marty being injured when he attacked Jan's killer, wasn't there?" Bud nodded. "Same thing with Angus; the tabloids raked over our relationship for weeks. All Zara would have to do is Google us; Google forgets nothing. Serendipity said there's internet service at the office, so Zara could have used that. Knowing the circumstances of Angus and Jan's deaths, and our relationships with them, it would be the easiest thing in the world to guess that you'd feel guilty about Jan's death, and that I'd have blamed Angus for the way he'd treated me. Researchable facts, and the application of a bit of basic psychology, that's all it was."

Bud's shoulders unhunched a little, and he let out a deep sigh. "Yes, you're right, of course. That's what it must be." His jawline firmed, and he looked grim. "I *have* forgiven myself about Jan, you know that, right? I had to work at it, but I couldn't have carried on for long with the weight of that guilt. It wasn't me who killed her, it was that creature – he's the one I'll never forgive."

"Good – I mean about forgiving yourself. And, you know what? Jan would have known that about you; even if she had managed to 'speak from the other plane' she wouldn't have sent those messages...so Zara missed the mark in that respect. And she was way off with Angus. Him saying he apologized for how he treated me? Well, unless arrival at the other plane really does lead to insights one never possessed in life, or else a complete and total personality transplant, no, that wouldn't be within the realm of possibility for him. When he was alive he was a great apologizer – but always with what I now realize was the insincerity of a narcissist who was gaslighting me. He used to beg forgiveness every morning after he'd been violent the night before. But that very last time I saw him alive – when I stupidly allowed him to stay at my place because he wasn't up to getting himself home – some of the last words I ever spoke to him were me taking the opportunity to make it quite clear that I'd never, ever accept, or even believe, another apology from him. The next morning I found him dead on the floor, so I'm as sure as I can be that he 'passed' knowing that apologizing to me wouldn't be the best use of his first chance to communicate with me from the other side. So, there – Zara got that wrong, too. She did her best to make a power play, using us and our losses, leveraging our grief, but didn't deliver. What was it Elizabeth said? Close, but no cigar."

Bud smiled, and I could tell he was rallying. Another sigh. "Yes, you're right about all that. A manipulative device that *we* know went awry, but I bet it hit home for the others there, as you say. Do you think that's what she does with everyone? Does Zara just do a bit of online research into people then use that information as 'proof' that she's communicating with a person who's able to know everything, because they're dead?"

I shook my head. "Given that quite a few people have – possibly – killed themselves on her say so, I'd have thought they'd need a bit more convincing than just having something they once put up in a social media post replayed to them…though, if they'd forgotten they'd done it, and she'd found it, then maybe they'd think it was something only an omniscient being could know."

"Like the argument KSue and Demetrius had?"

I had to admit that was unlikely. "That's more of a private thing, I'd say. But I stick to my explanation that Zara probably witnessed the fight in the first place. So…you know, putting it all together, maybe she was able to sway those people…"

"…because they were ready to be swayed."

We both smiled. Wearily.

I mused, "Linda had been suffering from rheumatoid arthritis for some time, which isn't a condition that improves with age. Who knows, maybe she *was* just tired of living without her beloved husband, and suffering terribly with pain. If what Ambroise said was true, Linda was pleased to receive the news that she was about to die. Maybe the others were, too?"

Bud stood, stretched out his back and said, "I'm with Ambroise on that one; I don't understand ending one's life…there's always something to live for, even if it's the unknown that tomorrow will bring."

"I agree, but – as you might imagine, given my background – I've studied the reasons behind suicide, largely through research carried out with those who've survived sometimes one, or even numerous, attempts. It's an extremely complex psychological picture: sometimes, the precipitating situation is an inability on the part of the individual to believe there's a time beyond their current circumstances that could ever possibly be any better for them – that there's 'no way out'. But – for some – the belief that 'things will be better for those I love, when I am gone' factors in, too…though not to the extent that we've seen here. If – and I repeat *if* – that's what's been going on. No autopsies means no proof, so we have to work on suppositions. Which could be a fruitless task."

"How do you mean?"

"Remember you flippantly suggested we shouldn't 'drink the Kool-Aid'?" Bud nodded. "Well, the mass suicide by over nine hundred people in Jonestown, Guyana back in the late seventies which led to that saying arising – because the folks there consumed cyanide-laced drinks, which, by the way, weren't made using Kool-Aid, it was Flavor Aid, but, there you go – was, I would say, mass murder. And – however Zara managed to get enough information to convince those people that it was Demetrius speaking, not her – if they then went ahead and took their own lives, I would say she's culpable. Which is…"

"…far from good, or useful, because, in order for there to be justice, we'd have to prove how she did it. And how would we ever do that?"

It was my turn to stretch. "Exactly. Standing looking down into those graves tonight, the flames illuminating those faces? Those people were happy, Bud – joyfully celebrating death in a way that suggests to me they don't see it as something to be feared at all. Which is dangerous. Because if you don't fear death, but see it as a gateway to something that's maybe even better than life itself, why wouldn't you take the steps needed to reach that other, seemingly paradisical alternative reality? KSue's delight at being spoken to by Demetrius? I suspect she'd be just as thrilled if she'd been told her time was soon, and her current mindset suggests to me she might be only too happy to go off to join her bosom buddy, Linda, on the other plane. Zara's power is significant, Bud. We just saw a glimpse of it tonight. And – notwithstanding all the organic, sustainable, low-carbon-footprint stuff being used here – it doesn't strike me that she's using that power in a healthy way. And can you imagine if we *did* accuse her without proof, how her followers would react? I can't see that going well, can you?"

I was feeling quite weary. Bud headed toward the bathroom and added, "First of all, I really cannot wrap my head around how she does it, and then there's your favorite question – why?"

He didn't wait for an answer, which was just as well, because I didn't have one.

Extraordinarily Ordinary

I felt exhausted when I woke, which annoyed me. I hadn't slept well, the twisted bedding and smashed-about pillow told me that much, and I felt about as fresh as a three-day-old daisy that's been picked and left to wither. Bud didn't look much better than I felt when he emerged from the bathroom, and there was no breakfast trolley laden with deliciousness either.

"What time is it?" I could hear the full-on grumpiness in my voice.

"Just gone eight. I couldn't sleep." Bud also sounded less than cheery, though his smile suggested he was prepared to make an effort.

"No breakfast this morning?"

"We were up and about a lot later yesterday. Maybe Serendipity reckoned half-nine was a good time? We could wander down to the restaurant to see if she's there, I guess. Maybe she'd rustle something up for us."

"I suppose that's as good an idea as any." I hauled my body out of bed. "I'll make myself presentable, then we'll head out. And we should make a plan...I'd really like a proper poke around the place today – there's so much we haven't seen. And we need to start talking to people about the whole Demetrius and Zara thing – try to find out how she proves it's him speaking; if KSue has one example of 'proof', others might have them, too. And I want to find out a good deal more about Oscar – I haven't any real mental picture of his personality yet, to be honest. Was he really the sort of man to take himself off into the desert immediately after his mother's body was found?"

Bud had stopped in the middle of the room, and looked taken aback. "Well, you've managed to go from washed-out and floppity to being in full flight in a heartbeat...what's eating you?"

"Zara essentially killing people, that's what." I hadn't meant to snap, so hugged my lovely husband before I disappeared into the bathroom, where I hoped the water in the shower would have magical properties.

Partially refreshed, but still not feeling as gung-ho as I'd hoped, I presented myself as ready to start the day just as there was a knock at our door. Bud opened it to reveal KSue beaming like a small child, and now completely dressed in yellow – which made a jolly change from her previous drab green.

"Oh, you're looking lovely and sunny," I said. "Want to come in?"

KSue entered and looked around. "They've set up this place real nice," she said, giggling a little. "It's fancy, like a hotel. All our digs are much plainer, though we can bring our own bits and pieces if we want."

"You rent them?" Given what Serendipity had said about Ambroise paying monthly fees, I wondered how the whole system worked.

"Yes, that's right. We have to be invited to stay, of course, but when we're here we're allocated a dig, and pay a fee. Like rent. I got a better deal than most because of my connection to Linda, and because I said I'd like to stay for three months, but that's about as much as I could afford. I'm due to leave in a few weeks, and have no idea when I'll be able to come back. But it's been worth every cent; this is such a life-affirming place."

"Despite Linda's death?" I didn't mean to hurt KSue, but wanted to understand what she meant.

She nodded vigorously. "Sure. Death's just part of life, after all. And I know she'd have wanted to go here – and stay here, if you see what I mean." She giggled again; I was starting to wonder if she even knew she was doing it – it seemed to be a habitual giggle, rather than one displaying any real merriment. "But let's not talk about that anymore," she continued, "I'm here because the chatter over breakfast was that you guys might like to see a bit more of the place; it's been a bit of an unusual time since you arrived, though today we're all back to normal. So, what do you say? Fancy the ten-dollar tour…for free?"

Bud and I nodded, but I said, "Is there anywhere we could get something for breakfast, KSue? Serendipity arranged it for us yesterday, and told us the refectory would have stopped serving by seven – so maybe just coffee? Though something to eat would be great, too." My mind returned to the salad and quesadilla we'd had before sunset the previous day – which my tummy was telling me had been a very long time ago indeed.

"Now there I can help." KSue beamed. "First stop will be the refectory, where I'm sure I can organize coffee and something to eat…not sure what, but there'll be something there. Then you're mine for the morning, and we'll all lunch at the refectory, too."

I hoped whatever food we might find would be filling. As we made our way out into the already-warm sunshine, and across the plaza, I asked, "Does it ever get old…the constantly perfect weather?"

"Honey, I'm originally from Colorado, so, no – especially through the winter months. I'll be back at my little condo in Sedona in April, but I have good A/C there, so even the summer months are bearable. To be honest, the real heat can get a bit tiring, especially if you want to be outside – it's quite something."

The refectory didn't loom up in the daylight the way it had when we'd first seen it, in fact, it was a bit of a disappointment; it looked like a commercial building, with dusty white stucco walls, a flat roof, and almost no windows. Inside, it was deserted, and I realized how kind the lamplight had been to it; quite how it had managed to develop its generally dilapidated air having only been built less than a year earlier, I couldn't fathom. The air was stagnant, and smelled of boiled vegetables; it was stifling. Suddenly, however hungry I was, the idea of settling to two meals in the place in one day seemed terribly unattractive.

KSue bustled through to the kitchen, with Bud and me in tow. "It stinks in here," he whispered as we lagged behind a little.

"I know – like school dinners," I replied.

"Here you are." KSue was fussing with a pot of coffee. "Goat milk, or black, and there's honey in that jug to sweeten it, if you like."

I opted for black and unsweetened – which was a great shame because the coffee was dreadful; I just hoped it contained enough caffeine to make drinking it worthwhile.

"I know we have some flatbreads left over, and let's see what's in here." KSue pulled open what I assumed was a "previously loved" fridge, and she shouted gleefully, "Oh goodie, hummus!"

The dish of reddish paste she revealed seemed an odd breakfast offering, but, frankly, I was so famished I could have eaten a lot worse. I tore chunks off one of the large, shapeless – but temptingly fluffy-looking – flatbreads in the basket KSue had popped onto the counter, and heaped spoonsful of the hummus beside it. Bud did the same, but with less enthusiasm than me, then we all took our breakfast into the dining area, where we sat around the end of a table.

"This is interesting," said Bud, tellingly, as he chewed. "What's the hummus made from?"

"Tepary beans and fire-roasted red peppers – all grown here. The tepary beans are wonderful, aren't they? The native peoples around here ate them for thousands of years. Brilliantly drought tolerant, and anything that crops without a great deal of water is good for us, and the planet. I'd heard about them, but hadn't eaten them before I moved to Arizona."

The way KSue spoke made me wonder about her duties at the Desert Gem. "Is gardening your strength, by any chance?"

The little woman glowed. "It is, though I say so myself. I've always had an affinity for dirt," she giggled with real mirth, "so I guess it's natural. Linda asked me if I'd like to help set up the gardens here, and I jumped at the chance. I don't do the hydroponic stuff, but everything that's in the ground is there because I wanted it to be."

"You use hydroponics here?" Bud sounded interested.

"Sure do. It's a surprisingly efficient way to use water – because it recirculates – and it means we can grow vertically, in controlled environments. You see, it's wonderful that we get so much sun, but it can scorch many crops – so our tenders are all grown in buildings down the valley a-ways, where we can control how much sun they get by opening or closing roof panels. Ambroise designed them. The hydroponic systems, and the roofs. He's so clever."

"But you're the plants woman," I said, keen to make sure KSue got some of the plaudits, "and without plants to grow that you've advised them about, they'd just be useless buildings."

KSue shrugged. "I guess." She tucked into her hummus. "I tend to steer clear of that area. Not my thing."

"I hope it won't be too painful, but Bud and I were wondering if you could tell us a little about Oscar? Being at his…funeral last night means we feel we'd like to discover a little more about him. Did you know him well?"

Once again KSue's little shoulders shrugged. "Linda loved him, of course, but I never really understood him." She paused, took a rag out of her pocket, wiped her mouth, then added, "I told Linda how I felt about him when she was on this plane, so don't mind telling you now – Oscar was loved, but didn't seem to know how to accept love. He was always cold…no, distant – that's it… toward his mother, and toward his father and sister, too, though he and Zara seemed to be getting along better in recent years. Well, maybe just since Demetrius died. Yes, I think that changed Oscar – he became the man of the family, and seemed to grow up a bit."

"I understood him to be around forty," said Bud, sounding surprised. "Wasn't he already grown up?"

KSue half-smiled. "Exactly my point. I know everyone parents differently, but Linda and Demetrius coddled him; he had no real responsibilities, ever. And that's not good for a child. I made sure my boy had chores he needed to complete every week to earn his allowance, and he's grown up to be a fine young man, even if I do say so myself; happily married with a couple of his own boys, now. But Oscar? It was sad, in a way; he dropped out of college, never had a real job, and took part in the Faceting movement in a very half-hearted way. It's probably why he got into so much trouble."

"What kind of trouble?" Bud was now really interested, as was I.

KSue waved her hand airily. "Oh this and that. Nothing too serious, but he was one of those people trouble seems to find – you know the type I mean? Tried various paths in life, but nothing ever seemed to go right for him. He liked nice things, but his parents eventually stopped buying them for him when he dropped out of college, so he took himself off and decided to start taking things he wanted, rather than paying for them. It was a terrible worry for Linda, I know. He ended up in jail, one time, and they had to bail him out. He was lucky – he had to do community service, and they paid his fines. He moved back into the family home after that. Not much use at anything, truth be told, though he was always very enthusiastic about pie-in-the-sky ideas and schemes. A dreamer, in many ways, but woefully lacking in direction." She paused for a moment, then her eyes twinkled. "A bit like Demetrius, I guess, but he *did* have direction. If he and Linda hadn't been prepared to make their dreams a reality, we wouldn't have all this today."

"But Oscar did a bit more than dream in the end, didn't he? You said that he and Zara were the ones who bought all this land, and talked Linda into creating the Desert Gem with them. When did the idea for this place begin? Was it before Demetrius died?" I wondered how the whole undertaking had transpired.

"It was spoken of, in general terms, within the family, and even among the elders at the original Gem in Sedona, but just as an idea, you know? A special place, just for Facetors, out in the desert. Demetrius wasn't keen – in fact, that was one of the things that surprised me most about his passing; it changed him so much. I told you he'd seen the light, and that must be a very powerful force so maybe it's *not* such a surprise, but to go from being so set against the idea of this sort of place, to being the one who talked Linda into investing in it, that was a big shift."

"And when was this specific site chosen?" Bud had cleaned his hummus off his plate and was sipping his so-called coffee.

KSue nibbled her bottom lip. "Oh dear, I'm not good with time, or when things happened. Maybe just after Demetrius died?"

"And…if you don't mind me asking, how did Demetrius die, exactly?" I really wanted to know.

KSue shook her head sadly. "It was a real tragedy: of all the things to be doing, he was cleaning the gutters at the family's home, fell off the ladder, and landed on spikes along the top of a metal rail. Such an ordinary thing to die doing, for such an extraordinary man. If only Oscar hadn't left him alone for a moment or two he might have been able to break his father's fall. Oscar was real upset; he'd left the foot of the ladder to do…something, I don't know what…and the next thing they all knew Demetrius was down, and quite dead. The only good thing was they said it would have been quick – one of the spikes went right through his heart, which is a blessing, in a way, don't you think?"

I couldn't imagine that dying like that would be any sort of a blessing, but nodded and smiled.

"Shall we clear away?" KSue was on her feet, and we all did what we needed to get going with our tour of the rest of the Desert Gem.

Lowest High, Highest Low

"I quite fancy seeing the swimming pool," said Bud, unexpectedly, as we set off. I turned and gave him a quizzical look, which he met with a bright smile. "Is it a fancy one, or what?"

KSue giggled. "Not fancy, but wonderful. Demetrius said it should be built in the shadiest spot possible, so we could use it without fear of burning – and he was quite right about that. It means you get a cool swim whatever time your booking is for."

"You have to book the swimming pool?" I thought that sounded odd. "Why's that?"

"It's meant as a place where we can undertake meditative activity, while also exercising – a truly multi-Faceted activity. I'm not a strong swimmer, so it's perfect for me because it's only four feet deep, so I know I won't drown."

I knew exactly what she meant. "I can't swim at all, so that depth would be perfect for me, too. But it's not a pleasure-pool, so I suppose we won't be using it. Besides, we didn't bring any costumes."

KSue looked blank. "Costumes?"

"Swimsuits," said Bud. "There are some things for which my wife seems incapable of using the correct North American terminology." He rolled his eyes.

KSue laughed heartily – the first time I'd heard her do that. Her laugh tinkled. "That's such a funny way to describe them – all oldey-worldey...like when they'd swim in waterholes in the days when they were out here digging for gold, and so on. But we don't wear swimsuits; part of the contemplation is to be able to feel the movement of the water against your skin. Oh no, a 'costume' would never do."

Bud and I managed to share a "Yikes!" look without KSue noticing before he said, "So I guess it's in a nice, secluded spot."

"See for yourself," said KSue as we stopped on the shoulder of the hill we'd walked up, and peered down.

The pool looked as odd in real life as it had on the map I'd seen: it was long and narrow, bordered with a plain stone coping, and was positioned in an isolated location, surrounded on all sides by desert. Someone was swimming languid lengths, and our birds-eye view was close enough that we could tell they were swimming *au naturel*, as KSue had said, but, fortunately, we weren't close enough to know if the person whose form we could see was male or female.

"You wouldn't catch me doing the backstroke down there," was Bud's wry observation.

"That's my favourite," said KSue, "and I like to float about on my back, too."

I couldn't unsee the picture that conjured in my head, so simply commented, "That must be very relaxing," and hoped the person using the pool at that moment didn't favor any such meditative methods.

"That's Jenn Okada," said KSue. "She's our communications guru – writes all the stuff that goes out to our followers around the world, and runs our online outreach. Wonderful swimmer – she'll keep going like that for almost her full hour, then she'll get back to the communications hub and do more in a day than some are able to do in a week. She gives to Faceting in every way she can. We're lucky to have her."

"Where next?" I asked.

"The gardens? Then the amphitheater?"

Both Bud and I nodded. "It'll be interesting to see some desert planting," said Bud, and I was pleased he sounded genuinely interested, as was I.

"Excellent," said KSue happily, "I'll lead the way."

We followed our guide to the top of the hill, rounded a bend in the suggestion of a path we were on, then headed down another depression in the hillside that led toward yet another little valley. I hadn't imagined there'd be so much hillwalking, and was getting quite hot. As we labored on – with my eyes firmly focused on where my feet were going – I asked, "Do you know where they found Oscar? Was he out this way when he…fell?"

KSue didn't seem to be at all interested in where she was putting her feet and replied by turning toward me and pointing back the way we'd come. "No, he was much further out. Over there, up on that hill. Lump Hill."

We looked and squinted. "That looks quite steep," I observed. "I wonder what took him all the way up there – presumably he'd had to go down into the valley below to climb back up; it looks like quite a hike."

KSue shrugged. "Not so far, really. It's a popular spot for people who want one of the best chances in the area of getting cellphone reception. If you look around, you'll see it's the nearest high-spot, though it's still relatively low, if you see what I mean."

I did. "Do you think he went there to be alone, after he found out about his mother's death?"

We continued to walk, carefully, down the hillside, as KSue gave her reply some thought. "I guess. He wasn't ever really alone, so maybe he felt he needed some space."

"So he was a sociable type?" I pressed. I was still trying to build a picture of Oscar.

"Not when he was younger. Kept himself to himself. That's what they always say, right? But, since the building began here, I rarely saw him alone. He was always with Zara, or Ambroise, or Don...or Jenn. That was an odd friendship right there – him and Jenn. They got along well, though they were a bit like chalk and cheese. She's such a good communicator – everything she says makes sense to me right away. But Oscar? You know how sometimes I don't know the right words to use? Well, he was the same, and quite often what he said made no sense at all to me."

"How d'you mean?" Bud was also concentrating on his feet as the stony soil rolled about beneath them.

"Well, like that last time I saw him, for example. I'd been sitting with Linda's remains for a while, as you know, then I'd finally left her and gone out into the plaza. When Don found me, I couldn't really speak – I was so very upset, you see, even though I knew I shouldn't be, because she was only passing on. But I was, and he was quite patient, but when I told him what had happened he went rushing off to see Linda, then headed straight for Oscar's dig. Don brought Oscar across the plaza, and they went into Linda's dig, and when Oscar came out he was like a different person. He was...well, now I don't know how to explain it, but he wasn't himself."

I sighed inwardly; I wanted to understand Oscar's mood after the discovery of his mother's body, so felt the need to say, "Oh come on, KSue, I'm starting to get to know you a little, and I reckon you're highly intuitive when it comes to judging people's moods," I lied, "so don't tell me what he was like, just tell me the answer to this question: if Oscar had been an animal at that moment, what animal would he have been?"

KSue looked surprised, but replied immediately, "A tiger. Yes, definitely a tiger. He roared at me that I should have fetched help as soon as I had found her. He was very...aggressive."

Interesting. "And what animal would you say he was normally?"

KSue gave that answer some thought. "An armadillo? They're slow, and roll themselves up into a ball, covered with armor, when they don't like what's going on around them, right?" I nodded. "That's what he was like."

Fascinating.

"That was fun," said KSue.

I knew I had a valuable opportunity. "Yes, it's fun, isn't it? So, what animal would you say Zara is?"

KSue stopped walking, so Bud and I stopped, too. "Zara?" She looked thoughtful for a moment, then her expression changed. "Zara's a white peacock. That's it! I've known her since she was little, of course, and that's not what she always was – not like Oscar who was always an armadillo – but that's what she's grown into, which is odd because she was a bit of an ugly duckling...oh, not that she was a hideous child, or anything, but her dark hair and blue eyes made her look very...intense, which isn't always attractive at a young age, right? And she was always very snappish – you know how ducks quack and squawk? She used to make a fuss like that if she couldn't get her way, or something she wanted, and Linda and Demetrius always used to give in, just to shut her up. Which I was never convinced was a good thing. But she did have a difficult life, being so clever, you see. And, of course, there was the fact she hardly ever slept. Not that she had the time, really, with all the studying she did. Such a voracious reader. Always with older kids in higher-than-age grades in school, then off to a special school, then to college at fourteen. She got her MBA at nineteen, so she's never really spent much time with people of her own age at all. But now that she's a young woman – and I try hard to think of her that way, even though she's still a *very* young woman – she's definitely a white peacock."

KSue's manner of speaking seemed to leave Bud with a bemused look every time she opened her mouth, and even I realized there was a lot to digest in what she'd said.

In an attempt to clarify the situation, I asked, "So Zara's got a Masters degree in business administration? She's got a good business brain?"

"Oh yes," replied KSue brightly as she marched off again, "quite brilliant. She was the one who set up the cooperative marketplace at the original Gem when she was still a teen, sourcing and selling supplies we Facetors used in our practices, and giving local artisans the opportunity to reach out to the community in Sedona – and a lot of tourists who came to Sedona for the art – as well as giving them a chance to sell to Facetors around the world. Not that there were as many of them then as there are now – but that's another thing she's been really good at, too: she's brought Faceting into the digital age. We are now many thousands, whereas before we were only a few hundred. And that's so wonderful."

"Was Oscar not as brilliant as Zara?" Bud sounded interested.

KSue stopped again, this time quite abruptly. "His ideas were beyond his capability to bring them to fruition." I was taken aback by KSue's pithy response, and wondered if they were her own words, or if she'd heard someone else utter them. I suspected the latter. Which was interesting in itself.

"And – to get back to your original point, KSue – what was it that Oscar said to you in the plaza that was so mystifying?" I was determined to get there.

KSue said, "He roared, 'She's gone too far!' Which I guessed meant Linda had gone too far from this plane for him to reach her. Though, of course, that might not be it at all."

I gave KSue a sideways glance – and wondered about what she'd just said.

"Here we are," she added as we finally reached a wide plateau which was a riot of greenery, especially when compared with the scrubby landscape around us. Instead of spiny cholla bushes, there were neat rows of greens, citrus trees, and a variety of vegetables and legumes being tended by about a dozen Facetors in their rainbow garments, all working diligently, and all – very sensibly – wearing wide-brimmed hats. I was beginning to wish I'd brought one, but at least my arms and legs were covered in cream flowing cotton – which I'd thought a sensibly neutral choice for the day.

"Amazing," said Bud, and I agreed. "Where do you get your water?" Now it was KSue's turn to look surprised, so he added, "At home we don't have city water, we get it from our well, so we're a bit more sensitive to the challenges of having a reliable water supply than some might be."

KSue clapped her little hands. "Quite right, too. And I happen to know all about our water," she said happily. "Because I care for the plants here, I need to be aware of our water management program. We have three wells in different parts of the overall campus, and we treat our gray water for reuse here, too. We also have a few strategically placed storage tanks, in case the wells or pumps are problematic and we have to get water delivered in a truck. But the wells are really good – wonderful pressure. We're on the edge of two watershed areas here, so it's all a bit complicated, but we're frugal with our use of fresh water – which all goes through our own treatment plant, so it's potable."

I could tell by Bud's expression that he hadn't expected such a comprehensive response, and he looked impressed. "It's a critical resource," he noted.

"Absolutely. And when Demetrius spoke about the original plans, water was his first priority, as it should be. You cannot build a refuge in the desert without it. In fact, if it hadn't been for Demetrius's foresight – and Ambroise being on hand to get the right sort of people involved – I don't think Oscar and Zara would have bought this specific piece of land."

"I didn't realize Ambroise had been as significantly involved at such an early stage," I said.

KSue looked surprised. "He and Oscar were very close. Knew each other for some time before this place ever got going. Something to do with diamonds in the Arctic Circle? One of Oscar's schemes or interests, anyways. Indeed, Oscar bringing Ambroise into our movement was a real coup, because he's such a lovely man – and not hard to look at, am I right, Cait?" She winked, then composed herself. "Not that looks are everything – well, they're not anything of any importance, really, though it doesn't hurt to have a big smile like he has. Oh, and those eyes – not too different from yours, Bud." Bud blushed. "But Ambroise is so much more than that – he's so helpful to everyone here. And, of course, then Zara encouraged Serendipity to come here to build her restaurant, which will do great things for us – because when folks see how wonderful life is here, they're bound to want to get to know more about our beliefs. So many young people these days want to try different foody things that they'll come to Serendipity's place and then find us here – and you know what these Millennials are like, so eager to really examine themselves. Such a healthy attitude, I think – though, of course, it's not for everyone."

As KSue's enthusiastic banter flowed over us, we were greeted with nods and smiles. We wandered among the rows of beans, peppers, cantaloups, okra, and some leaves I had to ask about. "Are those turnips?" It seemed an odd choice.

"Yes, they like the heat and the dry soil, as do the carrots, black-eyed peas, and cowpeas. Those are the tepary beans coming along – they'll be hummus before you know it." KSue had adopted a proprietorial air as we'd been walking the rows of raised beds. "Our compost is over there, but most of the kitchen scraps go to the chickens, along with some supplementary feed – which is, of course, completely organic, and free of any chemicals."

"Of course," I replied. "So where's the hydroponic area?"

KSue waved her arm. "The other side of the hill, nearer the water tanks. It's cooler there, too. Even here I've planned exactly where to plant certain crops so they avoid the worst of the afternoon sun, but the things we grow under cover can be anywhere, and don't need a prime spot like this. Not as beautiful, but so productive. Now, let's swing past the amphitheater on our way to the crafting shed."

"The crafting shed?" It was clear it didn't sound terribly appealing to Bud.

"Well, it's not a shed at all – in fact I don't know why it's called that. It's just a large open structure with a canvas roof – for shade, of course – where everyone gets together to…well, craft things out of…other things. It's not really my scene. Growing? Yes. Making something out of something else? No. But people do make such wonderful items. Of course a good number of stones and gems are used, but some collect dead cholla and clean it up to make it an attractive item for people to buy as home décor, or use local wood – from dead trees – to carve little boxes, or knobbly things that are…well, I'm never sure what they are, but they look good. That kinda thing, you know?"

"Did Linda have her jewelry made for her here?" She'd worn such a lot, I'd wondered when I'd seen the photos where she'd got it all; it didn't look as though it had come from any sort of place that mass-produced turquoise jewelry – if such places even existed.

"Not here, no. She used to make all sorts of turquoise objects, including jewelry, herself. Indeed, it sold real well at the original Gem. Over the years she built a good working relationship with the only remaining full-time turquoise mine in the country, right here in Arizona."

"Elizabeth told us that Linda was interested in Estsanatlehi, so turquoise was important to her?" KSue nodded. I continued, "I noticed her feet, in the photos. Her actual skin was turquoise. How did she manage that? Was she tattooed?"

KSue laughed. "Oh heck, no. Tattoos on feet are painful. She dyed her feet; sat with them in a bowl full of turquoise food dye that she mixed up herself. All natural. Totally harmless. She did it once a week. Said it helped her feel totally grounded and connected to Estsanatlehi. That, and her jewelry. She got all her stones direct from the mine I mentioned; they'd let her know when they'd found something special. More recently she'd get the stones made up into pieces by some of the professional silversmiths who used to sell their work at the Gem's co-op. When we're fully operational here, and folks come out to see what we have for sale, I expect some of them will sell through the Desert Gem, too."

I was still struggling with why on earth anyone would drive out so far into the desert to visit at all, so asked, "And are there plans for more facilities to appeal to visitors? Performances at the amphitheater, maybe?"

KSue looked uncertain. "I don't really know much about all that. I know we're trying to feed ourselves, and provide as much produce as we can for Serendipity's place, but, beyond that…well, it's not my thing. I have heard there'll be a sanctuary for rejuvenation – massage, reiki, acupuncture, all the good stuff – you know, for the realignment of body and soul. There'll be so many Facetors from all over who'll want to come here that I think that's the plan."

It didn't seem like much of a plan to me, but also didn't think KSue was the one to have that conversation with.

The amphitheater was quite large: stone benches lined a semi-natural bowl in a hillside, and a small stage, covered with canvas sails, suggested that performers would be arriving at any moment.

"This is impressive," I said. "It must have been a significant construction project, cutting all those tiers into the hillside. It looks like a big excavation took place here. What's the theater used for?"

KSue's face beamed. "Zara channels here sometimes, and we all come to watch. It's wonderful. Magical. The acoustics mean you can hear everything so clearly – she doesn't even need a microphone. All natural, you know? And those fire bowls along the front of the stage are lit during dark time, which gives the entire ceremony the most dramatic atmosphere."

I imagined Zara would enjoy that, and could picture how she'd be able to use the situation to impress her audience.

We walked on, and eventually reached the crafting shed, our next stop on the tour. My attention was grabbed by a small figure bent over a massive rainbow-hued quilt. "Good grief, that's huge," was out of my mouth in a heartbeat, and I realized I'd sounded quite rude, so quickly added, "and beautiful."

The head of the woman laboring at the piece popped up, and she smiled warmly. "Thank you," she said in a soft voice. "It's almost done. It's been my life for the past few months, and I can't believe it's almost finished."

"Dru Ann, meet Cait and Bud. This is Dru Ann, she's such a good quilter. We're lucky to have her. She's also one of our better sharers…you know, good at passing learning from one person to another." I didn't know, but flashed a smile at the woman whose passion project surrounded her.

"Wonderful colors," I said. Even Bud agreed, and we both drew closer to inspect the complex pattern she was crafting. Sinuous lines of colors that changed in half-shades from one hue to another snaked across the quilt. "Those pieces of fabric must have taken some cutting and sewing," I said, "though I admit I know nothing about quilting, that must be a lot of work." I looked around – not a sewing machine in sight. "Did you stitch the entire thing by hand?" I found it hard to believe.

Dru Ann nodded coyly. "It's a wonderful meditation," she said. "Now I'm almost done, I'm planning my next project."

"And what will happen to this?" Bud's tone suggested he couldn't imagine.

Dru Ann cast her eyes across her creation. "I was commissioned to make it for a friend of Linda's, so it's already sold. The next one is, too – a piece for a friend of Ravi, one of our elders who's also on the other side, now."

"How wonderful to be able to earn a living doing what you love." I meant it from the heart.

Dru Ann smiled. "The payment isn't for me, it's for this place – my way of supporting it, and helping it grow. I get to do what I love, and live the life I want to live here, though, of course, it's a little less like it used to be when Ravi and Linda were alive. I miss them."

"But they're all around us, everywhere, all the time, just like Demetrius, and they'll be back soon." KSue's tone was a little sharp.

Dru Ann nodded, then added, "I know…but still…"

"Oh look, there's Jenn – let me introduce you." KSue was immediately distracted.

Approaching us was the woman we'd apparently seen in the pool; she was about thirty, lean, and clad in a vivid orange outfit, her long, straight black hair still wet. She walked toward KSue, smiling, and they hugged, but not for very long. She bowed to us as KSue introduced us, and spoke with an unmistakeable West Coast accent.

"Great to meet you. Our first guests. Like the place?" She was direct, if nothing else.

"Loving it," said Bud, sounding as though he meant it. "Fascinating, in so many ways."

"Not as fascinating as you two; I wondered why Serendipity wanted you to be her guests of honor, then I found out all about you, and it became clear how special you both are. You know, we were almost, like, neighbors, once upon a time – I'm from Seattle, just down the road from you guys."

"Go Seahawks," said Bud, in what I could only assume was a bizarre attempt at bonding with the woman.

Jenn Okada's expression suggested she wasn't likely to be found wearing a shirt with a giant 12 on it during football season, and she stuck to her guns. "We have several local dignitaries and food writers visiting in a few days, but we're grateful you agreed to be the guinea pigs for the soft opening. Thanks."

I couldn't decide if what she'd said was a compliment or not; because of the way her voice rose at the end of every sentence, her "Thanks" sounded more like a question than a statement.

"Can't stop. I've got two podcasts to get up today, and we're hosting a live-stream discussion for Facetors in Australia and New Zealand later on, so I'll be at it until the small hours. Have fun at the dinner – and don't worry about the speeches."

Bud's brow furrowed. "Speeches? No one's mentioned speeches," he said. "Who's making speeches?"

It was Jenn's turn to look puzzled. "You two are; I'm having them filmed, for our website. Didn't Serendipity tell you?"

We shook our heads, and exchanged a horrified glance.

Jenn turned and waved. "A cop and a professor? You'll be fine – you've both done a load of public speaking, I'm sure. Don't be afraid to heap praise upon us. Bye."

I didn't want the chance to get an insight into what I suspected were the real money-making mechanics of the

Faceting movement slip out of my grasp, so called, "Just a minute Jenn…I have a special favor to ask."

I whispered to Bud, "Try to find out about this dead Ravi person from Dru Ann, and whatever you can about the other 'elders' who've died here – I'll meet you back at our dig; we'll give lunch at that depressing place a miss, okay?"

Bud appeared to still be reeling from the news that he was due to make a speech, on film, but nodded. I knew he'd do a great job of information-gathering, so made my farewells to KSue, thanked her for her time, and raced after Jenn, who was still in motion, and looking impatient.

"Let's take a shortcut," she snapped.

We passed through a most extraordinary area that was all but hidden behind a long, low building, very similar in style to the refectory; half a dozen clotheslines were filled with freshly-laundered rainbow outfits, gleaming in the sunlight, billowing in the slight breeze they were catching on top of the hill. It was beautiful, and surreal. I wondered who had picked the short straw and got stuck washing them all, and Jenn answered my unasked question by saying, "I'm on laundry duty for one day next week. I hate it – but it's a great workout and the sweating's good for my skin."

"Do you at least have washing machines?" I conjured visions of thrashing dirty clothing up and down an old-fashioned washboard.

"A dozen. Everyone gets a clean set of clothing, or more if they want, every day – of their chosen color."

"The orange suits you. Do all the different colors have a special significance?" I knew they must, but wondered if they played some sort of unique role for the Facetors.

Jenn gave me a sideways look. "Of course they do. You're a psychologist, so you must know that color's a strong mood influencer. Orange is an optimistic color, like me. It's youthful, and encourages good social communication. Very important in my role. The fact it complements my own coloring is an added bonus." All business.

"I went for cream today – I thought I'd try to blend in."

Jenn looked me up and down. "But cream's not really a color, is it? It's neither one thing, nor another. A bit indecisive. Lacking any statement. But maybe as a psychologist that's who you really are. I've found your profession to be almost paranoid about never stating a personal opinion about anything."

To be fair, Jenn's tone didn't suggest to me that she was trying to be scathing, but rather that she was just a direct person, who spoke her mind – whatever the effect might be. Rather than put her right, I thought it might be useful if Jenn continued to think I was indecisive, so replied by saying, "Maybe."

"So, what can I do for you?"

"Well, you see, while Bud's retired, I still work, and I didn't realize I'd be so out of touch while we were here. I really need to check in with my office. Is that something I might be able to do by using some of what I assume must be a good deal of communication equipment you use? If you're always filming, and uploading podcasts and so forth, I'm guessing you have internet access."

"Didn't Serendipity tell you we're all here because we want to be disconnected from the outside world?" Again, direct, yet cutting. *Heartless, or just professional?*

"Not really – she and I used to keep in touch by text and email, so it never occurred to me it would be so difficult to get a signal here, but there's no Wi-Fi either. I didn't think I needed to tell anyone I would be out of touch for a whole week, so I didn't even post an out-of-office notice on my email."

Jenn's reply was a short. "We decided against Wi-Fi. Disconnect to connect. Here we are."

The building we were about to enter looked like a double-sized dig – smooth, rounded, and blending into the ground beneath and beyond it – but this one differed insofar as, where the other structures had fire bowls on their roofs, this one had a large satellite dish. I also noticed we were at the top of a definite rise in the topography, even higher than the clothes lines, and above all the other structures I could see.

"Come in, I'll get you settled." Jenn sounded welcoming enough – for her – so I followed her inside.

The place was like something you'd see in a science fiction movie – with banks of screens double-stacked, keyboards covering several desks, and cables everywhere. Lights blinked, screens were populated with silently-speaking Facetors' heads, scenes showing landscapes, or nature in all her beauty. The room itself wasn't lit; all the illumination it needed was coming from the dozens of screens. The entire set-up was so overwhelmingly different from everything I'd been seeing for the past few days that it took my mind a moment to allow everything to sink in.

"Oh, that's a lot of technology," was all I managed.

"I know, and it all gets used, all the time, which is why this is the only part of the Desert Gem that has honest to goodness A/C," was Jenn's curt reply. "Just give me a minute and I'll clear a space for you. How does half an hour suit? I've gotta get some stuff set up in the channelling chamber, which is at the rear of Zara's personal dig, for later on, so you can have this place to yourself, but then I really will need you out of here so I can focus on my prep for our Antipodean special meeting, okay." It wasn't a question, so I stood back while Jenn fiddled with a few keyboards, finally allowing me to take a seat.

"Mouse, keyboard – that's your screen. You're already connected to the wonderful worldwide web, so have at it." She looked at her watch. "I'll be back in twenty-seven minutes. Have fun."

Harsh sunlight pierced the gloom as she opened the door, then I was alone inside what felt like a cave, with the internet at my fingertips, and twenty-seven minutes of freedom to roam at will. I had a plan, put my head down, and got on with it.

Understandable Misunderstandings

When I got back to our dig, Bud greeted me with: "I haven't a clue what to say," as soon as I'd closed our door. "I mean – what can I say? The food's been interesting? The sun's hot? Nice spot, considering you're in the middle of nowhere? And, in any case, don't you think it's a bit much, expecting us to allow our names to be connected with this place? I'm not at all sure I'm comfortable with that. We've both already agreed there's something not quite right about it all, and there's no shortage of dead bodies already buried here – and not just buried, but illegally cremated. No, this won't fly, Cait, we've got to talk to Serendipity about it."

"Feel better now?"

Bud harrumphed.

I smiled. "Sorry, I'd already put the speech thing to the back of my mind – but I agree, I don't think we should do it either. I don't mind saying a few words of thanks to Serendipity, and whomever else will have helped to feed us, but that's about it. And I have absolutely no intention of allowing myself to be filmed, let alone be named as a happy visitor to a cult's new headquarters."

"Good. Serendipity will understand, I'm sure."

I settled on the couch. "She might, but I'm not so sure about Jenn Okada."

"So, what do we do?" Bud looked simultaneously annoyed and helpless.

"Well, I'm going to have my second shower of the day – a short one, using almost no water at all, and think about it. I'm hot, sweaty, dusty, and my back's killing me; Jenn's computer room has gamer chairs, and they just don't seem to fit my body's shape at all. Once I'm fresh, I'm going to put my feet up and hope the swelling in my ankles goes down a bit, because they feel like they're going to explode after all that hillwalking in the sun. You can have some quiet time while I do that, okay?"

Bud sighed. "Good idea. I'll be outside, in the shade, feet up, too – you're not the only one with ankles, you know."

In the bathroom I was miserly with the water, but it was cool, and deliciously soothing. The idea of swimming naked seemed almost appealing, and I felt one hundred percent better when my hair was no longer a sticky mass and I'd taken off all my half-melted make-up. I also took the chance to chew on a piece of nicotine gum, which helped almost more than anything else. As I brushed my hair, I mentally corralled all the facts I'd gathered from my internet browsing, so I could pass them on to Bud in a cogent way, then thought through what KSue had said about Oscar, Zara, and the development of the Desert Gem. If what KSue had said was true, then it was Oscar and Ambroise who'd known each other first, but Ambroise had also known Zara by the time he was introduced to Serendipity, when they were all in Mexico at the same time as each other.

I stopped brushing, and gave myself a few moments to build a mental picture of the late Oscar Karaplis: a loner, a dreamer, a young man with big ideas that never came to be, who'd become friends with a man of about the same age with a strong academic and professional track record, who was anything but a dreamer. Two dissimilar personalities becoming firm friends; not unusual, but possibly noteworthy. And then there was the fact that Zara was something of a prodigy, who was now – apparently – applying her business acumen to develop what had been her parents' ideas into a global enterprise. An odd pair of siblings, to be sure.

"Will you be much longer in there?"

"I'll be out now, in a minute."

I heard Bud mutter, "You always say that," so I picked up my make-up bag, and really was out of the bathroom a moment later.

Bud was pacing about. "I took the chance of sharing some cold tea – well, lukewarm, in any case – when I was chatting with Dru Ann, and I'm paying the price. My turn."

He shut the bathroom door, and I settled myself on one of the loungers in our delightfully shady courtyard; I was glad to be out of the sun, but the air was still warm.

When Bud joined me he opened with: "I found out how all the elders died, and it's not good."

I perked up. "How?"

Bud looked grim. "Honestly, I try to not see crime where none exists, but it sounds to me as though we're talking about four more suicides. All 'peaceful' deaths, all found as Dr. Nderu said, and all taking place just a few days after Zara had foretold the deaths in question. From the way Dru Ann spoke, the nature of the deaths is common knowledge here – the prediction, then a peaceful passing, with no one caring to know exactly how that happened. It's not seen to be at all odd. Which is weird in itself. And more than unsettling. While she's obviously a delightful person, and a skilled quilter, Dru Ann is like all the others here – totally unable to talk about anything for long without mentioning Demetrius's omniscience, and how wonderful it is that Zara is connected with him…and is therefore able to know when deaths are imminent. It's alarming."

I sighed. "More than alarming. Okay, so that's that, then. Zara's definitely delivering death sentences, and it sounds as though the victims carry it out for themselves. No hints of outside intervention at all?"

"None, according to Dru Ann – but she's not us, so maybe doesn't suspect a murderous hand at work as we might. All the people who died were loved by everyone, she says, though, frankly, even that seems unlikely, because we both know that no one is ever loved by everyone – because no one's perfect, and they've usually crossed swords with someone at some point in their lives. But, if we do consider these elders as having been 'helped' to die, we have to consider where we are. If it were murder, I really think only those here at the time could be suspects, because who's going to keep visiting a place like this to knock off a series of people over a few months…with no apparent reason to do it? And all without being spotted. Seems unlikely, so any killer would have to be here, all the time, I reckon. If there is a killer."

I agreed. "I found out a fair bit, too," I offered.

"Go on then, let me have it. Where did you disappear to with the Faceting Queen of Communication?"

"There's a big dig, much bigger than ours, full of computer equipment, linked to Faceting sub-headquarters, and individuals, around the world. It's quite something. I was able to run a few screens at once, and took the chance to listen to a few of the podcast recordings of Zara doing her channelling thing – which were interesting insofar as she didn't say much at all, everything being very non-specific, allowing the listener to read into it what they would."

"Like horoscopes in the newspapers?"

"That sort of thing, but then she'd sort of pause, and give what seemed to be a very specific message to a specific Facetor."

"How d'you mean?"

"For example, the first one I heard was, 'Demetrius has a message for Eleanor in Tampa – your mother says you're not to worry about Binky because he's here with her and still enjoys chasing his yellow frisbee'."

Bud pulled a face. "Do you think Eleanor of Tampa and Binky are real?"

I chuckled, "And there you've put your finger on the crux of the whole matter…even if neither of them exists, nor Eleanor's late-mother for that matter, Facetors who are listening will have their belief that Demetrius is omniscient reinforced just because Zara said all those words. It's very clever."

"It is. And annoying."

"And I was also able to access some of the internal financial stuff; it was just lying around…a great big pile of it, in a folder that had been left on top of a printer. You might be surprised to discover that the Faceting empire is producing an annualized income around the mid-seven figures, which has spiked in the past six months."

Bud chuckled. "Annualized income? You mean if it had been a year that's what it would be…but it hasn't been yet?"

I shrugged. "Yes, that's what I mean. On track for more growth, it appears. The sales of books and subscriptions to the podcast channel net millions between them. Incredible. Oh, and the online store? I took a look at that, too. Good grief, they're charging through the nose for everything. And people are paying it. It's almost grotesque. Just because something has the Faceting seal of approval, it seems they can get away with charging double the amount, or more, than you'd have to pay for the same thing elsewhere online. I did a few comparisons, and it holds true across the board, for everything from the toiletries we've got in our bathroom, to the bedding – if you can believe it – to any number of potions and oils, as well as supplies of the actual Faceting gems."

"What are they?"

"Ah, now, they're special. From what I can see, there are dozens of Faceting Focus Gems available, ranging from small to large, and from expensive to ludicrous. I saw one that was about three inches across, a nice piece of cut glass, a bit like a paperweight, and they wanted fifty dollars for it. I found almost exactly the same thing online for less than twenty. And when you get to the fancy stuff? There was one necklace that was made to look like one of their faceted gems, but it was made up of different faces all encrusted with tiny diamonds. It was twenty thousand dollars. Twenty thousand!"

"Well, some people are known to like a bit of bling," said Bud nonchalantly.

I chuckled. "Well, there's bling, then there's bling, I suppose. But this bit of bling in particular had Zara's picture next to it, and it looks as though that's the thing she's got around her neck that she was twirling when she was channelling at the funeral. Oh, and in case you can't run to that one, there's a crystal-encrusted version that's a steal at two thousand. I bet they fly off the digital shelf."

Bud sighed. "As we agreed, it's the Facetors' money to spend as they choose."

"I know, but I hate thinking people are being ripped off. Who knows what spending decisions they're making to allow them to afford it all."

"They might be at home watching some sort of shopping channel instead." Bud was being sensible.

"True. Anyway, the other thing I discovered was that the land we're on here is owned by a private corporation, and it's leased by the Faceting movement."

"So the movement itself doesn't actually own the land? Who does?"

"A company called Karaplis-Longmuir."

"Who's Longmuir?"

"No idea. But the overall concept is a clever set-up: buy the land and lease it to the organization, meaning you've got income, but still own the land."

"Sounds even more questionable to me than it did before."
Bud's mastery of understatement was something to behold.
"The Karaplis clan as con artists? Okay, let's go with that.
Though possibly, or even probably, not Demetrius nor Linda.
So, just their kids. But killers, too? Do we think from our
conversations with KSue that Oscar really did have a nasty
accident?"

"Hmm, I've been thinking about that, and I wondered if he'd
run off to Lump Hill to try to reach someone on his cellphone.
Maybe the discovery that his mother had killed herself was just
one death too many for him? Or maybe the penny dropped
about all the convenient deaths he'd played no part in?
Remember his words to KSue: 'She's gone too far'? Could be he
wanted to reach someone to alert them to what was going on
here and…was stopped?"

"All possibilities." Bud looked as though he was flagging a
little. "But…and I say this with love, of course, we're still no
closer to really knowing what on earth is going on here, other
than we're witnessing a very successful scam with the reek of
death surrounding it. But it can't even be labelled a scam if the
people spending the money are happy with what they're getting
in return – even if that's a load of old horse manure."

"You're right; value is in the eye of the beholder."

Bud was scratching, with anxiety. "And the belief you're
working toward becoming the best version of yourself is
priceless, and – it seems – can even include killing yourself. It's
all a bit…dizzying. Anyway, it's my turn to shower, I think, Wife.
Then I guess we'd better decide what we're going to say in our
speeches this evening – or if we're even going to agree to do it
at all."

"Okey doke. My vote's for simple thanks, and nothing on
camera."

"Good, me too. By the way, we're out of here in half an hour, so if you're going to glam yourself up at all – even if not for filming purposes – then you'd best get to it, because *I'll* be ready on time, and I don't want us to be rushing down to the restaurant and getting sweaty all over again. By the way, I don't think that deodorant rock thing works at all – or else I'm a much smellier person that I ever thought I was. Thank goodness we brought our own stuff with us."

"You always smell lovely to me," I called at Bud's receding back, then I glared at my make-up bag, wondering why on earth I hadn't packed waterproof mascara, because at least that stands up to me getting melty. I pulled it open, and began picking out the bare necessities to make me look respectable, until it all slid off my face.

To be fair, we looked not too bad when we headed out; Bud was in navy dress pants, with a crisp white dress shirt, and I'd also plumped for white, which was set off nicely by the slight tan I'd managed to develop during our wanderings around our temporary desert home. At least the fact that I'd been glooping factor fifty on my face meant I wasn't pink-nosed and ruby-cheeked, which would have been annoying.

As we walked I whispered, "You don't suppose there's a rule around here that only Zara can wear white, do you? Everyone else has been in a color – oh, by the way, I also found out that the Facetors do get to pick the color they wear, except the novices, who all have to wear gray – the color of nothingness…which is what they are before they dig inside themselves to find their hidden gem."

"Good to know. But no one's mentioned any rule about white to me, so I guess we're fine."

As we approached the restaurant, we heard a wail. A female wail. Then Serendipity and Barbara rushed out, heading our way.

"What's the matter?" Bud called, instantly on alert.

They didn't stop to answer, but Serendipity screamed, "It's KSue…" as she ran past us carrying her first aid kit.

We grabbed each other's hands, then turned and followed. "Oh no…not KSue," was all I dared say.

Deadly Kisses

I was panting by the time we reached KSue's dig, so stopped at the door to catch my breath. "You go in," was all I could manage to wheeze at Bud, so he did. I sucked in lungsful of dry, warm air, but my throat told me it was all dust, and I ended up choking. Eventually I felt almost normal, and entered KSue's quarters, where the scene was chaotic.

I was greatly relieved to see KSue sitting upright in a chair, but was confused by why everyone else was acting so weirdly: Bud was tiptoeing about the place with a large candelabra in his hand; Serendipity was wrapping gauze around KSue's calf; and Barbara was out in KSue's little courtyard screaming "Elizabeth!" as loudly as she could.

Elizabeth appeared in the doorway behind me. "What now?" She sounded annoyed.

Serendipity looked up. "Careful – rattler somewhere about. Bit KSue. Can you and Norman take her into Flagstaff, as fast as possible, please? They've got antivenom at the medical center there, and that's what she needs."

I realized what Bud was up to, and wondered if I should leap onto a piece of furniture – then looked around for something I could wield as a weapon; the only thing that seemed remotely useful was an old bent fork I picked up from a little table.

Elizabeth sighed and said, "Sure. Can you lot get her as close to the entry arch as possible? We'll bring the car there."

"Will do," said Serendipity, rising from her crouched position. "Now don't move, KSue, we'll carry you. It's important you move as little as possible, and when you're in the car be sure to keep your leg below your heart at all times."

KSue was crying, silently. "I'm going to die, I know I am. But I'm not ready, I haven't prepared."

Serendipity touched her shoulder gently. "You won't die. Very few people die because of snakebites, not even if it really was a rattlesnake you saw. So just try to stay calm, okay? They'll be able to work out what bit you in the hospital, and will treat you accordingly. Try to not panic – it might have just been a Sonoran gophersnake – they look quite similar to rattlers. I can see you have puncture wounds, but you did say you stepped on it, after all, and they will bite, but they're not venomous."

"I can feel the poison inside me." KSue's voice was plaintive. "It's running around inside my leg. It'll kill me before they get me to the hospital. Can't you suck it out, or something?"

Serendipity shook her head. "No, that won't help – you, or me. There isn't a noticeable swelling around the wound, which is a good sign, but – like I said – try to stay calm, and as still as possible, and keep your leg down. Now, come on – let's all work out how we can carry KSue to the car, so she can be on her way."

Bud and Serendipity ended up lifting KSue on their own; her small frame meant it was difficult for Barbara and me to help, and Bud said she hardly weighed anything in any case. By the time we reached the archway, quite a few Facetors were in the plaza, hissing their wishes at KSue, which reminded me to watch where I was putting my feet because there might still be a very annoyed rattlesnake about the place.

We waved her off, and she was gone. When she and Bud rejoined me, Serendipity had a glazed expression – so much so that I had to ask her what was wrong. Her eyes were filled with confusion – or perhaps panic? She shook her head and pulled away from me. Bud caught her as she turned to leave. "You have to tell Cait," he said, "or I will. Tell her what KSue said to you."

I looked from one face, to another. "What?"

Serendipity sagged. "KSue said she was sure she was going to die, because Zara told her Demetrius had sent a message through from the other plane, but KSue said she wasn't ready to go. She said she wanted to go to her son and daughter-in-law's place in Sedona, go back to her normal life. She didn't want to go to Linda. She was frightened…and when she was bitten, she was convinced Demetrius had sent the snake to fulfill his prophecy."

Bud nodded. "I heard bits and pieces, and made Serendipity fill me in. KSue said she won't come back here, because everyone who dies, dies here. She reckons she'll be safe at home."

"Poor KSue," I said, thinking of how afraid she must have felt – convinced she would die, and trying to escape from danger. "I hope they can help her at the hospital."

"So do I," said Serendipity quietly. "But, for now, I guess I'd better get back to the restaurant. Coming?"

"We'll follow along in a moment," I said, and asked Bud with my eyes to hang back. He did.

Once Serendipity had disappeared beneath the archway, I grabbed Bud's hand. "KSue seemed truly scared about dying?" He nodded. "And she was certain about a snake biting her, wasn't she, so that can't have been a set-up…unless someone put the snake in her dig where she'd step on it."

Bud shook his head. "Knowing we were coming here I did a bit of research into things in the desert that can kill you…I know, I know, smile if you must, but I like to be prepared, and this is way outside my comfort zone. Yes, there are rattlers – several different types in fact – but as long as you keep away from them, you're usually alright. And Serendipity was correct to tell KSue that very few people ever die of rattler bites – that's the stuff of movies. But you know what? If you want to pick one of those things up, to move it to a particular spot, you'd better be an experienced handler. They reckon most bites are inflicted when guys spot a rattler lying about on their property and try to shift it themselves…that's when the snakes attack, and that's when folks get bitten. I'm not aware of any experienced snake handlers here – so I think it unlikely one was purposely placed in KSue's dig. The chances of it moving in of its own accord, on the other hand, are higher."

I shrugged. "Okay, let's walk a bit faster. And you'd better brush down your shirt – you're looking a bit crumpled and dusty now…but still the handsomest man in the world, of course. Anything else we need to discuss while we can?"

Bud swatted at his concertinaed sleeve. "KSue and Elizabeth had a bit of an odd exchange as I was arranging her in the back seat."

"That being?"

"She said she was glad Elizabeth knew where she was going. Elizabeth asked her what she meant, and KSue said, 'You're always going to Flagstaff.' Elizabeth's reply was surprisingly sharp – even for Elizabeth. 'How do you know that?' she said, and KSue replied, 'You told Barbara in talking therapy that the route is boring, and she used you as an example of how people can learn to make the most of downtime, because you'd told her you read aloud to Norman as he drives, and after Barbara said that, I've noticed you go there a lot, though I don't know why you'd bother.' What caught my attention was the tone of Elizabeth's original reply to KSue. Maybe KSue just annoys her? I can see how that might be the case. Anyway, by then I'd managed to stop KSue squirming about and I'd got her buckled in, which she seemed incapable of doing for herself – wriggling like a worm? Just fine. Helpfully clicking in her own seatbelt? Not so much."

"Excellent recollection, Bud," I said, patting him on the bottom.

"Thanks, Wife. It might be something I picked up during all my years as a cop...but I can't be sure."

"So they all talk to each other – not just about themselves, but about each other. Now that's interesting."

"Because it gives Zara lots more opportunities to pick up information folks think they haven't told anyone but maybe a few people, not being aware it's become common knowledge?"

"Exactly. Oh, you're quite good at this, aren't you?" I gave him my cutest smile.

"Why thank you...I have my moments."

We were laughing as we reached the restaurant; the sky was beginning its sunset symphony, and all the oil lamps were lit inside...the place looked truly inviting. As we entered, we realized we weren't the first to arrive; Dr. Nderu and a woman I assumed was his wife – suitably bedecked in beadwork – looked as though they were just settling at a table with another man and woman. He waved and smiled as we entered. There was another table of four people we'd never seen before, but none of them were wearing Facetor outfits, so I assumed they were "friendly types" who'd been invited for the trial run, too. Fortunately, there were name cards dotted about; I was delighted we'd been allocated a table for just we two.

I hadn't expected a welcoming committee but understood why Bud looked at his watch nervously. "We're not that early, or too late, are we? I know Serendipity rushed out of here to tend to KSue, so she must be trying to make up for lost time, but..."

A scream from the kitchen, followed by a loud smash, turned my tummy. "What now?"

We both rushed into the kitchen, where Serendipity was on the floor; half a dozen people wearing massive aprons over their usual Faceting gear were standing over her. There was blood, and moaning. One of the young people – they were all young – was on the floor, too, unconscious, and another scampered toward a sink, where they threw up.

Bud pushed through the circle to reveal Serendipity on her back, a large knife on the floor beside her, blood blossoming through her white top. Bud was wonderful: he barked instructions in a calm but masterful way, so that everyone he directed did exactly as he told them. A clean towel was brought for him to apply pressure to Serendipity's wound, and Dr. Nderu was summoned from the dining room to attend to her; the person who'd fainted was taken outside for some air, and the one who'd thrown up was given attention by a couple of fellow Facetors.

We made space for the doctor to get Serendipity's chef-shirt lifted far enough so he could assess her injury. "Okay, I need someone to keep applying pressure, and she might prefer a woman," he said curtly. "I have a bag in my car that I always carry with me. Do you know of any other medical supplies here?"

"Serendipity is the designated first aider – she had a sort of suitcase thing with her when she rushed up to KSue's place earlier," I replied.

"I know what it looks like," said Bud. "Cait, stay with her, I'll track it down."

"And I'll fetch my bag," said the doctor, pushing through the swing doors.

"Can someone go out and tell everyone there'll be no meal tonight – and apologize?" I shouted.

"Rusty should do that," said someone.

"Yeah, I'll do it." A tall young man with a close-shaved fuzz of reddish hair, dressed in gray beneath his apron, moved toward the dining room. "Leave it to me."

I pressed as hard as I dared on Serendipity's side, which was where the blade had sliced her. She looked up into my eyes, crying.

"How did this happen?" I asked.

"I wasn't paying attention," she blubbed, "and I was rushing, trying to make up for lost time. I was so careless – I know better than to do what I did. I allowed myself to be distracted, like Ambroise did last evening – but this turned out a lot worse for me than it did for him. I feel so foolish." A tear ran down her cheek. "Oh, Cait, what a disaster. Auntie Emily and Uncle Henry were right, I should never have come here, I shouldn't be trying to do this."

"Auntie Emily? Uncle Henry?" I reckoned if I could keep her talking it would distract her from her injury while we waited for medical attention.

"Mum's sister, my Auntie Emily, and her husband, Henry Zgorski. The wonderful, loving, perfect creatures who all but raised me in the vacuum Mom and Dad created with their so-called 'parenting skills'. They're the ones who really helped me become the woman I am. They did what they could to make up for Mom and Dad either never being around, or else being at each other's throats – or off on some sort of bender. Me working at the restaurant at Dad's vineyard was their idea – a way to allow us to all get to know each other as adults – and they were right, it worked a treat. Mom and Dad could sort of cope with me as a woman – at least, much better than they'd ever coped with me as an infant, a toddler, or a growing child. The Zgorskis filled that void…and any stability I ever knew came from them…but they both thought this place was a step too far for me. Suggested I waited. And they were right. Again. Oh how

I wish I could talk to Auntie Emily now...Mom and Dad's approach to solving a problem is to throw money at it, but she'd know just the right advice to give me. Oh, Cait...what have I done?"

I was at sea. "I don't know...what *have* you done?"

"Let me through..." Dr. Nderu and Bud arrived almost simultaneously, and bags were opened on countertops from which food had been hastily cleared. Dr. Nderu returned his attention to Serendipity, and I was relieved of my duties.

"Someone get busy disinfecting the largest stainless-steel counter, please," called Dr. Nderu. A number of Factors scuttled around, shifting boards, food, dishes, and equipment, then running about with spray bottles and rags.

Dr. Nderu pronounced himself pleased with the result, then several people lifted Serendipity bodily onto the surface, where he was better able to examine her injury.

The silence was profound, and the time it took him seemed interminable.

Eventually he said, "Okay, she's lucky; nothing vital looks to be affected – the ribcage has protected all her organs – and it's not a stab, but a gash. All of which is good. But she will need stitches, and it's some time since I administered those myself, so I'd like a volunteer to help me get set up, and be my general aide, but the rest of you can, and should, go. Who fainted? Did they bang their head at all when they came down?

A voice called, "No, thanks, I'm fine."

"Okay – get some air, drink water, rest up. The one who threw up? The same."

"Cait, will you stay, please?" Serendipity managed a weak smile.

"Of course. Would you like Bud to see if he can find Ambroise?"

She shook her head. "No…no, please don't." I was surprised by the sharpness of her tone. "Let the doctor get me sorted out first, okay? No need to bother him."

"Will we need to get Serendipity back to her dig when you've done what you can, doctor, or do you want her to go to hospital to be checked out?" Bud was using his professional tone.

"No need for the hospital; I doubled up on my rotations in the ER and should be able to manage just fine – I have everything I need. But, yes, she'll need to get to bed when I'm done – so maybe someone could get a vehicle to drive here there? And I would prefer to stay overnight, too – maybe my wife could drive our guests back home? I'd be grateful if you could see to all that while I deal with this – I think I can manage with just one extra pair of hands."

Bud nodded at the doctor and smiled at me. "They're good hands," he said, and left.

Dr. Nderu was efficient, professional, and possessed a delightful bedside manner – though, in this instance, it was a sterile-kitchen-island-side manner. Twenty minutes later, Serendipity was more than groggy – he'd given her some pretty strong painkillers – but she'd stopped bleeding, and her wound was stitched and bound. I was relieved…and grateful there'd a been a doctor on-hand, just when he'd been needed.

Finally, the doctor stepped away, looking satisfied, and said, "She'll need some help at her dig, and someone should be with her all night. I'm happy to offer, but maybe Ambroise? I believe they're friends…or maybe she'd prefer a female Facetor? I know she said she didn't want Ambroise taken from his duties, but it's almost dark time, so he should be finished by now. I think he should be told about what's happened; if he's the one who'll be looking after her, I'd like to talk to him, too. Whatever the folks around here think of big pharma, I need Serendipity to take the antibiotics I gave her – she's lucky I had them in my bag."

At that moment, Ambroise himself slammed through the swing doors. "What's happened? Is she alright?"

He was wild-eyed, his hair sticking to his sweaty face, his clothes soaked, and filthy...and he smelled strongly of...*eucalyptus? Odd.*

Dr. Nderu placed himself between the anxious man and his patient. "She'll be just fine, Ambroise, don't panic. But she'll need taking care of, and she's got a wound which I have dressed, but I want it to be kept clean, so no coming near her when you're like that, please. What on earth have you been doing?"

Ambroise stopped on the spot and looked down at himself – seeming to realize the state he was in for the first time. "I was on kitchen duty in the refectory, and clean-up got a bit messy, then I took the scraps to the henhouse, and I slipped and fell while I was feeding them. You are correct that I should not come close to her. I must clean myself..." He looked around, as though he were being hunted. "I must clean myself – I shall return! Serendipity is my friend, I must help her."

He ran out through the swing doors.

Dr. Nderu and I shrugged at each other. "Well, at least he didn't strip off in the middle of the kitchen," I said, with what I hoped was a winning smile.

Bud stuck his head through the doors. "There's a car outside ready to drive Serendipity to her dig when you say she's up to it, Doc, and your wife would like a word before she goes home with your friends."

Dr. Nderu turned to me, "Just wait with her for a few moments, until she's settled a little more, then we'll take her to her quarters. I'll be back in a moment. You okay to hold the fort?"

I mugged a salute, which seemed to confuse the doctor, but he left anyway, and Bud joined me. "She looks pretty out of it," he observed; Serendipity was all but comatose, flopped on the counter-top.

"Pills," I said. "It really wasn't a terribly deep wound," I assured him, "the blood made it look more frightening."

Bud nodded at me. "You're not kidding. How did she even manage it? What was she doing…just flinging the knife about?"

"Given what was on the counter when we first saw her, it looked as though she was slicing through some pretty tough-looking vegetables…and she said she became distracted."

Bud nodded toward my midsection. "Lot of blood, however it happened."

I looked down, and realized that maybe wearing white that evening hadn't been such a bright idea after all. I sighed. "Oh heck, I liked this outfit, but I really don't think there's any point keeping it. There again, after this evening, I'm not sure I'd want to." Bud came in for what I knew would be a welcome hug but I waved him off. "No, save your shirt – all that dust will come out in the wash, and those are your favorite pants."

"Stop…" Serendipity was mumbling, groaning.

We both gave her our attention. I stroked her forehead; she didn't feel hot, or cold, which I assumed was a good thing. "There, there, don't worry, you'll be fine," I said – in my mother's voice, as it turned out, which was unsettling.

"They'll find out…"

Bud and I exchanged a look that told me we were on the same wavelength. So, instead of comforting her, I let her ramble.

"Stop…too late…" Serendipity's head lolled, and she stopped talking.

Bud whispered. "Who d'you think she's talking about?"

"Zara?"

Serendipity groaned, then made an effort to sit up. We tried to make her lie down again as gently as we could, but she pushed against us, then her eyes flew open and she mumbled, "Norman...find out...prison...again."

Unnecessary Necessities

After the finally calm Serendipity had been carried to the waiting car, and everyone else had left, Bud and I checked all the switches, made sure all the oil lamps were out, and were just about to close the door of the restaurant to make our way back to our dig, when my tummy growled.

Bud chuckled. "Hungry?"

"I could eat one of my shoes, if you gave me a glass of water to wash it down," I replied.

We paused. I had to say it. "Look, we're walking away from a kitchen full of food – most of it not contaminated by blood – and planning to go back to our room, where there isn't even a cracker, and all I've eaten today is some hummus and bread. I know I probably shouldn't suggest it but…"

"…we should find something to eat here before we go back up there, even if it's something portable."

"Yes. Thanks. I'm not sure I could settle to eat in the dining room, but we'd have the place to ourselves." I used my cute smile.

"Tell you what, let's see what we can find, and then decide where we'll eat it, okay?"

We hit the kitchen and – being mindful of dark time rules, so only lighting oil lamps – it suddenly dawned on me that Serendipity was facing an uphill battle, and not just because she'd injured herself.

As I stared into the oversized refrigerator I said, "The light inside this thing is the brightest one in the kitchen. How on earth is Serendipity going to produce food in here by lamp light? It's going to be next to impossible."

Bud gazed around the entire kitchen. "She's got a lot of lamps up on the walls, and they've all got mirror things pointing down. Maybe she's planned for it, and she'll be fine? I don't know…but possibly the dimness in here contributed to her cutting herself? Tonight was her first night prepping food under real pressure."

"Hey – I've found some cooked ground meat in here." I sniffed. "I think it's lamb, and some marinated peppers, too. Have you found anything?"

Bud stood in the middle of the kitchen, looking lost. "Nothing that looks edible. Are these sweetcorn husks? You know, the stuff that you rip off before you cook them? They're not edible, are they?"

"Tamale wrappers," I said.

"Ah, yeah, there's a pot over there that I turned off earlier, full of them. You know I don't like them, but at least I recognize them."

I opened the pot Bud pointed at, and it was, indeed, filled with a spiral of tamales resting on a big lump of foil, but I had no idea if they'd been thoroughly cooked or not. "We could give these a go, I suppose."

Bud shook his head. "Nope, I'll pass, thanks. Why don't we just take some of the recognizable stuff, make up a couple of plates, and put the rest back into the fridge."

Five minutes later we were sitting outside, at a table on the expansive deck, the stars above us, with a plate each, a couple of bottles of beer, plus a large jug of iced water. We hardly spoke as we dug into our makeshift meal, which turned out to be surprisingly tasty, and satisfying; Serendipity had mixed the ground lamb with a fresh *salsa verde*, the peppers were both sweet and tangy, and the beer was cold, and really hit the spot.

Eventually we both unhunched a little, and it even began to feel as though we really were on a relaxing break at a swish desert oasis…but not for long.

"We need to come up with a strategy, Bud," I said.

My husband's voice was heavy with resignation when he replied, "I know."

"Do we really believe that KSue was accidentally attacked by a snake? And do we really believe Serendipity accidentally cut herself with that kitchen knife?"

Bud scratched his head. "I think KSue trod on a snake that found its way into her dig without human intervention. And I cannot imagine any scenario other than a carelessly self-inflicted wound in the case of Serendipity, given she was in a kitchen full of helpers; it was a slice, not a stab, and somebody would have said something if she'd been attacked. She said she did it herself, and I believe her. After all – why on earth would she lie about something like that?"

"I agree."

"Oh, good. What next?"

"You can lighten up on the sarcastic tone."

"I can?"

"Hmm…"

"I can't quite wrap my head around what Serendipity said when she was rambling…so maybe that's what we really heard: the ramblings of a woman under sedation. I cannot imagine what Norman's been up to that he should stop, or else he'll end up in prison." Bud mused.

"*Again* – don't forget she said 'again'."

"True. Now If I could only get access to the internet in the communications hub where you were today, I could get someone to check up on Norman McGlynn. His wife, too. And everyone else here, for that matter. Can you remind me of KSue's family name?"

"Henritze."

"Ah, right. Is that German?"

"Sounds it. Maybe her husband was from there originally?"

"Cait, you're very subdued. For you. What's going on in that busy brain of yours?"

I sat back and said, "This place is all wrong – and I don't just mean the absurdity of setting up a restaurant like this, here. But – and since it's just the two of us, let's be honest and open about this – we were always both likely to feel the entire Faceting thing was a weird set-up in the first place…so let's just try to set aside our skepticism about what the folks here obviously believe…you know, all the 'other plane' stuff, and so forth."

"Agreed."

"So, setting aside all that 'window dressing', if you will, what do we really have here? A total of five people who appear to have committed suicide on Zara's say-so. A fatal accident. Two non-fatal accidents."

"Let's not forget KSue having been told she was due to die, too. If she'd felt ready to 'pass on', she could have been the sixth suicide."

I smiled. "No, I hadn't forgotten that, thanks. We should also check if Serendipity received such a warning – because…well, who knows."

"You don't think she cut herself, meaning to end her own life, do you?"

I sighed. "I hate to say it, but stranger things have happened – well, let's be honest, stranger things have happened to us, let alone elsewhere in the world. So, if that's what we're facing – how do we investigate Zara? How do we gather proof to – and I think this is key – show the other Facetors *first*, *then* the authorities, because if the Facetors here aren't on our side, I think the chances of us managing to get Zara in front of the authorities are slim to nil."

Bud stood and stretched. "We need to find out exactly what it is she says and does to make people kill themselves, believing they are doing 'the right thing'. Until we know that, we can't do anything else."

"Any ideas *how* we do that?"

"You said you were able to hear podcasts of Zara doing her channelling thing when you were in the communications hub. Did you try to find her telling people they would die?"

"I couldn't. Not enough time, and no way to search for specifics – I just loaded up a couple of recent podcasts and let them play while I used the keyboards doing other things. Okay, let's think about this; I don't think Zara 'proves' she's speaking for Demetrius just at the time when she tells people they'll die – I think she's already built up their belief in her construct before that. For example, what she said about us, in front of that crowd at the funeral, will have bolstered the beliefs of everyone who heard it about Demetrius's omniscience, even if we can debunk the way she unearthed those facts. Which means Zara's had months and months to convince them all that she's speaking her dead father's words. Unless I listen to, or watch, hours of her channelling, I won't know exactly how she does it...unless..."

Bud sat again. "Unless...what?"

"Hang on, let me think." I stood and looked down at the table, visualizing the desk in the communications studio. In my mind's eye I looked at the folder names on the desktop screen. "Yes – there was a folder called 'Zara transcripts'. I could read transcripts of her sessions a heck of a lot faster than I could listen to them. Rats! Why didn't I think to read them there and then?"

"You did a lot in a short time, don't blame yourself. Do you think Jenn would let you back into the hub again? An emergency at the university, maybe? Student with a problem?"

"I'll do it first thing. And when I say 'first thing', I mean it. I'd really like to be up and about before dawn – to get out to see the ceremony when they all burn their notes from the night before. It's weird, isn't it, to think of them all sitting in their digs, right now, scribbling down all their thoughts and encounters from the day. I wonder what some of them have made of this evening's two emergencies."

"Oh, to be a fly on the wall, eh?"

"Yes, that would be interesting." I felt annoyance mixing with the beer in my tummy. "Oh, Bud, I'm a psychologist, I should be able to understand *why* what's going on here is happening. I suppose it could all be about money…but would Zara really talk her mother into killing herself for *just* money?"

Bud shook his head slowly as he replied, "Maybe Zara hated her mother for some reason we know nothing about…and it is a great deal of money, Cait. We've both seen people kill for a heck of a lot less."

I nodded. "Sad, but true. And maybe it's not just about the money, but about the money and the power." I gave the matter some thought. "I wonder how growing up with two parents dedicated to their own way of thinking, developing that into the Faceting movement, and having a brother who sounds as though he was a bit of an unstable dreamer, affected Zara – especially if she was grappling with the potential social isolation that dogs the lives of academic prodigies."

"You mean she could have grown up warped in some way?"

"Oh come on, Bud – nuts, warped, crazy – they aren't terms I condone or use. I'm not a psychiatrist, so not trained to diagnose or treat any mental illnesses, but, as a psychologist, I examine the behavioral patterns of subjects to try to determine why they do what they do. I turned my back on analyzing criminals in favor of analyzing victims because I felt that was the best way I could speak for those who could no longer speak for themselves…and the idea that victims here are taking their own lives because of the planned and intentional actions of another person horrifies, and disgusts, me. And it seems even worse, somehow, because Zara appears to be using people's own beliefs and hopes against them, in the most dreadful way possible. I have to understand the power she has over them. It has to be more than an unusually developed maturity and intense persona." I stood up, "I must read those transcripts."

Bud also stood, and grasped my shoulders, gently. "I agree, but first thing tomorrow, like you said, obviously not tonight, right?"

"Why not? Jenn said she'd be at the hub into the small hours working on that thing she was hosting online in New Zealand and Australia, and then I bet she has to do some techy stuff with it afterwards. Let's go now."

Bud let go of my shoulders, and I could tell he was having an internal debate with himself. "Only if I can come, too."

"Good idea – maybe you can connect somehow with someone via the hub who can gather information for you about the people here. It's worth a try, isn't it?"

He nodded slowly. "It really is good to be able to disconnect for a while, but there's nothing like the internet to allow the gathering of information – and that's what we need right now. So, what's it to be? You can't have heard of an emergency at the university…what did Jenn think you needed to do earlier today? Could you be following up on whatever that was?"

"Don't worry, Husband, I'll manage to come up with something plausible, and I'll make it as real as possible, so she doesn't work out that I'm lying through my teeth. What we really need is some way to get her out of the place so I can download what I need."

"Download? Onto what? You can't do that sort of thing with your phone."

"I have some handy-dandy thumb drives in my laptop bag, so all we have to do is collect them as we go past our dig – I can use those. At last, my 'fetish' pays off!"

Bud smiled. "How about – before we go rushing off to do anything at all – we grab some fruit from the bowl inside the restaurant, because we might be glad of that at some point."

"Food for midnight feasts needs to be more exciting than fruit, Bud, so you grab some of that, and I'll pop some of the desserts that were in the fridge into a container, and bring them."

Uncommunicative Communicator

I scrabbled around in my bag for the three thumb drives I knew were in there somewhere, and finally plucked them out, triumphant. "Give me a few minutes to wipe them," I said, powering up my laptop.

Bud wandered into the bathroom, then out again; he changed his shirt for a clean one, and popped on a pair of shorts. Then he took over watching the annoying countdown on my screen while I also changed my clothes – squishing the no-longer-white two piece into the tiny wastebasket in the bathroom.

Finally, we were both a bit cleaner, and so were the thumb drives, so off we set. There wasn't a single person about, and the plaza – indeed, the entire compound – looked and felt utterly deserted, which was a good thing, under the circumstances. Bud had brought an oil lamp, because I knew we had to go beyond the area where the fire bowls would illuminate our way, and – mindful of KSue's earlier encounter – I didn't want us to run into any dangerous critters as we wandered in what was basically open desert, at night.

The coyotes were serenading the dark skies above us as we plodded on until we reached the double-sized dig where I knew there'd be a frenzy of technological activity taking place. The door was closed, but I could hear voices inside. Many voices – laughter, snorting, and...was someone singing?

I knocked, then knocked again.

The door opened and Jenn's head popped out. "Hi. You need to connect to the rest of the world again?" I nodded. "Sure. Come in. I've got to get over to the channelling chamber as soon as I can because Zara's mic is sounding raspy, and that's not good. She's on again in an hour, for a big session, and she wants it adjusted by then." She looked at her watch. "I gotta go. Now. Listen – do me a favor? There's a woman called Glenda, from Bay of Islands, New Zealand – she's going to pop up on screen seven and I need you to tell her the answer is eighty-three. Could you do that for me, please?"

"Eighty-three what?" I asked.

Jenn was already in motion. "She'll know what it means – the answer is eighty-three. Back as soon as I can," and she'd disappeared into the dark.

"I always thought the answer was forty-two," I said.

"Hardy, har – Douglas Adams…see, I do listen to you, and even read the books you tell me I should, sometimes." Bud looked smug.

"Thank you, Husband. Now, let's not waste a minute…let's get going."

I left Bud to his own devices – literally, and figuratively – as I focused on three computers, and began to download folders from all of them simultaneously. Once I'd set all that in motion, I took another look through all the papers and folders I could find lying about beside the printer, and snapped away with my phone; it's all well and good having a photographic memory, but sometimes other people need to see what I've seen, too.

When Glenda arrived on-screen she wasn't what I'd expected, insofar as she was about twenty, extremely pretty and perky, and looked as though she'd just stepped out of the sea, because she was wet, and covered with sand. "Kia Ora, Jenn?"

She obviously couldn't see me, though I could see her. I replied, "Hello, are you Glenda?"

"Yes, I'm Glenda, but you're not Jenn, are you?"

The way she pronounced her name, it sounded like Glinda, not Glenda, so I wondered if I'd misheard Jenn. "Jenn had to step out. She said you needed the answer to a question – is that right?"

"Yes, I did…hang on a sec…are you Welsh? Grannie was Welsh – you sound just like her." She turned from her screen and called, "Mum, come and listen to this – there's a Welshwoman at the Desert Gem, and she sounds just like Grannie." She turned back to face the screen. "Could you say something for Mum to hear? She misses Grannie, you see. It would do her good. She's still upset."

"I'm so sorry, did your Grannie…um…I mean…"

"Grannie left this plane about a month ago. But it was a good passing. Peaceful. We all had a chance to say our farewells, and she's with Granddad now. Here's Mum – can you see us?"

"Yes, I can see you both, though you can't see me, and I don't know how to make that happen – sorry, I'm just holding the fort while Jenn's with Zara."

The youthful Glenda turned to her – in my view – almost equally youthful mother as she spoke, "Oh Mum, did you hear that? Jenn's with Zara." She turned to the camera again. "Have you met Zara? In real life? What's she like? Is she really as wonderful as she seems? Have you felt her heart beating as you bond?"

"Who are you talking to, Glenda?" The young woman's mother was peering into the screen, as though I might suddenly materialize.

"My name's Cait, and I'm visiting the Desert Gem with my husband. I understand your late mother was Welsh. I'm very sorry for your loss."

The mother turned to the daughter. "What a strange thing for her to say. Are you sure she's a Facetor?"

"Jenn left her in charge, so she must be right," said Glenda. "I thought you'd like to hear her accent. Don't you think she sounds like Grannie?"

"Would you like me to talk a bit more? Anything in particular I can say to cheer you at all?" Even though they couldn't see me, I was smiling at them as I spoke – because you really can hear a smile.

The mother looked suspicious. "Do the long Welsh word – that was her party trick, wasn't it Glenda."

Glenda beamed, "Oh yes, please do the big word."

I took a deep breath and – using my best pronunciation – uttered the word I've been asked to say anywhere and everywhere in the world when people find out I'm Welsh, which I don't mind one little bit.

"Llanfairpwllgwyngyllgogerychwyrndrobwllllantysilio…" I always like to pause at that point, for effect, "…gogogoch."

Both women clapped and laughed with genuine pleasure, and I felt as though I'd done at least one good thing that day.

Then the mother started to tear up. "Thanks for that. She was a good woman, and missed Wales. Loved it here, though, and we've had a good life because of decisions she took a long time ago. But you know what? And you'll understand this, being as close as you are to Zara herself…Dad's been waiting for Mum for almost ten years, so maybe now they're together they'll be able to break the veil and get back to us, right Glenda?"

Glenda hugged her mother. "Yes, Mum. So, do you have the answer for us? How many people helped Grannie to speed her piercing of the veil?"

I said, "Eighty-three."

Both women clapped and hugged each other again. "Good for us. Good for Grannie," said Glenda. "I didn't think that many people would come through for us. Eighty-three? That'll get her going, right enough. Eighty-three thousand dollars-worth of Faceting by fellow Facetors will see her right. I know we kicked it off with five, but that's an extra seventy-seven."

I needed to make sure I'd understood properly, "So you sent five thousand dollars, then seventy-seven other people have sent a thousand dollars each to the Faceting movement, to pay other Facetors to buff up Facets on your grandmother's behalf, to help her come through to you from the other plane?"

The women exchanged a puzzled look, then both nodded at the screen. "I've never heard it called 'buffing' before, but yes, that's right," said Glenda's mother. "Why do you sound surprised? Is that not much? Not enough? We were hoping it meant we'd start to get messages quite soon."

I pulled myself together. "No, sorry, it's just we're having a few technical difficulties here, and I wasn't quite catching everything you were saying." I could feel myself getting hot, then one of my thumb drives started blinking. "Can you hold on – I've just got to do something, I'll be right back now, in a minute."

As I lunged for the thumb drive, and popped it into my handbag, I could hear both women laughing like drains. "Oh, that was another one of Grannie's. Where are you from, Cait? Grannie was from a place called Port Talbot – do you know it?"

"I do," I replied brightly, "though the correct local pronunciation is closer to "P'Talbut."

More howls, and a few more tears.

Bud called. "What on earth is going on over there? I'm trying to have a sensitive conversation on this side of the room."

I mugged a shrug, then said, "Ladies, I've got to go now. Sorry. But before I do, can I just ask – are you both Facetors?"

They nodded.

"And your grandmother was also a Facetor?"

Laughing. "Oh no, staunch chapel, though she never went. She didn't believe in the whole Faceting movement. We tried explaining it to her, but she wasn't having it."

I allowed the implications to sink in. "So, to be clear, you organized for donations to be made by other Facetors to speed your grandmother's ability to pierce the veil, even though *she* didn't believe in your way of thinking?"

Glenda's mother jumped in. "Just because my mum didn't believe, doesn't mean she won't be able to come back. When she gets to the other side, she'll understand we were right – but because she didn't believe on this side, she'll need some extra help. That's what the 'paying our condolences' system allows for; we can all chip in and help those who didn't take the chance to believe on this side to still come through, when they've left us."

How clever, was what I thought; "That must be a comfort," was what I said. "And, other than this aspect, do you find that Faceting has made a difference in your lives?"

They exchanged a glance. "I hope this isn't some sort of test," said Glenda, looking nervous.

"No, indeed – it's just me, talking to you…Welsh blood to Welsh blood."

They hugged. "It's brought us closer in the past six months than we've ever been before," said the mother.

"We Facet together every day, and if we can't spend as much time as we'd like together, at least we now have so much in common that when we talk, we're really connecting," said Glenda, holding her mother's hand. "Dad thought it was all a bit sus to start with – but he listened to a few of Zara's podcasts and now he's as good as gold about it all. Does a bit of Faceting on the quiet, I reckon, but not much of a joiner, right, Mum?"

"Yeah, he'll be right."

"Great," I said, "well, that's good to know. Thanks. Shall I say it one more time, instead of saying goodbye?"

The women giggled. "Please," said Glenda.

"Llanfairpwllgwyngyllgogerychwyrndrobwllllantysilio…" I paused again, "…gogogoch."

The connection was broken at their end, leaving hoots of truly joyous laughter ringing in my ears. "Glad to be of service, ladies," I said to myself, as I removed the two other thumb drives, and popped them safely into my bag.

"Did she come through?" I hadn't noticed Jenn entering the dimness of the hub, and almost dropped my bag, she gave me such a fright.

I smiled. "She did, and her mother, too. I told them eighty-three. Apparently, Glenda's grannie was Welsh, so we had a lot to talk about. My accent reminded them of hers."

Jenn looked puzzled. "Glenda's grannie? Do you mean Mrs. Bessie Williams?"

I shrugged. "Sorry, no idea. I met Glenda and her mother, and the deceased was Welsh – that's all I know. And that the secret number was eighty-three. That's it."

"Secret number?" Jenn sounded confused. "Eighty-three is the number of condolence wishes they received from other Facetors. Zara asked me to give them the information, because it had come up as a question in one of the earlier sessions she was leading, and she'd said the answer was ninety-two, then realized she'd made a mistake, so had to check again. But, as my own grandmother used to say – even monkeys fall out of trees – though it was hardly a secret. Now, are you two done?"

Bud had wandered across the studio area. "What's all this about monkeys and trees?"

Jenn spun round. "Grandmothers' sayings, you know? People make mistakes – monkeys fall from trees. Oh, never mind. Now, if you please, I must get sorted out. Zara's back on in –" she looked at her watch – "ten minutes. Good grief, where does the time go?"

Bud and I headed to the door. "Don't worry, I dare say we won't need to come back again – we really appreciate it."

Jenn sighed, "'If it can happen twice, it can happen thrice'…another of the sayings I grew up with; the Japanese language is delightfully idiomatic. I'm happy to help, though a little stressed at the moment. The doors to this place are never locked, so feel free to come and go as you please. I'm not really supposed to tell you that, but I can't see the harm; it's all well and good that Facetors choose to cut themselves off from the outside world, but you haven't made that life choice, so I don't see why you should suffer. It's a bit of a sticking point when it comes to the plans for the guest quarters, to be honest: I think they should all have Wi-Fi installed, but a vote was taken, and the majority came down against that. Ah well, I'm not in charge, so I have to go with the flow. But now – I have to go to the channelling chamber. I'll see you around. Facet and Face it!"

She smiled and waved as we left, and I hugged Bud as we began our walk home.

He hugged back and said, "I have a feeling you have a lot to tell me."

"I do."

"Me, too," he replied.

"Oh my."

Uninformative Information

By the time we reached the plaza, a few Facetors were out and about, lounging on the wall surrounding the bubbling waters at its center, or sitting cross-legged on the ground in casual circles. The atmosphere was of people passing the time happily, and enjoying each other's company. Our passage across the plaza was accompanied by some nods and half-waves, but at least we weren't being treated as though we each had two heads.

Knowing I was carrying three thumb drives full of materials I didn't think for one minute I was really supposed to have meant I was a bit jumpy, so I was glad when we finally closed our door and were alone.

I flopped onto the couch, feeling exhausted.

"They could really do with some coffee-making facilities in here, if they're going to be as welcoming as possible to guests," said Bud as he poured himself a glass of cool water. "Want some of this? And I'm going to have an apple. You?"

"Brownie, please. I put them in a container in the bathroom – coolest part of the dig. Chocolate has caffeine, and I need some of that, I think."

Bud crunched into an apple as he wandered into the bathroom, and I happily sunk my teeth into a rich, yielding brownie that had a surprising tang of *chiles* at its heart. I gulped down a big glass of water, to cool my throat and un-coat my teeth.

"Right, laptop all fired up, and first thumb drive uploaded; I'll keep going with the second and the third, because it'll be faster to manipulate the data on the main hard drive – so why don't you fill me in on what you achieved while we wait?"

Bud saluted, consulted his notes, and began. "First thing you need to know – no one associated with this place is on anyone's radar, for any reason. Not a single red flag anywhere, about any of the names I was able to give them – I'll circle back to that in a moment. Second, records show Karaplis-Longmuir is registered in the Cayman Islands, so no information is immediately available on the corporation – though I can tell you it was set up about a year ago."

"Interesting."

"Possibly more interesting is the fact that Norman and Elizabeth McGlynn don't exist – at least, they don't exist as a married couple of their ages – so the guess is they're using false names. And, get this, there's no record of a French National named Ambroise Beausoleil residing in the USA. Suffice to say the McGlynns and Ambroise are being further researched."

"Interesting, and good. And what about Dr. Nderu? Anything off about him at all?"

"He has a pretty normal background: born in Tucson, did all his medical training in Arizona, and has always practiced here. Wife, no children, heavily involved in local pickleball leagues, and a qualified pickleball trainer, apparently."

"So, squeaky clean, other than for the fact he accommodates suicides when completing records of death."

Bud expelled a thoughtful, "Hmm…" as I changed thumb drives.

He continued, "Oscar Karaplis had a record: some dumb stuff in his teens – possession of marijuana – then, as KSue mentioned, he appeared in court on theft charges…twice, as it happens. Both times involved small items, of no great monetary value, and he got away with not much more than a rap on the knuckles; he's had a clean sheet since he hit his late-twenties.

Zara once got picked up and shipped off in a wagon at a demonstration by vegetarians outside a meat-processing plant, when she was nineteen. No charges. Nothing else. On anyone. But don't forget, I was only able to give them names I knew."

"Backgrounds on Demetrius and Linda Karaplis?"

"Demetrius's father was born in Greece, in a small mountain village not far from Delphi. He was brought to the USA by his parents as an infant. They all lived with the widow of his uncle, who'd migrated to the USA about a decade earlier – the uncle was killed fighting for the USA in 1944. Demetrius died last year; death certificate says accidental – and matches what we were told. Linda Karaplis was born Linda Olson, on the outskirts of Calgary, Alberta. She was Canadian – which I didn't know – and was working as a nurse here in the USA."

"I assumed she was American."

"Became an American citizen six years after she and Demetrius were married. Oscar and Zara were born in Arizona."

"Got it. And what about any response to our theories?"

Bud sighed. "Much as we'd expected: they're only theories; we've got nothing concrete to go on; paperwork regarding deaths of the four elders I gave them is all in order; suicide isn't illegal; where's the proof of fraud?"

"So that's it?"

"Afraid so. I got a fair reception, and as much cooperation as could have been hoped for, given the circumstances. Suspicions duly noted; warnings about me not having any standing whatsoever in these matters; the promise of expediting connections with local law enforcement as and when I have anything concrete – though comments were made about my not breaking any laws while I'm here. The usual."

"Thanks." I pulled out the final thumb drive.

"And what on earth was going on with you and those women on that screen?"

I explained.

Bud was aghast. "So there's a non-Faceting grandmother in New Zealand who died, upon whose behalf Facetors around the world donated eighty-three thousand dollars, to somehow magically streamline her reconnection to her living family?"

"Yes."

"And her family seemed quite comfortable with all this?"

"Yes. More than comfortable – happy. They were thrilled that so many people had sent money. And, like I said, overall they're delighted with their Faceting life."

Bud's head-scratching kicked in. "If Zara's pulling this off all around the world, all the time, whenever a Facetor loses a loved one – whether *that* person was a Facetor or not – it's a way of getting people to spend money to offset their grief. She's sucking money out of people's pockets when they're at their most vulnerable – and the way the system works means she's encouraging them to do a sales pitch to their fellow Facetors, asking them to put their hands in their pockets, too, with her as the ultimate beneficiary. Cait, we've got to do something."

"Bud, we've made a start. And at least I've now got a good idea where all that money's going; to the Karaplis-Longmuir corporation. I saw some more accounts, and the flow of money from the Facetors to the company that owns the land is a flood, not a trickle. The amount they're paying to have the right to build upon, and use, this bit of desert is astonishing."

Bud nodded thoughtfully. "While I was hanging on, waiting for intel to come through, I surfed about a bit. Focused on the Longmuir name – which isn't common. There are only two noteworthy mentions locally: one is a family-run company that specializes in landscaping materials, pool and spa supplies, and hydroponics supplies; the other was a kinda ghost legend, about the lost Longmuir Tunnel. Fabulous story about some young guy finding a bunch of gold in a small tunnel he'd dug into a hillside out this way, taking it into town to get cash for it, getting drunk for days, then forgetting where it was he'd dug his tunnel – because he'd hidden it so well. Spent the next twenty years of his life trying to relocate it – then just disappeared into the desert, never to be seen again. People swear his ghost wanders the desert even now, still searching for his lost fortune."

"The landscape and hydroponics supply people sound interesting; maybe they have something to do with this place – but it seems unlikely they'd be part of the land deal. Maybe your folks could look into that, if and when they get something out of the Cayman Islands. As for the ghost story? To be honest, that sounds less likely. There's a lot of copper around here – one of the things Arizona's known for: copper, cattle, cotton, citrus, climate – the Five Cs, they call them. But I didn't know there was a big gold mining thing going on."

"Well, not even you can be expected to know everything, Wife. But, as I said, those were the only Longmuir-connected bits of info I could find locally. But this is a big world, and 'Longmuir' doesn't really have to be something local at all, does it? Mind you, that ghost fella would be someone you'd hope would 'pierce the veil' and tell you how to find his tunnel, right?" I gave him an eye-roll, but he just replied with: "And what about you? Anything?"

I tapped my laptop. "All downloaded onto this baby. I snagged all the files I could – but the ones I want to start with are those transcripts. I hope they'll be the best way to work out what Zara's doing, and how she does it. I might have to put in a few hours tonight, but I really do want to be at the burning ceremony just before dawn – so why don't you get some sleep now, and I'll set an alarm, in case I drop off while I'm reading…which we both know has happened in the past. I wish I had something with caffeine in it, to help keep me going."

Bud popped into the bathroom and emerged with a couple of bottles of something purple. "I grabbed these from a carton in Serendipity's kitchen. Looks like it's all natural, and made locally. Want to try it?"

The pseudo-hand-drawn label told me the juice blend offered almost magical qualities when it came to focus and endurance, all through the amazing properties of various super-food berries. It looked like purple sludge, but I sipped it, and it didn't taste too bad – better than nothing.

"What time's dawn?" Bud was fiddling with his phone and charger as I got myself propped up on the lounger in our courtyard.

I checked my phone – no data. "About five-ish?"

"Okay, I'll set my alarm for a quarter to, so I can wake you."

"I'll be awake – I'll set mine, too."

"Okay. Good luck with that. Night."

I settled myself – the purple gloop at my elbow – and opened the folder containing the transcripts of Zara's channelling sessions. I worked out how they were organized, which was simply by date; sometimes there were several records for a certain day, then there might be a gap of several days – sometimes a week or more – then another flurry. Since I didn't really know what I was looking for, I decided the best thing to do was start at the beginning, and keep going as long as I could, unless I could spot a pattern that might suggest some keywords I could use to search.

I allowed my reading speed to gradually increase, which is the best way for me to do it; if I start speed-reading too quickly, I miss things, and that's not good. By slowly getting faster, my eyes and brain work in better harmony, and my personal preference is to place my finger on the down button – it gives me more control than scrolling. I kicked off at about ten seconds per page, and built-up speed from there, until I was in my comfort zone, zipping through the pages. I find I can keep up my pace if I give myself a break every fifteen minutes or so, just for half a minute, then I can keep going again.

I was getting along quite well when a shadow loomed over me, giving me a bit of a shock: it was Bud, standing at the patio door, looking snuggly, with crease-marks on his cheek. "You haven't slept at all, have you?" He sounded groggy.

I checked my watch. "Apparently not. I honestly have no idea where the time went." I looked at the two empty bottles beside me. "That stuff's as amazing as they say it is; I feel fresh, and still quite sharp."

"Good," mumbled Bud, heading off. "More than I do."

I set aside my laptop, and was poking my head out of the front door when Bud returned from the bathroom. "Anyone out there yet?" He still sounded less than wide awake.

I replied quietly, "No one. What should we do? I don't want them to think we're spying on them."

"Despite the fact we are."

I let my tone convey how wounded I felt. "Not really – I mean, they're out there doing something completely innocent, in public. In what way are we 'spying' on them?"

Bud shrugged. "In that case. Let's just stand outside, in the darkness of our doorway, and hope we don't offend anyone. Don't forget, we're not really supposed to know about all this writing and burning stuff, because we haven't committed to joining up."

We hovered in the darkness; the air was as cool as I'd felt it since we'd arrived, and I wondered if I was imagining a little moisture in it.

"What's that smell?" Bud spoke quietly.

"Night blooming jasmine. Strong, isn't it."

Bud was waggling his hand under his nose. "You're not kidding. It's overpowering. And not nice."

"Yes, it's a bit sickly for my tastes, too."

He peered around. "I can't see anything around here with flowers on it. How far does the smell travel?"

"A long way. Ssh…someone's coming."

We pulled back even further into the arched entrance surrounding our door, as barefoot Facetors, in many different colors of outfit, emerged from their digs. I'd expected to see them all approach with sheafs of paper in their hands, but they were empty handed, to start with. Then each person reached up to what appeared to be a little door in the wall of their dig, opened it, pulled out a bowl, and carried that to the circle of fire at the heart of the plaza. Once there, they each bowed four times, then pulled papers from their bowl, which they dropped into the fire. Then they bowed four more times, replaced the bowl in the little chamber in the wall of their dig, and disappeared inside. No words, or even hugs, were exchanged. It was eerie and lasted for about five minutes – then the plaza was deserted again.

Once we were sure we were alone, both Bud and I made our way to the same point on our outer wall where they'd all accessed their little door: no door was to be found.

I began to creep toward the dig next door, and made signs suggesting Bud did the same, but heading in the opposite direction. There were no little doors at the next three digs, then every one thereafter had one. I reached up to the first one and pulled – it opened easily, making no noise, and I was able to retrieve the bowl – which was empty. I replaced it, and scampered back to our dig, where I dragged Bud inside.

We agreed it seemed that guest digs had no receptacles containing bowls, but Facetors' digs did.

"We haven't got a little niche above our bed in which to place our notes, either," I noted, "so I'm guessing that's all part of it – write up the notes, bung them into the bowl above your bed to contemplate their meaning, then take them out on the other side in the morning. There's probably some idea that they don't weigh you down if you put them 'away' at night and don't bring them back into your living space – but that's me guessing. Just give me a minute while I recall KSue's dig…"

Bud stood patiently while I summoned the visual image of KSue's dig, and I gave myself a chance to re-examine it in my mind's eye. "Yes, there was a little door above KSue's bed, painted white, so it blended into the wall. So it must be a two-door thing – with the thickness of the wall – which is quite considerable with this style of building – being used to accommodate the bowl."

"Sounds very complicated to me," said Bud, "unnecessarily so. Why do they make everything so fiddly?"

"Ah, now that's a part of the charm of every organization like this – the more detailed the ceremonies, the more complex the required activities and observances, the more opportunity there is for layers of significance to be built in…then the process of following those practices becomes a part of the contemplation of their meaning, which increases the importance of their role, and so the cycle goes on."

"Not my thing at all," said Bud shaking his head. "Now they've done that for the day, what do you reckon they'll do for an encore? I guess they all get ready for breakfast at the refectory now."

"I expect so," I said. "I don't suppose you got another bottle of the purple power juice, did you?"

Bud chuckled. "I thought two would be enough. But they might have some at the refectory, I guess, or we could go back to the restaurant to look. But before we do anything else, please tell me what you've been doing. What was it that kept you up all night, Wife? And do you feel okay? Should you grab a nap?"

I sat on the edge of the bed, bouncing on the lumpy duvet. "Zara kept me up all night…and I think I've made a bit of a breakthrough…though I won't know if I'm right until I've been able to carry out a bit of an experiment…and you know what…the refectory might be just the place to do that…do you fancy joining the Facetors for a spot of breakfast…I bet they wouldn't turn us away…they might have some nice things for breakfast…they work hard enough outside to need a good breakfast…I don't suppose there'd be sausages…but they might have some tasty stuff like that hummus…and there were flatbreads left over after yesterday's breakfast….so it's likely they'd have them…"

Bud's eyes were round. "Woah…just a minute, Wife, take a breath. You're…well, you're racing, you look flushed – and your eyes are badly bloodshot. Hang on, I've got some eyedrops in the bathroom – stay there. If you've been speed-reading all night, I bet you haven't been blinking enough, have you? You never do." He handed me a little bottle. "Go on, use these, then just lie back and close your eyes for a couple of minutes – let them work, and let your brain slow down to normal human pace."

I did as I was told, because my eyes were, in fact, a bit sore. He knows me so well.

As I lay there, Bud bustled around. "I think it's a good idea to go to the refectory for breakfast, but I don't like the idea of you conducting an experiment. Explain to me exactly what that means."

I allowed my body to sink into the mattress as I said, "I think I've worked out a part of how Zara does what she does, but I need to test my theory, by having a conversation with someone here – anyone really – wherein I tell them something I've never told anyone else…and I tell them in such a way that they believe I'm sharing a valuable life lesson with them."

"Okay…you still need to slow down. But why do you have to share a secret?"

"Because I want to find out what happens to that knowledge – discover the life it takes on once it's left my lips."

I opened my eyes to see Bud staring down at me, looking puzzled. "I don't understand. Do you think – what – there are microphones around the place recording every conversation?"

"Sort of, but not quite."

Bud tutted. "Oh come on, Cait, don't go all enigmatic on me now. This is important – and we're talking about a woman who thinks nothing of encouraging who knows how many people to go off and kill themselves. She's…well, she's not normal. This could be dangerous."

"All I'm going to do is share a lesson I've learned. How can that be dangerous?"

Bud harrumphed. "Well, at least you look and sound a bit more normal, now. Should we head on over to the refectory? Just arrive there, unannounced?"

"Why not? But, first, bathroom, teeth, hair, clean clothes…then breakfast."

Bud peered out into the courtyard. "You'd better get your skates on – remember, they have to have everything cleared away by seven."

As I headed for the bathroom I couldn't resist muttering, "First you want me to slow down, now you want me to speed up. Make your mind up, Husband!"

I heard him chuckle as I shut the door.

Publicly Private

I wondered if we were acclimatizing to the temperatures, because I felt a little chilly as we approached the refectory. Entering, we managed to create one of those fabulous movie moments: as we stepped inside, all the chatter stopped, and every pair of eyes turned in our direction. We paused in the doorway.

"Okay if we grab some breakfast here with you good people?" Bud was using what I recognized as his masterful but calming tone – usually held in reserve for deescalating potentially dangerous situations.

A figure seated on one of the long benches rose; I recognized Don. "Sure, let me show you around."

Bud waved, and we set off, passing Elizabeth and Norman as we headed for the serving area; they were hunched over bowls of something completely ignoring us, which – given that we now knew they were probably using false names – I thought highly suspicious.

"Thanks for the welcome, Don," said Bud quietly, as we perused the variety of breakfast offerings.

Many of the items were easily recognizable because they were fruits, all presented in shiny, stainless steel bowls. Yet more bowls contained various ingredients from which I assumed one could mix a muesli-type dish if one wished – which I didn't. I grabbed a flatbread, some of the hummus we'd enjoyed the day before, and a couple of muffins, then I hunted about to see if I could spot any bottles of the magical berry juice Bud had brought me the previous night, and found a pile of them in a bowl full of rapidly-melting ice. There were also little cotton bags promising to contain all sorts of "teas", but they just seemed to be a sneaky way of getting me to steep a variety of plants and vegetables that were anything but tea in not-quite-boiling water, which didn't appeal at all. So, more purple gloop it was – I couldn't bring myself to face another cup of the dreadful coffee they served there.

The folks Don had been sitting with either left – quite amiably – or scooted along, so we could join him, and I tucked into my food as fast as I could, because it was quite obvious that folks were nearing the end of the breakfast period, and were clearing away after themselves as they headed off to what I assumed would be their daily duties. Given there were fewer and fewer options available to me for secret sharing, I realized Don would have to be the person I would – quite casually – confide in.

"What will you be doing today?" asked Bud in his best jovial-small-talk tone.

Don had finished eating and was remaining with us to be polite; at least, that was what his body language was telling me. "I'm on laundry duty today," he said, "which isn't my favorite thing to do, but we all take turns."

I was about to ask a question, but Bud beat me to it. "I guess you see all sorts when you're doing laundry. Get to know who the real messy ones are, eh?"

Don chucked amiably. "Not really, all the Faceting clothing is one size and omnigender, so people just dump what they need laundered into baskets we leave outside the laundry building, we wash and dry them all, then return them to the central supply room. You can go in there and take whatever color you want, whenever you like, and even change your clothes as often as you need throughout the day. Some of these guys need to do that a lot; working under the sun gets hot, and a change – of clothing – is as good as a rest."

"So you never know whose laundry you're doing? Very egalitarian," said Bud, unpeeling his second banana.

Don leaned in. "Well, sometimes I have an inkling. For example, Jenn's the only one who wears orange, so hers are easy to spot, and – I don't know if you've noticed – but quite a lot of the people here like to wear perfumed oils. The scents are mood enhancers, and we get to take our pick of those from the general supply room, too, but you get to know who favors what, and the smell lingers, even on very dirty laundry."

I spotted the chance I'd been wanting. "Could we go to the supply room and have a sniff of those oils? Some people around here smell absolutely fantastic." I sounded as fluffily enthusiastic as I could.

"I don't see why not." Don was smiling. "I have mentioned in a few conversations how we should think about bottling them for sale, and I think that's being planned. They'd be popular, I believe."

I agreed, then gushed, "I learned a valuable lesson because of personal perfume choices when I was at university," I mused, seemingly distractedly, I hoped. "A housemate of mine wore a particular brand that everyone else in our shared house agreed was making them feel nauseous. One girl went so far as to cough and splutter when she came into a room, and started spraying air freshener whenever she left. Eventually, the girl wearing the strong scent pulled me aside and asked if she had a problem with body odor that no one had the guts to mention to her. I took the opportunity to tell her about the effect her perfume was having upon everyone, and she burst into floods of tears. It turned out that her grandmother had recently died, and the brand of perfume she was wearing was to help her remember her beloved grannie. But she'd gone a bit 'nose blind' to the scent, so just wore more and more. She was devastated when she discovered how much discomfort she'd caused her housemates, and she and I came up with a plan whereby she'd launder, or get rid of everything with the perfume already on it, then she'd have a special tin, in which she could keep a scent-drenched hankie, so she could sniff – and really smell – her grannie's perfume, and thereby recall her grannie better, whenever she wanted…in private. And do you know what that taught me?"

Don was agog, and shook his head.

"We really can never imagine the true motives behind the actions of people we think we know well – so I learned to never judge before I know all the facts. It's a lesson that's stood me in good stead since then. I hope you can see why."

Bud almost choked on his last bite of banana, but I chose to ignore him.

Don nodded vigorously. "Indeed I do understand. Profoundly. In a similar vein, I gained insight from a situation where I truly believed I knew why a person was doing a certain thing, only to discover I was completely wrong. That taught me, I can tell you…but your example is both instructive, and touching. I shall think on it."

I beamed at Bud, who was looking pink in the face, and added, "Thank you, I like to share the lessons life has taught me, when I can. So come on – can you tell me the specifics of the lesson you learned."

Don looked about – the place was all but deserted – then leaned even closer. "I thought I knew why Oscar spent so much time in his dig. But – and I am ashamed to admit this, but I must, because it highlights a weakness of mine that I've been working on – I later discovered I'd jumped to a completely wrong conclusion. You see, I thought that – because he was Demetrius and Linda's son – he felt he could shirk work duties and responsibilities, and was just a bit lazy. But then I discovered he went into his dig after meals, but left again almost immediately, climbing over the outer wall, to head off into the desert. I saw him present his mother with an impressively large fossilized snail that he'd found on one of his excursions, and I asked him where and how he'd found it, so he explained to me how he liked to walk in the desert. He wasn't being lazy at all. Imagine that – it turned out he was fascinated by the ancient history of this area, and got out into the desert as much as possible, but would climb the wall behind his dig to get there so his mother wouldn't worry about him being out there alone. After that, I would often join him on his walks. He had great knowledge about the desert – so all our time there was highly informative. He was wonderful at navigating without a path, even at night. He said he used the stars to make sure he kept going the way he wanted. Amazing – and I had made some terrible assumptions about him, to my shame."

"So Oscar was a bit of a fossil hunter? Interesting." *Interesting.*

Don shrugged. "Well, I thought so to begin with, but it turned out the fossils were something he picked up when he was out indulging his love of geology. That's how he and Ambroise met – both nuts about rocks."

Bud perked up. "I didn't know that about either of them."

Don beamed. "Oscar was very clever, but quiet, you know? Didn't like to blow his own trumpet. I…I understand that; I've been working on my assertiveness, and I'm starting to feel a little better about myself. Oscar helped me with that a great deal. He was a very kind person."

"Would you say he was happy here?" I hoped Don was going to help me better understand the man who'd died before I'd had a chance to meet him.

Don stared at the ceiling, and I suspected he was trying to prevent tears from rolling down his cheeks. "He was, in his own way," he replied softly. "But he could have been so much happier, I know, if only…no, it's not for me to say. He's gone now, and I have no doubt that Ambroise made his peace with him when he found his body."

Bud and I managed to exchange a puzzled glance. "I understand Ambroise and Oscar were good buddies," said Bud.

Don managed a weak smile. "You could say that. Knew each other for years." Finally, gravity won the battle and a tear fell. Don looked directly at Bud and added, "They were close. Their friendship meant a great deal to Oscar. Ambroise's ability to help Oscar understand his purpose was quite extraordinary. But I guess you could say that about all the people Ambroise chooses to help, like me, for example. He's developed his Faceting skills so far that he's way beyond most of the rest of us. And he's given me a good deal of responsibility when it comes to coordinating the other novices. We all hope to become like him, one day."

"Ambroise sounds like quite the role model," said Bud gently.

Don nodded, his eyes glistening. "He is. But he's not Oscar," he said, pulling a rag from his pocket.

All three of us were startled by a hooting sound. "What's that?" Bud and I chorused.

Don was on his feet. "It's a call to all Facetors. We meet in the amphitheater whenever that horn sounds."

Bud and I also stood, picked up our used dishes, and dumped them unceremoniously on the counter as Don told us to be quick; the horn meant there was an urgent need to congregate.

I wondered what was so important.

Illogical Logic

When we arrived at the amphitheater, the rows of stone benches were a-buzz; every face showed puzzlement, and anticipation. We didn't have to wait long to find out what was going on: Zara appeared on the stage, once again dazzling us all with a gleaming white dress, and accompanied by Jenn, who hovered behind her.

Zara stepped forward, and complete silence descended upon the gathered crowd. Once she had everyone's attention, she spoke quietly, with a warmth to her voice that was both commanding, and alluring. "I am pleased that our valued friend KSue is about to be returned to us in good health, and we will celebrate that fact presently. I know you've all heard about her encounter with a snake; it was not a rattlesnake, and she will be just fine. I called this gathering so you could all hear the good news as soon as possible."

At just that moment there was a bit of a kerfuffle, and we all looked around to see KSue, Norman, and Elizabeth enter the auditorium. People stood, there was a lot of bowing, and KSue was greeted with a great deal of Faceting well-wishes – so lots of hissing, which seemed exceptionally inappropriate, under the circumstances.

The woman we'd come to know a little took a seat on the front bench. Elizabeth sat one side of her, Norman the other. She seemed to shrink from them both, and I was close enough that I could tell this was a different KSue than the one who'd been our guide the previous day: she looked drawn, diminished – and scared. She waved away hugs being offered, then sat as immobile as a statue.

"Welcome, KSue," said Zara. Everyone sat down again and stopped hissing. "Our thanks to Elizabeth and Norman who, once again, sacrificed their time to drive to a place we all know they'd rather not have to visit. Your kindness is noted." She bowed deeply toward the beaming McGlynns.

Once everyone was seated again, Zara continued, but now her voice carried a slight edge – it was more ominous. "Demetrius has told me that there has been some talk about my brother's death. How it happened. Why it happened. My father has conversed with my brother and has asked me to pass on this message: Oscar became disoriented, and stepped off a ledge he didn't see in the dark. It was an accident and, yes, sadly, he did feel pain as he fell." Zara held up her hand as "Oh dear" and "Oh no" rustled through the crowds. "But he is now at peace, the pain is behind him, the challenge to pierce the veil is before him. So we should rejoice!" She threw her arms into the air, and twirled on tiny feet.

A cheer went up – a cheer of genuine, heartfelt delight.

"Doesn't sound like the same Oscar that Don was just telling us about," I managed to whisper to Bud, who replied with a nod.

Zara calmed the crowd, and everyone sat again. "Those who have been trying to suggest that Oscar passed in some other way are being heard by Demetrius, and he is displeased." Zara's voice had taken on a distinctly threatening tone. Looking around, the body language of her followers told me she didn't need to make any specific charges – they were all immediately cowed. I found the reaction of the group to be fascinating – and more than a little worrying; this young woman had tremendous power over them.

Zara's chin, and voice, dropped as she added, "I shall speak more of this at another time – but Demetrius wanted me to remind you that he sees all, and hears all." She shook her head, tossing her hair from her face, and her tone changed – it dripped with sweetness when she said, "Facet and Face It." She bowed deeply, then turned and left the stage.

Facetors stood and began to amble off, or huddle together in small groups. I spotted KSue almost scampering through the crowd, her head down, making for her dig. I had no hesitation – nor did Bud; we followed her as closely as we could until we all reached her place. She rushed inside, and was about to push the door closed in our faces when Bud stuck his foot beside the jamb.

"KSue, you can trust us – please let us in." Bud used his calming tone.

KSue bobbed about, then opened the door so we could enter, pushing it closed behind us. Her chin puckered as she spoke, her voice quavering. "I'm not staying. I must go. I phoned my boy and told him to come get me. He has to work today, but he'll take a personal day tomorrow and get me then. Until I open that door to him, I'm not going anywhere, and no one else is coming in."

"Do you think your life's in danger?" Bud's words were spoken evenly.

KSue said nothing. A tear rolled down her face. She swatted it away.

I reckoned she needed a push. "Okay, listen, KSue – we can see you're terrified, you've admitted you're trying to get away from here…if you're not in fear for your life, what *are* you afraid of?"

KSue swallowed, her eyes wide. "I think…I think someone might try to make Demetrius's prediction that I'm going to pass come true, yes. And I'm not ready. I don't want to die yet."

Bud put his arm around KSue's little shoulders, and she dissolved in a tide of tears. I could tell there was nothing I could do to help, so spent my time examining the details of KSue's home away from home, going so far as to enter the bathroom under cover of grabbing a length of toilet roll, which I stuffed into the weeping woman's hands.

Eventually Bud got her settled on her sofa – which was a much less plush affair than the one in our dig – and she stopped crying, though her body continued to be wracked with sobs. Her face was puffy, there were sagging bags beneath her eyes, and she looked a lot older than the day before. My heart went out to her, and I knew the only way we could help was for Bud and me to follow through with our desire to somehow understand, undermine, and stop Zara.

When Bud managed to get away from KSue – she'd clung to his arm the entire time – he motioned to me to join him in the bathroom.

He whispered, "Do you think we should tell her our beliefs about Zara? I think that might calm her, and she might even know things she could, and would, share with us. Or do you think she's so enthralled that she'll poo-poo our theories, and maybe even tell Zara what we say?"

I looked out at KSue, sitting on her sofa in the other room, and said, "I believe she's a decent, honest woman, who's been – as you said – enthralled. However, I think she's now coming to terms with what death really means to her, and not liking the prospect. She's not as stupid as she thinks she is; her gardening abilities clearly illustrate the fact she's capable of learning and applying a great deal of knowledge, but her lack of belief in herself is a real problem. It seems to me she's developed a pattern of behavior throughout her life that she hopes will get people to like her – and she might say almost anything to achieve that."

"So…?"

"I think we should let her work it out for herself – then she might believe it."

Bud shook his head. "How on earth are you going to do that?"

"Not sure, but here goes…I'll get her chatting, first." I left the bathroom and sat beside KSue on the sofa. "I'm sorry you're so scared. We are, too. We understand."

KSue's eyebrows suggested she didn't quite believe me. "You're scared?" She glanced at Bud.

I smiled. "Well, I'd be a lot more scared if I didn't have Bud, so for now, how about we share him?"

KSue nodded, and managed a smile.

I decided to open with: "I have an idea, and I want to run it past you, to see what you think."

"Me?" KSue sounded amazed.

"Yes, like I've said before, I believe you have excellent intuition about people – you see through what's not real, right to the heart of things." The little woman shrugged. "And I think you realized when you heard that Demetrius had said you would soon pass, that, if you didn't help that happen, someone else might do it for you."

KSue's breathing quickened; she was becoming agitated.

I used my calming voice. "It's alright – don't panic. We don't believe that suspecting that makes you a horrible person; we know how the Faceting movement encourages folks to envisage dying as another part of the overall process of existence, but it's scary to think you'll be leaving all this behind, not knowing exactly what's waiting for you."

KSue nodded. "There's that, yes…and…I didn't want to die without having a chance to tell my dear boy that…that I didn't mean what I said the last time I saw him. And that I forgave him for the things he said. I need to see him before I…before I pass. I can't have that last terrible argument on my conscience for eternity."

I hadn't seen that coming, but decided to follow the path KSue had presented. "Did you two have a falling out? About you coming here?"

KSue nodded. "He said I shouldn't spend all my money on coming here for such a long time, but I said it was my money, that I could do what I liked with it. And he said I wouldn't have had any money if his late father hadn't worked his you-know-what off for all those years, and that he'd hate to see me wasting all his hard-earned cash on this place. It was dreadful. His wife's on his side, and they stopped me seeing my grandkids. Which was very hard. So I…so I came here anyway, because it *is* my money. I can spend it how *I* want, and I know it'll be a bit more difficult to afford my little place when I get back to Sedona. But that's not his problem, it's mine. But, now that Linda's not here any longer, I don't mind going back sooner."

"You miss her a great deal, don't you?" I used my most sympathetic tone.

"I do."

"Tell me about her. You've known her for a long time. When did you two meet?"

KSue looked wistful. "Over a quarter of a century ago. Zara was about two. They were good times."

"And was Oscar around then?"

"Sometimes, but he was usually off, doing his own thing. Liked adventurous places back then; you know what young men are. There was such a big gap between him and Zara they didn't really mix at all. So it was just Linda, Zara, and Demetrius – and the birth of Faceting. I remember how Linda and Demetrius loved to visit Taliesin West, and how they really took Frank Lloyd Wright's Organic Commandment to heart – that was what inspired them when they first defined the fourteen critical facets, you know."

"I didn't," I replied, but realized it all made sense; Wright's four key points had morphed to become fourteen critical facets, and I could imagine the thrills Demetrius and Linda must have had as they developed their ideas, and thinking. Given its simple beginnings, I was truly curious about how Linda could have allowed her daughter to push the movement as far as she had in such a novel direction.

"Were Linda and Demetrius a happy couple?" Bud was following a different line of inquiry.

KSue gave her answer some thought. "When I knew them, yes. They first met when they were quite young – she nursed him, in a local clinic – and always knew they were meant for each other. But Linda told me about a few problems they'd had in the early days – before they had Oscar – before they were married. You see, Demetrius had his mid-life crisis young, she said, went off travelling to Greece – which he always thought of as his homeland – which it was really, of course. He spent a good deal of time studying up on all the ancient ways of Delphi. He came from not far away from there. Then he visited lots of other places across Europe, and Linda thought he was never coming back to her. But he did, and brought some wonderful wisdom with him. They married, then along came Oscar, and they were set. But it was a long engagement, because of his travels, and that was very difficult for Linda. They never really left Arizona after that. They were truly settled here."

"That's good to know – I like to hear about happy families," I said – possibly too brightly.

"Yes, I have fond memories of those times. I had my own family as well, of course, but our families never mixed; my husband wasn't into Faceting, which was a great shame. He even set my son against me on that front. But now, with Demetrius saying I'm going to die soon, I told my boy how scared I am, and he's said he'll look after me. I know he loves his mother really. He said so on the phone. I could hear it in his voice. As soon as I said I'd learned my lesson, he said he'd come fetch me."

"And what lesson is that?" I was truly curious.

"That not everyone's exactly who or what they say they are, or make themselves out to be. Especially…especially not the younger ones. The novices – you know, the ones who wear gray?" I nodded. "I don't think they understand how very precious time on this plane is."

"Why do you say that? What's happened to make you feel that way?" Bud stepped forward, in full protective mode.

KSue wiped her nose. "A couple of the new ones – I know I should know their names, but I don't, because they all look so much alike to me, but I think these two are both the children of people who work in that Silicone Valley place – well, a couple of them said before dinner last night, in the refectory, that they'd heard I was going to pass soon, and they asked…they asked if I needed any help. It frightened me so much I left before eating. I've never heard of anything like that happening before."

"Did you ask them what they meant by that?" Bud squatted beside KSue. "Did they actually offer to help you commit suicide?"

KSue sobbed. "One of them said he could get me some datura, like Linda used, or some of the peyote or ayahuasca they use in some of the new dreaming and connecting rituals."

Bud and I exchanged a worried glance. "Psychotropic drugs are being used here?"

KSue nodded. "Yes, but that stuff's all for the young ones, it's not for me. Faceting used to be so simple, just doing nice things with friends, now it's…well, it's changed a lot since we came here. The novices? They're all so young…so…I don't know. It's like they'll try anything, and if they like it, they'll keep doing it, but if they don't, they'll just stop. I'm pleased there are young people joining the movement but they're all so…I don't know. Oh – yes I do! You know you got me to do that thing with animals? Well, they're all like donkeys – braying, and running about, or being stubborn when you don't need them to be. And they all do a *lot* of the drug therapies – they're all so keen to find themselves – but fast."

"So, to be clear, you were offered access to drugs that could be harmful to you, or at least make you unaware of what was happening to you?" Bud pressed, clearly not wanting to allow KSue's chatter to sidetrack him.

She nodded. "They said it helps with the passing. Promised it would make it painless. And I know Linda took datura all the time, so it really isn't harmful, unless you take a lot. You know, too much."

I could feel myself getting angry. "And do you know how much is too much, KSue, or would you have to rely upon someone else to tell you that?"

KSue's chin puckered. "They aren't the sort of plants I know anything about, not like Linda did, so I'd have to trust them, and that's the thing, you see – I don't. Which is one of my weaknesses – I haven't developed my Faceting skills well enough to be able to trust."

I replied, "I think you've shown great good sense in knowing you cannot trust everyone – because, sometimes, people don't have your best interests at heart."

"But they said I was so loved that a lot of Facetors would pay their condolences to help me pierce the veil more quickly – like they have done for Linda. I've heard that Facetors all around the world are supporting her journey back – which is only to be expected. We'll all value her insights as much as Demetrius's, so we all want her back as soon as possible. I've paid two condolences myself."

I sat back. The wickedness of how Zara was monetizing grief made me feel hot, and angry.

"You haven't mentioned these condolence payments until now," I said gently, "is there a reason for that?"

KSue looked genuinely surprised. "No. They don't have anything to do with anything you've asked me about so far."

To be fair, I could see what she meant – we hadn't suspected they were happening, so had never asked about them. With that in mind I said, "So are there any other things – not connected in any way with what we're talking about – that have started up during the time you've been here? New rituals, new or different ways of doing things?"

KSue sucked the end of her thumb. "The condolence payments are new, and the dreaming rituals the younger ones do. There's more marijuana being grown than was ever the case – though, as I told you, that's not my area of oversight."

"Marijuana?" Bud sounded grim. "Hydroponically grown, I guess?" KSue nodded. "Any idea how much?"

She shook her head. "A lot of us use it, for our aches and pains. Some had medical cards for it, even before they came here. Quite a few of the older ones, like Elizabeth, find it helpful – she's been having a bad time with her back, you know."

I didn't, but said, "It's not illegal to grow it in this state, but there are limits, and selling it is tricky."

KSue looked shocked. "It's not sold here, it's free. For us. When they put up the four new hydroponic buildings they said we needed them because there are more of us here now, so we need more plants…though I didn't think we were using that much more." KSue shrugged, then added, "But, I guess almost everyone eats the brownies and the cookies, so maybe that's where it's all going. They say the cookies help them with their Faceting, you see, though I find they just make me sleepy."

Bud stood and stretched out his back – he'd been crouched down for a long time.

Immediately, he started to pace. "I have to be honest, KSue, and tell you that it's all sounding as though there's quite a drug culture being cultivated here. Aren't you worried about that?"

The little woman looked surprised. "It's all natural, not like the chemicals and the meth and the other terrible things you see in so many places. And no one needs to steal or commit crimes to get it because it's just here, to use when you want it. So the problems you get with drugs in the outside world don't exist." She made it all sound idyllic. "And, of course, the amount of additional successful Faceting means those who do choose to use all the new dreaming methods are able to learn more about themselves and the movement so much better, so they stand a greater chance of progressing, and coming closer to their goals."

"And this is the environment into which you want to attract more members?" Bud was just about managing to keep his anger in check.

KSue looked a bit miffed. "Up in your part of the world you have cannabis stores in every mall, and I happen to know you have home delivery services for it, too. Your government sells licences for the stuff, but here, it's free, which I think is better for everyone. It's a very amiable way of life all round...except when you're told you're about to die, then it's not as nice anymore."

"You're not kidding," was out of my mouth before I could stop it. KSue immediately looked deeply wounded, so I added, "Which is why you did the right thing asking your son to come to collect you. In a way, being bitten by that snake was fortunate – it meant you were taken somewhere where your cellphone would work." A cog rolled into place. "Or did that bent fork I picked up from your table have something to do with it?"

Bud looked puzzled. "Bent fork?"

KSue flushed pink, and I knew I was right.

"You stuck your own leg with two prongs of a bent fork, then screamed that you'd been bitten by a snake, knowing you'd get out of here, and to a place of relative safety, didn't you?" I tried to not sound as though I was accusing her of being a bad person.

KSue nodded, chewing her lip.

"Very clever." I allowed myself a chuckle. "So why did you come back at all – why not wait in Flagstaff for your son to collect you there?"

KSue's eyes widened. "They made me come back. The McGlynns. They said that if I didn't, I could be chipped off, and I don't want that."

"Chipped off?" Bud and I chorused.

"Excommunicated – like the church. Thrown out. Oh – that's another new thing, now I come to think of it. There was never any chipping off in Demetrius's time. But it's a good idea, I guess, in case people break the rules…but not when you think it's going to happen to you. I mean, where would I be if I was chipped off?"

Alive, safe, and with a much healthier bank balance, was what I thought; "Even after what you've told us about being scared for your life, you still feel that way?" was what I said.

KSue nodded. I decided to try a different approach. "Is there anything about Zara that you haven't told us?"

KSue looked genuinely curious. "Like what?"

"I tell you what interests me," said Bud, who'd paused in front of the fireplace, "you told us how you knew it was Demetrius talking through Zara, because he mentioned an argument the two of you had had, right?" KSue nodded. "Do you know why everyone else knows it's him speaking? Does Zara give proof – or maybe I should ask does Demetrius give proof – to everyone he talks to?"

KSue brightened a little. "He speaks to many people, all the time."

"And an example of that would be?" I asked politely. I certainly had no intention of giving away the fact I'd read so many of the transcripts of Zara's channelling sessions, and was interested to see what KSue would offer up.

"Well, you saw it yourselves – when he spoke to you two. How would Zara know those things about your loved ones on the other plane unless Demetrius had told her?"

I replied gently, "Everything Zara said about us is on the internet; she didn't need to get those bits of knowledge from Demetrius."

KSue looked puzzled. "But they were personal messages."

"Which didn't ring true for either of us," said Bud. "One of the messages was supposedly from my late wife; if it had really been her, she wouldn't have sent the message she did."

"And my dead ex-boyfriend wouldn't have apologized the way the message said he did," I added.

KSue nibbled her lip.

"And maybe little Zara was in the house, or close by, when you and Demetrius had that argument, all those years ago?" I decided it was worth pressing on. "Children do remember the strangest things."

KSue's eyes were darting. "She always was a bit of a lurker, I suppose...but, no, there are too many examples."

"Like?" Bud pressed.

KSue scratched her forehead. "Oh, I don't know, I forget things – specific things – but there's a general...oh, I know...here's one: Demetrius told Ravi – he was one of our elders – that his father was asking about a necklace he'd gifted to Ravi's wife, when they married. I remember that one because Ravi himself had told me the necklace had been so ugly that his wife had only worn it once, then she'd intentionally broken the clasp and said it couldn't be repaired, just so she'd never have to wear it again. And he'd only told me that about a week…or maybe more…earlier – and I'd learned from his story that sometimes you have to do a little bad thing to avoid doing a big bad thing, like telling his father she thought it was ugly. Then there Demetrius was, not long afterwards, saying Ravi's father was asking about the necklace, telling him he knew what his wife had done, and asking why hadn't his wife just said she didn't like it? Oh, Ravi and I laughed about that one. There you go – that's an example. Only Demetrius could have known about that."

I weighed my response, and decided I had to try. "But you knew about it, KSue. So it's not as though Ravi kept the whole thing a big secret."

KSue looked blank. "Yes, I did. But what of it?"

"Did you tell anyone about it?"

KSue looked hurt. "No, I didn't. And even if I had – it was still Demetrius who was hearing about it from Ravi's father, on the other plane."

I couldn't help myself. "But that makes no sense, KSue. You're ignoring the reality of the situation. Zara isn't hearing anything from Demetrius, he's dead. She's somehow gathering information about people from different sources, and replaying it in a way that makes you think she's hearing it from her father."

Bud glared at me, and KSue's chin went into puckering overdrive. "You asked for proof, and I gave it to you. If you don't believe the basics, then no amount of proof will persuade you – but I've seen it with my own eyes. So there."

Bud sighed. "Okay, KSue, yes, that's a useful example, thanks. That helps us to better understand what we're facing."

"Now, do you think you should try to get some sleep?" I realized we weren't going to make any headway with KSue, so wanted to get out of her dig and back to the rest of the compound, where Bud and I stood a better chance of making some progress with…something…anything.

KSue looked at Bud, then me. "Will I be safe?"

"Are you planning on eating or drinking anything that someone tells you to?" Bud sounded as though he were speaking to a child.

"No, but I'm going to need to eat at some point. You don't think anyone would try to sneak something nasty into my food, do you?" She sounded alarmed.

"No, we don't think that, but how about we bring you some fruit and some other food you can eat here, from the refectory. Everyone eats from the same bowls there, so you'd know it would be safe." I was trying my best to placate her. "We could bring enough to get you through until tomorrow morning, then bring some more. How about that?"

"So should I not drink my tea tonight?"

"What tea is that, KSue?" I looked around the dig, but couldn't see any sign of a kettle, or any other way to boil water.

KSue looked puzzled. "The tea, tea. The tea we all drink every night. It's delivered to each dig, every night. It's what we drink before going to bed to help us distill our learnings from our…" KSue stopped, clapped her hand over her mouth and said, "Oh, nothing. Forget I mentioned it."

"Do you mean to distill the learnings from your talking, listening, and writing therapies?" Bud smiled as he spoke, which made KSue giggle.

"Oh, you know about all that? I thought it was secret. But…well, if you know then it's alright, I guess. Yes – that tea. Will I be able to drink that? It really does help me sleep. I didn't have any the night I slept beside Linda, and I didn't have any last night, of course. I quite miss it. It's wonderfully relaxing. Would I be able to drink that?"

Bud and I exchanged a glance, and we both shrugged. "How's it served?" I asked.

"The person – usually it's Don – brings a big container on a little trolley and he ladles it into your own cup. It saves waste."

Bud said, "In that case, I'd say yes, drink it, because it's coming from a source used by many, so it's likely to be safe. But don't consume anything that's given to just you, or that has been prepared solely for you. The refectory stuff, and the tea you describe, should be safe enough."

She brightened. "That's a good idea. I'm not a fussy eater, and everything at the refectory is vegetarian in any case, because so many people said on their commitment paperwork that they preferred to not eat animals – so bring whatever looks tasty. The food at the hospital was just packets in vending machines, and it tasted of dust."

"What's 'commitment paperwork'?" I had to ask.

KSue seemed surprised that I didn't know, "It's the paperwork you fill out when you make your commitment to Faceting. Everyone does it. It takes a long time to complete – pages and pages of it. But it's quite enjoyable, in a way. It made me think, to be honest – but I had to keep looking things up all the time, because I don't have a good memory for all that stuff, so maybe I took longer than some do."

"What sort of stuff do you have to look up?" I was intrigued.

"All the usual – the numbers the government gives you, all your family's names, going back aways, schools, places you've lived, that kinda stuff. You know, ordinary. Then there's all the medical side – allergies and what-not – and then all the funny questions that didn't make much sense to me."

"Like what?" Bud was now interested, too.

"Oh…I don't remember. Things like do I enjoy parties, or my own company. I remember that – because I like both. Weird questions, and they went on and on forever. But they said to do them fast, so I did my best. Like that. Oh – there you go – that's a new thing, too. We never did anything like that paperwork in the old days, you just said you liked the idea of Faceting and did it."

Interesting.

I checked my watch. "We'll be back with something for you to eat as soon as we can, but try to get your head down for a couple of hours first, okay?"

"Thank you. This has all been very stressful." KSue smiled weakly.

"I'm sure it has been," cooed Bud. "You stay there, we'll see ourselves out – or do you want to lock the door?"

"There's no lock, so just close it behind you. See you later, and thank you. Facet and Face It."

Outside in the heat again I said to Bud, "She might quote the mantra, but she doesn't want to face the truth, does she?"

He shook his head. "Do you think anyone will?"

"I hope so."

Faultlessly Flawed

I was getting tired of the sun. It makes you feel invigorated for a while, then it becomes a tyrant: sunglasses on, sunglasses off; gloop your face – so sunglasses slide down your face; sweat a lot, so you have to shower and wash your hair again…and so on, and so on. Bud was glowing with sweat, I was flapping my multicolored overthingy around to try to make a breeze, but nothing helped. I couldn't imagine what it would feel like to be working in the gardens in the summer; at that precise moment, meditative swimming seemed like a very good idea – even without a swimming costume.

Pulling Bud into the shadiest corner I could find, I whispered, "You need to get onto your people and tell them about the drug angle. Maybe we should have seen that coming, but I didn't. And as for the marijuana thing? No wonder everyone's so laid-back all the time – they're probably half-stoned. I understand that psychotropics have proved useful in pushing the boundaries of perception, and it's popular with those for whom seeking an understanding of themselves is a priority. But a large and increasing quantity of marijuana?"

Bud shook his head. "I know we agree that a bit of self-analysis is a good idea, but I've got to say I find this whole thing to be…totally self-indulgent. Can't these people just get out there and help those less fortunate than themselves to find out how that feels, instead of trying to find themselves by getting high on psychotropics?"

I shrugged. "To be fair, that's what Elizabeth and Norman McGlynn – or whatever their real names are – have been doing, with regard to developing adult literacy skills. But – talking about them – what do you think about what KSue told us? It sounds as though they forced her to return here against her will. Why?"

Bud looked perplexed. "Order from on high? Which means Zara. Do we think KSue knows something she isn't even aware of?"

I chuckled. "I think that might well be the case, but – as we've just seen – trying to get anything useful out of her is more difficult than getting beer from a stone."

"Shouldn't that be 'blood'?"

"Not when you fancy the idea of a cold beer as much as I do at this moment."

Bud tutted. "The fact that KSue was offered a variety of ways to kill herself concerns me most at this point." The skin around his eyes crinkled as he pondered this thought. "I wish she could have been more specific in her description of who did that; I guess we could ask a few questions around the place, trying to establish which newbies are the offspring of Silicon Valley parents."

"If that's what they really are. That might be an 'impression' KSue has, which isn't based in reality – or it could apply to other gray-outfitted novices who aren't even the ones who spoke to her. I really think we have to treat her as an unreliable source of precise information, even if we accept the generalities of what she's told us."

Bud nodded. "Right – what's next? How about I head over to see if I can use the internet at the communications hub to try to gather some more information about the folks here – there might be some news about the so-called McGlynns, for example. And I want to pass on the word about the drugs doing the rounds here, too; I could ask them to dig deeper into any possible drug connections Oscar might have had. While you…what?"

"I think we need to find out more about how Oscar died. Look, if we're facing an uphill battle regarding proof about how Zara's doing what she's doing, maybe if we focus on what might be a more 'traditional' murder, we'll have more luck."

Bud's thoughtful response was: "Given everything we're learning, I'm much more inclined to think Oscar's death was not as the result of an accidental fall. What's your plan?"

"If rigor had set in by the time Ambroise found him, that puts the likely time of death during the night, when we were still in Phoenix. I'd like to find out more about what was going on here that evening – because we know basically nothing about it, so far. I think I've become a bit too transfixed with the Zara thing, but – having now taken steps on that front – I think it's time to put a bit more effort into Oscar and his death. Maybe that will help."

Bud kissed my cheek with an "Eww", as he managed to catch a little rivulet of sweat.

"Love you, too," I called at his receding back. Then I squared my shoulders, and headed off to the plaza – to see what I could see.

Unfortunately, the place was deserted. I weighed my options: head to where I thought people would be – in other words, the areas where they'd all be working in the sun – or try Serendipity's restaurant, hoping she might be there. I decided that a downhill walk, followed by at least the opportunity for a cool drink, was my preferred alternative, so headed off, having an internal conversation with myself about how our hostess factored into everything I'd learned.

Having grown up with parents embroiled in the world of sex, drugs, and rock and roll, Serendipity Soul might well take absolutely no notice of people around her indulging in any number of consciousness-altering substances. Yes, she was generally level-headed, but clearly a true devotee of the Faceting movement, and even seemed to be on board with all the more novel elements of it. But…might she be the one Bud and I could bring around to our way of thinking about Zara? Might she see the sense of our explanations for what Zara was up to? I paused as I gave the matter some thought, and was busy analyzing the "how" of it all, when a figure ran up the hill toward me, stirring up masses of dust. All I could tell was that it was a novice, but they had their head down, and the top of it gave me no more clues that that, because – regardless of gender – they all seemed to have closely shorn hair. The novice in question continued running past me at an admirable pace, with the canvas bag they had on each shoulder bouncing about.

The only thing I was certain of was that it wasn't Rusty, or Don – because I'd have recognized both of them – and they were well past me before I had a chance to ask what they were up to, so all I could do was quicken my own pace, and hope there wasn't a fresh disaster waiting to greet me at Serendipity's.

When I got there, everything looked normal: no cars parked anywhere; no strange noises; nothing out of the ordinary at all. I peered into the restaurant – empty, and not a hint of any foody aromas. Odd…or maybe not; there was a distinct possibility that Serendipity wouldn't be up to cooking, given her injury the previous evening. I shouted, but there was no answer – so I stuck my head into the kitchen. It was also deserted.

I let the door swing closed behind me and scanned the place. Clearly someone – or maybe even several someones – had cleaned the place since Bud and I had left it the night before. Every surface was gleaming, and there was a fresh smell in the air that wasn't disinfectant, but hinted at cleanliness. No food was waiting to be prepped, every knife and other implement was in its assigned spot. It didn't look as though there were any plans afoot for this kitchen to produce a meal anytime soon.

Though Jenn hadn't been specific about when the food

writers and local dignitaries were due to be hosted, I couldn't help but feel that none of this was a good sign.

I heard what sounded like a muffled thump, and…was that a voice? I looked around. Nothing. No one. There it was again. I tried to work out where it was coming from, but it didn't happen often enough for me to make progress quickly. I gradually realized it was in the vicinity of one particular corner – the corner with the giant door to what I'd assumed, when I'd first seen it, was a freezer room. I hauled on the substantial handle, and the door pulled open. To my horror, Serendipity slumped out on her side, her hands and feet tied, and looped together in front of her; her face was pale, there was blood on her shirt.

"Help me," she croaked.

I grabbed a pair of scissors and cut the plastic tie holding her wrists, which released the one attaching her hands to her feet, then I cut off the ties on her ankles; there were two of them, so someone had been taking no chances. She immediately put one hand to her bloody side and groaned. She looked up at me. "Cait? Oh, thank you. Thank you. Can you help me up?"

I did my best, as did she. There were no seats in the kitchen, but I wanted her to move about a bit in any case to get her circulation going. I helped her out to the deck, where she eventually collapsed onto a chair in the shade, rubbing her wrists, and her eyes. I peppered her with questions about how she felt, and so on, trying to work out if she was hypothermic.

"Where do you keep your kitchen thermometers?" I asked, hoping she had something I could use.

"Above the biggest sink, in a cupboard. Three digitals."

I brought one of the thermometers to her. "You know how to work this pad thingy, so stick it into your mouth to take your temperature – okay?"

She did. We waited. Eventually she said, "It's ninety-four. Is that bad? I feel a bit cold, still."

"Around ninety-seven point five to ninety-nine is normal, so you're definitely cold, but ninety-four means you only have mild hypothermia. We can deal with that here. I'm going to bring you some water from the tap, and a banana – neither of which can hurt, and your body needs fluids and fuel, so you can get those down while I rustle up a cup of tea, with three sugars," I said. "Don't worry, I'll work out how to do it all – just let the warmth of the air bring your temperature up slowly – stay here, out of the sun, and come back inside if you begin to feel too hot, or too cold, okay? Are any of your clothes wet?"

Serendipity felt herself all over. "I don't think so."

"Good. Stay here."

She nodded, and I did what I'd said I would.

Ten minutes later she was hugging a mug of something that was similar to tea, with honey in it rather than sugar, but at least it was hot, and sweet, and that was all that mattered.

"How long were you locked in there?" I asked.

"What time is it?" Her voice was weak, but at least she wasn't slurring her words – and she'd asked a sensible question, so it seemed she wasn't confused.

I checked. "Eleven."

"I finished clean-up around nine, then I was doing some menu planning. I pulled out some supplies that had been requested by the refectory and bagged those up…I guess I must have gone in to get the frozen pork around ten-thirty, or so. So not long, really – but it felt like an age."

"Do you know who tied you up?"

Serendipity shook her head. "Everything went dark – like someone had shoved a bag over my head. I know I screamed – anyone would – then I turned, or at least tried to…then someone grabbed both my arms – which really hurt because of the stitches – and then they zip-tied my hands. I could hear the zipping sound, and I knew what they'd done. Next thing I knew I was on the floor, on my back, and they were tying my ankles, then they sort of hog-tied me and rolled me over so I was facing the back of the freezer…then the hood thing had gone, and the door slammed shut. I wriggled as much as I could, but my side was so sore…and I couldn't get up to reach the handle inside the door to get out. It was so hard to bang to door, and it hurt to shout…but that was all I could do."

I gently lifted Serendipity's arm. "I think you might have torn some stitches. If Dr. Nderu's still here we should get him to take a look at that again before he leaves."

"He said he'd leave after lunch; Elizabeth and Norman are going to drive him to Phoenix this afternoon. They volunteered, because his wife took his vehicle last night, to take their friends home."

I checked my watch. "Once I feel I can leave you alone for a while, I'll go up to the refectory and find him there – get him to come here before he leaves. You need to keep moving about – which I'll help you with in a moment, when you've finished that drink – but I'm not convinced that walking all the way back up to your dig is a good idea. However, I need to be certain you're okay to leave. Oh heck, living without a cellphone is a right pain; if I could just get hold of Bud – or any number of other people – instead of having to go to find them, it would all be so much quicker. If my time here's taught me anything it's how very much easier cellphones can make life."

"True," said Serendipity over her tea. "How do you know so much about hypothermia, by the way? I mean, I'm glad you do – but why do you? We didn't cover it in any real detail in my first-aid sessions."

"I was a Brownie, then a Girl Guide, and finally a Ranger Guide – when I reached those dizzying heights I belonged to a search and rescue team. We used to train in the Brecon Beacons – where hypothermia is a very real danger. I learned a lot."

Serendipity's color was returning, which was a good sign. "Other than about hypothermia?"

"Well…there were scouts on the team, too," I replied with a little twinkle, "and the bloke who trained us taught us all about surviving in the wild for days with no more than a knife, and an OXO cube. Oh, and he showed us how to eat a worm sandwich…which was as disgusting as it sounds."

My patient managed a laugh. "But where would you get the bread?"

"Exactly my point."

I could tell that Serendipity was feeling more like herself, and that the trauma of having been attacked, as well as the effects of being in the freezer, were starting to wane a little.

"You've no idea who did this to you?" I pressed. She shook her head. "And do you have any idea why someone would? Did they say anything – any threats, or even questions?"

She shook her head again. "Not a word. But I can tell you they were strong, and they had big hands – so a man, I reckon. Or maybe even two. You see, I can't understand how they managed to do what they did, as quickly as they did it. I didn't want to be tied up, but the way they moved me around it was almost as though I was helping them. It was weird."

"As I was walking to the restaurant, a novice ran past me, carrying two canvas bags. I don't think he – or she – could have had anything to do with this, because of the timing, but do you know what that was all about?"

"The supplies for the refectory, I guess. I grow herbs out on the deck." She moved as though to wave an arm, but grimaced. "I cut whatever's ready, that I don't need here, and they collect them every day. If someone was doing that when you say, it was probably Hans; he's Swiss, which makes it all the more ironic that he's always – and I mean *always* – late for everything. If he's on kitchen duty at the refectory today, lunch will, inevitably, be late."

"So when would someone usually come to collect those herbs? Is there a set time?"

"Around the time I was slung into the freezer, or within a few minutes of that."

"Would someone other than Hans be here earlier, and might they therefore not be in such a rush to get out?"

Serendipity looked to be deep in thought. "Yes," she said quietly. "On a normal day, the person would be here from the refectory by half-ten at the latest, and they always stop for a chat. It's a thing. There's a person who does the cooking, and a runner – who, quite literally, does all the running about, gathering the ingredients for the day's meal. The runners are always novices, and I like to get to know them. It's my routine."

"And everyone would know that?"

Serendipity nodded. "I think it's important that I connect with the novices, and I believe that's well known. Some of them are very young – and, yes, I know I'm not that old myself –" she managed a smile – "but even though I have a few years to go before I hit forty, my early twenties seem like a lifetime ago – and that's all that some of these people are. Yet still I learn from them – some of them have an enviable outlook and attitude toward life – they're really living on their own terms…though it has to be said that quite a lot of them – like me – are relying upon their parents to keep that lifestyle funded." Serendipity sighed. "This attack's really rattled me, Cait – I don't mind admitting it. I mean who would want to hurt me like that? And why? It has to be someone from outside – someone who's come here hoping to get their hands on something valuable. It couldn't have been a Facetor who did this. That's impossible."

I didn't comment about that assertion, instead replying, "Right, let's get you moving about – I want to see how steady you are on your feet before I leave you alone. Off you go, once around the deck, please."

Serendipity stood and walked. She seemed to be fine – no thanks to whomever had attacked her.

"That looks good, but I wonder if you'd also take a walk around the kitchen and the restaurant with me – so you can tell me if anything's been disturbed, or if there's anything missing."

"You also think someone did this because they wanted to rob the place? An outsider coming here to take…what?" She sounded surprised. "That's what's confusing me, you see. There's nothing worth taking. It's all just kitchen equipment, and décor – there's not a thing here with any real value."

"How about we just take a look?"

"Okay."

As we made our way around the dining area I asked, "What's the most expensive single item in the whole place?"

"The freezer they locked me inside."

Ah. "No rare pieces of artwork missing? No ingredients worth thousands of dollars?"

Serendipity looked at me as though I was losing my mind. "Nothing. Not one thing. This?" She gazed around. "This all arrived in two trucks, delivered from the decorator who'd been putting it together in her warehouse over a few months. There are older pieces here, and even a few honest-to-goodness antiques, but nothing to write home about. And all the paintings are by local artists – see? They all have price tags on them, because they're for sale. And none of them is worth much at all. Not even what most of the price tags say, if you ask me – but art is subjective, I know, and if folks are prepared to pay over the odds for a piece, then that's up to them."

I scanned the pieces she was referring to and had to agree: it looked as though most of the artists were happy amateurs rather than gifted professionals, and the majority of them had decided to portray the local landscape in their own way – which ranged from hyper-realistic to something closer to a drug-induced nightmare. "That one of a rattler's rather good," I said.

"That's by Norman. He'd love to hear you say that, because Elizabeth told him it was woefully out of proportion when we hung it."

"Unless she's cooing about how much she loves him, she's constantly putting him down, isn't she?" It was out of my mouth before I could stop it.

Serendipity gave me a suspicious look. "That's quite a personal thing to say."

I shrugged. "Sorry – but you know me, I do tend to say what I think." As the words left my lips, I realized Serendipity had no true idea about who I was, or what I was really like; we hardly knew each other, in the real sense.

"I guess she can be a bit sharp," was her telling reply.

"Where's that stack of canvas bags, with the Faceting logo on them? They were hanging there, inside the vestibule." I waved at an empty hook.

Serendipity looked around. "No idea. They're just bags – I'll replace them."

"Anything else gone?" I pressed.

Flopping on a nearby chair, Serendipity answered weakly, "I didn't even notice they'd gone – so I guess I can't be sure, but I don't think so. But they're just gone gone…why on earth would anyone tie me up in a freezer to take a pile of canvas bags?"

I agreed it made no sense, then was just about to reconsider leaving, when Ambroise ambled in, smiling. As soon as he saw Serendipity's face, his expression changed.

"Serendipity, are you okay?" He looked panicked.

"She seems fine, now, thanks, Ambroise," I replied. "Don't you, Serendipity?"

Serendipity nodded.

Ambroise seemed to calm down immediately, and I saw my chance to escape.

"Right, I can leave you in Ambroise's capable hands, and you can tell him all about what's happened. I'll go to see if I can track down Dr. Nderu. Stay here until he arrives to check you out – those stitches might need attending to."

I grabbed a few bottles of what I recognized as the magical berry juice from the cooler, and, when I left Serendipity, I felt confident she'd be well looked after by her friend, Ambroise.

Unoriginal Originals

Just as I entered the plaza, I spotted Dr. Nderu heading toward me, accompanied by Norman. They had their heads together and both looked quite earnest. I explained the situation and they high-tailed it off to the restaurant, which was just what I'd hoped would happen. I checked in at our dig, but Bud wasn't there, so decided I'd try to find Oscar's dig, hoping it wouldn't be locked.

But how to work out which was his? They all looked identical. I knew where his mother and sister resided, and they were within a few doors of each other, so I headed in that general direction, trying to spot a dig that looked Oscar-y, which was quite a feat, considering the man had been dead before I'd even arrived at the place.

A couple of novices came running from the direction of the refectory, seemingly buffing up the "playing" Facet, by kicking a soccer ball between them.

"Which one was Oscar's?" I called. "Serendipity asked me to drop this off." I waggled the first thing that came out of my handbag, which happened to be my cellphone.

The pair looked puzzled, yet still playful, and pointed toward one of the anonymous dwellings. "The one with no flowers," was shouted at me, then they ran off, chasing their ball.

They were right – only one of the houses in that row had no pots of flowers outside it, so I tried the door. It wasn't locked – indeed, upon checking, I could see it had no locking mechanism; it seemed that only the guest houses locked.

I stepped inside and allowed my eyes to adjust to the dimness. The place smelled and felt completely desolate, so I also allowed myself a moment to adjust to the mood, too, but scanned the room as I stood inside the door, not wanting to waste any time. Like his mother's, Oscar's dig was much more personalized than KSue's had been – which I assumed was because it truly was his home, as opposed to rented, temporary accommodation. Lacking the flamboyance of his mother's decorative touch, the bare bones of the structure were more obvious, and I could see that almost every item that wasn't functional was something taken from nature: behind the door he'd nailed up a couple of dead cholla branches to serve as a rack for jackets; on his bedside table he'd placed a fossilized ammonite; a shelf displayed several examples of different types of rocks – including glittering pyrites, and gleaming hematite, and there was a collection of beautiful stones of varying hues in what I recognized as the sort of pan that's used to find gold in riverbeds.

I opened the small closet: one gray outfit. Had he, the son of the founders, chosen to wear gray as a sign of solidarity with those at the beginning of their journey in the movement? Or because he had, in fact, still been a novice?

I pulled opened a few drawers, and finally found what I'd hoped I would: his phone. I had no idea if he'd had it with him when he'd died, but suspected he had – because I was still thinking he might have gone to Lump Hill to try to phone someone…though why he wouldn't have gone to the communications hub to use the phone there was a puzzle; surely Jenn would be as welcoming to Oscar as she had been to Bud and me? KSue had said they'd been close, after all.

I turned on his phone, and it came to life, which was good. I was keeping all my fingers mentally crossed that I could work out his password. It was six numbers, and I tried 000000, which worked; it's amazing how many people use that code – so lazy, and guessable. Thank goodness.

I opened up his email. Nothing. Contacts? Empty. The same thing for texts – nothing. I was starting to think his phone had been wiped clean – which annoyed, and intrigued, me.

Next, I checked his photo gallery. Nothing. That was a terrible disappointment. In a last-ditch attempt to find something, I checked the trash for the phone itself, rather than the communications applications, and there they were – all his photos. Deleted, but not double-deleted. I was thrilled. I sat on the edge of his bed to scroll.

The most recent shots had been captured the day before his mother's death – nothing since, though just before that were a few shots of what was clearly another phone, showing some of its contacts pages. Most entries were just first names and what looked like cellphone numbers, though there were a couple with email addresses, too. Only two had physical street addresses listed, both in Saint-Laurent-sur-Mer, which is a place few people have heard of because the area's better known to most as the location of "Omaha Beach". I wondered if Oscar had an interest in World War Two; his father would have been too young to have been involved. Maybe there was some other reason for him having taken a photograph of these particular pages of someone else's contacts. *Odd.*

I pondered that as I scrolled all the way back to the earliest pictures, which mainly featured people I'd never seen before, in places I couldn't identify – but something told me they were significant, so I kept looking. In many the setting was rugged, there were mountains, evergreens, and bald eagles. Lots of shots were of cliffs, rivers, and rock faces, some were definitely taken in a town or towns – though on a small scale, and with the sort of architecture you'd see in an old western. In one, I spotted a building behind the people posing: white wooden siding, with something painted on the wall. I enlarged the photo to its fullest extent, but all that had been captured in the shot was "ED", above "ON", above "OON", painted in red and black on the white wall. I had no idea what it was a part of, but filed it away mentally for future reference. Before I scrolled on, I spotted an almost-familiar face. Was that Ambroise? A slimmer version, with very short hair, but it could have been him. The next shot showed the same person – and another bloke who looked quite similar, who I was pretty sure was Oscar, though I'd only seen a few photos of him on KSue's phone – and they'd lacked good resolution. The two were with a small group outside a yellow building with "Claim 33" painted on the front; almost everyone was wearing a plaid shirt of some sort, and there was a pile of backpacks on the edge of the shot.

I continued scrolling, moving forward in time. There were more faces I didn't know at all, a lot of photos of Oscar's mother and sister, and I finally got to see a picture of his father, Demetrius Karaplis. It was a photo of a photo that had been displayed in a plain wooden frame; it showed Oscar as a small boy, gazing up at his father in awe. Demetrius was a good-looking man with a fine head of dark hair, startling blue eyes, and a distant gaze. I took my own snap of it, so I could show Bud.

Then there was another picture of a framed photo of someone I could now more happily identify as Ambroise; yes, if this was him, the earlier shots had also been of him. In this one he was a very young man – maybe in his early twenties – with much longer hair than he now had, or had been sporting in the intervening pictures. In this one he was carrying a backpack, and standing beside some sort of monument; I stretched the photo as far as I could, but the resolution was dreadful. Try as I might, I couldn't decipher the inscriptions on the monument, which was about as tall as Ambroise, with some sort of carved pot or vase on top of it, with a draped piece of cloth carved into the stone. A memorial of some sort? I zoomed in and out, and it looked to me as though I was seeing a list of names. But the characters didn't look right. Cyrillic? No – Greek. It was some sort of Greek war memorial, of that I was sure – though I couldn't make out where it was. The area was anonymous – certainly not a major city, so probably a small village, with mountains in the background. *Odd.*

Among Oscar's more contemporary shots, the most noticeable thing was that there were a great number of photos of the desert: up close, wide-shot landscapes, hillsides, rugged rock faces, rocks lying on the ground, some fossils in situ, even the ammonite that now sat on his table was there. There were also a lot of holiday snaps – certainly some of them taken in Puerto Peñasco when Oscar was there with Zara, Serendipity, and Ambroise, and a fair number of just Serendipity and Ambroise – plus quite a lot of selfies with Ambroise. The more photos I saw of Oscar, the more certain I was that'd he'd been in many of those early shots I'd seen. I scrolled back to be sure: yes, there he was, always toward the back of whatever group it was, almost hidden. What had those groups of people had in common with each other? Where had they been at the time…and why?

Overall, returning to the more recent holiday snaps, it seemed Oscar enjoyed the odd beer or ten, and appeared pretty well-oiled in a number of the shots, but the party photos, views of the beach, bars, and sunsets over the sea weren't as puzzling as the hundreds he'd taken of the desert. It seemed that what Don had told me about Oscar was true – he really did spend a great deal of time out there, combing the place for geological samples, and fossils, some of which he'd brought into his home.

I took a few more snaps of his photos, for Bud's sake, so we could discuss them, then turned off the phone, and put it back where I'd found it. I was puzzling over who had cleared all the emails and texts from the phone, when I heard a noise outside.

I wondered if someone else was sneaking into Oscar's place, but the noise passed, and I put it down to Facetors leaving the refectory and making their way back to their digs for – what? Did they have a sort of siesta time, during the hottest part of the day, or was it still to early in the year for the temperatures to require that? I realized I'd already been at the Desert Gem for a few days, but still didn't have a clear idea of how it operated.

I scoured the bathroom for anything out of the ordinary – anything that might give me more of an idea of who Oscar had been, or what might have got him killed – if he had been – but I didn't find anything remarkable. His home suggested he'd been a man of relatively simple needs, with an interest in desert geology, and having a good time. I read the titles of the few books on his bookshelves – and realized a couple of them were about Faceting, but weren't the ones listed in the volume in our room – so, presumably, titles only available to those who were at a higher level in the organization. I picked them up, and sat down to read. One was a level four book, another was a level eight. I worked my way up; half an hour later, I was none the wiser – it was all twaddle. I weighed the idea of taking them with me to show Bud, but decided against it, however, I did take photos of a few of the pages so he could read them for himself; I knew it would be interesting to get his take on them.

I was just about to leave, when the door opened. I jumped up, and dropped the books.

"I thought it would be you. My brother's home gave off an unusual vibration." It was Zara.

I didn't say anything, there was no point; my expression was already blurting out my guilt.

Zara closed the door and moved into the room as though she were on wheels beneath her flowing dress. It was eerie – and I had no idea how she did it.

"Don't feel guilty, I believe you are genuinely concerned about my brother's passing, and you have quite a reputation as an investigator, so I expect that's what you're doing."

I nodded.

"I, too, am worried that he passed alone in the desert, though maybe you have already worked out, from his home, that he loved the desert with a passion. His passing was as the result of an accident, and sometimes those things happen – though I believe it was his time to pass, and that's why he fell."

"But…"

Zara raised a hand, and I shut up; I couldn't help myself, which made me cross, and curious about the power she seemed to have over even me. "No, don't say it. It was not a suspicious death. He was greatly upset by our mother's passing, and his beliefs failed him, when they should have comforted him. This is my only regret."

My mind was whirring – was Zara going to have an entire conversation without my saying a word?

She carried on speaking, her voice mellifluous, calming, oozing confidence. "You want to understand more about him as a person, to try to work out who might have wanted him to die, which is understandable, of course," she continued, "but you won't be able to work that out, because no one wanted him to. So you might as well stop wasting your time." She sounded as though she felt terribly sorry for me, which was infuriating. "You and your husband will leave here soon – and I can tell you're both anxious to get back to the outside world – you both seem incapable of leaving it alone while you're here. Of course we're happy for you to use our communications hub, but surely your university can get along without you for a while." Now she was sounding a little patronizing. "Or does Professor Frank McGregor work you that hard, even when you're still on a sabbatical? I didn't realize doing research meant you had to keep in touch with the office so frequently when you're not teaching. But there, what would I know about it? The academic life's not for me – I prefer the application of theory in the real world." She smiled. Like a shark.

I was using all my willpower to consider my words carefully; these days I count my teeth with my tongue when I'm trying to hold back, which sometimes helps slow me down a little. Zara had an air about her that made me want to slap her down – not physically, but with words – however, I didn't want to get into a slanging match. Indeed, watching her performance was fascinating, and I did my best to work out how to make the most of this opportunity.

"It's rather a flattering photo of Frank McGregor on the University of Vancouver's website, I've always thought." *Stick that in your pipe and smoke it.*

"Almost as flattering as the one of you. Was it taken some years ago?" *Touché – and ouch.*

I counted my teeth. Again. "You've created an impressive empire, using your considerable business acumen," I said, hoping flattery might get me somewhere.

Zara beamed with an almost-genuine bonhomie. "Ah yes, KSue has told you about my MBA, of course. She attended my graduation for my first and second degrees, with my parents. They were very close. She was always a big part of my life, and I of hers; her pride in my achievements is a joy. I shall be sorry to see her leave, though I understand her son will be collecting her tomorrow. How was she when you and Bud saw her? Well, I hope. I should drop in to see her myself, to say my farewells – or maybe she wouldn't let me in? You both seem to be very protective of her. I understand from Norman and Elizabeth that she was keen to return to collect her possessions, so we can have use of her dig. KSue is always so thoughtful of others."

"She'll be sorry to leave, despite the fact she's returning to her family," I replied, aiming to take the conversation in a slightly different direction. "You'll be sorry to see her go, too, I'd have thought, with her having been such a large part of your life. With the rest of your family now gone, she must be a wonderful reminder of happier times."

Zara almost sneered; I was thrilled, because I felt I was getting somewhere. "I don't need reminders, I have my memories," she said unctuously.

"She spoke of you as a child, always being around, happy to share everything with your parents…enjoying your family life. She said she always knew you had the potential to achieve great things, and is proud that you have."

Zara's eyes widened. "She said that? Maybe you haven't realized it, but KSue's not really that bright. A very average woman. For her to believe she spotted my potential is a little ridiculous, but typical."

At last, an insult – I knew I was getting somewhere, and decided to press my advantage. "She spoke of your sixth birthday, said you had the best time with some sort of fabulous gift given to you." I was vamping, but needed to confirm a suspicion that was wriggling in my head. I hoped she'd bite.

Zara's eyes looked through, and beyond, me. "My sixth birthday was not unusual."

"KSue said you looked so pretty, in a blue dress, with a pink bow in your hair. Kept saying what a special day it was."

Zara shook her head. "I wore a lemon dress, two sizes too big for me, and my hair was too short for a bow – it was cut like a boy's, at the time. I wore red pumps. Patent leather. They were quite special – Mom found them at a thrift store. My birthday cake was a plate of six cupcakes with lemon toppings, each with one candle. Dad helped me blow them out."

"But it clouded over and threatened to rain."

"It was a hot day, too hot to be outside, so we sat indoors."

"KSue said your mother and father had a row that day – was that why it was special?"

"Mom and Dad didn't row that day. They'd spent time decorating our kitchen with banners they'd cut from paper they'd also found at the thrift store, and we had balloons – six of them, all yellow, like my dress. It wasn't a bad day."

"No cross words?"

"Dad had a little difficulty lighting the candles, but there were no cross words at all." She sounded genuinely puzzled.

"KSue mentioned she wore a special outfit herself that day. Was there maybe a color theme?"

Zara tutted. "No, I wore lemon, KSue wore a striped blue top with cargo pants, khaki – not so very special. Mom always wore turquoise, even then, and Dad was in his usual array of indigo everything. Normal."

"Ah well, it seems you don't need KSue here after all, to be able to relive family memories."

Zara's disdainful expression sharpened. "Yes, and at least I recollect them accurately, unlike KSue, who is clearly – judging by what she told you – a highly unreliable source of information."

"Do you really think she's going to die – sorry, pass on – soon, as your father has told you?" I did my best to make my intonation suggest I was asking a question in earnest.

I watched every micro-expression, every blink, every movement of the pulse in her neck – and nothing missed a beat. "I know we have to become accustomed to outsiders visiting our new home; some will come with open minds, but some will be closed to new ways of thinking, as you and your husband are. We have beliefs you do not share. Our beliefs embrace the fact that we spend some of our time on this earthly plane, then move to a mystical plane; even those who are not Facetors on this plane will journey there. We Facetors all expect to go there, of course, and we all hope we will know when we will pass from this plane to the next – because it's only natural to want to say a proper farewell to the earthly life one has lived. It is a blessing to be given that knowledge, not a curse. But, Cait, I do not think you will ever understand this – you do not possess the insight to do so. If you don't have faith, no amount of proof will convince you of these truths, whereas if you do have faith, you need no proof. My father's ability to speak through me is an amazing gift that's been granted to those who have faith – because they now also have proof – but even that's not enough for the non-believers, like you and your husband. For us, this is difficult, but something we will have to work on coming to terms with, because the only way we can grow in number, is by helping those who do not currently believe, to understand." She was sermonizing, talking to me almost as though I was some sort of pondlife.

Questions buzzed in my head like flies. "When you told your mother she was to pass soon, how did she take the news?" I decided to be direct.

Zara tossed her hair, resetting her expression to calm and confident. "As I knew she would – with grace."

"Then she killed herself, to make sure your words came true."

"My mother was ready to pass. If she chose to use an aid to help her passing, that was her decision."

"Datura isn't a painless poison."

A flash – definitely dismissing me. "Her decision. Her choice."

"Has grieving her and your brother, but maintaining your leadership role here, been difficult for you?"

A nostril flare – *good.* "We all have difficulties we must face and overcome. Facet and Face It, Cait – it's more than a mantra, it's a way of living. I'm sure if you delve deep enough, you'll realize that you do, in fact, understand: your parents' deaths must have been a terrible shock for you, especially coming so soon after you'd run away to Canada, following your ex-boyfriend's death. And there have been so many more deaths you've been involved with in some way, since then, haven't there? Those people are all over there, on the other plane, with my father; maybe they'll tell him more about you, if he asks. Then he can tell me. My father sees and knows everything, Cait – remember that."

I was livid. "As you say, we all have difficulties we must face. I don't believe communication from the dead is something I shall have to grapple with."

Zara was a little taller than me, and her gaze bored into my forehead. "We shall see," she said, then turned toward the door. "Let us alone to live our Faceting life in peace, Cait Morgan. That will be better for everyone."

"Is that a threat?"

She looked over her shoulder. "Call it a prediction, if you will. My father was born not far from Delphi, which – as I am sure even you know – is one of the most important mystical places in this world, and has been for thousands of years. It gives him powers it is difficult for even me to understand."

I screwed my fingernails into my palms until she'd closed the door, then had a really good, long talk with myself after she'd gone – because I didn't dare allow myself to be seen in public when I was that angry.

I told myself that at least I knew one thing about her that was critically important: her sixth birthday had been perfectly normal, in every detail.

Even so, I was still fuming when I stomped back to our dig, where I found Bud snoozing on the sofa. I slammed the door, and let out a stream of profanities. He woke up, and sat there open-mouthed.

"Is now a good time to tell you I took food to KSue?" he said when I'd stopped ranting.

"Sorry. Yes. I've had a bit of a morning of it, and I didn't get any real sleep, as you know. I'm sorry. And thank you." I hugged him. Hard.

"Right then, tell me all about it," he said, patting the cushion beside him, so I sat down, and I did.

Ups and Downs

By the time I'd finished telling him all that had happened to me that morning, and all I'd learned about Zara – as well as assuring him I'd done as much as I could for Serendipity along the way – I felt exhausted. As did Bud, by the looks of him. He'd scratched his head, paced, exclaimed, and pored over photographs on my phone that I stuck under his nose.

"Do you think Zara was really threatening you? With what? Voices from beyond?" Bud sounded both annoyed, and incredulous.

"It's all a power play," I said, dismissing her words for being as toothless as I knew they were, "but she's obviously been researching me – or us. She seems to have gathered a lot of information."

"As they say – knowledge is power."

"Pithy, and true. And I'd like some more power myself – so what knowledge have you gained since we parted?"

"Nothing more on the McGlynns or Ambroise: photos of them might help in that regard. Nothing on the Cayman Islands company either. But I did learn a lot from Jenn, who was enjoying a bit of a lull – though, to be honest, she seems to be set to run at full speed all the time, so downtime isn't something she truly grasps, I don't think. And I was rather pleased with myself for having taken your thumb drives with me, because, when she left me alone, I managed to download what I think might help me find out more about our nameless friends, and help you understand more about the whole Faceting organization."

He held up the thumb drives, looking triumphant.

"What did you get?"

"The members' commitment questionnaires KSue told us about? There are thousands of them on these three sticks – I could tell that much, but I haven't had a chance to open any of them – so why don't we look together?"

We did, and I knew we'd struck gold. The first breakthrough was that we now had photographs of Ambroise and both McGlynns for Bud to send to his contacts; the second was that it was clear every person who'd ever committed to becoming a Facetor had not only shared personal information about themselves, their families, and their extended families, but had also been profiled using a psychometric test, which evaluated their personality type.

"This is amazing, Bud. This is part of how Zara does it – understands how to speak to different groups and types of people in different ways. It's a break-down of how best to manipulate people – a blueprint for milking them. Look, all their finances are here – how much they earn, what they're worth, what their family is worth. It allows for targeting. Good grief – this is nuts."

"I thought we didn't use that term around here." Bud smiled. "I did the right thing, then?"

"As you said, knowledge is power, and this offers untold power. No wonder she's so smug – she's got an attack plan for everyone based upon the information they've given her. I've been annoyed with myself that I couldn't put my finger on how such a comparatively young woman could be so self-possessed. Now I know – she feels that way because she really does have something on everyone."

Bud shook his head. "But wouldn't she need someone with computer knowledge to be able to access all this data? I mean look at it – there's so much. From all around the world.

Thousands and thousands of forms, each containing a mass of data. I had no idea there were so many Facetors, and I mean…how would she even navigate it all? I know you've told me what you found at Oscar's dig, and it sounds very much as though he really was the dreamer KSue said he was, but do you think he could have been some sort of computer whizz, on the side?"

I didn't think so, and we talked about the possibility of there being someone else involved in the Faceting organization at a high enough level to be able to set up all the computing systems it would take to allow so much data to be trawled and put to use.

"KSue's donkey-like novices with family in Silicone Valley – do you think that might be a lead?" I could tell Bud was reaching – and so was I.

I gave the matter some thought. "Husband, tell me your impression of Jenn."

Bud looked surprised but responded thoughtfully. "To be honest, she doesn't seem to fit in here. She's the only person I've had a conversation with who hasn't almost immediately started going on about Demetrius's omniscience, and the role of multiple planes. She's…she's not exactly heartless, but certainly coolly task-focused. Efficient, rather than emotionally connected to Faceting, like everyone else we've met. She told me earlier that she'd always worked doing what she's doing here, so I believe she's a true professional – rather than someone who happened to be here and has taken on a particular project."

"Do you think she might be a person who would, let's say, be swayed by our theories?"

Bud ran his hand through his hair. "In my opinion…of all those we've met so far, I'd say yes. But, to be honest, I'd have said that about Serendipity, too – but she seems pretty stuck into the whole Faceting thing…deeper than I'd imagined."

"About Serendipity – we need to keep an eye on her. There's something in play there we don't yet understand. My instincts tell me it's connected to Oscar's death, rather than Linda's."

"But you've no idea what that might be?"

"I think it's got something to do with the missing canvas bags…" I mused.

"What canvas bags?"

"The pile that went missing from…oh, didn't I mention that?" Bud made his playfully-annoyed face at me. "Sorry – got a bit sidetracked with the whole Serendipity-locked-in-a-freezer thing. Yes – there was a stack of canvas bags with the Faceting logo on them at the restaurant, and they're missing."

"And you think these bags are connected to Oscar's death, in some way?" I nodded. Bud pulled a face suggesting he thought I was a bit batty. "And what else do you think it's connected to?"

I shook my head. "I need a nap." I could feel myself falling into a stupor as I sat there – which is quite unlike me.

Bud looked concerned. "What have you eaten today? You have eaten something since that breakfast, right?" I shook my head. "Oh, for goodness sake, Cait. What have you drunk? Any water?"

"I drank another one of those juice things." I could feel myself going.

"Right, into that bed now. Drink the water I'm about to bring you, then sleep. That's it, Wife – you need your rest."

"But there's so much to do…"

"Sleep. That's an order. You promised to obey me, in our wedding vows."

"Oh no I didn't…"

The next thing I knew it was a few hours later, and I could smell coffee. Until I opened my eyes I thought I was dreaming, but it was real enough, and I gulped it down, hot though it was. I felt as though I'd been put through a wringer, then hung out to dry in the sun for hours – my skin actually felt crispy.

"I knew you'd want coffee, but now you have to drink two glasses of water…and have a shower. You've been drained by that juice. Do you know what's in it?" Bud sounded cross.

I was confused. "You said berries. The label said berries. I thought it was berries. Why? What's in it?"

"I checked with Serendipity – yes, I've seen her, and she's fine, by the way, still pretty rattled, but fine – and I told her how you'd been up all night on that juice and she said she wasn't surprised; apparently it's full of guarana, which technically are berries, I guess. That juice has about six times the caffeine that's in coffee – which is why you didn't sleep, and why you just kept going all day, too. This coffee should give you a bit of a boost, without taking you back to the levels you've been at for so long."

I sat where I was and took my telling off; Bud was right, I should have known better than to pound something down without really knowing what was in it, though I did mention once or twice that he was the one who'd brought it back to the dig. It was ironic, really, because I usually avoid fruit, berries, and other healthy things, like the plague, and the one time I'd actually enjoyed the flavor of something that was seemingly good for me it turned out it was anything but. *Lesson learned.*

"So why does Serendipity even have it in her restaurant if it's so overstimulating?" I thought it a reasonable question.

Bud sighed, and sat beside me. "It's favored by the drivers who will be ferrying her guests back and forth. She also stores it at the restaurant then sends it over to the refectory where it's a very popular drink among those who do the more energetic tasks around the place, apparently. But she reckons a person should be limited to just one bottle per day. How many have you had, since last night?"

I felt guilty as I replied, "Three."

"Well, no more." Bud hugged me, then added, "Now hit the shower – we're due to meet Serendipity at the refectory for dinner – she's not up to working in the kitchen this evening; Dr. Nderu had to re-do a few of her stitches, and he's forbidden her to work at all. In fact, he's decided to stay on, so he's on hand if needed. She can tell you all about it herself, but she's still hoping that she'll be good enough to open up again tomorrow, if the doc gives her the all-clear."

I felt a bit wobbly when I stood up. "I'm sorry, Bud, I feel as though I've let the side down a bit. But you're right, I need to get myself cleaned up, and I should feel a lot fresher after a shower. By the way – how long before we have to get out of here?"

Bud checked his watch. "You've got thirty minutes, tops, so you'd better get going. Then we can get some food into you, too, and I'm sure that'll set you right."

Three quarters of an hour later we were seated at one of the long tables at the refectory with plates of vegetarian goulash in front of us – though, sadly, the only thing that could be said to be remotely goulash-y about the dish was the overwhelming aroma of paprika. But I knew I needed to eat, so wolfed it down while Bud just picked at his, peering about.

"I don't know what's happened to Serendipity," he said, "I hope she's okay."

We weren't particularly near any of the other diners, so I whispered, "Where was she, when you saw her earlier on? You haven't told me what you were up to while I was asleep yet."

Bud finished chewing. "She was on her way back to her dig. Norman was with her, and she was going to have a lie down after the doc had fixed her up. He'd given her some more of those painkillers. Maybe she fell asleep and no one woke her –

though I'd have thought Ambroise would have looked in on her, wouldn't you?"

"They're not a couple, Bud. Just friends." Though I share most things with Bud, I hadn't mentioned the thing about Ambroise swearing himself to celibacy, because I felt Serendipity had told me that in confidence, and it didn't really seem pertinent to our inquiries. "Maybe he was tied up doing something else?"

"But she was attacked, Cait, and literally tied up!" Bud was hissing. "What I can't get over is the way no one's running about trying to find out what happened to her...and it's yet another incident no one has called the cops about. That's not normal. I know we could have done more – or maybe not. By the time I saw her she was downplaying the whole thing. Kept saying it would all be fine...though she looked pinched, nervous...far from happy about it all. Tell me, how shaken was she when it happened?"

I took a moment to recall every detail of finding her, and being with her immediately afterwards. "Initially she was still in shock, and overwhelmed with relief at being found – and feeling the physical effects of hypothermia, of course. But, as we talked, I got the impression she was much calmer than one might imagine, despite saying she was shaken by it, her demeanor suggested she was coping quite well. Better than I would have been, in any case."

"Do you think the Faceting thing was helping her cope? You know, was she doing any 'buffing' while you two were together?"

I gave Bud's question some thought. "Hard to say – she's seemed a bit up and down since we got here, not calm like she was when we first knew her. But she's facing a great deal of responsibility here, and her stress levels might be through the roof because of that."

I was about to add another observation or two that I'd made, when Serendipity herself entered the refectory, and made a beeline for us. She was accompanied by Norman and Elizabeth, who were both wearing expressions of concern, and appeared to be making a distinct effort to not physically help Serendipity cross the room.

"You sit there, and we'll sort out some food for you," said Elizabeth solicitously.

"Yes, just wait, we'll bring everything you need," agreed Norman. "Leave it to us."

The pair headed for the serving area, and Serendipity slid onto the end of the bench, which was by far the easiest seat for her to take, given her injury.

"How are you feeling?" I was genuinely concerned for her; her face was drawn, her complexion had taken on a sallow hue, and her entire body was sagging just a little. She looked completely...defeated.

"I'm fine, thanks," she lied. "Just a bit tired, you know."

Bud leaned across. "Did you manage to sleep?"

Serendipity nodded, gently. "Yes, those pills are pretty strong. Knocked me out. Still a bit groggy, to be honest. And not much appetite – though I know I must eat – my body needs fuel, to heal."

"Quite right, too," said Elizabeth, as she placed a plate of goulash on the table, and Norman matched it with a tumbler of water, and another of milk. "Solids, and fluids – come on now, get it all down."

Elizabeth sounded as though she were talking to a pet, rather than a person.

"Don't rush it, though – take it easy," added Norman, sounding a little more sympathetic to Serendipity's condition.

"I had a nap, too – I drank too much of that purple juice stuff, and crashed and burned a bit," I admitted.

"Bud asked me about that," said Serendipity, eyeing her food with trepidation. "How much did you drink?"

"Three bottles."

"Good grief, that would keep me awake for a week," said Norman, tucking into his own food.

"You're familiar with it then?" I wondered why.

Elizabeth jumped in. "Our drivers use it…the restaurant drivers. Helps them keep sharp on the roads. It might not look as though there's a great deal of traffic out this way, but there are all sorts of creatures and other hazards that can catch out an inattentive driver, aren't there, Norman?" She was now speaking to her husband as though he were her child; she was starting to annoy me.

"Indeed there are, dear. Any number of hazards." Norman spoke through his food. "But they've all had good journeys so far."

"Why have they had any journeys at all?" I asked. "The restaurant hasn't opened yet – so who have they been driving?"

Elizabeth replied, "Norman thought it best that every driver had a few test journeys, always leaving here after dark – so they'd know the road for when they're carrying passengers. They were paid the going rate to do it, of course, and Serendipity's been most accommodating in serving them refreshments, even before the restaurant was fully equipped. Such a professional. It was a sound idea, and it's run smoothly, so far. My husband has recruited some excellent drivers."

"Thank you, dear. The fact we only wanted drivers of electric vehicles meant it took me a little longer than I'd hoped, and the ones based out of state took a little convincing, of course. I guess we'll need to keep recruiting over time, but I'm sure that will be easier, once the word gets around."

"I bet," said Bud. "Being paid to drive, getting a full charge for their vehicle, and a slap-up dinner for free? It's a good deal for the drivers. They come from out of state, too, you say? Wouldn't restaurant guests coming that far just plan to stay overnight in any case?"

"It's all about options, isn't it, Norman?" Serendipity spoke quietly.

Bud shrugged. "I guess." He sounded doubtful. "But you're right about one thing, Norman, night driving's no joke, though I expect the challenges are a bit different here than they are at home for us. We have pretty temperate weather, but snow and ice are a problem at certain times of the year – then there are the wild animals too, of course – and some of those are pretty big."

I suspected we were about to have a conversation about bears, but Serendipity interrupted with: "I think whoever put me in that meat locker today did take something. Other than those canvas bags."

We all gave her our attention. "What?" I asked.

Serendipity pushed her food around her plate. "We haven't had any paying customers yet, as you know, and we'll only be dealing in cash when we open – one of the downsides of not having any connectivity at the restaurant. Oddly enough, it's been something those who have booked already have commented upon – the novelty of using actual cash."

"And?" Bud leaned in.

"Well, because of all that I haven't kept much money in the till – you've all noticed it, right? It's that lovely old brass piece – beautiful, but not terribly secure – so I just keep enough in there to pay any suppliers I know are delivering that day, or to pay the drivers for their test runs, as Norman mentioned. But there was quite a lot of cash in the safe."

Bud and I chorused, "What safe?"

Serendipity addressed the tabletop. "The safe in the kitchen. Hidden inside one of the under-counter cabinets. It's empty."

"How much is missing?" Bud sounded grim.

Serendipity took a deep breath. "I'm not absolutely certain – but something over sixty-five thousand. To be honest, there's been a lot more in there at certain times during the past few weeks, but I think that's about how much was left."

"How'd they get into it?" Bud was on full alert.

Serendipity shook her head. "I don't know. It was open when I checked. It didn't look...broken."

"Sixty-five thousand dollars?" Bud spoke quietly.

"I can't be sure without Elizabeth going over the figures." Serendipity was almost whispering.

I looked at Elizabeth. "You keep Serendipity's books?"

"She's wonderful with numbers," said Norman, proudly.

"I keep my own records," replied Serendipity, "but I'm not up to the accounting and reporting, so Elizabeth does that. Or she will be, when we get going, won't you? All the systems and spreadsheets are ready to go."

Elizabeth nodded.

"She does all the accounting for the Faceting movement, overall," boasted Norman, "and she's agreed to do this as well. I couldn't be prouder, though we both know it might eat into the literacy effort, which is getting harder to sustain from out here anyhow. But there are other ways to give, and we're doing our part in that respect, I believe."

"You should definitely report the attack and the theft to the police," said Bud, clearly not about to allow himself to be sidetracked. "This is a crime – no question about it. A felony."

Serendipity pushed away her plate. "Would...the person who did it go to prison?" She sounded horrified.

Bud's tone was professional. "If I remember correctly, it could be three or four years, up to maybe twenty-five, I believe. But you should call the cops. If you're insured and intend to make a claim, you'll need a record of the police report in any case."

Serendipity stood, swaying a little. "No. No report. No claim. It's just money. I'll call Dad about it. He'll replace it. I don't want the movement to lose that much – Dad won't even notice."

I said, "That's a great deal of money, Serendipity…but the main thing is that you were attacked, quite ferociously, don't forget that. Whoever left you in that freezer could have killed you. This is serious – you need to deal with it through the proper channels. You could have died." I couldn't understand why I couldn't get through to her.

Serendipity raised her head. "No. No. I shouldn't have said anything. I'm going to bed. I need rest. Dr. Nderu said I need rest. Goodnight."

She tottered off; Elizabeth followed her, and tried to hug her, but was fobbed off. As Serendipity left, Dr. Nderu rose from his seat near the door and followed her out, but her departure went generally unnoticed otherwise – except at our table.

Elizabeth chatted to a few people on her way back to us, and by the time she returned, Bud, Norman, and I were experiencing something of an awkward silence.

"That's a great deal of money," muttered Bud. "Why is everyone so set against using law enforcement out here?"

Both Norman and Elizabeth shrugged, as though it were natural, or at least of no consequence. I was counting my teeth to force myself to not ask the pair why they were using false names, when Bud said, "There's a lot going on here that would interest the cops. Oscar's 'accidental' death, Linda's convenient passing, now theft with potentially deadly assault – and yet no one, not one person here, is interested in a formal investigation."

"Why would we need one, when we have you and Cait here?" Don had appeared from the kitchen, and was beside us. He spoke loudly enough that a few heads turned; his tone angry.

"What do you mean?" Elizabeth snapped.

Don continued, "I thought we were just having a friendly chat earlier on, Cait, but you were grilling me about Oscar and his background – that's right, isn't it? And Dru Ann told me that Bud was questioning her about our elders, who have passed. Wanted to know all about how they'd died. Isn't that right?" Gone was the chummy Don we'd chatted with earlier in the day – this version of the man wore a frown, and his voice carried an edge.

More heads had turned, and the murmur of general chatter that had prevailed throughout dinner stopped altogether. I could sense a shift in the atmosphere in the room, and it wasn't good.

Don realized he was the center of attention, and addressed everyone in the refectory. "These two are poking into our business, wanting to call the cops on us. He's a retired cop himself – and not just that, but a homicide detective, and then involved with some anti-drug squad. That's the kind of guy he is – probably more rotten than the people he helped lock away. And her? Cait Morgan isn't just a professor of criminal psychology, oh no, she's a busybody who leaves a trail of death and disaster in her wake wherever she goes. Keep an eye on these two until they leave…you have been warned." He glowed with anger as he spoke, then turned – his work done – and disappeared into the kitchen.

I noticed that both Elizabeth and Norman physically recoiled from Bud and me as Don was speaking, and they didn't make eye contact at all after he'd left. The rest of the diners stared at us – and the looks we were getting were far from friendly. Hissing and whispering followed as conversations started up, and I could only imagine the nature of those comments.

Norman and Elizabeth stood, picked up their dishes – and Serendipity's – and cleared them away. All we got were two curt "Goodnights" as they left us alone at our table.

Bud whispered, "There goes any chance of having more investigative chats, I believe, Wife."

I nodded. "I agree. No help from anyone – except maybe our hostess?"

Bud stood. "Come on, let's get back to our dig. This place doesn't feel…healthy any longer. We need to regroup."

Nothing, and Something

It was still quite early – the sun having only just gone down by the time we reached our dig, but I knew I needed a nap to allow me to be able to do what I needed to do while everyone slept that night. I hadn't shared my plan with Bud yet, and I wanted to explain my idea to him, but that needed to be done privately, and we hadn't had a lot of alone time.

But, before I explained what I had in mind, I wanted to hear what Bud had been up to while I'd been asleep, so we settled ourselves on the loungers on the patio, and I pulled a wrap around my arms.

"I see you're acclimatizing to the temperatures," he observed. "What felt delightfully warm a few evenings ago is just normal now, right? I can see why the fireplace might come in handy during winter nights."

We shared a chuckle, then he pulled out his pad, and began to read, putting flesh on the bones of his notes as he went.

"So I managed to have a good long chat with Dru Ann again – as Don just mentioned – and she did indeed tell me a lot more about the elders who had passed. It turns out that Ravi was a computer whizz; he came up through the ranks at the same time Bill Gates and that lot were out there creating what we now all take for granted. Dru Ann told me he was the one who set up all the computing systems the Faceting organization benefits from. 'Scalability' was his big thing, apparently, and while I'm no expert, I know enough to understand that means he developed systems that can start small but grow to accommodate large amounts of data. He also developed the Faceting app

Serendipity told us about, which isn't free by the way, and has to be used by all Facetors. That's where the note making and burning thingy is – and the app also connects Facetors around the world in various chatrooms and so forth. Basically, once you're in, you're connected to all the other Facetors – which is pretty ironic, considering how the big thing around here seems to be that 'disconnect to connect' mantra. Anyway, because this is the Shangri-La of Faceting, everything's a bit different here…more basic, but more real. The other three who 'all passed peacefully'? She had nothing more to share on how they might have all achieved such a peaceful passing, by the way – just an unquestioning acceptance that they all did – but she did tell me a lot about what they all did on this plane, and – like Ravi – they all had significant roles."

"Which were?"

"One had set up the online store; he had a background in retail, and was the person who set up all the deals with suppliers to gain the Faceting seal of approval, for which they pay a hefty fee, it seems. Another was the lead architect for this place; she worked with local authorities organizing permits and so forth, then hired and liaised with contractors. The third was the person who coordinated the production of all the literature – a publishing background helped with that."

"Good job, Husband. That's illuminating: all the creators of Faceting as it is today are now dead…with the exception of Elizabeth, who came up with the therapies they use. That's interesting – and significant, wouldn't you say?"

Bud nodded, looking grim. "They really did give their all for Faceting, didn't they?" I nodded. "Funny thing is – even though she was happy to tell me all this, that connection didn't form for Dru Ann. She doesn't strike me as a stupid person, but it seems her faith in the organization has blinded her to quite a lot."

"I don't think she'd be alone in that, Bud. Anything else?"

Bud looked pleased with himself, "I managed to send the photos of the McGlynns and Ambroise to my guys. But it's still a long shot – they really cannot search photos of every face in the world, despite what the movies might suggest, but they can have a go at trying to narrow the parameters, and see what they find."

"So you went back to the hub?" He nodded. "How was Jenn?"

Bud gave me a knowing grin. "Not happy...not happy at all. She was stomping around the place complaining that Zara's expectations of her were ridiculous. Moaned about how she'd taken a pay cut to come here – so at least now we know she's here in a professional capacity, rather than as a talented volunteer, though a few things she mentioned told me she really is enamoured of Faceting, but more as...well, as a hobbyist, if that makes sense."

"Likes the general ideas; not a strict adherent, or evangelist?"

"Yeah, like that. Though, talking about evangelizing – she told me about a new member-get-member scheme that gives a Facetor points toward moving up a rung when they recruit a new sign-up...which seems to have created quite a lot of work for her. I admit I took the opportunity presented by her anger to perform a little test of my own; I wanted to get a sense of how she's into it all. "

"Do tell."

Bud's eyes twinkled. "I managed to let it slip that 'paying condolences' meant just that – slapping a thousand dollars at a time in the hands of the movement."

"And how did she take that information?"

"Told me there was no way that could be right."

"In your judgement, she knew nothing about it?"

"Correct. She'd been annoyed when I arrived, but that just about sent her over the top. She marched out of the hub saying she had to speak to Zara right then. She didn't come back."

I gave what Bud had said some thought. "I think she might be swayed, Bud, and she could be so useful if we could get her to see things our way. She's got access to all sorts of information that could help us prove to the Facetors here what Zara is up to – they'd believe her more than they'd believe us. And, after the looks we got earlier on, I'm even more firmly of the opinion that any accusations we might make against Zara would not only be dismissed, but that taking such a step without irrefutable proof could actually put us in danger; the mood was downright threatening in the refectory when we left. And – while I know you could probably get us out of here in a pinch, I don't fancy the idea of having to; it would be easy to follow a fleeing vehicle out here. I also don't like the idea of slinking away to Lump Hill to make a call and wait for help – if the communications hub became somewhere we were no longer welcome."

Bud nodded. "Reckon that's what Oscar thought, too?"

I nodded. "I find the fact that his phone, text, and email records were wiped clean to be highly suspicious…though, to be honest, why whoever did it didn't just destroy his phone completely is a mystery. We're in the middle of the desert after all…all anyone had to do was break it apart and drop bits of it around the place; no one would be any the wiser. And yet there it was, in his dig, neatly stored away."

"That is a puzzle," replied Bud. "Maybe it had to be found with him, or raise alarm bells? So wiped, but not discarded."

"Good point. Yes, good point. Anything else?"

"You were only asleep for a couple of hours, I think I did rather well."

"You said you'd seen Serendipity?"

"Yes, but I've told you everything that passed between us already. However, since we're on the subject…that stolen cash? She thinks she knows who's taken it, doesn't she? Covering up for someone. Pretty obvious. But who? Who would take it…and who would she protect?"

"It's a lot of cash, so anyone might want it. But who would have known where it was? And who *would* she protect? She's the protective type, so, to be honest, she might cover up for any number of people. She told me she likes to get to know the novices…maybe one of them? They're…well, they're a strange and troublesome bunch, aren't they? I know they're not an amorphous blob of people, they're all individuals, but they seem to have more of a pack mentality than the others. There really is a noticeable difference between those in gray, and those who choose their colors – and I don't mean in terms of Faceting, but in terms of personality. Those who've moved up the ranks seem much more aligned with what I'm thinking of as the core old-Faceting process, of buffing up Facets each day to be a more rounded person, live a more fulfilled life. The novices – the donkey-like ones as KSue thinks of them – seem to be much more interested in using drugs to achieve an almost instant result."

"Kids these days, eh?" Bud grinned at me, so I swatted at him. He mugged a dramatic flinch. "I know, I know…and I agree with you; there's a significant difference in general attitude, however, I refuse to attach the 'it's a Millennial thing' label to it. It's more than not liking their attitude, it's a feeling that they're all up to something." Bud sighed. "Am I hunting for criminal activities that don't exist, or am I responding with my cop instincts to something that really is wrong, but pretty well hidden. I feel unsettled about them all…their presence always throws me. I feel they're always rushing, pushing, jostling…but toward what, and why, I can't say."

"Me, too. But what does it mean?"

"We're not of their generation, and they have less patience? They want results now, then they can get on to the next tier? Like with computer games – use your tools, or weapons, or magical abilities, to win battles, gather the points, and move up a level."

"Tools they've had to buy from the Faceting organization – though it appears all the drugs they might want are free, which is nice for them, isn't it? Good to see them getting something back for their investment in books full of platitudes, woolly psycho-babble, and vague promises of wonderful revelations once they reach the top of the tree."

"Do you think anyone has?"

"What?"

"Reached the top of the tree. The highest level."

I shook my head. "I have no idea, but that would be risky. Unless someone reaching the top has a vested interest in keeping the illusion intact, why wouldn't they blow the whistle when they find it's no more than smoke and mirrors?"

Bud stood and stretched. "True. Unless they get a cut, why would they add to the mystique – because they would be, wouldn't they?"

I nodded.

"And on that topic, are you going to tell me what your plan is? You have one, or you wouldn't have been wittering on to Don about some old housemate of yours – who I happen to believe doesn't exist – wearing her grannie's perfume. I hope you appreciated my silence this morning by the way, because that required an enormous effort. And yet – despite the fact that you were lying was pretty much stamped across your forehead – Don lapped it all up, didn't he? Until he went off on one at us tonight, I'd thought he was a decent sort; a bit gullible, and innocent, maybe, but decent. He certainly liked the way you learned from your experiences with your non-existent friend. So? Plans?"

"Good question. I had an inkling overnight, tested my theory with Zara, and you're right that my yarn about perfume was a bit of a trap. But I need to do something else that you might not like too much; we have to stay up all night and maintain a lookout for anyone coming into the plaza."

Bud's eyebrows told me he hadn't been expecting that. "And how do you suggest we do that, exactly? And why?"

"Well…I thought the roof would be a good place to – quite literally – lie low, and yet be able to have a good field of vision."

"This roof? The roof of our dig?"

I nodded.

"Why?"

"I want to see if someone is doing the rounds of the digs in the dark, when everyone is asleep and under the influence of the tea KSue mentioned…which I think might contain a mild sedative, by the way."

Bud started his head-scratching. "I've got to be honest and tell you that hadn't occurred to me…but, now that you've mentioned it, I don't like the idea one little bit, and yet I think you might have something there. KSue mentioned missing it – which I know can happen even if you're just talking about consuming anything regularly. But a sedative? Really? More drugs? And what if someone decided to put something stronger in it? Are we back to not-Kool-Aid?"

I shrugged. "Stranger things have happened."

"Well, not on my watch, they don't, and – now that you've mentioned it, and before we even consider going clambering about on roofs, which is not an idea I'm wild about, by the way – I'm gonna run to KSue's dig to tell her to give her tea a miss tonight; when we told her it would be safe, the idea you just mentioned hadn't even crossed my mind. If anything were to happen to her the night before she leaves the place, I'd never forgive myself. You okay here? It shouldn't take me long."

"Yes, I'll be fine, you go. We were wrong to make her feel comfortable about consuming anything at all that we didn't take to her."

"Agreed. What are you going to do?"

"I want to go through the commitment records you snaffled. They sound fascinating in the broad sense, but I want to see them for myself, and focus on the questionnaires completed by some specific people, because I think that's where I might find out something that'll answer the riddle of why Serendipity isn't keen to report all that cash as having been stolen."

"Divide and conquer," said Bud, as he headed out of the door.

Brilliant Darkness

I never have any grasp of time passing when I'm speed reading – which is one of the reasons why I find what appears to be a mentally draining activity to be so restful. But, on this occasion, I snapped out of it when I realized Bud had been gone for about half an hour. I couldn't imagine where he'd got to; maybe KSue had trapped him, nattering away at him because she was glad of a bit of company.

I tried his method of pacing to help me decide what to do, but that didn't work, so I pulled on my spudgy old lace-up shoes – because I wanted my feet to be comfy if I was going wandering – grabbed an oil lamp, and headed out of the door. I made sure my phone was in my pocket, and I even left Bud a note, saying I would first go to KSue's, then the refectory, then the hub, then back to our dig, along with the time I was writing it: all of which I thought eminently sensible.

The plaza was empty, and I was grateful for that, because I didn't think I'd get the friendly waves and nods I'd received on previous occasions. The fire bowls illuminated my way as far as KSue's dig. I knocked, but there was no answer, so I opened the door and stuck my head in. The place was in complete darkness, and silent. I told myself to not think about graves as I walked in, held up my oil lamp and checked the bathroom. No one. *Odd.* There was a noticeable lack of ornamentation, and a couple of lumpen bags beside the bed; KSue had packed in readiness for her departure, so that was a good sign. At least, I took it to be so, though I couldn't imagine why Bud and KSue had left her dig at all.

Having said in my note I would do so – and keen to track down my husband – I headed for the refectory. No light showing, door shut, no activity at all. I went inside and walked around the place – kitchen and all. Nothing.

I was beginning to feel disheartened, and more than a little worried. Where on earth had Bud and KSue got to? I did my best to push my worst fears to the back of my mind, however eager they were to place themselves at the front of it, and headed for the communications hub.

Even before I got there I could see the lights, and knew it was the most likely place for at least Jenn to be working at that time of night. I opened the door and heard the now-familiar electronic buzzing of the computer equipment, but the place was deserted. Where was everyone? It was like one of those episodes of *The Avengers* when Mrs. Peel and John Steed arrive at an English village to find not a soul there, but milk on the table, tea in the pot still warm, and then get overwhelmed by some sort of gas. I sniffed the air – just dust, and heat. No gas.

I had to admit I was at a loss as to what to do next. I'd said in my note to Bud I'd head back to our dig after I'd tried the hub, then realized I had an ideal opportunity to use the internet for whatever purpose I chose, without anyone looking over my shoulder, though I knew Jenn might return at any moment. But, given the chat I'd had with Bud earlier, and our agreement she might be able to understand our reading of the organization, I decided to risk it.

I took a seat, extinguished the oil lamp, and began to search a range of topics I knew were important: famous saloons of the Alaska gold rush era; the history of Delphi and its environs; two farms on the coast in France; any mentions at all of Demetrius Karaplis; a list of names of novice Facetors who were at the Desert Gem, that I'd gleaned from the questionnaires. Then I made a phone call. Having finished that, I'd just typed in

"Longmuir Tunnel" when I heard the door open behind me. I clicked to close the browser, then started to turn to greet whomever it was who'd annoyingly stopped me from finding out more about the ghostly legend Bud had told me about – and felt the whoosh of something beside my ear…

I was in the dark, hunched on my side on the floor. A dirt floor. That was all I knew. My head hurt like nobody's business; I've been knocked unconscious before, so know exactly how it feels – it hadn't been a pleasant experience that first time, and it wasn't now. The other thing that certainly didn't help was the fact I was tied up the way Serendipity had been, with zip-ties around my wrists and ankles, held together by another looped strap.

I stared into the darkness, and it stared back at me. I knew it would take a while, but gradually my eyes grew used to the dimness and I began to make out shapes. I was in a room full of boxes – cartons. Small cartons, not great massive things. There were a lot of them. Hundreds, maybe. Neatly stacked. The walls above them seemed to be made of cinder block; I hadn't seen any buildings constructed that way at the Desert Gem. It dawned on me that I could be anywhere.

I wriggled about and managed to get my back against a stack of cartons, so I could sit with my knees bent up to rest my arms a bit. There was no question of my being able to stand. I was stuck. Helpless. And without Bud. I couldn't help worrying about him, and KSue.

What if I'm not alone in here? What if they're here, too? Dare I shout out? Might there be someone silently standing guard somewhere, and they'll come and do something…unpleasant…when they know I've regained consciousness?

The thoughts flashed through my mind and I made an instant decision. "Bud? KSue? Anyone?" I shouted as loudly as I could, then listened. Nothing. Not a sound. It was the loudest silence I'd heard in some time.

I focused on the problem of my bindings. Once upon a time, when I'd been teaching a course on the role of toolmarks in forensics, I'd invited a guest speaker to address my class who'd brought an array of deadly items that my students had found ghoulishly fascinating. He'd been one of those yompy types, and had enjoyed showing us how to get out of zip-ties that day. One of the methods he showed us was to make a friction saw out of…well, in his case, almost anything. I reckoned the laces in my shoes might work, so spent the next who-knows-how-long unlacing one spudgy shoe, then I threaded the lace through the looped plastic tie that connected my hands to my feet, and sawed away as hard as I could. It was amazing – in only half a dozen strokes the plastic snapped, and at last I could separate my arms from my legs, which felt wonderful. I used the same method on the tie on my ankles, and was thrilled to be able to get up and walk about a bit – my circulation needed that.

Then came the problem of the tie on my wrists: I couldn't hold the lace in my teeth and my feet to saw through that, so I tried what our well-built guest speaker had done, and raised my arms, pulling them down and my wrists apart with all my might. Of course, he hadn't had boobs that got in the way of him doing it, and I was convinced it wouldn't work. I tried four or five times, and all I seemed to be achieving was two very sore wrists. I was exhausted, and frightened, and getting very, very angry with whomever had done this to me – and it was when I used that anger that the zip-tie finally, wonderfully, delightfully snapped. I wanted to cheer, but thought better of it, so rubbed my wrists instead; my guest speaker had obviously been far too roughty-toughty to mention the extremely painful results of managing to get the tie to break, but at least all my limbs were my own to direct, and I directed them around the perimeter of the room. I also checked in my pocket for my phone. It was there! The screen was cracked, and – though there wasn't a signal, of course – at least the flashlight app worked. I cheered for my small victory.

I looked around; boxes were piled higher than I could reach on a couple of walls, and were stacked along a corridor, just on one side. I crept forward; I'd been brought into the place somehow, there was no way out of the room I'd been in, so there had to be a way in, and out, somewhere else, I reasoned. And then I found it: a metal door, with substantial, knobbly hinges, barred my way. I tried the handle; it wouldn't budge. A ramp led to it – so I reckoned it allowed for equipment to come in and out, perhaps for loading all the cartons?

Since there obviously was no way I was getting through the door until someone unlocked it, I decided to open one of the cartons, because I really, really wanted to know what was inside them – though I reckoned I could guess.

I ran my thumbnail along the packing tape on one of the cartons and managed to get it open. Inside were brick-shaped packages wrapped in a yellow plastic material. They felt lumpy, but it was more difficult to break open the yellow membrane than it had been to get into the carton itself. Both my thumbs were sore by the time I managed to open it. Inside, it was filled with individual, vacuum-sealed plastic bags full of a lumpen substance. When I sniffed inside the brick, I could smell lemon and musk…and something like the beach. I nibbled at the plastic of the lumpen bag – my thumbs were too sore to use them again – and I made a little hole, then ripped it open. Marijuana. Of course. I returned to the carton and poked about a bit, finally finding a few rags soaked in the aromatic oils I'd smelled on so many of the Facetors; a clever way to disguise the drug's pungent odor. I took lots of photos.

Cogs clicked into place, and I cursed myself for having put a target on my back, and possibly Bud's, too. In that moment I realized coincidences can and do happen, and this was one I could have well done without.

Wakeful Dreaming

I put the carton back, and opened another, just to make sure my findings weren't a fluke. They weren't. The second carton was also full of the yellow bricks and scented rags. I fumed at myself – and did my best to keep down the panic that was growing in the pit of my tummy. Now I was even more worried about Bud and KSue – and yet I knew I could do nothing…about anything. I stamped my feet like an angry child out of pure frustration. How could I have been so stupid? *Oh Cait…what have you done?*

I sat down on the floor and allowed myself to cry. I knew it wouldn't achieve anything, but I hoped that by letting the tears flow I'd be able to emerge on the other side and at least think straight. Of course, no handbag meant no hankies, so I had to use the overthingy I'd pulled on before I'd left our dig to wipe my eyes and nose. Horrible.

Eventually I was past the tears, and started to try to come up with a plan, which I knew was ridiculous: I had no idea where I was; I didn't know where Bud and KSue were; I did, however, have a much better idea of why I was wherever I was, and of who might have played a part in me being there.

I grasped at that straw, then decided I needed to think a few more things through.

Sitting there, in the silent darkness, I knew I was in the ideal situation to use my wakeful dreaming technique – when I allow my mind to flow uninhibited by my preconceptions and assumptions, allowing it to make connections where it wants, not where I want.

When I'm recollecting, I like to hum, but for this technique I prefer it to be quiet and dark, so I made use of my surroundings, closed my eyes, settled back against the cartons of marijuana and allowed my mind to float freely…

I'm sitting in a black hole, a cavern, but it's warm and comfortable because I'm nestled in a bed of enormous leaves with an intoxicating aroma. I look up and see a circle of turquoise sky, which gleams like a stone, shot through with veins of gold. I push myself up, then climb, using the jewel-encrusted rungs of a ladder, until I emerge into the brilliant, blinding sunlight, which burns my skin with its touch. I shield my face from the glare and spot a person dressed in multicolored clothes wandering, far away, in the moonscape surrounding me. I call to them, but all that comes out of my mouth is a rasp – my throat is too dry for me to speak.

Above me I see a flock of gray birds, with huge wings and beaks, all braying; they wheel and swoop as one, so I duck to avoid them, but they keep attacking me, and I run…but there's no cover, anywhere. I stumble on rocks, find myself impaled on cholla bushes that spring up in front of me…blood is pouring from my arms and legs, though I feel no pain…and I feel no terror when one of the birds picks me up in its huge claws and carries me off to an eyrie on top of a gigantic saguaro cactus that's appeared on the horizon. The eyrie turns out to be the communication hub, from which I have a view of the entire Desert Gem compound, but now, instead of being built across a series of hills and valleys, it's all spread out flat, like a map…and I see dotted outlines on the desert plain – the ghosts of buildings yet to be…as I watch, the lines sprout rows and rows of adobe bricks, which shoot into the sky, creating four tall towers, with fountains of water pouring from their roofs.

An old man with a beard, wearing a filthy, rainbow-hued plaid shirt appears on the edge of my lookout – he's scaled the cactus using a pick, but as his head pops up, we both plummet, along with dozens and dozens of computer screens, down to the flatlands, where we're both overwhelmed by what feels like an army of tiny gray people who have emerged from the soil itself. A voice calls, and the attack upon us stops. I see Zara: she's standing in the back of a ruby encrusted pick-up truck, being driven by Elizabeth and Norman, who are both human and also racoons, simultaneously. I look up, and see that it's snowing in the desert, then realize it's not snow, but millions of sheets of paper turning to ash as they fall, never reaching the ground. Zara's watching them, too – I see her lips moving, her eyes fixed and unblinking, her face alight with joy, and malevolence.

Zara glows white in the sun, dazzling me with a faceted jewel on her forehead; in one hand she carries a branch with lemons growing upon it, in the other she holds her brother's cellphone, which is massive, and is displaying a scrolling presentation of photographs of Zara, Demetrius, Linda, Oscar, and Ambroise. They all look strangely alike, and begin to morph into one genderless person, who's projected from the photographs onto the turquoise sky, translucent, massive, and with eyes that burn like fire bowls…seeing everything.

I feel afraid of the giant figure floating in the sky, but know that running away isn't possible, because they can find me anywhere, at any time. Then I hear a voice – it's Bud, calling to me from a hole in the desert, an entry to a safe place…I know this. I try to drag myself across the rubble-strewn ground, but keep getting pulled at by fossilized creatures that are alive. Bud grabs my hand and tugs at me, telling me that the darkness is safe…to come to the darkness, and I'm trying my best to get there but I need to put my hands over my ears because there's a sound that's so painful…

I opened my eyes and realized that the horn used to call all Facetors to the amphitheater was sounding; it was close – so close that I had to be at the amphitheater itself – maybe behind, or under the stage? Either way, I reasoned that if people were coming to the area I might stand a chance of someone hearing me if I made as much noise as I could. I reassessed my surroundings – as best I could in the dark – but there didn't seem to be anything hard that I could use to bang on the metal door. While my shoes had been useful in providing laces that helped me get out of my restraints, they were too soft to be of any use, and I didn't think using my phone would be a good idea. I hunted about for a stone, or a rock, then crept along the corridor, pointing the beam of my light into every corner. Eventually I found a stone that filled my palm; it wasn't terribly hefty, but it would have to do.

I returned to the metal door, and pressed my ear against it. Yes, there was definitely some sort of hubbub beyond it. I hammered on the door with the rock in my hand. The dull banging reverberated in the darkness of the corridor, and I did my very best Morse code of dot-dot-dot-dash-dash-dash-dot-dot-dot – anyone hearing it would surely recognize my SOS. I kept repeating the pattern, banging as hard as I could. Nothing – no response. I kept at it, hoping against hope that someone would hear me.

A clunk, a squeal, and the door opened. The light beyond it was soft – not sun, but fire…an oil lamp.

"What are you doing in there?" It was Dru Ann. I stepped out and hugged her, and she hugged back. It was a wonderful feeling.

"I don't know – someone put me in there after bashing me unconscious," I replied, when we'd pulled ourselves apart, and bowed.

Dru Ann's expression suggested she thought I'd lost my marbles. "Really?"

"Yes, really," I said – more snappily than I'd meant to. "Where are we? Have you seen Bud?"

Dru Ann stepped away from me, but answered quietly, "We're behind the stage at the amphitheater. We were all listening to Jenn, who summoned us here...then we heard banging – it was plain to hear, because of the acoustics. I was the one who tracked its source." She leaned to my ear. "Be aware that everyone can hear what you're saying both here, and in the amphitheater." She stood back and added, "Bud's out front, with everyone else, why don't you come join him? He'll be so pleased to see you."

She led me around the cinder-block structure that formed the corridor I'd been in, then we emerged at the side of the bowl-shaped auditorium. Everyone was looking at me, and Bud's face was a picture – he looked horrified, and leapt to his feet.

"Cait – oh Cait...where've you been? I've looked everywhere for you...you've been gone for hours. What's happened to you? Was that you saying you'd been knocked out? Are you okay? Who did that to you? When? Where?"

He was beside me in a moment, holding me, pushing my hair back from my face, checking my body for injuries, and examining my head. "There's a bit of blood," he said, "but not much, for a scalp wound. How do you feel? Woozy?"

"If you ask me to count your fingers, I might snap," I hissed into his ear. "I'm fine – honestly. But angry. And sick to death of everything that's going on around here. It has to stop. But listen, don't speak – everyone can hear every word, because of the acoustics. It's so good to see you – I didn't know where you were. Quick, tell me what I've missed."

Bud pressed his lips to my ear and whispered, "I went to KSue's and she was feeling real lonely, but I didn't want her at our place, so I took her to Serendipity's, for safety's sake; I hoped they could look after each other, but when I got there Serendipity was pretty groggy, so KSue fussed over her for a while and I kinda got stuck...you know how she can be. By the time I got back to our place you were long gone; I read your note and followed your trail. But I couldn't find you. Anywhere. While I was at the hub Jenn arrived and I knew I had to go for it – I laid it all out for Jenn, and got her on-side. Once I told her about our theories, she went all in to help. She's been great, Cait: she took me over to the administration building, where the doors have locks, and it was much more private there for me to be able to make the calls I needed to. And she was totally supportive of us needing to get the authorities involved, given the fact you'd vanished. She's the one who blasted the signal for all the Facetors to come here – so she could organize search parties. I haven't got any more info on the McGlynns or Ambroise...sorry – not even the photos helped. But the good news is there'll be a significant force here in about an hour. You going missing was something my contacts were finally able to act upon, so there's that. And, of course, I'm so pleased that you're safe. You're okay, really? You're sure?"

He pulled back, and I could tell from his tight lips, and worried eyes, that he knew things were looking grim. I kissed him on the cheek and whispered, "Husband – I'm fine, just fine. But it sounds as though I've got to put on a bit of a show – something that'll keep everyone here until help arrives. I've worked it all out, and I'll need to explain to everyone here what's been going on." I felt the anxiety in the pit of my tummy. "This is all going to be a bit weird...even for me...so follow my lead, if I call on you, okay?" He nodded, and we broke apart – with him taking a seat between KSue and Jenn, both of whom looked apprehensive.

Zara was on the stage, perched on the edge of a gold chair that had obviously been designed to suggest a throne. She spoke softly, her tone mocking me, "I'm so pleased that Jenn's surprising plan for everyone to go hunting about in the desert for you won't have to happen now, Cait. Won't you join your husband in the audience? Since everyone has been summoned here in the middle of the night, robbing them of their sleep, I feel I should say a few words."

I looked at the assembled crowd: very few favorable expressions returned my gaze. I took a deep breath, and climbed the steps to the podium; it was time for me to do the best I could to keep everyone exactly where they were until whomever it was that Bud had contacted turned up. Given the number of Facetors in the place, I hoped the 'significant force' they were sending would be sufficient.

Beginning the End

My hair and face were bloody, my overthingy torn and filthy, and I was entirely covered with dust, but I didn't care. Zara might have appeared gleamingly white on the outside, but I knew for a fact her intentions were anything but pure, so I pushed back my hair, and said, "You all know my name's Cait, and you've probably heard quite a bit about me and my husband. But what you might not know is that we've been here under false pretences."

Knowing looks were exchanged throughout the audience., lots of shoulders being squared.

Right, Cait – give it your very best effort…recall every dramatic mystic you've ever seen portrayed on screen, and use those memories now.

I continued, "And no, I don't mean that my husband and I have been here snooping; we've been here studying you, as a movement, and Zara most of all. You see, news has traveled fast about the new leader of the Faceting movement – and the word is she's managed to achieve what so many have hoped and dreamed of for so long: real, and meaningful, contact with someone on the other plane."

Nods of appreciation, and surprised looks all round. *Good. Get them to take the journey of discovery with you, Cait, like you do in lectures.*

"For those of you not familiar with it, what you're hearing is a Welsh accent. Why is that relevant, you might ask? Well, we Welsh have a long and storied history when it comes to mystic connections. It's not just Faceting that has a set of beliefs which include multiple planes of existence, you see. On the Gower peninsula, not far from where I grew up, there are burial chambers built by my forbears about five thousand years ago to honor their dead and show respect to their deities, a great deal earlier than the oracle at Delphi uttered her first prophetic verses. And those of us who have Welsh blood in our veins know how special that heritage is…going all the way back to the earliest inhabitants in our area, almost thirty thousand years ago. Let that sink in for a moment – yes, I can tap into all that history, though I don't usually…because it terrifies people."

There was a slight hissing in the crowd, which I hoped was a lot of people doing their Facet and Face It thing – though the effect was a bit off-putting. *Come on, Cait, get them on your side.*

Zara replied sharply, "Well, ain't that grand, Cait Morgan. But don't try to make out you're something you're not; you're just a busybody who manages to get into trouble wherever she goes, who's intent upon undermining all the good work we're doing here." She turned to her audience, dropping her voice into the register where it sounded powerful and commanding. "This woman, and her husband, have been prying into our movement since the moment they arrived. Demetrius has been keeping an eye on them – and he's told me *all* about them."

I wanted her to think I'd bitten. "Has he told you how I ended up unconscious, and tied up in a locked room back there for who knows how long?"

Zara dismissed me with a toss of her hair. "Why would he bother talking to me about that?"

"Of course, I forgot, he only speaks to you about matters that concern Facetors, doesn't he?"

"Usually." *Disdainful.*

"Which is a great shame, and something Bud and I came here to better understand. You say Demetrius speaks to you – through you. That you and he have pierced the veil in a way that's unique, and special."

I turned to the audience, stepped forward so the flames of one of the fire bowls illuminated my face from below, and flung my arms in the air.

"But what if I told you there are many more voices on the other side, and that those who are beyond are able to see a great deal more than merely what's going on here, now. Their vision is boundless in terms of space, and time…" I dropped my arms, and faced Zara. "I think your father's efforts are wonderful, Zara, but limited. And that's what our time here has revealed – you're pretty small fry, and those who've been connected to the other place for centuries, but have kept that knowledge and power a secret, will be relieved to know it."

The audience buzzed. *Good, they seem to be buying into my Mystic Cait act.*

Zara's face betrayed her emotion – for once. She was clearly completely puzzled, yet still happy to dismiss me – which was what I'd hoped for. "You're talking rubbish. What do you know about connecting with those who've passed?"

As I pulled myself up to my full five-four, I dropped my chin and my voice, "I speak to you with the voices of all those who have passed, not just one." *Come on, Cait – you can do this, remember those diaphragm control lessons in all those choir practices…project!*

I searched the faces in the crowd. "Janis, from Flagstaff – yes, you." I pointed. "Stand up, please." A young woman stood – she was dressed in purple. "Your father Frank, and mother Irene, say you haven't been looking after your asthma properly, and they're worried about you…please get your inhaler prescription renewed; your mother's also terribly concerned that you're losing too much weight."

A few gasps and murmurs swept around the audience. Janis sat, looking confused.

I continued, "Would Zachary from Lisbon in Portugal please stand?" A novice rose somewhat hesitantly. "Oh Zachary, you've been telling a few fibs, haven't you? Your grandmother Ines says you've been hiding out here to escape some debts you built up in Portugal. She says you should go home and face the music – which won't be too bad, because your father has paid them all off. But you'll have to face him, of course. Facet and Face It." The other novices sitting around Zachary looked up at him, puzzled; the young man sat down, chastised.

"Very clever, Cait – but what do you think you're doing?" Zara snapped.

"Exactly what you do, Zara – I'm passing on messages from the other plane."

"But what you're saying proves nothing."

"You don't think that what I said proves that Zachary's grandmother, and Janis's mother and father, are speaking through me in the same way that Demetrius does through you? Well, maybe this will convince you...there's something else I have to tell you. All."

The audience was absolutely silent.

"What?" Zara's tone told me she was calling my bluff.

"What if I told you your mother has chosen to speak through me, rather than you? Maybe she thinks you're too busy listening to your father to hear her as well."

A real gasp of astonishment, and a widening of Zara's eyes, told me I was making a dent in things.

Zara stood and addressed the audience. "My mother will speak through me, when she's ready."

"Well, it could be that she's ready to talk to me right now...you see, now that she's passed, she can understand what you've really been up to, and she's angry about you using the movement she and your father set up to make millions of dollars, which you pay to yourself – the owner of the land upon which the Desert Gem has been built."

A gratifying rumble of consternation met my ears.

"These are merely *your* words, not those of my mother. You have no proof that she is speaking to you." Zara tossed her hair haughtily.

"Proof?" I turned to the audience and said, "Would you like proof that Linda is talking through me?"

There was a general nodding of heads, and a few, truly aggressive, "Yeahs" could be heard.

I held up my arms again, and the crowd became quiet. "Linda, as you all know, never was a show-woman…she preferred to do the work of Faceting quietly, always staying in the background; she doesn't want me to speak to all of you on this occasion – she wants me to talk directly to her daughter. But, of course, that means only Zara will know if I am speaking the truth – I hope you're all okay with that."

Nodding from the crowd, but there was a challenging toss of the hair by Zara as she retook her seat, as nonchalantly as she could.

"Zara, your mother is sorry she used to look at you with fear in her eyes when you were a child; it is only now that she finally understands what it was that made you the way you always were. She wishes she had understood at the time, and is saddened that you did not tell her."

You could have heard a pin drop.

"My mother never looked at me fearfully." Zara's voice betrayed her lie.

"Oh Zara, your mother and father both loved you, but you terrified them…because they didn't understand you. They were also constantly worried about you – and *for* you. You rarely slept, which of course gave them cause for concern, but your mother was also troubled by the fact that you had no friends – no real, close friends, in any case. Not ever, at any time in your life. She knew you were lonely, and hurting, because she heard you cry at night – sometimes right through the night – but she couldn't console you because you were utterly dismissive of her, all the time. But now she understands. You found everyone to be incredibly stupid, didn't you? Your contemporaries didn't see the world as you did, and were unable to learn the way you did. And your schoolteachers? They had no real understanding of what they were talking about, did they? They simply passed on facts from books they'd read, without having the ability to see how those facts fitted into a much bigger, more complex picture. School work was a joke for you – you didn't understand why people around you couldn't learn the way you did. And exams? You had no idea what all the fuss was about. You made almost no effort, yet gained perfect marks – in anything, and everything. Even when you attended a school for gifted children, you were still the only one there who could do what you did. And you gradually grew to hate everyone who wasn't able to keep up with you, or challenge you."

Zara's body language told me I was hitting home – her eyes darted, and she was shrinking into her ridiculous golden chair; I hoped everyone in the audience could also work out that what I was saying was true.

I pressed on, "One great irony in all this is that the Faceting for Life movement focuses on self-awareness, but you never took the time, nor did you do the work, to truly understand your gifts, yourself, or your fellow human beings, did you? Instead, you chose to look down on them, never tried to, or learned how to, fit in. You didn't sit down with your parents as an eleven-year-old girl to tell them about your problems – so they could help you to understand your gifts. You never had the joy of knowing that even if your parents couldn't possibly understand the way life felt for you, that they loved you because of, and in spite of, your differences. Doing that might well have changed the path you chose to tread, Zara. As it was, you preferred to allow your disdain for all those around you to grow, eating away at you over the years, until all you were left with was a view of the world where you were on one level, and everyone else was on another, beneath you, inferior to you in every way."

KSue's awe-filled voice sliced through the silence. "Could Zara hear the voices of those who had passed even then, when she was a child? Is that why she was so…different?" She turned to face the audience, "I knew her when she was young, and she always was an extraordinary child."

Facetors leaned forward on their stone benches, Zara turned to face me.

"You're talking nonsense," she all but whispered. *Liar!*

I continued, "No, KSue, Zara couldn't hear the dead back then, and she can't now. But she is clever, and she is gifted. She has an eidetic memory – which is what some people call a photographic memory. She's used it throughout her life to benefit herself – only herself…never others, because, sadly, her gift has also left her with a very poor opinion of humanity."

I saw Zara exhale deeply. *A direct hit.*

"I speak with my father," she shouted – quite unnecessarily.

I snapped back, "No, you don't. Our investigation of your technique has proved to us beyond doubt that you do not communicate with your late father. Your 'new rules' require Facetors to complete questionnaires that give you a great depth and breadth of knowledge about them, then you use that to research their family backgrounds, and that allows you to 'prove' to them that Demetrius is in contact with their dead loved ones, 'on the other plane'. You've also gathered information about every single person here that allows you to understand their psychological profile. None of this is difficult to do, and it requires no contact with the dead; it just takes time – less time if you can speed read, which many with eidetic memories are able to do. And if you suffer from insomnia, which you do, you have several extra hours each day to read and remember information which you can call upon during your so-called 'channelling sessions', which are nothing more than you using your enhanced recollection abilities to make it sound as though you're hearing information passed on from an omniscient being."

As I began my accusations against Zara, the amphitheater started to feel a great deal less welcoming. This was what I'd expected and feared – I needed these people on my side, I had to sway them…or things could get dangerous for me, and Bud.

"Zara knows so much – no one could do what she does unless Demetrius was telling her." I didn't know who had spoken, but the deep male voice sounded quite threatening. "You're lying – and prying, and we won't stand for that."

I knew the gloves were off, so I went for it. "I understand why you might think that – but let me give you some specific examples of what I mean…"

I spent the next twenty minutes or so stating the dates and times of certain of Zara's channelling sessions, then repeating what she'd said to a specific person in the audience in front of me – verbatim. I then followed up with a detailed explanation of how Zara had gleaned that insight from the forms completed by the audience member in question, as well as citing the specific online sources she'd used to find out more than they'd originally told her…even stating the dates of the social media posts from which she'd gained her insights. I couldn't keep going for much longer, because I'd only had a chance to do that depth of online research for about ten of the files I'd read.

Thankfully, the effect was cumulative: angry voices became guffaws, ridiculing my examples; then the guffaws were silenced; the silence morphed into nods of recollection and agreement; nods became whispers and then shaking heads…with more people glaring at Zara than at me.

Zara stared at me, pink with anger. "I speak for Demetrius."
Weak.

She looked scared, and I knew why; she'd finally recognized the fact that I was like her…probably the only other person she'd ever met in her entire life who shared her abilities. She'd worked out there was no other way I could have done what I'd just done. But, other than Bud, we were the only two people there who knew that, and she couldn't reveal my secret without also admitting her own. *Checkmate.*

I addressed the audience. "By giving Facetors 'proof' that she's connected to the non-existent omniscient Demetrius on another plane, Zara has come up with a clever plan to get as much money out of as many bank accounts as possible: the books you all have to read to progress through the Faceting hierarchy; the courses and workshops you attend; the condolences you pay; the Facetor-approved supplies that cost more than their non-approved counterparts. These are all ways to generate income for the Faceting movement – which is not being invested in Faceting at all, but is being paid to a company she owns, registered off-shore, in the Cayman Islands."

"But she, Oscar, and Linda spent their entire inheritances building this place," shouted KSue, loyal to the end.

"A good investment, for which she's been repaid many times over. But it's not all about money, folks – let's not forget the deaths of your friends and colleagues. If Demetrius Karaplis is *not* speaking from beyond the grave, there are *no* predictions of imminent deaths from the other side – so it's Zara who's marking people for death, her mother included. Just think about that for a moment – do you really believe that five good people would have surrendered their lives if they hadn't been convinced by Zara's words that it was their time to die? And why were they convinced by her words? Because of Zara's manipulative construct – the story about the non-existent voice of her dead father."

Serendipity spoke quietly, sounding stunned, "I truly believed they all wanted to pass. We all did. We all believed what Zara told us – and they did, too. So…so they all killed themselves for no reason? It *wasn't* really their time?" The horror in her voice told me she was truly doubting Zara, and I knew she wasn't alone.

An anonymous female voice spoke, "But even if Zara has that memory thing, and could do it all that way…why would she? Are you saying it was all about money? And for that she killed her mom…or at least made her mom want to kill herself?"

"Why don't you tell them?" I stared at Zara, daring her to speak.

"I speak for Demetrius, that is all." Her voice cracked as she spoke.

"Very well then, allow *me* to tell *you*. All the people who have died here were the architects of the new Faceting for Life business – your empire. They created the computerized infrastructure, the online store, oversaw the building of this place, and helped get all the books published you now sell around the world. And then, of course, there was Linda herself, your own mother. One thing I'll give you, Zara, is that you understand the power and anguish of grief very well. And you've used that knowledge – paired with your eidetic memory – in the most wicked of ways. You've exploited the desperate desire of those who are grieving to believe that their lost loved ones are still somehow present…*or can be.* You convinced your bereft mother that your father was waiting for her on the other side, telling her to come to him – and she did, by taking poison. At the time she did it, she believed it was of her own free will, but you manipulated her grief – as you have done with so many others – for your own gains. She had to die so you could take the reins of the Faceting empire, and gain sole ownership of this land."

"No – that's not true," Zara pounced, "Oscar owned it with me."

"And he himself died the very next day. How convenient."

Zara's expression changed, there was a glint of…anger? "His death was an accident."

"Yes, Oscar's death was an accident," shouted a voice; Don stood in the audience – I recognized him at least.

"Let's talk about Oscar for a moment, shall we? The story is that he ran off into the desert in a fit of grief and fell – somehow – to his death. But he was often in the desert, and was knowledgeable about how to spend time there safely, wasn't he? In fact, you know he was, Don…you told me so. Right?"

His bravado faded a little. "Yeah, well, that's true, I guess."

"He loved geology, was fascinated by rocks…indeed, KSue, you told me Oscar was always a dreamer, interested in madcap schemes. Yes, he invested his inheritance here – but why? He wasn't a particularly devoted Facetor, was he? Why not keep his money and invest it in a scheme of his own – maybe something he'd dreamed of his whole life…like finding gold. Over the years he'd visited many places where gold rush fever had reigned – enjoying a few pints at the Red Onion Saloon in Skagway, or listening to tales of hard-earned fortunes in Dawson City, where the folks at places like 'Claim 33' offer bags of pay-dirt for sale, as well as pans you can use to find grains of yellow in the sand. That was where Oscar went once, KSue, not to a diamond mine in the Arctic."

I addressed the audience as though they were one of my classes. "For those of you who don't know, there's a local legend around these parts about a man finding a fortune in gold in a tunnel he dug, then promptly lost. He spent years trying to find it again – his ghost continuing the job after his death. Just the sort of story that would appeal to Oscar – an enthusiast, and a dreamer. He was the sort of person who might be persuaded to invest in buying land – if someone who really should know what they were talking about told him it contained the most likely spot for finding the lost tunnel."

Heads turned, and there was a low-level buzz.

I directed my gaze toward the front row of the auditorium. "I'm so sorry to tell you this, Serendipity, but Ambroise Beausoleil doesn't exist – at least, he's not a French citizen residing in the USA – so who exactly is the man who claims to be 'an engineer', and who's been so helpful in getting the Desert Gem set up?"

Serendipity shifted uncomfortably. Ambroise was sitting beside her, and stared me down.

I continued, "Ambroise Beausoleil is such a lovely name: 'Ambroise' lived in twelfth-century Normandy, and famously wrote poetry about the Third Crusade; the locals there are extremely proud of him and his links to their region. And Beausoleil? It means 'beautiful sun'…which sounds just the same as 'beautiful son', as in child, doesn't it?"

"And what of it?" Ambroise's hands and shoulders had become quite Gallic.

I stepped toward the side of the dais, in front of where Ambroise sat, and I noticed quite a few Facetors leaning to try to see him – which was good.

"Demetrius Karaplis was born in Greece, and was brought to the USA as an infant. At a certain point in his life, before committing himself to Linda in marriage, he went travelling across Europe, to visit places that were of significance to his family. He certainly visited the home they had left behind in the Greek mountains, near Delphi, but he also visited the war memorials in Normandy…one of which bears the name of the uncle he never knew, the uncle who died on Omaha Beach back in 1944, with whose widow he and his parents shared a home in America. Could Ambroise Beausoleil, from near Caen, in

France, be Demetrius's son – his firstborn son? He *could* because Demetrius Karaplis was in the right area of the world at the right time…but is he? He has similar physical features to Oscar, Zara, and Demetrius – they're all dark-haired and blue-eyed. But that's not much to go on."

"It is nothing at all," said Ambroise angrily.

I returned to the center of the stage, and pointed as dramatically as I could at Ambroise.

"Before she died, about twenty years ago, your mother finally revealed to you how she'd fallen for a young, good-looking, Greek-American who'd stayed at the farm in Saint-Laurent-sur-Mer, near Omaha Beach, run as a guest house by your aunt and uncle. By the way, your uncle is recovering well from a recent surgical procedure, and when I brought our conversation on the phone earlier this evening to a conclusion, he asked me to tell you how sorry he was that your busy job in America had meant you were unable to attend your aunt's funeral last year; I understand it happened just about the time when you were holidaying on the beach in Puerto Peñasco, Ambroise. Or would you prefer me to use your real name: Demetrius Dubois. Your uncle told me your mother named you for your absent father, which was a nice touch. After her death you completed your studies as an engineer, sold off the farm you'd lived on not far from your uncle's, then took yourself off to discover your roots in Greece. Eventually, you hunted down the man himself, your father, Demetrius Karaplis, in Arizona, and travelled to meet him. But he snubbed you, didn't he? Your mother had never been able to tell him she was even pregnant, and there was Demetrius settled with his seemingly perfect family – of which you were most definitely not a part. Your uncle told me how sad and angry you were about being treated like that, then added how different you'd seemed when you'd told him all about your big job with an American hotel chain, and how you planned to stay in the USA."

I glanced across the stage, and Zara's face told me she didn't like what she was hearing – I could almost see the wheels turning behind her eyes, and she was trembling.

I returned my attention to the audience. "You had a plan, alright, but it wasn't what you'd told your uncle. Oh no – your plan began with needing to find out what it would have been like to have grown up as a real Karaplis. But how to do that, if Demetrius wanted nothing to do with you? Oscar Karaplis became your mark; you discovered he was interested in geology, and managed to strike up a friendship with him by joining tours organized for those who enjoy travelling the old gold rush trails. You stayed outside the Karaplis family circle until after Demetrius's death – because you couldn't have him recognizing you, could you...not with your assumed name and persona. But then the gloves came off. You were finally able to begin to take your revenge upon the entire Karaplis clan – the people who were living the life that should have been yours. I wonder if it was a coincidence that you were in Sedona at the time Demetrius fell from his ladder? You attended a lapidary event with Oscar there the day before Demetrius died, according to Oscar's Instagram account."

Zara gasped, and I saw her visibly blanch, which was fascinating.

"As Ambroise Beausoleil, Demetrius Dubois put his plan into action: having established yourself as a great friend to Oscar – the loner, and dreamer – you somehow managed to convince him that this bit of the desert was worth buying. I've pondered that, and I reckon your time spent as a geological engineer in Mexico, advising on a hotel-building project near the beach in Puerto Peñasco, was what gave weight to your claims that this was where he could find gold. Ever since he arrived, Oscar's been out in the desert searching for the lost Longmuir Tunnel – with absolutely no luck. You're also the one who got Zara on board; she wouldn't buy into your madcap lost-gold scheme, of course, and you never expected her to...but you offered the lonely girl who'd never had any friends, who could never really connect to anyone around her, the sort of acceptance and flattery she'd never known before. You managed to get her to buy into the idea of setting herself up as something not far short of a goddess, to be worshipped by people in awe of her so-called 'abilities'. The notion of a sham resort in the desert from which she could build her own physical and digital empire appealed to her enormously; her intense dislike of most people, those she always thought of as inferior to herself, meant she loved the idea of taking hundreds, then thousands, then who knows how many of them for a ride. You sweetened the pot with the added attraction of a restaurant – funded entirely by someone else – that would bring more *bona fides* to the place. For which you targeted Serendipity, through Zara initially, who'd invited her online chum to holiday with her in the sun; and Serendipity fell prey to your charms, didn't she? The desire to find a partner who is a true soulmate is something most humans yearn for – it might even make a person so trusting that they'd do almost anything for the one true love of their life. That's such a clever way to manipulate people, Ambroise – making them trust, love, and desire you...but never delivering anything tangible. Serendipity agreed to get her parents to bankroll a restaurant because of it...and what did Zara agree to because of the same desire...the same hope? A great deal, I believe – though let's not forget that there aren't many people in this world who wouldn't want to be worshipped. Especially when it allowed Zara to achieve another goal of hers: of making lots and lots of money – and I think everyone here is starting to understand just how much she loves that."

I could sense the unease in the amphitheater; more and more Facetors were working out that they'd been duped, which had been my intention all along…though I understood how very carefully I still had to tread; everyone struggles with the idea that they've acted stupidly, and will seek to blame almost anyone but themselves for their own fallibility.

I looked at Bud and he made the motion with his hand that meant I had to keep going, so I plunged in.

"So, folks, let's Facet and Face It – you've all been tricked by Zara Karaplis, a young woman pretending to be able to communicate with the dead, when all she has is a good memory, and a determination to suck as much money out of your bank accounts as possible. I dare say that's making you feel pretty annoyed right now…but I'm guessing you're just as annoyed with me as you are with her. So I think it's time to remind you that Zara's desire for control, power, and money has led directly to the deaths of five people…suicides, maybe, but suicides instigated by her lies, nonetheless. And I think we can all agree that losing money is nowhere near as dreadful as losing one's life."

An actual shudder ran around the amphitheater.

I continued, "But even *that's* not all that the Desert Gem is about. I know there are many novices here, all recruited and overseen by Ambroise, through Don, who work hard – like donkeys – and are eager to please; the fact they're all putting in long work hours is expected, and accepted. But let me tell you about KSue Henritze for a moment. She's a wonderful woman, underestimated by most – and she's bright…much brighter than you – or even she – thinks. You see, she's noticed that these novices are just a little…shall we say 'different' than the usual Faceting types. I bet some of you others have noticed that, too – they really only mix with each other, don't they?"

A few nods from those in rainbow colors, shrugs from those in gray.

"So let me tell you what else has been happening under your noses…your hydroponic marijuana crop is hidden away, out here in the desert, in the middle of nowhere, with fabulous growing conditions; but it's not being harvested and packed just for your use. Oh no, it's being distributed across the state, and beyond, by a network of drivers who've been recruited by Norman." I stared down at my next target. "Oh Norman – for someone Serendipity told me was a timid person, that's a bold move. And with your wife keeping all the accounts for the Faceting movement, she knew exactly how to hide the money, didn't she? You see, folks, drugs are sold for cash, and that's tough to cope with these days, unless you've got a convincing-looking source of cash income. Most of the money flowing into the Faceting business from around the world arrives electronically; anyone examining the accounts of the Faceting for Life movement would be able to see that. So a restaurant that has to deal in cash, because it's completely offline, is an excellent way to show anyone who might ask where all that cash is coming from. Right, Elizabeth? Oh hang on, that's not your real name, is it? Elizabeth and Norman McGlynn are aliases. Did things get a bit hot for you both in the world of banking?"

Both Elizabeth and Norman looked like the proverbial deer caught in headlights – it was a wonderful sight.

Serendipity rose to her feet, and stood in front of Ambroise, facing the audience. She was aglow with anger. "You used my parents' money, my name, my reputation, and my restaurant to cover up drug dealing? After knowing how I feel about drugs?" She was shouting, and many of the people in the auditorium looked most uncomfortable. "That's what it's all been about, has it? I thought…I thought it was…something else." She looked up from Ambroise to face her fellow Facetors. "Which one of you novices tied me up and locked me in the freezer? I know it was one of you lot. You could have killed me. I was lucky to not freeze to death. I talked to you all, accepted you all – I made an effort to get to know you all, as individuals, not just a herd of gray animals. Even…even the ones who made me feel uncomfortable. I gave you all the benefit of the doubt. The cash you took? That Ambroise told me to keep in the safe, and use for all the payments for supplies? Is that all my life was worth to you? Just…money?" Her voice broke, and she collapsed in tears onto a part of the stone bench that wasn't beside Ambroise.

Ambroise stood and looked around, pointing at me. "Everything this poor, deluded woman has said about me is a lie. It is true that we grow marijuana here, but only small amounts. We use it here. You all know this. It is not illegal." Ambroise managed to sound quite hurt by my accusations, and I could see a few Facetors acknowledging that he was speaking at least a little truth.

I wasn't having that. "I was just knocked out, tied up, and dumped in a massive storeroom full of boxes of packaged marijuana – I've seen it, lots of it, so I know it exists, Ambroise. And I also know why I ended up in there, unconscious and hog-tied – in exactly the same way Serendipity was. And this is where I have a confession to make myself, which should interest all the true Facetors here: I made a mistake – a big mistake – and that mistake has taught me a valuable lesson…coincidences *do* happen. Earlier today I set a trap – a trap I intended to use to prove that Zara has been reading all the notes you store in your little cubbies in the wall overnight before you burn them – oh, by the way, did you know that all the notes you enter into the Faceting app are not 'burned' but are sent directly to Zara so she can pick out what she wants, and use it when she does her channelling sessions? No? Well, you do now. Anyway – back to me making a mistake…I told Don that I'd once had a housemate who sought to keep her late grandmother's memory alive by wearing her perfume. I knew the 'lesson' I'd learned from that experience would end up in Don's notes about today, that Zara would read them, and she'd replay that information when I forced her to take the opportunity. And that would be proof she wasn't talking to Demetrius because, if he existed, he would know there'd never been a girl, no grandmother, and no perfume – because I'd made it all up. But what I didn't know at that time was that the idea I told Don I'd come up with to help this fictional girl – to take a perfume-soaked handkerchief and keep it in a box – would be so close to the method being used to cover up the aroma given off by the marijuana harvest in its cartons that I'd spook the people here whose purpose is to run their drug business out of the place."

A buzz…an angry buzz. *Good.*

"And that's why you grabbed me, wasn't it? Yes, I'm talking to you 'Norman' and 'Elizabeth'. Don raced off to you two – who he knew were completely tied up in the marijuana business, and told you about what I'd said…that I'd mentioned perfumed cloth, and you reckoned maybe I'd worked out what was going on. You two are quite the pair – between you, you managed to cart me away from the communications hub to the storeroom, and I reckon you'd have left me there all night while you made off with the cash you took from the safe in Serendipity's restaurant – stuffed into a bunch of Faceting canvas bags – because that was your intention, right? You knew the game was all but up, your trip to Flagstaff with KSue proved that. KSue had noticed that you both went there often, as had Barbara, and you wondered how many others had others noticed your odd travel patterns. Could it be long before your critical roles here weren't deemed so critical any longer? All those marked for death by 'Demetrius' were the ones who'd built what the new Faceting movement had become; about the only two left who'd played significant roles in its current formation were you Elizabeth – who designed the special therapies which Zara used to gather daily information from Facetors around the world that she was able to put to good use in her channelling session, and you Norman – who'd set up the distribution network for the drugs. Time to cut and run, right? When Dr. Nderu said he didn't want you to drive him to Phoenix this afternoon, you were stuck here. Then Don told you about what I'd said to him about a perfumed handkerchief, so you decided you had to shut me up until you could get away in the dead of night. But you got caught up by Jenn calling this special gathering."

The so-called McGlynns were Serendipity's next target as she leaped up. "*You* two did that to me? *You* nearly killed me? I thought we were close...I always made allowances for you." She lashed out with her fists at Norman, causing Bud to pull her off, while Elizabeth hugged her shocked husband to her chest. He was crying.

I knew I had one last push in me, so steeled myself. "But, in all of this, what about poor Oscar? A dreamer, with a love of geology...and a weakness for gold. Was he just enchanted by the idea of a lost gold mine – or did he have a few grains of the desire for riches his sister had? Did he have any idea that the man who'd talked him into putting all his money into this place was, in fact, his half-brother? I believe he did. He'd found photographic evidence of Ambroise traveling to Greece in his youth, and he had the telephone number of the man I spoke to in France today – Demetrius Dubois' uncle; I'm sure he had, or would have, worked it all out. But he wasn't driven in the same way his sister was, so there was no great hurry. Everything was going just fine for him here...until it wasn't. He knew his sister wasn't talking to his dead father – he'd never been a great devotee of Faceting, and didn't have the personality to seek out, or believe in, great spiritual revelations. All he wanted to do was find that lost tunnel, full of gold…until his mother died. KSue – your insights once again proved invaluable in this respect. You told me that Oscar was like a tiger when he found out that his mother was dead, that he screamed, 'She's gone too far!'"

KSue stood and addressed the audience very formally. "This is exactly what he said to me – and he *was* like a tiger. He wasn't an armadillo anymore." She sat, looking pleased with herself – though I could tell that her armadillo comment had puzzled more than a few people.

"Thank you, KSue. Now that comment by Oscar might have meant that Linda had been dead for too long for her to be reached on the other plane…or it might have meant he knew his sister had played a role in their mother's death – that she'd finally crossed a line."

I faced Zara. "Did your brother confront you about your mother's death?"

She nodded, dumbly.

"Would you like to tell us about that meeting?"

Zara's body was half-slumped in the chair, and I could see she was not the person she'd been even half an hour earlier. Everything I'd said was taking its toll; not only had she been unmasked, but I'd also revealed some truths not even she had guessed at. I wondered how she'd react – and gave her a moment to do so.

Eventually she stood, looking much younger than her years. Her head was bowed, her hands hung by her sides. She spoke softly. "Oscar was distraught. Mother hadn't wanted him to know about the prediction that she'd die, so it was a dreadful shock for him. And he was already in a bad state because he couldn't find the gold…which I knew didn't exist, and he was starting to work that out, too. Indeed, he was beginning to think that Ambroise had…led him on." She paused and stared at Ambroise, her face contorted with pain. "I…I only ever told people they would die when I honestly, truly believed they were ready to go. I didn't ever force anyone to kill themselves – not even Mom. She was in terrible pain, and even talking to Dad through me wasn't helping her the way it once had. I'd…I'd been told – by Ambroise, who I believed – that Mom was in a bad way; not sleeping, hardly eating. I felt awful for her…so…so I gave her a way out. I told Oscar all that, but he was inconsolable. He told me he'd had enough of this place…that he wanted nothing more to do with Faceting…and wanted his money out of the business. I told him I'd organize it all, so he could live whatever life he wanted, wherever he wanted, but I needed a couple of days to get the money. He said he'd wait – but he needed some time alone, right then, to think things through. For Oscar, I knew that meant he'd go wandering in the desert – it calmed him. Then…then he never came back. I honestly don't know what happened – it really was an accident, right, Ambroise? You found him – you said it was an accident."

I pounced. "And I bet you told Ambroise all about these conversations with Oscar, didn't you?" Zara nodded. "And did he tell you everything would be alright – the way he always has." Again she nodded.

I was quite impressed she'd managed to say so much, without actually confessing to her lies – and I even had a little sympathy for her – but not so much that I wasn't prepared to go in for the kill.

"When Bud and I arrived here, it didn't take us long to work out that Zara was somehow coming up with 'proofs' that meant she convinced people sufficiently about the existence of another plane, where loved ones waited for them, that they'd take their own lives. We knew *who* was doing *what* – but didn't understand the *how* or the *why*. But – and here's another, much more dreadful confession, folks – we were wrong…so terribly wrong. Because, while Zara *was* the one using her special memory to build the body of proof needed to convince folks there was an existence beyond that which we know…she *wasn't* the one doing all the talking. And the irony of this entire situation? Zara maintained all along that Demetrius was speaking through her – and it turns out that was the truth – but it wasn't Demetrius Karaplis doing the talking, but Demetrius Dubois. Zara was the face and mouthpiece of Faceting – the reason thousands have been drawn to it, and are ready to pay through the nose to be a part of the movement. But – other than the excellent business plan – how much of what was being done was Zara's idea? Very little. It was all Demetrius. Demetrius Dubois. He explained to Bud and me how – as an engineer – he liked to deal with systems in their parts, and that's what he did here – with no one person knowing everything that he was making happen. Only he had that overview, only he gave the entirety direction. And his overall plan was working well, until Oscar blew a fuse, and threatened to bring the whole thing tumbling down. Imagine…Oscar Karaplis, the son of the founders of the Faceting movement, being seen to not support it. Imagine him taking his money elsewhere, to do other things…maybe even slightly madcap things. Oscar had lost confidence in Ambroise – maybe he'd even talked to Ambroise's uncle, so knew the real story…and that's not something Ambroise could tolerate. So what was it, Ambroise? A promise of a heart-to-heart in the darkness of the desert, late that night? 'Let's meet on Lump Hill and talk about it?' Oscar wasn't running about on a hilltop trying to find cellphone reception to call for help – he'd have used the communications hub overseen by his friend Jenn if he'd needed to do that. No, Oscar was under your spell – had been for years – Oscar *wanted* to believe in you, and gave you one last chance…which you used to kill him. How very convenient that it was you who 'found' him, who helped establish the time of death, who supported the immediate burial and cremation. Did it also give you the chance to clear Oscar's phone of what you hoped was any evidence that might incriminate, or point toward, you? I think so – but you didn't do a good enough job of getting rid of his photos. Big mistake, that. Thank you. Then there was only one Karaplis left – and you controlled her completely, though she didn't see it that way. You were the one feeding her false information about the people she should mark for death. You were the one who'd recruited a pack of novices who were eager to do your bidding, because you could get them accepted into an organization where all the drugs they wanted were free, just as long as they worked hard supplying your marijuana trade. You were the one who got Norman and Elizabeth involved, and made sure your drug distribution network was established. You were the one who pushed, and manipulated, everyone. Your charisma is not something you flaunt, you use it quietly, just on a one-to-one basis…and it's not only about making people lust for you, it's about making people trust you first, because you give them what they've always lacked – a true friend…a confidant, someone in whom they have complete and utter faith. Only then, when they have come to see you as their soulmate, comes the promise of the possibility of a physical relationship…but, oh dear, no…you can't do that, can you? Because you're sworn to celibacy."

Serendipity stood again, her emotional exhaustion written all over her face. "He's done all that to me. Ambroise…Demetrius, whatever his name is…he became my best, my *only* true friend. Told me I'd never need anyone else. That I was the only one who might make him want to break his vow of celibacy. I can't believe I fell for it…but he was such a good listener, so sensitive to my needs, and weaknesses – obviously. I fell for him, and I fell for his act. I've been so foolish. I admit it. Who else here is brave enough to admit the same?"

Don stood. "I thought we were good friends…no, I admit it, too…I thought we were more than that. I thought we were connected in the most meaningful way possible. He got me to tell him everything that Oscar was up to, and he's made me feel good about my management abilities by letting me oversee the work rotas to build, maintain, and produce crops at the hydroponic center. I thought…I really thought we were sticking it to The Man, together…as a team…that I had a future here…with him. That's…that's what he made me believe. Let me believe." He slumped back onto the bench.

Norman stood next; I wondered if he was about to be truly brave. "I've been a complete fool," he said quietly. "I'm so terribly sorry about what we did to you, Cait, and especially to you, Serendipity." He gave his full attention to her. "You were good to us – you knew about our past…and you even guessed we were skimming a bit off the top of the drivers' payments, yet you said nothing. But, you see, we knew we had to get away…we knew about the money in the safe, and knew we needed it to be able to make a fresh start. We honestly thought someone would come to the restaurant just a few minutes after we left you, Serendipity…we had no idea you'd be locked up for so long…didn't think you were in real danger. We don't deserve your forgiveness, we know that, and we really wish we could turn back the clock. But we can't – neither of us can…we couldn't twenty years ago, and we can't now."

Norman paused, and looked down at his wife, who was hugging herself and rocking backwards and forwards.

He continued, now addressing me, "That was the problem, see? When we first met Ambroise he worked out that we weren't who we said we were. I still don't know how he did it, but he found out that we left our life in California because I'd borrowed some money…" His wife kicked him. "Okay, okay…I'd embezzled some money from a small bank we'd once worked for, and I got caught. Spent…some time in prison. When I got out we'd both decided to start over, clean. Even though we didn't know how he knew, Ambroise was so forgiving, so it didn't matter; we really thought he understood why we'd done what we'd done…how we really did want to give our lives to something that mattered. Then he asked us to do little things for the Faceting movement, then a few more little things…then I ended up doing exactly what you said – I've set up a huge drug distribution network for him, but no one involved with it has ever so much as set eyes on him – they think it's all my idea. It's not me, it's him, but the cops won't believe that – they'll just know about me."

Ambroise stood and turned to face the audience. When he spoke, his tone was warm, comforting. "Please don't listen to them. You all know me – I haven't changed. You know I'm the sort of person who likes to help, listen, and encourage people. None of this is my fault. Of course I've been supportive of Zara, and Serendipity, and even Don, Norman, and Elizabeth – but the idea that I'm the son of Demetrius Karaplis, and have done all these terrible things, is ridiculous. However, I understand that my being here might be difficult for you all, so I shall leave. Then you can continue to enjoy your lives here, undisturbed by drama. I believe you will miss me as much as I shall miss all of you. You each have a space in my heart – especially you, dear Zara." He turned and faced the stage. "You are a most talented young woman, and you have the potential to build an empire that will sustain many around the world for years to come. Do not allow these people to undermine your faith in yourself. Nor you in yours, Serendipity; you are a talented chef, and will do great things, I know it."

Zara moved toward the edge of the stage, her eyes and her diamond-encrusted jewel blazing in the firelight. "You *are* all the things Cait and the others have said you are, and you *have* done the things they are saying you have done. You said you loved me. Only me. That we would be together as soon as you felt complete. That I was the most attractive, desirable woman in the world. Just like you told Serendipity. The big difference is…you're my half brother. My blood. How could you do that to me? How could I have let myself feel…the connection was so…you knew all the time, yet you led me on until I…how could you? *You* are the person behind everything bad here, the poison we have all drunk and thought tasted good…the evil corrupter of everything that started out clean and pure…and you will stay here until you answer for your deeds. Convince me my mother is ready to die, when she's not? Kill my brother…*your half brother*…in the dead of night? Make me feel the way I felt about you? Those are actions that cannot be tolerated. Demetrius Dubois – my father's son – you are dead to me. Time to Facet and Face It."

I caught the glint of something out of the corner of my eye. Zara pushed past me, then leaped down onto Ambroise, screaming. As she flew at him, he turned his back, covering his head with his arms. Zara pulled at his hair, beat him with her fists, and lashed out at his face with her bejewelled gem. He yelled in pain, blood pouring from his ripped cheeks. He tried to push her off., but she clung on, howling, and slashing at him, until uniformed officers who seemed to materialize from the darkness beyond the amphitheater pulled her off. They handcuffed her, Ambroise, Norman, Elizabeth, Don, and several of the novices.

Ending the Beginning

Half an hour or so later, the panic, horror, and anger still being expressed by the large crowd, and the effect of the acoustics, made the amphitheater an uncomfortably noisy place to be…so Bud and I took ourselves off, until the furor was just a rumble in the background.

We walked toward the plaza; the flashing lights of the police cruisers blended with the orange glow from fire bowls, and the place looked bizarrely festive. We both knew we were unlikely to get any sleep that night, because we'd be talking to cops for hours, but I wanted to shower and change my clothes, so that I at least looked and smelled fresh, even if I didn't feel it.

We didn't talk immediately, but soon the words flowed.

"I'm so proud of you," said Bud.

"I didn't frighten you with my awesome powers, then?"

"You're always awesome – in a good way. But tonight you were brave, too. When you were telling Zara about her childhood, you were really talking about your own, weren't you?"

I nodded. "But I was lucky – I was the girl who *did* share her secrets with her parents, the people who truly loved her, and I did have the support I needed to be able to learn how to fit in. But I have to say it was odd, to understand how things might have gone so differently for me."

"She's still relatively young – maybe she'll have time to understand…change…put her gifts to good use, like you do. But do you really think Zara was influenced by Ambroise to such an extent that she didn't understand what he was getting her to do when she was telling people their time was up?"

I shook my head, sadly. "I'm delighted that's a determination that will have to be made by people other than me, or you. I believe she had such faith in herself and her abilities that she was probably blind to anything that tarnished her opinion of herself. Possibly her desire for Ambroise played a part, too. Maybe she *allowed* him to dupe her – the way so many of her followers allowed her to dupe them. Truly hoist by her own petard – which is a saying I rarely get the chance to use. So there's that."

Bud chuckled wryly, "Yeah, there's that."

"How do you think Serendipity will come through all this?" I was deeply concerned about her.

Bud shrugged. "I reckon she'll be okay – eventually. While the cops were taking Ambroise away and the medics were checking you over – after they'd patched up his face – she told me she's going to leave here immediately, to spend some time with her Auntie Emily and Uncle Henry…the Zgorskis. They sound like just the folks she needs to be with right now – they'll help her come to terms with what she's been through better than her parents ever could, I reckon. And KSue's son will be here in the morning; she'll be even more glad to get away after all this, I'd have thought."

"She's a sweet woman."

"She is. Sharper than she thinks, too. But, hey, you look pooped. Maybe I shouldn't suggest it – but do you fancy a drop or two of the purple gloop…you know, just to get you through the night? We could share the equivalent of a couple of cups of coffee each?"

I laughed. "Great idea – purple gloop it is…because you're right, I'm exhausted. And my head hurts."

"You're sure the paramedics gave you a clean bill of health — that amazing head of yours is going to be okay? Those wrists, too? They look sore."

I nodded. "I'm going to be fine. Honest."

Bud hugged me. "Here's our dig, then…our last night here, I should think. You do know you only have to say the word and we can go straight home, right?"

I sighed. "At the moment, pulling the plug on the whole idea of traveling on to the National Parks seems very appealing. But wouldn't we be running away if we did that? Our time here was supposed to be just the first part of our trip to see the wonders of nature. I feel the need to do that even more keenly having spent so many days contemplating the horrific things people can do to each other. I think that when we've seen this all through, tonight, we'll be ready for the big, open skies and the grandiose landscapes we'll see over the next few days. Then we can go home."

"There's no place like it, you know."

"You're right, Husband, there isn't."

Acknowledgements

Writing and publishing a book is never the work of one person alone...though, sometimes, it feels that way. But even then, in the darkness of the small hours, the knowledge that others are willing me to write something that will engage and entertain them is a great boost, because they are out there, somewhere...and I can connect with them through my work.

For this book, I contacted some of the people who've encouraged and supported me over the years to ask if they'd be prepared to allow me to use their names, or at least a version of their names, in this book. No one said no, which was a relief!

Thank you to KSue Anderson (Henritze), Linda and Pantelis (Demetrius) McNab/Karaplis, Colleen (Elizabeth) (Mc)Glynn, Dru Ann Love, Kristopher Zgorski, and Jenn and Don Longmuir for all agreeing to "lend me your names". I hope none of you have palpitations when you see the uses to which I have put them. You all know each other, and now my readers know at least a version of your names, though nothing of you, as real people...so what should I tell them about you all?

Hmm...I met you all because I write mysteries, and because you're all involved in that world. Dru Ann and Kristopher both run wonderful review blogs which I heartily recommend folks follow (*Dru's Musings* and *BOLO Books*, respectively) and have each been recognized for the stellar work they do by – among other bodies – the Mystery Writers of America, of whose prestigious Raven Award each has, quite rightly, been a recipient. Linda and Colleen were the moving forces behind organizing the 2019 Left Coast Crime convention which was held in Vancouver, BC, where I was honored to be Toastmaster. Jenn and Don are booksellers (*Scene of the Crime Books*), whose support of our community is second to none, often overseeing and organizing the entire book room at many crime writer/fan conventions in North America. KSue is one of my valued early readers, and we have become firm friends, after having met at the first Left Coast Crime convention I ever attended, in Monterey in 2014. What a wonderful group you all are – thank you for your years of friendship and support...and for now giving me permission to "immortalize" you, here.

I must also acknowledge the inspiration of the works of L. Frank Baum, whose characters terrified me on the screen as a small child, but entranced me on the page in later life. I hope you enjoyed spotting my nods to the world we all connect most closely with Oscar Zoroaster Phadrig Isaac Norman Henkle Emmannuel Ambroise Diggs!

I suspect you're wondering about the Faceting for Life movement itself. No, it's not real. I invented it to use in *The Corpse with the Golden Nose*, the second Cait Morgan Mystery referred to in this book. It's a complete fabrication, so don't even bother trying to hunt it down...though I will tell you that I found myself with an unexpected and unique opportunity to spend some time in the company of several hundred members of an organization that shares many features with what the Faceting movement "became". It was an intense period, with many eye-opening discoveries, but I must emphasize that the Faceting for Life cult described in this book is not based on any specific movement.

I want to thank my editor Anna Harrisson and proof checker Sue Vincent, both of whom put hours and hours into knocking my work into shape. Without them doing that, this would all be a lot messier than it is, and I might well have lost my mind.

I also want to thank my husband, whose continuous support also contributes to me hanging onto my sanity, even when I feel as though I am juggling soot – which happens at (apparently predictable) points throughout the writing, editing, re-editing, and publishing process.

To the bloggers, reviewers (including those who leave remarks and reviews at online stores, where they really do make a big difference to the visibility of a title on what is an extremely crowded virtual bookshelf), social media sharers and boosters, booksellers, librarians, and those for whom the good old "word of mouth" still means something out there…what you all do is *critically* important in allowing readers to find my work. Thank you.

And last, but by no means least, thanks to *you* for choosing to spend time with Cait and Bud; maybe this was the first time you met them, or maybe you've been with them since the beginning…either way, I'm grateful.

About the author

CATHY ACE was born and raised in Swansea, Wales, and now lives in British Columbia, Canada. She is the author of The Cait Morgan Mysteries, The WISE Enquiries Agency Mysteries, the standalone novel of psychological suspense, The Wrong Boy, and collections of short stories and novellas. As well as being passionate about writing crime fiction, she's also a keen gardener.

You can find out more about Cathy and her work at her website: www.cathyace.com

Made in the USA
Coppell, TX
24 November 2023

24665204R00194